C000163131

RESERVATIONS OF THE HEART

RESERVATIONS OF THE HEART

TB MARKINSON

Published by T. B. Markinson

Visit T. B. Markinson's official website at lesbianromancesbytbm.com for the latest news, book details, and other information.

Copyright © T. B. Markinson, 2019

Edited by Kelly Hashway

This book is copyrighted and licensed for your personal enjoyment only. All rights reserved. No part of this publication may be reproduced, stored in a retrieval system, or transmitted in any forms or by any means without the prior permission of the copyright owner. The moral rights of the author have been asserted.

This book is a work of fiction. Names, characters, businesses, places, events, and incidents are the product of the author's imagination or are used fictitiously. Any resemblance to actual persons, living or dead, events, or locales is entirely coincidental.

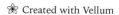 Created with Vellum

back of her sister's head, her broad shoulders hunched in that way of hers that made it clear Rosie was annoyed, and truth be known, she had every right to be.

Stella sighed as she got the attention of the usual hostess, who was surrounded on all sides by eager people wanting a table, and motioned that she would seat herself. The hostess smiled and waved for Stella to go on, before addressing a man who clearly was upset about having to wait. It paid to be such a loyal patron coupled with having a sister who'd been annoyingly on time since arriving on her exact due date.

"What took you so long?" Stella goaded as she claimed her seat.

"Oh, I have zero respect for people's time." Rosie made a la-di-da motion with her hand.

"Ouch. I'm sorry. Truly. I got held up at the hospital, and then a student corralled me to discuss Monday's test." Stella failed to mention she'd made the student walk with her to the bus stop, nullifying that excuse.

"Was the emergency at least life-threatening?" Rosie's shoulders were already relaxing, and the steeliness in her eyes softened.

"Aren't they always?"

"Considering you transplant kidneys and teach future doctors, I'm going to take a wild stab and say yes." Rosie motioned for the waiter to bring another margarita on the rocks.

Stella raised her hand to their usual server and indicated she wanted a marg, knowing she didn't have to specify what kind. "Well, I teach more these days and write fancy schmancy articles in journals no one reads." She stopped for a cleansing breath. "You look good."

"So do you, baby sis. Have I mentioned lately how much I hate you for barely being in your forties?" Rosie smiled, causing the lines around her eyes to crinkle even more.

"Pul-lease! You look years younger than I do." Stella waved for Rosie to stop feeling sorry for herself.

"I only look more relaxed since I spend more time on the beach. When was the last time you took a vacation?"

"Can you define that word?" Stella laughed. "How was the Caribbean? From your tan and super blonde locks, I'm guessing sunny."

"Hot and humid. Just the way I like it."

"You're the only person I know who loves humidity." Stella leaned back for the waiter to set down her drink, minus the salt on the rim, her preference. "Thanks, Jimmy."

He smiled, but given the place was hopping, he didn't stop to chew the fat.

Rosie pressed on. "Can't get enough, but it's nothing like here because there, I'm sitting on the beach reading saucy thrillers, not nineteenth century English novels trying to figure out ways to get my students excited about Austen or Dickens. And I can drink beer that's brought to my lounger. Now that I think of it, I wish I were still there, not back in the Boston grind. The older I get, the less I want to be in the classroom teaching English lit to little shits who can barely read. I'm waiting for some smart-ass to craft a paper only using text acronyms or emojis."

"Surely the state of English majors hasn't reached that level at your forty-thousand a year university, or the parents footing the bill would yank them out faster than you can say Jane Austen."

"Maybe I can spread the word. Unemployment doesn't sound all that bad considering classes start tomorrow, and I'm not ready." Rosie's face reddened, and she cradled her drink against her cheek.

"Tomorrow! What a luxury. My students started two weeks ago and have their first big test coming up."

"Mine aren't dedicating their lives to saving others. So, how are you, really?" Rosie seemed to examine Stella's face as if doing her best to root out the true answer.

"I'm hanging in."

"Even today?"

Stella stroked her chin. "What's so special about today?"

Rosie leaned back into the hand carved, brightly painted chair and crossed her arms. "Don't try that with me."

Stella flicked up a hand. "What?"

Rosie's eyes widened. "You really don't know?"

"I have no clue what you're going on about. It's not your birthday. Nor mine. What am I missing?" Stella shrugged.

"It's your wedding anniversary."

"Is it?" Stella closed one eye, consulting her mental calendar. "Huh, I guess you're right. But…"

"But what?"

"Does it really matter now? We've been divorced for a few years." Stella hefted one shoulder, determined not to let the date bother her. But, how had she'd forgotten? Her ex-wife, Kim, had always accused Stella of being a bit cold when it came to the sentimentality of their relationship. Was this further proof Kim had been right? That got under Stella's skin more than she liked to admit.

Luckily, Jimmy arrived to take their orders, bringing Stella out of her head. Neither of them had consulted a menu, but they'd been coming to the Mexican restaurant once a month for years. Stella ordered the enchilada platter while Rosie opted for her usual chiles rellenos.

"Thanks, Jimmy," Stella said when she handed him the menu.

"You got it. I love regulars. Easy peasy." He whirled around, heading for the kitchen.

"He's got such a cute ass." Rosie licked her lips.

"If you say so." Stella raised her glass to her mouth.

"What do you think of the hostess? What's her name again?

She's a looker." Rosie pivoted in her seat to check out the perky brunette.

Stella forced down the mouthful of margarita, trying not to choke. After swallowing, she said, "Andrea is a baby."

Rosie rolled her eyes. "She's got to be in her early twenties. Come on. You're a hot and successful doctor. Most girls who are into girls would kill for a date. Play your cards right. You might get more."

"It's weird to have my middle-aged sister call me hot." Stella shifted in her seat.

"You are hot, and don't call me middle-aged. Forty is the new thirty." Rosie shook a finger at Stella.

"You're forty-five."

Rosie mimed for Stella to zip it.

"What? Are you trying to pick up someone?" Stella scouted the area for viable contenders. "I have a feeling your husband would object."

"No, I'm not. That doesn't mean I want my age spoken aloud. It gives it too much power." Rosie shook her upper body as if warding off an evil spirit.

"I wasn't aware that's how age works. How is George?"

Rosie's face lit up, melting twenty years. "He's good. God, I'm lucky to have a guy like him. Especially after my terrible first marriage. Why'd you let me marry Steve? The only redeeming factor of that union was ditching the last name Gilbert. Not that Butler was all that much better. Thank God George has a decent last name." Rosie swigged her drink. "Dr. Rosie D'Angelo sounds so much better."

Stella crossed her arms. "You know, Gilbert is still my last name."

"No one stopped you from taking Kim's last name or just changing it. Part of me wonders if that was the only reason I married Steve. We both know I'm the emotional one. You were supposed to take care of me."

"You're four years older! Besides, if I remember correctly, I told you he was an ass when I met him."

Rosie pressed her finger to her nose and pointed at Stella with her other hand. "Exactly! If you'd liked him, I would have ditched him way before he worked up the courage to pop the question."

"I was supposed to pretend I liked Steve? But, wait, I like George. That blows your theory out of the water."

"Everyone likes George. And I met him in my thirties. I'd matured some."

"A teensy bit." Stella raised her glass. "To George."

Rosie clinked her glass and swallowed a hefty portion. "How can we find you a George?"

"No offense, but Georges do nothing for me."

"Okay, a Georgette."

"Again, they don't do anything for me. People. I'm just not into them." Stella sipped her water since her margarita was gone.

"That's interesting coming from a woman who works eighty plus hours a week saving people's lives."

"I like them that way. I don't want to be in a relationship." Stella slapped her palms together, implying *never again*.

"I really thought after a few years your aversion would have softened some." Rosie held her hands a foot apart.

"It's not an aversion. I've learned to accept medicine and love don't mix. Besides, I have Mackenzie to think about. It wouldn't be fair to her. It hit her hard when Kim and I separated." Stella didn't understand why she had to state the obvious to Rosie. Then again, Rosie was the romantic sibling.

"A lot of divorced moms date." The left side of Rosie's mouth curled upward.

"Not this one. No more relationships. I'm much happier alone."

"Is that right?" Rosie's pale blue eyes had a gotcha glint. "What are you doing this weekend?"

"When not getting caught up with work, I plan on sleeping."

"Sounds thrilling and totally not a sign of depression." Rosie waved to get Jimmy's attention to order another margarita.

"I'm not depressed. I'm exhausted from the start of the semester and long hours at the hospital. It takes time to get back into the groove at the start of a new school year. And, Kenzie will be with her mom, so I have zero obligations."

"You know, not all women will—"

"Where's our food? It's taking longer than normal. I'm starving."

"That's my cue that you're done with this conversation thread, but if you'll permit me to say one thing before we talk about how awesome I am and how you couldn't have asked for a better sister..." Stella groaned, but Rosie pressed on. "I wasn't lying earlier. You're a great catch, but you aren't getting any younger. Don't wait much longer."

"Or what? I'll miss my chance?"

"It's possible."

Stella leaned on her forearms. "Fine by me. I'm not having a pity party for myself or whatnot. I don't want a relationship. End of subject. How's my favorite niece, Charlie?"

"If she makes it through her first year of college, it'll be a miracle."

"Oh, don't be that way. She's clever. Too much for her own good."

"Tell me about it. I'm afraid to ask what she did while her dad and I were out of the country." Rosie's face went a shade whiter.

"Well, when I popped by to check on her, she was running a brothel. A very stylish one, I might add." Stella grinned.

"Oh, good. That totally puts my mind at ease. Not."

Stella shook her head. "I don't know why you're so worried. Charlie's at school now and settling in. She reminds me so much of you."

"That's exactly why I'm worried." Rosie waggled a finger at Stella. "I can still remember all the trouble I got into during my time in college. Do we need to circle back to Steve?"

"Please, no." Stella laughed. "I remember the summer before your first year in college, when Mom had the oriental rugs cleaned and they all came back with cigarette burns. She threatened to sue the cleaner until Mom figured out you were responsible."

"I would have gotten away with it if she hadn't sent them out. It took me hours to shave off pieces with a razor to get enough fuzz to fill in the holes. That was an epic party the weekend before I left for college." Rosie's eyes glazed over with nostalgia.

"I wouldn't know. I was at Grandma's."

"You were just a baby. Besides, you weren't the partying type. You preferred having your nose in a book." She let out a puff of air. "Now that you're older and getting older by the day, I just don't want you to wake up in ten years with regrets about being alone. I truly believe there's someone for you. But you have to look."

Stella placed a hand on her sister's arm. "Trust me. I'm happy with my life. I love my career. I have the best daughter. And, as much as it pains me to admit this, I have the most supportive and funny sister. My life is perfect."

CHAPTER TWO

"OH MY GOD, AURORA. WHAT'S WRONG?" BECKY, IN A retro 1977 Star Wars T-shirt and cotton pajama bottoms, rose from the battered couch and went to her best friend and roommate.

Aurora collapsed into Becky's arms. "My life as I know it is over."

"Come on. Sit down." Becky, almost a head taller than Aurora, steered them to the couch. "Does this conversation need alcohol?"

Aurora burst into tears.

"Tears already. Beer won't cut it. How about tequila?"

Aurora wiped her eyes with a tissue she'd snagged from the Kleenex box on the coffee table from the previous night's viewing of *Moulin Rouge*. "No, not after last time."

"Oh, I know." Becky snapped her fingers. "Whiskey. That fixes everything or does a mind erase so you can't remember why you were upset. Either way works." She zipped into the kitchen, which was less than ten feet away. While gathering two mismatched tumblers, Becky asked over her shoulder, "What happened?"

"I don't even know how to put it into words." Aurora sucked in a breath, let it out, and repeated the action to try to gather her wits.

Becky opted to bring the bottle. Sitting on the couch, she twisted off the cap and poured two healthy portions from the primo whiskey one of her clients had given her last year for Christmas. "Start off slowly."

"My dad… nnn-not dad," Aurora stuttered in a shaky breath and tossed back half the glass.

Becky blinked. "Okay. Try using more words."

Aurora set her glass on the coffee table, collapsed back into the seat, and tossed her arms over her head. "He's not my dad, Becks."

"How is your dad not your dad?" Becky covered her mouth. "Oh, did your mom have an affair with the mailman or something?"

"The mailman?" Aurora's voice crescendoed.

"Oh no! I was only teasing. Honest." Becky's face drained of all color.

"She didn't have an affair!"

"But how is your dad not your dad? Was she married before or got knocked up and your dad married her to save her good name? He's the kind of man who would do that." Becky nodded in a decisive way, indicating that was the only explanation.

"You need to stop watching so many made-for-TV romances or whatever. They're seriously warping your brain."

"I'm sorry. Accountant, remember. I like things to have simple explanations. Two plus two is four." Becky repositioned, with her back against the arm of the couch, and sat cross-legged facing Aurora. "Walk me through it."

"Okay." Aurora's eyes darted to the ceiling. "It's weird to talk about, but here goes. When my parents wanted to start a family, they couldn't get pregnant. They had to use a sperm donor…" Aurora couldn't state the rest.

Becky didn't speak for several seconds. "Is that all?"

"What do you mean *is that all*? All my life, I thought he was my dad."

"He is. He's more of a father than mine, who left mom and me when I was three." Becky splashed more whiskey into her glass.

Aurora sighed. "I know that, but it's weird to learn at the age of twenty-nine. To find out he's not—"

"It doesn't mean he doesn't love you," Becky rushed out. There was opinionated, and then there was Becky.

"I never said he didn't. I don't know how to explain how I'm feeling to you. I know you have daddy issues."

"Not really. You have to have a father to have those issues." Becky stated the words with venom.

"Uh, I'm not sure what to say after—"

"We're not talking about me. Let's get back to you." Becky sipped her drink as if needing a second to regroup. "I understand why the news would be upsetting and it'll take time to set in, but how is your life over? That seems a bit dramatic, even for you."

"Don't you see? The two people who raised me have been lying to me my whole life. I feel it here." Aurora clutched her floral blouse over her breast. "How can I trust anyone if my own parents kept this from me?"

Becky's brow crumpled. "How'd you find out anyway? Did they just decide to tell you?"

"I went to his doctor's appointment to find out if he needs a kidney transplant—"

"Does he?"

Aurora shook her head. "They're starting him on dialysis, but the doctor says he's a good candidate for a transplant if need be."

"Wow. That's heavy. And that's the moment they revealed this secret to you?" Becky's upper body slumped.

"No. When I heard the news, I offered to donate mine because I thought I'd be a match."

"Let me see if I'm following everything now. Your dad may need a kidney, and you found out his swimmers didn't really swim, meaning you can't donate." Becky let out a tiny whistle.

"And I just started my temp job today. Rather, I spent the morning in a training program and then met some of the people I'll be working with. But, with this… family stuff, I feel like calling and saying I just don't have the headspace for this temp job when everything around me is tumbling down."

Becky refilled their glasses. "You can't quit. Aren't you the one who said this could be your way in at the medical school? You've wanted to be a nurse your entire life."

"Not anymore."

"No!" Becky held up a *stop right there* hand. "Don't let one bad teacher in high school discourage you from pursuing your dream."

"Mr. Huff called me an idiot in front of the entire class."

"He called everyone idiots. And need I remind you he taught geometry? He has zero clue what it takes to be a nurse. Mr. Huff was a bitter old man who never married and took his revenge out on anyone in his path, especially bright and beautiful young women."

"He never called you an idiot. No one has. You're twenty-nine going on sixty when it comes to life choices. Everyone always seeks your opinion."

"Only when it comes to finances. I'm a math geek. I would like to add, though, that if you're correct that everyone wants my opinion, you should listen to me about nursing school and everything else for that matter."

"I don't want to talk about nursing school. Not right now." Aurora took a belt of whiskey. "Let's talk about something happy to get my mind off everything. How's the wedding planning?"

Becky blew her bangs out of her eyes. "I don't know why Nate and I didn't decide to elope. So much for being the wise one."

"It would have been easier for all of us."

"Have you found a date yet?" Becky's eyes narrowed.

"Uh, did you not hear about my day? How was I supposed to find a date while dealing with... everything?"

"Okay. Putting a pin in it for now, but don't you think all of this would be easier to handle if you had a girlfriend to go home to?"

"I have you." Aurora patted Becky's thigh.

"I'm getting married in the spring. Nathan will have completed his PhD and will be back in Boston. You need a plan, Aurora. Either get a girlfriend, or start looking for someone to pay half the rent here. The months will fly by, and you have a tendency to put off unpleasant tasks."

"I can't stomach the idea of living with a stranger. We've been roommates since college. And, no way do I want a girlfriend. Will you be off-limits for when my life crashes and burns? It happens on a regular basis for me."

"I know. Of course, I'll be there for you, but it's different when you're dating someone." Becky tugged her shirt away from her chest, their *older than dirt* window A/C unit not doing much to combat the heat.

"Dating is so last century. Study after study shows women are better off alone. Besides, men just want women who remind them of their mommies who they can fuck and who'll also cook and clean for them." Aurora emphatically raised a fist to hammer this point home.

"That's disturbing, and news flash—you dig chicks."

"Exactly. I love women, who can be, well,"—Aurora motioned to her emotional state—"hot messes."

"I'm not."

"You're also straight and getting married. Although, you've been getting your panties in a bunch about my dateless state for your wedding since you got engaged, so there's an argument you're just as unbalanced as the rest of the female species."

"You try balancing the pressure of work, a long-distance relationship, and planning a wedding. But you're trying to distract me. Do you plan to stay celibate?" Becky raised a thin, dark eyebrow.

"Fuck no. I love sex. I plan to have lots of sex, just not a relationship. Know any women who are only interested in being fuck buddies? Commitment is a hoax forced upon society by religious nuts. No one can stay faithful to one person for their whole life. Not with all the options on the table." Aurora made a sweeping motion with her hand.

"You do know I'm getting married, considering you asked me how the wedding plans are going and you're going to be my maid of honor?"

Aurora backtracked quickly. "You and Nathan are different. You two are perfect for each other."

"I'd almost given up, and now I'm getting married. There's someone out there for you, too."

Aurora shook her head. "No. I used to think there was, but after today, I know it's not in the cards for me. My entire life has been a lie."

"Oh, please. I know the news is a big deal, and it'll take time to adjust, but don't forget the big picture. Your parents adore you. I used to wish I was their daughter." There was wistfulness in Becky's eyes.

"They lied, Becks." Aurora drew in a sharp intake of air.

"When? Did you ever ask if half of your DNA actually came from your father?"

"I didn't think I had to!" Aurora slapped a palm on her thigh.

"And what about kids who are adopted? Do you think they aren't loved by their adoptive parents?"

Aurora's head snapped up. "Does this mean I was adopted in some way?"

"No!"

"I think in some way it does." Aurora slouched down and swallowed more whiskey.

"How's your dad doing? With everything?" Becky asked.

"He's staying strong for Mom and me. As much as he can. He's always so exhausted and barely leaves their apartment."

"Is he being added to the list, then? If he needs a new kidney?"

Aurora sniffed. "It's being considered. They have to run more tests, and there's the complication that others who are worse off are already in line. Hence why I wanted to give him one of mine."

Becky pulled Aurora against her. "Everything's going to be okay, you know. No matter what, Aurora Borealis, he's your dad. He loves you, and you love him."

"Why didn't they tell me, though?"

"Have you asked them?"

"I—I was in shock about everything."

"Do they know you're upset?" Becky smoothed Aurora's hair.

"Of course, but I didn't want to make a big deal about it. Not after learning my dad is starting dialysis and may need a transplant."

"Do you think maybe you're more upset than you may have been because of the magnitude of everything? It's been a difficult few years with your dad's illness."

"Maybe. But, I can't get it out of my head that everything I thought I knew about myself isn't true."

CHAPTER THREE

AFTER GETTING OFF AT THE HYNES SUBWAY STOP, Stella elected to walk down Massachusetts Avenue instead of taking the dreaded bus that was perpetually late, smelly, and overcrowded. She needed to clear her head from the previous night, even though she'd only had one margarita, while Rosie had demolished three. Of course, Rosie didn't have to teach her first class until tonight, allowing her plenty of time to put herself back together. Rosie was a pro at tearing herself up and banishing the ill effects of a hangover in record time. And dinner with Stella was one of Rosie's new semester rituals. Tying on one last doozy before getting back to the grind. During the semester, she'd limit herself to one small glass of wine per evening just to take the edge off until winter break, when she'd head back to the Caribbean to cut loose and recoup.

Stella had always been the moderate one in all things. Hence why one drink left her mind fuzzy at best. The walk would do her some good, and it'd make up for Stella skipping her run home the previous night. Not to mention, Stella loved traversing the quaint tree-lined side streets with brownstone apartment buildings and brick sidewalks. Back in the day, when she was still married, she'd lived in one. Now, just her ex and child resided in their apartment with a small garden out front enclosed by a black iron gate.

Twenty minutes later, she stepped into her office at seven on the dot, not too much later than normal, but she had a packed day so perhaps the stroll down memory lane hadn't been the wisest choice.

Mia knocked on the door one minute after the hour, not allowing Stella to tidy up her emails before hitting the ground running until the end of the work day.

Half past nine, her desk phone rang. "Dr. Gilbert."

"Stella, we have a problem with Dr. Howie." It was Vera, Dean Andrews's assistant.

Stella stifled a groan. "He's only been on staff for a few weeks. How do we already have a problem?"

"He doesn't like the classroom he's been assigned and wants to change to one he happened upon during orientation."

Stella reached for her squeeze ball, which was a silly blue dog that her daughter, Kenzie, had given her for Christmas last year. "That involves me how?"

"My schedule is packed today." Vera spoke the words as if the world would cease to rotate if she stopped whatever it was she did all day. "Can you personally go to the Scheduling office to plead Dr. Howie's case?"

"You can't be serious."

"I am. This is part of your new role as course manager to liaison between the hospital and school. That includes scheduling. I'm certain Dean Andrews explained this to you."

"Nope. I would have remembered, considering it's no secret that department is one of the worst run branches on campus and I'd rather perform a lobotomy on myself than speak to anyone there. Can my admin—?"

"Scheduling listens better to people in white coats." Vera

supplied the details of the assigned room and the room change request. "I hope you got all that. I gotta run."

There was a click on the line.

Stella tapped the receiver against her forehead before replacing it on the base. "I hate that woman."

She exited her office and hung a left, walking down the characterless but pristine hallway, making her way to the bridge on the second floor that connected the hospital to the campus building where the majority of classes were held. She nodded to a few doctors on the way, not stopping. Not that she was expected to since everyone was just as harried.

In the stairwell of the instructional building, she climbed to the fifth floor on the far side of the building. Perhaps it was the dean's way of protecting everyone else from Scheduling hell. The department was responsible for making room reservations for classes, student organizations, special events, and other campus-wide activities for the medical and dental school, in addition to the school of public health. Moreover, it coordinated all AV and lab requests. Every professor had had at least one run-in with Scheduling that left a sour taste in their mouth.

The door to E507 was propped open, and Stella marched in, doing her best to look like she wasn't a woman to be trifled with.

Sitting at the front desk was a woman she'd never seen before. Stella would have remembered the woman's dark roast espresso eyes and hair almost the same color falling in waves to her shoulder.

"Good morning," the woman said in a pleasing tone.

"Morning. Where's Winnie?"

"Who's Winnie?"

"Isn't she the boss here?" Stella peered at the three empty workstations right behind the front desk.

"Oh! I think I remember Shelly saying Winnie had quit or

something recently. Shelly's in charge as far as I know. But I'm new, so…" The woman let out an adorable nervous giggle.

Stella had to stop staring into the woman's entrancing eyes and focus on the task at hand. "Okay. What about Shelly? Is she nearby?"

"Running late, I'm afraid. Something about a smashup on Route Two."

Stella checked the time on her watch. "You're new, and you're here all alone?"

"Seems so. Shelly had security open the door for me when I arrived. And she was able to talk me through getting logged into the computer. I've temped in many offices, but so far, this has been different. Kind of a *toss you into the deep end and see if you survive* mentality." The woman let out another nervous bout of laughter.

"I see. Maybe I should come back then." Stella sighed, not liking the idea of leaving and having to deal with the wrath of Vera later if the matter wasn't resolved soon. Vera was the type who expected everything to get done last week.

"If you'd like, but I can try to help you. I've been reading this for the past two hours." She lifted a blue binder. "It's a step-by-step for making reservations, and Shelly gave me a crash course with the software yesterday morning."

Stella didn't want to burst the young woman's enthusiasm, but she wasn't sure reading a manual would be sufficient. Although, this was the only free time she had the rest of the day, and she doubted Vera would give two shits about the situation. This was Scheduling to a T.

Stella rested her arms on the counter of the front desk. "Here's the problem. One of our new doctors doesn't like his assigned classroom and wants to switch. I'm sorry. What's your name?"

"Aurora." She stuck out her hand.

Stella took it, noticing Aurora's skin was soft and warm. "Dr. Gilbert."

Aurora moved the mouse, presumably waking up her computer. "What's the name of the class? No, wait." She flipped the binder to a certain page and ran her finger down the paper. "Yes, that's right. It'll be easier to find the reservation if you give me the room number, day, and time."

"C309, on Tuesdays and Thursdays at ten in the morning."

Aurora moved her mouse, clicking here and there. "Got it. I can see what other rooms are available during that time."

"He has his heart set on one in particular. E405."

"Let's take a look-see." More clicking. "Oh." Aurora's face inched closer to the screen. "This doesn't make sense. The room is free, but the system won't let me reserve it."

"Can you override it or something?"

"Uh, hold on a second. I remember reading that some rooms need setup and breakdown times." Aurora consulted the tabs in the binder. "E building." She flipped the pages. "That's what I thought. The room has a partition. In order to seat forty-five—the number of students in the class—the partition has to be opened." She paused to read. "And facilities needs thirty minutes to open it and reposition all of the desks."

"What class is in there before or after? Maybe we can move them."

Aurora's eyes widened. "Is that normal?"

"Not really, but Dr. Howie is special. He's new here, and wooing him to our school was a major pet project of the dean."

"Translation: what the doctor wants, the doctor gets."

"Exactly. So, who's in the way?"

"Dr. Beacham. It's not a class but a weekly admin meeting. I can see what's available—"

"Damn. He's the big dog in neurology and has worked here since the beginning of time, or so it seems. Come to think of it,

Dean Andrews attends the meetings." Stella tried to think of a workaround to the dilemma.

"Oh. This seems like a problem, then." Aurora's brow crumpled.

Stella rested her chin on her palm, unable to solve it. "Yes, it is."

"What if we moved Dr. Howie to a different room and told him it was one of the best rooms on the campus?"

"Which room would that be?" Stella asked hopefully.

Aurora's cheeks tinged with pink like two tiny apples. "I don't really know. I was hoping you did."

God, she was adorable. Stella straightened. "Of course. I'm sorry. Can you check A203?"

CHAPTER FOUR

AURORA TAPPED ON THE KEYBOARD, HER EYES wanting to find the doctor's penetrating sky-blues again. They were the color Aurora associated with a brilliant summer day when the horizon seemed to go on forever, as if beckoning her to dive in and get lost for an eternity. Aurora was fairly certain she was picking up a prominent come-hither ping on her gaydar.

Not that it was wise to get involved with a doctor while employed by the university, but it didn't hurt to daydream. What would Dr. Gilbert's full lips feel like on Aurora's bare skin and other areas? How could she get the doctor's deets for when Aurora's temp job ended in two months? The school had to have a who's who page for employees. She made a mental note to check, secretly wishing the page would list Dr. Gilbert's likes and dislikes. Or she could research the woman on social media.

Aurora had always been a sucker for blondes, and Dr. Gilbert had her tresses up in a messy up-do. Another weakness of Aurora's, forcing her to cross her legs so she could concentrate on the job and not on... "Shoot, that room is also taken."

"Any room on that floor? All of them were upgraded this summer."

Aurora searched each room with little success. "Tell you what. Why don't you leave me your number, and I'll puzzle this out and get back to you as soon as possible? I'm sure there's a solution. There's always a solution."

Dr. Gilbert seemed to hesitate, but after consulting her sports watch, she said, "Yes, I think that's the best course of action." She pulled a business card and pen out of her lab coat pocket and clicked it. "Here's my office line, and I'll add my personal number." She handed it to Aurora.

Aurora read the name on the card. Stella. Aurora had never met a Stella in real life. "Do you have a preference for which number?" Aurora practically wanted to high-five herself for getting the sexy doctor's number.

"Whatever one works for you. This is important."

Aurora had an important idea for the personal number after the temp job was done and over with, leaving her a free woman. "Of course. And, just in case." Aurora jotted down her name and personal number on a Post-it note.

Stella looked at it and grinned. "You have distinctive hand-writing. The type you don't forget."

That made Aurora blush, but it also gave her a burst of confidence. "Don't worry about a thing, Dr. Gilbert. You're in good hands."

The doctor smiled. "Good to know." Her voice was sexy as hell. "I better get going." She didn't move right away, staring into Aurora's eyes. "Call me."

"Will do." Aurora shook the card to solidify her determination.

Stella wheeled about, charging out of the door in the same manner she'd waltzed in.

When the coast was clear, Aurora fanned her face with the card still in her grasp. "Oh, my," was all she said.

Moments later, Shelly, Aurora's supervisor, rushed in, her hair looking as if she just rolled out of bed. "Morning, Aurora. Everything okay here?" Shelly's eyes panned the three empty desks. "Are you alone? I phoned Kip to tell him to stay with you when he wasn't on a job."

"Oh, he was here earlier." Aurora had only seen him for a hot minute, but she didn't want to be that employee that got others into trouble. Not so soon, at least.

"The lack of professionalism in this office is mind-blowing," Shelly said.

Aurora had to curb a smile, considering Shelly had been missing in action, and upon further inspection, her blouse was buttoned wrong and she wore one navy and one black shoe. At least they were the same style, but they weren't a matching pair, unless Shelly was the trendy type. Was looking like one got dressed in the dark a thing these days? The outfit made it seem like Shelly may have fibbed about being stuck in traffic to cover waking late.

"I'm going to get breakfast from the cafeteria, and then we'll chat." Without another word, Shelly left, her rapid footsteps in the hallway echoing in the empty wing.

"Oh, I don't need anything. Thanks for asking," Aurora muttered under her breath.

Next to appear was Kip, the head AV tech. "Hey there, Audrey."

"It's Aurora."

"That's what I said. Have you seen Isaac?"

"Who?"

"The other tech. The scrawny one." Kip puffed out his chest some, but it didn't make him appear all that manly, and the pastiness of his skin only reinforced the nerdy tech vibe.

"Can't say that I have."

Kip consulted the AV schedule. "He's supposed to be in A301. Do you know if he's there?"

Let me consult my crystal ball. "I don't, actually. Sorry."

The phone rang, and Aurora pounced on it, not wanting to continue the conversation with Kip, who had an innocent face, but something about him gave her the willies. "Scheduling, this is Aurora."

"Where's my tech?" the man on the other line barked.

"Uh, can you hold on?"

"Kip," she said out of the side of her mouth, covering the phone with her hand. "There's a man wanting to know where his tech is."

"What room is he in?" he whispered.

Aurora put the phone back to her ear. "What room are you in?"

"E203. This is Dr. Greene."

Aurora jotted the info down on a pad and held it up for Kip. He was already pale, but Aurora was certain he lost the last remaining color in his face.

Kip took a massive step back. Another bad sign.

"Dr. Greene, I'm sending a tech to you right now." Aurora snapped her fingers to get Kip's attention, but he seemed to be having a staring contest with a ghost, given the frightened expression on his face.

The doctor thanked her, and from his tone, Aurora guessed Kip was in for an ass chewing.

Aurora hung up the phone. "Kip, I think you should go before he calls back."

"Let me see who should be there, first." He ran his fingers down the printed sheets tacked to the board, the words *Daily Jobs* written at the top. "Is this for a ten or eleven o'clock class?"

"Does it matter? He's there now and wants a tech. You're the only tech I know."

"Oops." Kip swallowed and then headed out of the office, dragging his feet as if he didn't plan on ever returning.

Five minutes later, a man in the same type of polo shirt Kip had on, although this guy had his sternly tucked into his pressed khaki pants, with a seam that could slice cheese, walked in. Aurora guessed the tech was a good inch or two taller than Kip. "Have you seen Kip? I just bumped into Dr. Greene, and he's hopping mad."

"Kip's on his way there now. Are you Isaac?"

He smiled. "Yes, I'm sorry. I wasn't here when you stopped by yesterday, but I heard you'd be starting full-time today. Aurora, right?" Isaac tendered his calloused hand to shake.

"Yes. Nice to meet you."

"I'm going to take a break. Got here for the weekly 6:00 a.m. surgical residents meeting." Isaac yawned and made his way to the break room. Soon Aurora heard what she assumed was *SportsCenter* on the TV in there.

Does anyone actually work a full day here? At least Isaac had the best excuse so far.

Kip returned ten minutes later. "Dr. Greene is a piece of work." From the whiteness of Kip's lips, Aurora guessed he'd received a spectacular dressing down. "Is Isaac back?"

Focusing on her computer screen, Aurora said, "Break room."

"Isaac, get your scrawny ass out here!" Kip shouted.

Aurora flinched, unused to people screaming in an office.

The TV noise stopped. "What do you want? I'm eating breakfast," Isaac called out.

"Bri's coming back to cover the night shift. Alice is tired of hiring temps," Kip hollered, cupping his mouth megaphone-like.

Aurora sank down into her chair some.

Isaac rushed out into the main area. "What?"

"Bri's coming back." Kip's thin lips puckered.

"I thought she was dead."

Kip laughed like that was the funniest thing he'd heard all day, much to Aurora's confusion.

"No, really. I thought she died when she didn't come to work after getting kicked in the head by a horse." Isaac whacked the side of his head, making a thudding sound that rattled Aurora.

Kip eyeballed Isaac. "What are you talking about?"

"Her last day here before summer, when we didn't know it was her last day, she'd told me she'd been kicked in the head by a horse. Remember? She worked at a stable on the weekends."

"If you spoke to her after it happened, why'd you think she'd died?" Kip rolled onto his tippy toes. Was he trying to appear taller?

"I never saw her again." Isaac hefted one shoulder. "I thought it might have been one of those injuries that no one knows about for a day or two and then—" He made a slicing motion across his throat with his hand, implying death.

"Dude. Alice transferred her to the main campus."

"Really. No one told me that. I've been wanting to get transferred there for ages."

Kip scratched the back of his head and furrowed his brow. "Why didn't you tell me about the horse?"

"Are you sure I didn't?" Isaac ran a hand over his crew cut.

"It seems like something I would remember."

"Must have slipped my mind." Isaac pulled up his pants, his belt cinched tightly in an effort to keep them in place. The tall beanpole of a man didn't have an ass to speak of.

"Did you also get kicked in the head?"

"W-what? No." Isaac seemed perplexed.

Aurora watched the two of them, stunned they were actually having this conversation. She was thanking her stars the job was only a two-month stint working the front desk while the regular scheduler was on maternity leave. Already Aurora had to resist the urge to etch tick marks onto the brick wall like prisoners do. And this Alice person Kip had spoken of, was she the big kahuna? Higher up than Shelly? Where in the hell was she hiding? Aurora, though, had learned from previous temp jobs not to ask too many questions. Toxic work environments like this one could suck the life out of someone.

"When's she coming in?" Isaac asked.

"Couple of hours from now." Kip flipped about. "Aurora, can you schedule a tech meeting for noon today so we can all get on the same page and avoid more Dr. Greene situations? Someone dropped the ball, and that can't continue to happen." He slammed a fist into his other hand.

Aurora was positive Kip had dropped the ball on the Dr. Greene reservation and wondered if he was the type to always pass the buck.

"Won't we meet in the break room?" Isaac asked.

"Yeah. That's where we usually meet."

"You want me to schedule the break room for noon?" Aurora asked, wondering if the space even had a designation in the scheduling database.

"Yeah." Kip fled the office, nearly crashing into Shelly, who was carrying a tray from the cafeteria.

"I'll be in the break room," Shelly said without stopping, her tray loaded up with a bowl of fresh fruit, a muffin, and bacon slices on a white plate.

Aurora tried scheduling the room, but as she suspected, it didn't appear as a resource. Not wanting to trouble Shelly, Aurora printed a note stating the room was booked for noon. When Shelly left again, which Aurora was now betting would happen within the half hour, she would tape it to the door.

"I better get to the E building for my eleven o'clock recording." Isaac left.

Aurora flipped through the binder, determined to solve Dr. Gilbert's dilemma.

Midday rolled by, and Aurora hadn't seen the mysterious

Bri, who may or may not have a horse's hoofprint on her head. When the clock struck twelve-thirty, Kip paced the office, huffing and puffing behind Aurora. By one, he was hopping mad.

He snatched the phone off his desk. "Bri hasn't shown up!"

There was a muffled voice that Aurora thought belonged to a woman. The mysterious Alice, perhaps?

"Why is Bri setting up the dean's conference room? I usually do that." Kip turned around and whispered, "She hasn't even stopped in to report for duty."

Did anyone take their job seriously in this office?

Aurora's desk rang, and she answered.

"This is Mary, Dr. Beacham's admin. I need to cancel a weekly meeting in E405."

Aurora's heart raced. "Oh, really? That's a popular room."

"Is it? Dr. Beacham hates it."

Aurora did a mental high five. Dr. What's His Name wanted it, and it would allow Aurora to impress Dr. Hottie. "I understand. Should I look for a different room?"

"No, thank you. He's decided to use our break room instead."

"Okay. I'll email you the cancellation. Thank you for letting me know."

Within minutes, Aurora had moved everything around and called Stella's desk line.

"Dr. Gilbert."

"Hi. This is Aurora in Scheduling. We spoke earlier—"

"Yes, Aurora. I remember. I'm hoping you have good news for me."

"I do as a matter of fact. Dr. Beacham moved his weekly meeting, so E405 has been reserved."

"And the partition? There's time?" Dr. Gilbert's voice sounded eager.

"Plenty." Aurora dragged out the first syllable.

Kip slammed his desk phone down, letting loose a string of curse words that startled Aurora.

"Everything okay there?" Dr. Gilbert asked.

"Oh, yeah. The door accidently slammed shut," Aurora covered for Kip, praying Stella hadn't heard Kip's colorful outburst.

"Well, thanks for everything. I won't forget this."

Aurora said goodbye and hung up. *Oh, I hope I can cash that in some day.*

Shelly popped her head into the office. "I'm going for lunch."

Good grief, the woman spent more time eating than working.

Aurora sighed and counted how many more work hours were left in the day. Three. She could hold on.

CHAPTER FIVE

STELLA STOOD IN THE DOORWAY OF HER APARTMENT, looking Kim in the eyes. "Anything to report?" Stella asked her ex, who was wearing tight jeans and a tank top, showcasing Kim's toned arms.

Kim's gaze darted heavenward. "Not on my end, Dr. Gilbert. Yours?"

Stella sighed. "I'm sorry. I didn't mean it that way. Sometimes, I don't know what to say to you."

The expression on Kim's face softened some. "I know what you mean. Even after all this time, I kinda dread this."

"Thanks for that reality check." Stella chuckled despite herself.

"Kenz has a school project due on Tuesday. Being the precocious eleven-year old that she is, she hasn't started it yet, and I thought it'd be great for you two to work on it together."

"Sounds great!" Stella wanted to groan in frustration, but it wasn't about helping Kenzie. It was Kim's passive aggressive way of saying, "You need to get more involved with our child's education." Stella paid their daughter's tuition, thirty thousand a year, and had to move into a small two-bedroom apartment in

Brighton near Boston College so she could continue supporting Kim, who had only recently rejoined the working world and still didn't have her feet under her, and their daughter.

"Have fun this weekend. Do I need to pick her up—?"

Stella raised her hand. "No worries. I'll drop her off at school on Monday."

Kim remained frozen for five excruciatingly long seconds. "Okay then. I'll see you in two weeks." She flipped around and wandered down the cracked pathway to Commonwealth Avenue.

Mackenzie, her wild red curls the spitting image of Kim's, sat on the couch, playing a game on Stella's tablet.

"We got our orders."

Kenzie looked up. "I heard. We have to work on the school project."

Stella practically fell onto the couch next to her daughter. "What's it on, kiddo?"

"Ohio."

"I know nothing about Ohio," Stella admitted.

"So far, I only know they claim that eight presidents had a strong connection to the Buckeye state."

"That's two things. Presidents and the nickname. You're on a roll, Little Mac!" Stella held her hand up for a high five.

Kenzie smacked her mom's hand hard. "How do we construct a float?"

"Come again?"

"I have to make a float that symbolizes everything I know about Ohio for the project."

No wonder your mother left this for us to work on. "That's interesting. I'm really praying you don't mean a parade-size float."

"Get real, Mom."

"Just checking and very relieved. We should brainstorm this later. It's Friday night, and you know what that means."

Kenzie pumped a fist. "Pizza and movie night!"

"Darn tooting."

"Mom, no one says *darn tooting*."

"I do."

Kenzie eyed her cautiously. "Maybe you should try not to. Try saying something cooler, like *totes*."

"Why?"

"Do girls like it when you say things like that?"

"What are you talking about? You're a girl. Do you like it?" Stella bumped her shoulder into Kenzie's.

"I wasn't talking about—" Kenzie blushed. "Never mind. Too hungry to think."

"Me too." Stella took the tablet from Kenzie and placed their usual order: large cheese pizza, a chicken Caesar to share, and cinnamon bread twists. "Okay, twenty minutes. I'm going to hop in the shower and rinse off the day."

Kenzie reclaimed the tablet. "Yeah, yeah. I know the drill. I'll set the table," she said in a mocking tone.

"Such a smart aleck." Stella stepped into the bedroom to grab a clean pair of green scrub pants and a white T-shirt before heading into the bathroom. "Oh, Kenzie," she hollered from the bathroom, "what time does a cat see a doctor?"

"Me-ow time!" Kenzie hollered back, annunciating both syllables as if separate words so it sounded more like, "Me. Ow!"

Stella chuckled as she cranked the water to hot.

Ten minutes later, with her hair dripping down the back of her T-shirt, Stella was back in the front room with Kenzie. "Good. You didn't burn the place down, and the table is set."

There were two plain white plates, red checkered napkins, salad forks, and two glasses of Perrier on the coffee table.

"Do you ever plan on moving into a bigger place where you can have an actual table to eat at?" Kenzie set the tablet on the side table.

"When you start chipping in on rent." Stella tickled her

side. "Besides, there's a small table in the kitchen, but you can't see the TV from there. And, I like this place. It only takes an hour to tidy it up. What movie would you like to watch?"

"*The Parent Trap*."

Stella arched one eyebrow. "Again?"

Kenzie nodded, taking the remote from her mom's hand. "Yep. It's my all-time fave."

They settled on the couch, Kenzie snuggling against Stella's side. This was Stella's favorite ritual with her daughter. Stella had never been a snuggling person, not until she'd held her daughter for the first time. She couldn't prove it, but Stella suspected her ex was jealous of how much Stella doted over Mackenzie. Kim also adored their daughter, but when they were still a couple, Kim seemed to comment how often Stella cuddled with Kenzie, but then later when it was just the two of them, Stella would rebuff Kim's attempts. The majority of the time, Stella hadn't been aware she was doing it until it was pointed out, but looking back on it now, Stella realized she'd been freezing her wife out for some time.

"Mom!" Kenzie snapped her fingers in front of Stella's face. "Someone's at the door. Where's the tip?"

Stella pulled out the little drawer of the table on her side of the couch. "Here ya go."

Kenzie paused the movie and hopped up to answer the door, Stella right behind her.

A kid barely old enough to shave stood on the front stoop with the blue hot bag in both hands. He handed the items to Stella and accepted the dollar bills from Kenzie with a polite dip of the head. The transaction lasted a little longer than a minute.

When the door shut, Kenzie asked, "What's he going to do when robots take over his job?"

Stella's eyes widened. "That's an intriguing question for a Friday night."

"Meaning we should discuss it another time."

Stella placed the pizza box on the hot pads Kenzie had set out. "Are you worried about robots?"

"Nope." Kenzie shrugged. "I want to be a doctor like you."

"Since when? Last time you wanted to land on the far side of the moon." Stella ripped off a slice, put it on Kenzie's plate, and then selected one for herself.

"The Chinese beat me to it," Kenzie said with a heavy heart.

"Okay, but going on that logic, you won't be the first doctor. Hippocrates beat you by hundreds of years."

"I know, but it seems more useful than landing on the moon."

"Good point, unless we all have to leave the planet."

"We'll still need doctors in space. Duh!"

Stella swallowed a bite and chased it with sparkling water.

"Do you ever go on dates?" Kenzie asked.

"Um, what?" Stella shook her head as if to clear her ears.

"Do you date? Mom has been going on dates for months now, and well…" Kenzie picked at the crust on her pizza. "She introduced me to her last week. You haven't introduced anyone to me, and from the looks of this place, no one besides me visits."

"Oh." Stella's mind had to downshift to understand Kenzie's words. Kim was dating? This was the first Stella was hearing about it. Why hadn't Kim told her? How long had her ex been dating before introducing their daughter? Kenzie mentioned months, but that was vague.

"So, do you have anyone you want me to meet?"

Stella shook her head. "Sorry, Kenzie. Between you and my job, I don't have time for anything else."

Kenzie rolled her eyes, looking so much like Kim. "But what will happen when I grow up? You'll be all alone. That makes me sad."

Stella wrapped an arm around her daughter's shoulder.

"Hey, there. Don't think things like that. Your mom is fine." Feeling like she had to clarify, she added, "I'm fine."

"But—?"

"Seriously, Kenz. I'm not sad at all. I like my life. I have the most amazing daughter, who'll be the first doctor in space, and I love my job. What else do I need?"

"Have you considered getting a dog?" Kenzie looked overly eager.

"Oh, boy. Did you set this whole thing up?"

"Wh-what? No. I wouldn't do that." Kenzie attempted to appear completely innocent.

"You've been trying to con me into getting a dog since you could talk." Stella poked Kenzie's side.

"Have not!"

"Have to!"

Kenzie bit into a pizza slice, taking longer to chew than her normal inhalation method.

"Is your mom really dating someone?" Stella asked.

Kenzie nodded, still chewing.

"Do you know how long?"

"For a while now." Mackenzie shrugged.

"What's she like?"

The child swallowed. "She's okay."

"Just okay?" Stella arched her brows.

"Yeah." Kenzie avoided Stella's eyes.

"It's fine if you like her. It won't hurt my feelings."

"Are you sure?"

"Yes. Of course. If she's going to be in your mom's life, I want you two to get along. Do you?"

"Before I answer, do you pinky swear it won't hurt your feelings?"

Stella presented her pinky for the sacred vow.

After sealing the deal, Kenzie said, "She's pretty cool. She works with dinosaurs."

Stella's face crumpled into confusion. "What?"

"At the museum."

"Your mom is dating a paleontologist?"

"Yeah. I think that's the word mom used."

"Impressive." Stella whistled.

"She's going to give me a behind-the-scenes tour next weekend. Michael is so jealous!"

Michael had been Kenzie's best friend since they were two.

"Can't Michael go?"

"That's what Mom said," Kenzie pouted.

"You should invite him. He's had a rough year with his dad—"

"Dying. I know."

"It's important to be there for the people you care about." Stella tried not to sound like she was lecturing.

"Fine, but if his mom dates someone cool like Rooney, I hope he remembers this."

"Rooney," Stella parroted.

"Yeah, that's her name. Cool, huh?"

"Totes."

CHAPTER SIX

AURORA GAVE BECKY A HUG BEFORE TAKING HER SEAT in the faux black leather chair in the fashionable bar around the corner from their apartment. The high-top table wobbled to the left when Aurora steady herself with one hand. "Why do all tables, no matter where you are, have one bum leg?"

"It's the law. That's the only explanation."

A waitress zipped by without noticing Aurora, not for a lack of trying on Aurora's part to flag down the server.

"Next time, flash your boobs. Who knows? She may play for your team."

"Is that the type of woman I want to attract, though? One who only gives my boobs the time of day?"

"Depends. Are you looking for a connection or sex?" Becky asked as if she was deadly serious.

"An excellent point. Hey!" Aurora shouted at the woman's retreating back.

"Yes?" The waitress clearly wasn't impressed by Aurora's *hey* given her tight smile.

"May I have a whiskey neat?"

The waitress quirked a bushy eyebrow to Becky, in what can

only be described as her accounting outfit: cream colored blouse and black slacks.

"Make that two." Becky held two fingers in the air.

Without a word, the woman left.

"I bet she doesn't shave her armpits," Aurora said to Becky.

Becky puckered her face in disgust. "Those are the thoughts I wish you'd keep to yourself, because now I can't get the image of armpit hair floating in my drink out of my mind. However, I'm going for the world's worst segue, so hold on. Have you found a date to the wedding?"

Aurora raised a hand in the air. "Question."

Becky's expression was a mixture of annoyance and curiosity. "We haven't been in school for a long time. No need to raise your hand. Go on."

"Does said wedding date have to shave in all the appropriate areas?"

"Which areas do you classify as appropriate?" Becky's smile was proof she found Aurora goofy in an adorable, albeit frustrating way.

"Underarms, legs, and upper lip if need be."

"I'm getting to the point that I won't be so picky who you bring as long as you bring someone."

Aurora groaned. "It's months away, Becks! Way too early to ride my ass like this all the time."

"Don't start. You're the maid of honor. You can't come alone."

"Why the hell not? You're being prejudiced against singles."

"Singles?" Becky crossed her arms and narrowed her dark eyes, which had matching bags under them.

"Yes. I'm tired of people forcing women into coupling. It's misogynist or patriarchal." Aurora scratched her head. "I get the two confused."

Becky's eyes practically spun in their sockets. "It's not men doing it. It's mothers!"

"And brides from hell." Aurora waved to Becky. "Exhibit A!"

Becky brandished her knife. "Don't you dare call me that!"

"Which? A bride from hell or exhibit A?"

"I don't like either." Becky still clutched her knife in a threatening manner.

Aurora showed her palms. "Hey, put down the weapon."

"Not until you promise you'll find a date to bring to my wedding."

"It's weird that you're having your first wedding before you're thirty."

"First wedding!" Becky put the knife back onto the hunter green napkin, shaking her head. "You have high hopes for my marriage."

"Statistically—"

Becky shook both hands in the air. "Oh, stop reading shit on the internet. Most of it is made up to please people like you."

"People like me?" Aurora positioned both hands on her chest.

"Desperate to prove a point. But the only person you're trying to convince is yourself, I think."

"I'm not trying to convince myself of anything. It's all of you I'm fighting. There is nothing wrong with being alone." Aurora pressed a finger onto the tabletop.

The waitress set down the drinks on black cocktail napkins. "Do you want to order any food?"

"We should get an appetizer if we're starting right out of the gate with whiskey," Becky said. "I don't want to carry you home like last time."

"We were at home the last time I drank whiskey."

"And I had to help you to bed." Becky ran her finger down the menu options. "The artichoke spinach dip with pita chips and the calamari."

The woman nodded, but she still wore a sour face.

When they were alone, Aurora commented, "That's a weird combo. You aren't pregnant, are you?"

"How would I be preggers if I haven't seen Nathan in four months?"

"That's weird. You're getting married this spring, and you haven't seen him much in over a year since you live a thousand miles apart. Are you sure this is the best course of action?" Aurora placed a hand on Becky's. "There's no shame in calling things off."

Becky slipped her hand out from under Aurora's. "Stop. I'm not going to cancel my wedding because you don't want to find a date."

"But it would save me so much time and energy." Aurora wilted in the chair, suggesting just thinking about the prospect was exhausting.

"Oh my God. I can't handle you sometimes. You're hot. Intelligent. Currently employed." Becky ticked off each with a finger. "Why is it so hard for you to find a date?"

"Because I don't want one. Women are complicated. I don't want complicated."

"Consider this your gift to me." Becky dramatically smothered her heart with a palm.

"I've already got my eye on the salad plates you've picked out. Seriously, why do you need sixteen? Do you even know sixteen people that you'd want to have over for dinner?"

"Aurora." Becky pronounced every letter in the name.

"Fine! Are you against me paying someone to come as my date? That's the level of commitment I want right now."

"At this point, not at all, but if you do go that route, make sure she shaves all the visible areas even if you have to pay more."

"What do you think the going rate is?"

"They probably make more than you and I do in a week."

"Really?" Aurora's eyebrows shot upward to her widow's peak. "Maybe I should look into it."

"What's wrong with you these days?"

"Nothing. Why are you looking at me like I have termites crawling out of my ears?"

"Because I can't figure you out. You didn't date much in college, but that was normal. Something's changed. The old Aurora wasn't dead set against relationships. Can you explain it to me?" Becky's eyes showed concern.

"I told you about my parents."

"But they love you and are supportive. Not once did they bat an eye about you being gay." Becky flicked her hands in the air. "A lot of people would love to have parents like yours."

"They probably accepted I was gay from the guilt eating them alive since before I was born when they'd concocted the plot to hide the truth of my conception from me forever," Aurora blurted out in a rush to avoid Becky cutting her off.

"Oh, wow. You really want to hold onto this one, don't you? Have you considered it wasn't a big deal to either of them? And that they wanted you so much they went to fertility doctors to ensure they had a child? You may be the most wanted child on the planet."

"They could have told me, though. You keep forgetting that part." Aurora circled a finger in the air.

"Maybe they planned to. On your wedding day." Becky winked.

"How do you turn everything around to weddings? That may be the other reason I'm resistant to finding a date."

"I'm not sure that's the reason either."

"Oh, please. Let's put your psychology minor to use." Aurora placed her hands on the table. "Why do you think I don't want to find a date?"

"You don't want me to move out?"

"It's not like you'll refuse to get married if I show up without a date." Aurora crossed her arms.

Becky drilled her eyes into Aurora's. "Prove me wrong."

"I have been. You chatter too much about weddings. It's making me sick."

"You may be in contention for the world's worst maid of honor. Keep it up." Becky tossed back her whiskey.

Aurora's shoulders sagged. "I'm sorry. I didn't mean it to come out so harshly. I am happy for you, Becks. You and Nathan are like peanut butter and jelly."

"I suggest writing that line down for your speech."

"Speech?" Aurora's spine snapped into a perfect line. "What speech?"

"At the wedding. The maid of honor and best man have to give speeches."

"Have to!" Aurora screeched. "Another thing couples want to force upon the singles."

"You know that's not a thing, right? Singles?"

"I'm going to start a movement. Rights for singles. This tyranny has to end!" Aurora slammed her glass down onto the table.

Becky laughed with Aurora caving in and laughing with her.

"Please don't become that bitter old lady in the neighborhood everyone hates." Becky's expression was sincere. "You have so much to offer. Any woman would be lucky to have you."

"Do I not have anything to offer as a singles?"

"Is it plural when only referring to yourself?"

"It's my movement, and I say yes." Aurora stuck out her tongue.

"Warped. You're becoming more and more warped the closer you get to thirty. It's like you're regressing back into a teenager, and I have to be honest; it's not pretty."

"No. I'm becoming more clearheaded, honestly. Since

getting the relationship monkey off my back, I've felt lighter."
Aurora pantomimed this and added, "Happier. Do you know
what I did last Saturday?"

"What?" Becky's eyes widened with anticipation.

"I went to the art museum and sat in front of one painting
for thirty minutes, completely lost in the amazingness of it."

"Who was the artist?"

"I have no idea. That's not the point. The point is I can do
whatever I want, whenever I want, even if that is to sit and
stare at something I don't understand but can still appreciate."

"You've pretty much summed up what it's like being in a
relationship, FYI. It's nearly impossible to understand how you
can love someone so much, but you still do."

The waitress set down the apps.

Aurora shoved a pita chip nearly knuckle deep into the dip.
"You're missing a key part. The best part of a painting is you
don't have to speak or explain anything. Girlfriends like to
dissect everything."

"Are you worried you won't be able to explain things to a
partner? That's a weird phobia." Becky popped calamari into
her mouth, which must have been scorching since she frantically waved her hand to cool off her tongue.

Aurora shoved a glass of water to Becky. "I don't have a
phobia. I have peacefulness. I'm feeling so zen-like these days.
Maybe you're jealous of me. Most married women are."

"Is that right?" Becky, after swallowing more water,
gestured for Aurora to fill her in. "This I've got to hear."

"Not just of me. I haven't lost my senses completely. But I
have read articles—"

"Oh my God, stop reading shit. It's seriously distorting your
mind. Start living. You'll be amazed by how much easier it is to
do that instead of tracking down information to reinforce ideas
you know you don't truly believe."

CHAPTER SEVEN

STELLA'S DESK PHONE RANG. "DR. GILBERT."

"Ah, Stella. I was hoping you wouldn't be in and I could just leave a message." It was Vera, the dean's admin.

"I'm not liking the sound of this." Stella held the phone between her right shoulder and ear, while trying to finish crafting an email.

"It's Dr. Howie. While he truly appreciates you accommodating him by making the room switch, he's not happy."

"Really?" Stella massaged her left temple. "Why not?"

"The carpet."

"What about it?" Now Stella was intrigued, although slightly miffed Dr. Howie kept going over her head to the dean's office to make these requests. Stella, the course manager, or her admin, really, should be his point of contact.

"It's brown."

Stella silently inhaled a deep breath. "I'm almost afraid to ask if there's a deeper meaning to the color brown."

Vera let out an exasperated tsking sound. "Apparently, this particular shade of brown is disturbing, and Dr. Howie can't focus on teaching."

"But he has been teaching in the room for a couple of weeks now."

"He's reached his breaking point, I suppose."

Stella made a gun with her fingers and pretended to blow out her brains. "Got it. Is there another room that's less... disturbing?"

"He's decided he'd like C430. I looked at the schedule online, and well... it isn't available. I'm heading to the main campus for a team building thing... otherwise I'd take care of it."

Vera's crucial pause was a crystal-clear signal she was lying, but it wouldn't help Stella's long-term career plans to call the dean's assistant a big fat liar. "Let me guess. You want me to work my magic and see if it can become available?"

"Bingo."

There was a knock on her office door. Stella covered the mouthpiece and said, "Come in." She then spoke into the phone, "I'll do my best, but I can't make any promises this late in the semester." Stella had her hand covering her eyes to shield whomever had entered her office from the fire in them. She probably shouldn't have said the last bit, but Vera, a thirty-year veteran at the school, was well versed in how things operated. Most doctors would be told to get over it and pay closer attention when receiving room assignments months in advance of the start of the semester. Those with Dr. Howie's clout were hardly ever told no.

"I understand Dr. Howie is peculiar, but I don't think I have to remind you that getting him on our staff was a major coup for the school."

You just did. "Leave it with me, Vera."

The line went dead.

Stella looked up from her desk. "Oh, I wasn't expecting you."

There stood Kim in what Stella always referred to as her

take no prisoners pinstripe suit. "Sorry to pop in like this without calling ahead, but I decided to take a chance to see if you would be in your office."

"Unfortunately."

Kim's hand shot to her hip.

Stella quickly corrected herself. "I didn't mean... I just got off the phone with Vera." Stella's wave implied *you know who she is.*

Kim's hand slid off her hip indicating the crisis was averted. "It appears she still has your number."

"And everyone else's on campus." Stella massaged the crease in her forehead, hoping to curb an oncoming headache.

"I've always liked her style. I think in a former life she was a general of some sort. Maybe she planned the storming of Normandy." Kim set her bag down on the chair opposite Stella.

Stella rose from behind her desk. "Can I get you anything? Tea? Coffee?"

"A coffee would be great. Two—"

"Sugars and a splash of milk. Take a seat, and I'll be right back."

In the breakroom, Stella took several sharp intakes of breath until her heart rate steadied to semi-normal. *Pull it together, Stell.* She popped a Donut Shop Extra Bold Coffee pod into the machine and hit start. While the cup brewed, she focused on the sign instructing staff members to clean up after themselves, which for the most part wasn't enforced considering the sticky round table and empty sugar packets and stir sticks strewn on the counter. Stella wondered what their homes looked like if this was how they treated a shared area.

She poured two packets of white sugar into the steaming cup and added a splash of milk from her carton, which was much lighter than when she'd made her own cup of coffee first thing that morning. Stella grabbed her homemade green machine juice.

Reentering her office, she said, "Here you go."

Kim took the cup. "Thanks. I'm dying today and I'm not too excited to get back to work, but the finance world never seems to stop."

"Are you enjoying being back in an office?" Stella retook her seat on the opposite side of the desk and twisted off the cap of her Nalgene bottle.

"It's nice to be among adults during the day, mostly, after staying home with Kenzie all those years. The life of an admin isn't glamorous, though."

"No, I imagine not." Stella waited a second or two to see if Kim would say more. When she didn't, Stella prompted her, "What brings you by?"

"I had an appointment and thought it would be good for us to touch base, not just during the kid handoff."

Yeah, right. "What appointment?"

"Just my yearly exam. Nothing of significance."

Stella nodded and took a long swallow of the kale, spinach, celery, apple, lemon, cucumber, and ginger concoction that she drank every mid-morning.

"I see you still love to blitz your veggies."

"Not sure love is the right word, but it helps me keep going." Stella swallowed another mouthful. "Are you sure your appointment was fine? You look a bit pale."

Kim set her cup on Stella's desk. "It was fine. I promise."

"You've been having your thyroid levels checked regularly?"

"Yes." She brushed a pesky red curl behind her ear. "I'm not here because of that. I thought I should tell you something before you heard it from Kenzie."

Stella adjusted in her chair. "Is she okay?"

"She's fine, Stell."

Stella controlled the urge to cringe over Kim's use of the nickname. She wasn't the only one to call her that, but it seemed like a privilege Kim had lost with the divorce.

"It's just, well, I've been dating someone." Kim's eyes avoided Stella's by staring blankly into the light brown coffee.

"Yes. A paleontologist."

Kim sucked in her lips. "I see I'm too late."

"Or the first to date. Depends on how you look at it."

"Are you okay with...?"

"How long have you two been dating?" Stella held a pen with both hands, staring at the worn lettering of the university's name.

"A little over six months."

Stella met Kim's gaze. "Why didn't you talk to me first before telling our daughter?"

"I was going to, but it just kinda happened."

"How does it just happen? You introduced Kenzie to a woman you're dating. What happens—?"

Kim showed her palms. "I'm sorry. Truly, I am. But I wouldn't have made the introduction if I wasn't sure about the relationship. I'd never put Kenz through that. Not after—"

"Are you telling Kenzie to worry about me?" Stella demanded in the tone she used when in the operating room.

"What? No."

Stella tapped the pen on the desktop. "I don't believe you."

"Why would I do such a thing?" Kim's pinched face reminded Stella of all the arguments they'd had the last couple years of their marriage.

"Oh, I don't know why you do anything. Like when you slept with Jess."

"Jesus! You'll never forgive me."

Stella raised a placating hand. "It doesn't bother me. Just using it as evidence as to why I can't trust you."

"Yeah, right, it doesn't bother you. That's why you throw it in my face every chance you get." Kim squared her shoulders. "Maybe you should ask yourself why I did."

"Why you did what?"

"The thing you can never forget."

"Go on. Say it." Stella waved for her to say the words aloud.

"Is that what you want?"

Stella continued to prod her ex by cupping her hand behind an ear.

"Fine. I slept with Jess. I can admit I made a terrible mistake. Can you admit to yourself why I did it?"

"I have absolutely no idea why you did it, besides to hurt me in the worst way possible."

"You still haven't figured it out?" A look of bewilderment marred Kim's face.

"Because you could? Because during our entire relationship, everyone threw themselves at you?"

"I did it to get your attention! Our marriage was collapsing."

Stella let out a bark of laughter. "Are you saying you slept with Jess, my backstabbing colleague, to what... save our marriage?"

"It wasn't the best course of action. I know that now. But I'd tried everything else to get you to realize what was happening, and I wasn't getting through."

"Oh, I disagree. It was the best course of action, to use your words. It woke me up to the type of person you are." Stella made a light bulb going off motion over her head.

"And what type am I?"

"A woman."

Kim glared. "That's rich, coming from you. I remember you chasing me when I was dating Matthew."

"Casually dating! Not married. Nor living together. And you had admitted you were unhappy and wanted to end things. You and Matthew didn't have a child together." Stella released a cleansing breath. "I wish you wouldn't fill Kenzie's head with these thoughts."

"What thoughts?"

"I don't want her to worry about me. I'm the parent. It's my job to worry about her." Stella chugged more of her veggie concoction.

"Are you worried about her?"

"Of course, I am. Aren't you?"

"About anything in particular?"

"Is there something you're not telling me?" Stella demanded.

"I think you're the one holding things back. Or in. Have you considered therapy? We talked about it when we were still together."

"You want us to go to couple's therapy?" Stella said in a disbelieving voice.

"No. I wasn't suggesting that, but if you needed me to go with you, I would. I care about you. I want you to be happy."

"Says the woman dating Rooney. What kind of name is that, anyway?"

Kim's thinning lips made it appear she was digging deep not to take the bait.

Stella finished her juice, shaking off the tartness of the lemons. "I need to take care of a work matter. It's urgent."

Kim started to rise. "By all means. We can talk about our child when you have the time."

Stella jabbed a finger in Kim's direction. "That was low."

"Are you surprised? I'm the woman who cheated. That's the only thing that matters to you when dealing with me. Everything has to be a battle." Apparently, Kim could only let so much roll off her back.

"Please, just stop telling Kenzie to worry about me or stop saying things that make her worry."

"I don't, Stella. Take a hard look at your life, and maybe you'll realize why our daughter worries about you."

CHAPTER EIGHT

AURORA TWISTED THE PHONE CORD AROUND HER finger. "Are you really calling me at work to nag me?"

"I have to. I'm kicking wedding planning into high gear." Aurora could picture Becky elevating her hand in the way she did to indicate that shit was about to get real. "And it would be nice to cross this item off the list. I don't think you're taking this very seriously."

"What do you want me to do, Becks? Ask the next woman I see?"

"If necessary, yes. Just say, *I need you.* Chicks dig vulnerability." Becky dragged out the word *dig.*

"How do you know? You're marrying a man."

"I've read my fair share of lesbian romances."

"I haven't." Aurora sat up in her desk chair. "Why have you? It's weird."

"Research. Someone has to take your love life seriously. As your best friend, I won't let you live this way." Becky sounded legitimately concerned.

"And your solution is reading books that have *happily ever after* endings? That's not real. Listen to me very carefully. Love does not exist." Aurora pressed her index finger onto her desk, whitening the knuckle, to emphasize each word, even if Becky couldn't see her.

"Again, not something you should say in your speech at my wedding."

"About that. Is it really necessary I speak? It's just not in my wheelhouse. Or do I need to remind you about the speech I gave in the tenth grade?" Even the memory caused Aurora's heart to flutter.

"No need to remind me."

"You see! I think it'd be a serious mistake to set me loose at your wedding."

"I'm not asking you to pontificate about the American Revolution. Are you saying you can't think of anything nice to say about me on my special day?"

Aurora groaned and closed her eyes. "Oh, wow. That was a great twist on that. Why do I need to date a woman when my best friend is a pro at guilt trips?"

When Aurora reopened her eyes, there stood Dr. Gilbert.

Aurora stiffened in her seat. "Hey, Becks, I have to jump."

"Hopefully, you mean you have to hang up and not jump out of the window because I'm such a terrible female."

"Nope. Not jumping out—I'm only hanging up. Work." Aurora knew she wasn't making much sense, but Dr. Hottie had that effect on her.

"Find a date!" Becky yelled before hanging up.

Aurora felt her entire face shoot up in flames as she replaced the phone onto the cradle. "Sorry about that."

"Everything okay? I hope I didn't interrupt anything." Stella placed a black bag on the counter between the two.

"Not at all."

"Are you sure? Threatening to jump out of a window seems kinda serious." Stella wore a puzzling smile.

"Ha! I didn't. Becky can be a wee bit dramatic." Aurora held her thumb and forefinger in the air with plenty of space between the two.

"Becky?" Stella arched her brows.

"My best friend."

"Ah. And, she wants you to date because?"

"Not date. Find one." Aurora added, "For her wedding."

"Well, that explains it." Stella's expression relaxed, but confusion still resided in her eyes.

"How can I help you?"

"I'm a bit embarrassed to broach the subject after you were so kind to help me out of a jam last time."

"It's my job." Aurora consulted the clock on the wall to her left. "For the next six weeks." She laughed, fully aware the clock didn't measure days, only hours.

"I didn't know this was a temporary thing."

"Yep."

Stella's forehead puckered. "Oh, that's too bad." She glanced about. "Are you the only one here?"

"As usual." Aurora cleared her throat. "Now, what's the dilemma you don't want to tell me about?"

"It's Dr. Howie," Stella said in a confessionary tone.

"Okay." Aurora tried to remember who Dr. Howie was. She dealt with twenty to thirty requests daily, but the name tugged at the corners of her mind.

"He's not happy with the room you went out of your way to assign."

"Oh, that's right." Aurora snapped her fingers. "But I thought that was the room he wanted, if memory serves correctly."

"It was until the carpet got to him."

"The carpet?"

"Yeah. It's brown." Stella hefted a shoulder in a helpless fashion.

Aurora slanted her head, trying to puzzle that one out.

"What color is it supposed to be?"

"Brown, I'm assuming. Most of the classrooms in the area have that color. Apparently, he has a thing with the color. Messes with his chi or whatever." Stella waved a hand, making it clear she thought that was total bullshit.

"Is that a condition of some type? An aversion to brown?" Aurora studied the blue carpet in her office, trying to determine if it affected her in any way. The stains grossed her out, but overall, nothing.

"If you mean he's a moron, yes." Stella flinched, seeming appalled she'd said that aloud. Leaning her forearms on the counter, she said, "Ah, that's just between you and me."

"Good thing I'm not the type to gossip. For a price."

Stella grinned. "What price would that be?"

"Oh, I'm easy. Bring me a Snickers or something."

Stella tapped the side of her head. "Logging that for the future."

"Damn. I should have asked for more."

"Such as…?"

Aurora gave Stella what she hoped was her sexy, confident smile. "All good things come to those who wait."

"I can be very patient."

"I'm learning that." Aurora waggled her brows. "Now back to the matter at hand. Tell me more about Dr. Howie."

"He's a brilliant doctor, but everyday life seems to get the best of him."

Aurora had to muffle a snicker. "I've been noticing that trend here. So many special snowflakes."

Stella grinned. "So you have a high opinion of me, then?"

Aurora's eyes widened. "I didn't mean—"

"Don't worry. I was just teasing you. It's been one of those days, ya know?"

"Tell me about it. I spent the morning being chewed out by a doctor who didn't know how to hookup his laptop to the

LCD. He didn't request a tech, but apparently, I should have used my special scheduling powers to deduce he needed one. I wanted to go do it myself, but it seems I'm always alone here and can't leave the phone." Aurora jerked her thumb over her shoulder to emphasize all the empty desks.

Stella laughed. "This department has a certain reputation."

"I picked up on that during my first few days when I was the only one who seemed to work a full day. I've only been here two weeks, but I'm exhausted."

"Do you have a new temp job lined up when this tour of duty is done?"

Aurora sighed. "Not yet. But you didn't come here to talk about that." Not wanting to think about possibly being jobless, Aurora steered the conversation back to work. "Does Dr. Howie have another room he's interested in?"

"Yes. C430. And before you look, I know it's taken."

"I see. You doctors. Always wanting a miracle," Aurora teased.

"Yes, but now I know you can be bribed. Shall I dash out to get a Snickers and come back?"

"This may cost you more. Let me see how bad the situation is." Aurora clicked her mouse. "Ah, it's an admin meeting scheduled for the office of the dean of Public Health this time. Dr. Howie has a special skill when it comes to being difficult."

"Dr. Phillips has the room," Stella muttered, realizing why Vera had wanted to leave a voice mail. "She's a ballbuster."

Aurora nodded. She hadn't personally met the dean of Public Health, but if her take-no-prisoners assistant was any indication, Dr. Phillips was a piece of work.

"Does that mean this request isn't happening?" Stella's expression darkened in a sexy way.

Aurora scratched the side of her head with a mechanical pencil. "It doesn't look good. From what I've learned, everyone in Public Health thinks they get the shitty rooms because they're not medical doctors, only PhDs. If I have to hear that one more time..."

Stella nodded as if in tune with Aurora's misery. "Is C430 shitty?"

"What?"

"You said the school of Public Health complained about shitty rooms."

"Oh, I didn't mean to say that part out loud." Aurora slapped a hand over her mouth.

"I won't tell anyone if you don't."

"Does this mean I now owe you? What's your price?"

A blush tinged Dr. Gilbert's cheeks, somehow making her even more attractive. "I'm not a fan of Snickers."

Aurora placed a hand on her chest as if about to faint. "I'm not sure I can handle this news."

"Do you need medical attention?"

"Got any procedures in mind?" *Like mouth to mouth?*

"I'm a pro at figuring out someone's needs." Stella, seeming to try to get back on track, or possibly to showcase another one of her strengths, leaned over the counter to see Aurora's computer screen, and Aurora had a hard time taking her eyes off the way the shirt strained over Stella's chest. Stella said, "Is there a room comparable to C430?"

"C432." Aurora entered the information to check its availability. "Oh, we may be in luck. It's free. Do you want to ask Dr. Howie if that'll work? It's identical aside from having a different number on the door."

"I'm going to make an executive decision and say reserve it."

"Living on the edge." Aurora gave her an admiring look.

"I'm trusting you when you say it's comparable."

"I promise, everything is exactly the same, even down to the faux wood floor, which is more of a maple color. Not the turd brown in his current room. Is that okay?"

Stella laughed. "It is that color. Where he is now. And, only one way to find out about C432. I have a feeling he'll have an opinion about something."

"If he does, do you promise to come to me right away? I'm not sure I can live not knowing how it works out."

"I wouldn't have it any other way."

"Considering his next class is tomorrow, we'll know sooner rather than later. Although, it took two weeks for the carpet to get under his skin." Aurora shrugged.

"I just may have to camp outside his class to find out right away and report back."

Aurora liked the sound of that. She completed the reservation. "Do you want me to cc you on the room confirmation?"

"Please do."

A tingle worked through Aurora, but she was unable to come up with a zippy reply.

Stella consulted the clock on the wall. "Unfortunately, I have to get going. Here's hoping everything works out tomorrow." She crossed her fingers before securing her bag onto her shoulder.

Aurora hoped for the opposite so she'd see Dr. Gilbert again.

CHAPTER NINE

STELLA LEFT THE OFFICE MUCH LATER ON A MONDAY night than she would have liked, but the September evening was warm, making her decision to walk to the Hynes subway stop easy. Selecting her route wasn't as straightforward. Should she cut through her old neighborhood in the hopes of bumping into Kenzie? Knowing Stella's luck, she'd spy Kim with her new girl.

It was nearing nine, meaning Kenz would be getting ready for bed soon. Her daughter loved to read before going to sleep. At Stella's, the two of them had started on the Harry Potter series, each taking a turn reading a chapter aloud. Stella remembered Kenzie saying she and her mom were starting the first Percy Jackson book. What was the name of the first book in the series?

Stella wished the divorce didn't put Kenzie smack dab in the middle. Just the reading ritual caused a wrinkle, such as the two-week lag in between chapters. While Mackenzie said it didn't bother her to wait, Stella knew her daughter was trying to make things as easy as possible for both moms. She was that type of kid. Kind, thoughtful, and smart. Stella cringed to think just how much Kenzie knew and understood.

Her phone rang. "Hello?"

"I hope you're not home yet."

"I'm close enough where I can turn around. What's up, Vera?"

"Oh, no need to come back. I'll make this quick. There's a potential med school applicant for next year. The dean wants to do a full-court press."

"What's so special about the student?"

"Her name is Tracy Ang, and she'll be the youngest ever to enter medical school. Not just here but in the country."

Ah, the dean wanted the press for the school. "Can you email me the details so I can start laying out a plan to woo her?"

"I knew I could count on you."

They disconnected, Stella kicked some gold and red leaves on the bricked path. *The Lightning Thief*. That was the name of the book. "This old lady still has it," Stella muttered to herself, perhaps proving she didn't really.

Someone called out her name, and Stella slowly turned. "Oh, hey." She smiled at Melissa, a former neighbor.

"How have you been?" Melissa asked in the tone used by many who knew about the divorce.

"Great. You?" Stella put on a brave face.

"Oh, you know." Melissa's shoulders hunched.

Stella didn't, but she wasn't inclined to dig deeper, so she asked, "How's Carrie?"

Melissa's face fell. "That's right. There's no way you'd know. We split up a few months ago."

Now that she mentioned it, Stella kinda remembered hearing that from the old neighborhood grapevine via Facebook. "I'm so sorry to hear that."

Melissa stared as if wanting Stella to say magic words to make everything better. Now what?

Fortunately, Melissa's phone rang, and Stella jumped at the chance to make a clean getaway. Turning left at the next cross street, Stella headed for Massachusetts Avenue, where she was less likely to bump into someone from her former life with Kim. Part of her felt bad leaving things like that with Melissa, but what could she say that Melissa didn't already know? Breakups sucked. It was best to move forward, and at least Melissa and Carrie didn't have a child together. Not even pets.

Melissa had the luxury of a clean break.

Not that Stella wished they didn't have Kenz. She'd rather gnaw off her own leg than give up her child. Since the breakup, Kenzie had kept Stella grounded. Stella didn't have the option to breakdown. She had to get up every day to support her daughter and Kim. Stella had promised when they married to always take care of Kim, and Stella fully intended to keep that promise, in spite of them living apart. Stella was many things, but dependable most of all, for better or worse.

CHAPTER TEN

TUESDAY EVENING, AURORA GLANCED AT THE CLOCK, wishing the second hand would move faster. Twenty more minutes to go before she was a free woman for the night. For how many hours? She had to laugh at herself if she was already thinking that way about the job. This quite possibly was the most difficult temp job she'd been assigned, and she started to count on her fingers how many hours before she had to return the following day. The phone rang before she got past five.

"Scheduling. Aurora speaking."

"Hello, Miss Aurora."

Aurora beamed. "Hello back, Dr. Gilbert. I was starting to think you'd forgotten all about little old me."

"Not sure that's possible. I'm calling to report, so far, Dr. Howie likes the room. He did mention that one of the markers for the whiteboard was almost out of ink, but given his track record, I think you knocked it out of the park."

"Which color?"

"What?"

"The marker. What color? I'll have a tech replace it."

"Oh, I... This is going to sound idiotic, but I didn't think to ask."

Aurora jotted a note down in the next reservation for that room. "No worries. I'll have a tech replace all of them. Just to be safe."

"You really are the best. What will I do when you leave?"

"Luckily for you, that's not happening for several more weeks."

Stella laughed. "We should do lunch later this week. You do get a lunch break, right?"

Aurora usually ate at her desk, but she answered, "Affirmative."

"Would this Friday work for you?"

"Couldn't think of a better way to end the work week."

"Alrighty then. Friday at one?"

"Perfect." Aurora made a Victory V in the air with her fingers but tried to sound completely calm when she asked, "Where shall I meet you?"

"I know the best cafeteria at the hospital."

"Is there more than one?"

"Nope."

Aurora's grin widened. "I have a feeling I know which one you're talking about. See you on Friday."

They quickly said goodbye, and Aurora hung up the phone when Kip breezed in.

"I need your help."

"Hello, Kip. How are you?"

Kip studied her face. "You seem peppier than usual. What gives?"

Aurora pointed to the clock. "Almost quitting time, so if you want me to do something for you, ya better get to it or forever hold your peace."

"I don't want to marry you."

"We're so on the same page. Seriously, what do you want? I

got things to do and places to be."

"Like what?"

"Kip!" She pretended she was throttling his neck.

"Okay, okay. I just like it when you're in a good mood and not grumpy."

"Don't make me grumpy all the time. It's not fun getting chewed out on the phone when you forget one of your setups."

He started to defend himself but looked at the ground instead. "That's what I came to ask. Tomorrow's setup—Dr. Greene's. He hates me. Can you reassign Isaac to it?" Kip whispered the last sentence.

Aurora knew this to be true. "Okay, let me look at the schedule." She clicked a few buttons. "Isaac has a recording in the auditorium."

"I know. I used to do those recordings."

Aurora sensed there was a story behind that.

"I spoke to Isaac. He doesn't mind switching." Kip bounced on the balls of his feet.

Aurora picked up her phone and dialed Isaac's number. "Hey. Quick question, did Kip speak to you about switching jobs tomorrow?"

"Yep. And it works out for me since I have a dentist appointment right after the recording and that professor has a habit of running long."

"I guess everyone's happy. Thanks, Isaac." Aurora replaced the phone.

Kip grinned, wagging a finger. "You thought I was lying."

"I absolutely did." Aurora made the modification and reprinted that page for the jobs board. "Since I did you a solid, can you cover the phones on Friday at one? I have a thing?"

"Is that code for the lady's doctor?"

"Seriously, Kip. Every time I start to like you, ya have to do something like that."

"Like what?" he asked with a look of bewilderment, clearly

not understanding where he went wrong.

"You can't ask a female you work with if she's going to the gyno. It's uncomfortable."

He nodded as if this was the first time he'd ever been told something along those lines. "Got it. I'll never ask about the lady's doctor again."

Kip seemed so sincere Aurora softened her tone. "Can you cover for me on Friday?"

"Sure can." He saluted her.

Aurora logged off her computer but didn't shut down completely since the IT department regularly ran updates overnight. "I'm out of here then. Have a wonderful night, Kip."

"I plan on it. A big night ahead." He rubbed his hands together.

"Oh, really? Whatcha doing?"

"D&D. It's going to be epic!" He made a roll the dice motion.

"Sounds fun."

"You want to play? We need a female."

Aurora laughed. "I appreciate the offer, but I'm having dinner with a friend."

"She can come, too. Two females are always better than one."

Aurora had to smile. "That's probably another thing not to say to a woman you don't know all that well." She skedaddled before Kip could trap her into another conversation thread or guilt trip her into coming to D&D. The more she got to know Kip, the more she realized just how socially awkward he was, but underneath was a sweet guy. At least, she hoped so.

* * *

On Friday, Aurora waited at the entrance of the cafeteria, giddy as a school girl. *Get a hold of yourself.* It was just lunch with Dr. Gilbert. In a hospital. This wasn't *Grey's Anatomy*, although Dr. Gilbert was way hotter than McSteamy What's His Name. Aurora's eyes panned the two hallways that converged at the entrance of the cafeteria.

"Looking for anyone in particular?"

"Just some doctor," Aurora replied. "Know one?"

Dr. Gilbert crossed her arms. "One or two. Do you have any other criteria? Specialty, perhaps?"

"Good question." Aurora tapped a fingernail against her front tooth. "Preferably one with a good bedside manner."

"Ah, yes. That's key for any good doctor. Go on." Stella waved for Aurora to continue.

"One who knows his or her shit. I'm so over charlatans."

"Have you encountered many?"

"You mean like the doctor who told me to have a hysterectomy because I have really bad cramps?" Aurora wanted to die. "Not that you needed to know that tiny detail about my life."

"Let me guess. A male doctor?"

"Yes."

Stella's eyeballs bulged. "I'm really hoping the male doctors I teach won't blow off women like many of my generation do. And the ones older than I am..." She shook her head.

"Your generation. You make it sound like you're oh so much older than I am."

"At least a year or two." Stella winked, and Aurora felt weak in the knees. "Can I buy you lunch?"

"I'm a woman of my generation. Dutch, okay?"

"If you insist." Stella gestured for Aurora to go ahead, bringing up the rear.

"I could murder a burrito." Aurora playfully gnashed her teeth over her shoulder.

"What have I unleashed on the hospital grounds?"

"Yes, burrito eaters should be feared. I can spear a tomato from fifty paces with a toothpick."

Stella laughed. "I'm not sure I know what that means, but I won't get in your way. I'm heading for the pasta section." She pointed to a table in the back next to the window overlooking Whitaker Green. "Meet you there."

Aurora grabbed a spicy beef burrito loaded with extra salsa and cheese and then headed for the drink section, choosing a raspberry iced tea. In line to pay, Aurora wondered how much everything would come to. She'd heard from Kip the place was cheap, but she'd never been before, aside from grabbing a yogurt in the morning when she didn't have time to eat at home.

The woman rang up her items. "Five fifty."

"Really? Wow, that is cheap."

The woman didn't respond either way, breaking Aurora's twenty as if she was actually a robot, unable to express any human emotion. Actually, Aurora wondered if some robots had more personality.

Stella sat at the table, glancing at her iPhone.

"Are you really eating mac and cheese?" Aurora set her tray down and took a seat to Stella's right.

"Totes."

Aurora laughed. "Totes, huh? Being around the students seems to have rubbed off on you."

"Are you saying I'm not a natural *totes* kind of person?" Stella placed a hand over her heart. "You wound me."

"Hey, you could be. I'm curious to find out."

"How do you plan on doing that?" Stella forked in a bite.

"Observation will be key." Aurora peeled back some of the foil from her burrito.

"Are you going to stalk me?"

"Would it be considered stalking if I'm doing it for research?"

Stella pointed her fork at Aurora. "Oh boy, this could get interesting."

"I'm down with interesting. You?" Aurora wanted to run her fingers over the doctor to find out if the few freckles on the back of the doctor's hands were an indication of more in secret places.

Stella's lingering gaze seemed to explore the depths of Aurora's intent. "Depends who I'm going down with."

Aurora burst into laughter. "Oh my, Dr. Gilbert. I'm not exactly sure what I should say to that."

"Stella."

"I should say Stella?"

"No... well, yes. That's my name."

"Oh! Right. Stella, it's very nice to meet the real you."

"Have I been faking?"

"Clearly, or at least hiding the *totes* side of you." Aurora gave Stella her best *I think your fucking hot* grin.

"Mockery? Really?" Stella didn't seem put out at all. More like she wanted to put out.

Aurora leaned closer to Stella. "All in good fun, my dear Stella. I've found humor is a great way to get to know a person."

"What if I'm not funny?"

"You're in luck. I am. I'll teach you a few things."

"I have no doubt. When do the lessons start?" Stella eagerly leaned in.

"Pretty sure things are in motion."

"Oh." Stella reached into her lab coat pocket. "For dessert." She placed a Snickers in front of Aurora.

"Aw, thanks. Now for research purposes, what kind of treats do you prefer?"

"And taint the data by telling you?"

"You do understand this means I'll have to kick my so-called stalking into a higher gear?"

Stella's pupils tripled in size. "I'm all for things done properly."

CHAPTER ELEVEN

STELLA SHOOK OFF A SHIVER FROM THE CHILL IN THE October air and knocked on the newly painted peacock-blue door of her old apartment.

"I'll get it," Kenzie screamed from the other side. The door swung open. "Mom!" Kenz seemed shocked to see Stella.

"Do I have the wrong night? I thought this was Tuesday." Stella glanced at her watch to check the date.

"Yes, it's Tuesday. You're just super early. Also, I'm really happy to see you. I'm starving. We should go. I'm ready." Kenzie started to head out the door.

"You don't have a coat, and don't you think you should say goodbye to your mom?"

"I won't get cold. Did I mention I'm starving?" Kenzie rubbed her belly. "So hungry."

"Kenz, it's not summer anymore. Please, go get your jacket," Stella instructed in her mom tone.

Kim appeared in the hallway. "Kenzie, why aren't you letting your mom in?"

"Uh…"

Kim waved for Stella to enter. "We're in here. Would you

like some wine before dinner?" She headed in the direction of the kitchen.

"We?" Stella asked, starting to figure out the reason behind her daughter's odd behavior.

"Rooney's here." Kim glanced over her shoulder. "Is that okay?"

"It's your home." *That I pay for.*

Kenzie looked to her mom and then back to Stella, a pained expression on her face.

Stella knew she had to act like this was a normal situation. "Not sure about the wine, but I should say hello, right Little Mac?" She tossed an arm around Kenzie's shoulder, pulling her daughter close like a shield. Walking together, they entered the kitchen.

The woman in their—Kim's kitchen was a slight brunette, with nerdy glasses and an expression that conveyed she'd rather be eaten alive by a T-rex than meet Kim's ex-wife. Stella tried to squash the cheerful thought of feeding Rooney to said T-rex.

"Hi, I'm Stella." She didn't let go of Kenzie, making it impossible to shake the woman's hand. As if Kenzie understood her role, she went limp noodle in Stella's arms, a thing she did, and Stella playfully swayed Kenzie back and forth.

"Rooney."

"Nice to meet you."

"Likewise." Rooney seemed to be blinking abnormally fast, and Stella appreciated the woman's discomfort. Was that wrong?

Kim squirmed in her heels, and Stella had to wonder why she still had on her shoes and not her tattered house slippers.

"I hear you're into dinosaurs." Stella couldn't think of anything else to say.

"Ever since I was a kid. I guess you can say I never really

grew up." The paleontologist laughed nervously, with Kim joining in, sounding even more ill at ease.

"Do what you love. Isn't that what they say?" Stella looked down into Kenzie's eyes. "I'm with you and starving. Shall we jump?"

Kenzie's bones seemed to magically reform in her body, and she hopped on her feet. "Only joking. I know you mean let's go. I'll get my jacket."

"Please, kiddo. Feels like snow tonight." Stella involuntarily shuddered.

Kenzie dashed out of the kitchen.

"Do you really think it'll snow?" Kim asked, wrapping her arms around her stomach as if the mere mention of the weather caused her body temperature to plummet.

"It's cold enough." Stella kept her gaze on Kim.

The three women didn't speak until Kenzie returned, shoving an arm into her jacket and then the other. "Ready, Freddie."

"It was lovely to finally put a face to the name," Stella told Rooney before nodding at Kim, who gave a tight-lipped smile.

Outside, Mackenzie looked her mom over. "That wasn't as bad as I thought it would be."

Stella, starting to unclench her muscles, laughed. "Did you think I'd kill her or something?"

"Way to put that thought into my head." Kenz wiggled her head like she wanted to evict the statement from her brain.

Stella did her best to straighten her spine to regain the confidence she didn't feel. "What are you in the mood for?"

"Chinese."

"Now you're talking."

They walked toward the neighborhood restaurant two blocks over.

"Mom?"

"Kenzie?" Stella said breezily.

"Are you okay?"

Stella placed a hand on each of Kenzie's shoulders. "You really need to stop worrying about me. I'm okay."

"But... it was awkward."

"I'll give you that. It was. It doesn't mean anything, though. All of this is new for everyone. I need you to know I'm good. I promise. Are you fine with everything?" Stella examined her daughter's eyes.

Kenzie nodded. "She's nice to me."

"That's all that matters. You are my number one priority. Always will be. Don't you ever forget that."

"Me forget? You're the old one!" Kenzie's carefree smile returned.

"Then I'm tasking you with reminding me."

"Oh, don't worry, I will. Does this mean we can stop for ice cream after dinner?"

Stella stuck her palm out. "I think that was a snowflake. You want ice cream?"

"I always want ice cream. Old people are wimps. Now come on. I'm a growing girl. I need Chinese!" Kenzie dashed off in the direction of the Lucky Seven.

Stella was hot on her heels. "Loser has to pay for dinner."

Kenzie giggled. "You know I don't have any money on me."

"Better win, then."

By the time they reached the front door of the restaurant, Kenzie was huffing and puffing but smiling victoriously. Stella hoped her daughter always looked this happy.

CHAPTER TWELVE

It was the third Thursday in October, and for once, the Scheduling office was fully staffed. Although, the reason behind the attendance was Kip bringing in cupcakes for Aurora's last day.

"Is the pink one mine?" Aurora asked, observing it was the only one of that color.

"I've noticed it's one of your favorite colors. You wear it at least twice a week. Usually on Mondays and Fridays, not Thursday. I tend to notice patterns," Kip explained and then bit into a plain white one with rainbow sprinkles on top.

"I wasn't aware of my color preferences on certain days. Makes sense, though. I need extra pep on Monday, and the end of the work week should be celebrated." Aurora chomped into hers and, around a bite, said, "These are good. Did you bake them all on your own?"

"Mom helped."

Aurora had wondered if Kip still lived with his parents or mom, at least. He seemed the type to need some looking after.

Shelly polished off her orange cupcake with brown sprinkles

in the spirit of Halloween. After licking her fingers, she said, "I better get going. I have a meeting with Alice."

After Shelly grabbed her bag and left, Isaac took a second cupcake. "She didn't even say goodbye. I swear the woman has a recording playing in her head to remind her to breathe."

Bri laughed, shaking her head. "She's the perfect example of the lazy American manager who knows nothing about her job." The woman had jet-black hair and stunning deep-blue eyes. She turned to Aurora. "I know we didn't get much of a chance to speak since I work nights, but thank you for making my transition back on the medical campus smooth. The reservations used to be so messed up all the time." She made a hand motion that implied crazy. "It was nice not to have to struggle on my own each shift."

"I kinda liked being here. I've always liked jobs that involved solving puzzles, and this one allowed me to do that every day. I won't miss being screamed at on the phone by doctors who are overwhelmed by something simple like their laptop battery dying in the middle of a lecture."

"I swear half the time I feel like a babysitter." Bri sucked frosting off her finger.

"What's the deal with Alice?" Aurora asked. "I was here for two months, and not once did she call or stop by the office."

Isaac sighed. "She runs the Scheduling and AV departments on the medical and main campuses, and between us, the woman is about as competent as Shelly, except Alice has been able to hide her idiocy from the higher-ups. Alice is the type who never asks questions to understand even the most basic protocols, but she's the first to place the blame on someone else. Nothing is ever her fault."

"Glad I never met her then. I'm not a fan of those types."

Isaac tossed his cupcake wrapper into the trash. "I have a setup in the C building." He put his hand out to Aurora. "Don't be a stranger."

"It's been a pleasure working with you."

Isaac left, and Bri soon followed.

Kip perched on the edge of Shelly's desk. "You won't actually call Isaac or anything, will you?"

Aurora spun in her desk chair to face him. "Oh, stranger things have happened. Besides, it's always good to have a competent tech on hand."

"I'm better than Isaac," Kip said without gloating. Stating facts, like her color preference, was simply his style.

"Why are you the one who's always getting into trouble, then?" The question had been on Aurora's lips many times.

Kip sucked in a breath. "I'm not good with people. I don't see why they can't understand things that are so simple for me."

"Are you good at everything?"

He shook his head.

"Can you give me an example of something that's difficult for you? Besides communicating with doctors?" Aurora laughed to ease the situation.

"I can't drive a car. Not well, I mean. I'm not aggressive enough for city traffic."

"Does it scare you?"

He looked away, shoving his glasses up his nose and nodding.

"Next time you're dealing with someone who's struggling with a tech issue, remember how you feel when driving, and be patient."

"I'll try," he said, not sounding entirely convinced.

"I know you can do it, Kip."

"Thanks." He got to his feet. "You're nice. I'm sorry you're leaving."

"Me too. Thanks again for the cupcakes. That was very sweet of you."

Without another word, Kip left.

Aurora let out a cleansing breath, once again alone in the office, much like the way she'd started, so it seemed a fitting way to say adios.

"Oh good." Stella rushed in. "I didn't miss you."

"Almost. Under twenty minutes to go. Help yourself to a cupcake." Aurora waved to the Tupperware container with three left.

"Thanks. Who made them?"

"Kip and his mom."

Stella nodded, taking the last orange one. "Any idea how she's doing?"

"His mom?" Aurora's brow crinkled.

"She had a stroke a few years back. Kip moved in to help care for her."

"I had no idea." Aurora tried to replay her interactions with Kip, but she didn't think she'd missed any clues. All along, she'd thought Kip needed to be with his family so they could look after him, and the whole time he was taking care of his ailing mom. There was much more to the man than she'd given him credit for.

"I'm sorry to see you go. It's been a delight working with you. And, I enjoyed our Friday lunches."

"Same here, Dr. Gilbert."

"We're back to Dr. Gilbert, are we?" Stella's sapphire eyes sparkled.

Aurora craned her neck to see the clock behind Stella. "For the next sixteen minutes. Not that I'm counting or anything."

"What are you doing tonight to celebrate your freedom?"

"Starting the quest to find a date for a wedding that isn't even happening until the spring, or my best friend may disown me."

"Oh."

Aurora sensed she missed an opportunity. "I was kidding. I have zero plans. You?"

"I don't have any either."

"It's a shame that neither one of us does. We should do something about that."

Stella appeared interested. "Like what?"

"Let me buy you a beer."

"Sounds like a plan, but I think you have that wrong."

Aurora looked at Stella questioningly.

"You've saved my bacon with Dr. Howie, who is now happy in C432, meaning I should buy you a beer." Stella consulted her watch. "You said sixteen minutes. I need to grab some papers from my office. Shall I meet you out front in twenty?"

"It's a date. As work colleagues, I mean. Or former, I guess since I won't be employed by the university by then." Aurora realized she was rambling, unsure why she was suddenly nervous around Stella.

"Yes. I better get back to the hospital. Out front at seventeen hundred hours."

Aurora saluted Stella, who smiled awkwardly in return.

When the coast was clear, Aurora palm-slapped her forehead. "Way to go, moron."

CHAPTER THIRTEEN

STELLA WAITED ON THE BENCH FACING THE GLASS doors of the sixteen-story medical school. She'd managed to escape her office without being stopped by a student about the test the following day. A rarity. The mid-October air had the earthly smell she associated with fall—crisp and invigorating. The temperature wasn't cold enough to keep her in the lobby. That risked being spotted by a needy student or professor. Under the yellow, red, and orange leaves of a massive oak tree, Stella watched two finches hop around pecking at crumbs on the ground.

Right at 5:01, Aurora, looking killer in a black skirt, dusty-rose blouse, and stockings, emerged from the building. Her black hair had been let down and shimmered in the fading daylight. Aurora looked around the quad, not spying Stella. Aurora seemed to check the time on her phone before slipping it back into her purse. With the bag between her legs, Aurora started to put on her tweed jacket.

Stella, who'd been enjoying watching Aurora without her knowing it, leapt up from the bench. "Here, let me help you."

Aurora stilled, allowing Stella to ease the jacket first onto Aurora's left and then right arm. "Thank you."

Stella smiled, but her gaze dropped from Aurora's piercing dark eyes. "Where to?"

"Is there a decent bar nearby? I haven't really had much of a chance to explore the area." Aurora glanced around the quad, but only office buildings were in sight.

"That depends on how far you want to venture. There's a suitable one across the street, but if you don't mind legging it a few blocks, there's a gem of a place." Stella purposefully eyed Aurora's three-inch heels. "I'm okay with the place across the street if you rather."

"And miss out on the gem?" Aurora shook her head. "Lead the way." Aurora motioned for Stella to go ahead.

"Are you sure? I don't want you to get a blister. I don't have any Band-Aids on me. We could Uber it."

"And you call yourself a doctor. Aren't you supposed to have a black medical bag or at least one bandage in case of an emergency?"

"Apparently, I'm a bad doctor."

"How bad?" Aurora's voice practically purred.

Stella's cheeks prickled with heat. "That remains to be seen."

"I'm curious to find out. Seriously, though, I'm used to walking in these. My mom loves to joke I was born with heels on."

Stella laughed. "Okay, but if you do get a blister, I'll have to treat you free of charge."

"You've already admitted you aren't prepared for anything, so I'm curious what type of treatment you're considering. Kissing a boo-boo better?"

Stella grinned. "Improvising is necessary for surgeons."

"Of that, I have no doubt. Only one way to find out what your capable of, Dr. Gilbert."

"And here I thought I'd graduated to just Stella."

"That's right. The work shackles are off." Aurora motioned they should begin the adventure.

They headed north on Massachusetts Avenue, quickly turning right onto a side street, and then making a left, ending up on a residential street.

"I've always liked these apartment buildings." Aurora's eyes panned the brownstones, the black metal fences, and small gardens. "Do you think they cost a fortune?"

"Most assuredly." Stella kept her gaze from glancing at her old apartment across the street, even though it was the night Kim took Kenzie to dinner, so there wasn't a chance of bumping into them. Was Rooney now part of the Thursday night tradition?

"Do you live near here? Is that how you know about this gem?"

"Nope. I'm much closer to the Charles." Stella cringed over not telling the whole truth and rambled on, "But I've worked at the hospital for fifteen years, so I've gotten to know the South End." They walked side by side, and Stella had to turn her head to see Aurora's expression. "I just dated myself, didn't I?"

"A bit, but it wasn't that much of a secret. Have you signed up for AARP yet?"

"Harsh, man. Harsh." Stella laughed. "Although, retirement does sound nice. I wouldn't have to lug around work all the time." Stella patted her bag, which seemed to get heavier with each step.

"Do you usually bring home work?"

Stella nodded. "I always seem to be a week behind no matter how hard I try to get ahead."

They walked in silence for half a block before Stella said, "It's just around the corner here. Are you Irish?"

Aurora seemed puzzled by the question. "Like most Bostonians, I have some Irish relatives on my mom's side I've visited a handful of times."

"Good news, because I think having an Irish connection will help you appreciate this place more."

O'Shea's Irish Pub was a quaint establishment that boasted the perfect Guinness pour. Inside, every square inch of wall had old-fashioned posters depicting Guinness ads. The low ceiling, dark furnishings, and dim lighting made the place feel homey.

They approached the bar.

"What'll you have?" The red-haired man with burly arms asked.

Aurora placed her hands on the bar, checking out the beers available on draft, and asked with a straight face, although Stella detected a twinkle in her eyes, "Do you have Guinness?"

He narrowed his eyes. "What else do you think we serve here?"

"Given the décor, I'm assuming it's illegal to order anything else in this establishment," Aurora spoke with confidence.

"Ah, a wise guy. Let me guess. You'd prefer an appletini." He made a dainty gesture with his pawlike hands accompanied with a girlish oohing sound.

"Never had one and I don't plan on ever trying it. I want a Guinness. For reals." Aurora motioned for Stella to select her drink.

"Make that two, Conor. And you'll have to forgive Aurora. Young people today can be so impertinent." Stella flashed a self-satisfied smirk.

"Says the old lady," Aurora bumped Stella's side with an elbow.

Conor laughed. "How are you, Stella?" He placed a pint glass at an angle under the tap, the dark brown liquid and milky foam slowly filling the glass.

"Not too bad. Will be much better in a few." Stella motioned to the glass.

"Take a seat. I'll bring these out to you when they're ready. You can't rush the proper pour."

"That's a criminal offense." Stella guided Aurora to a small round table with two worn brown-leather club chairs.

Aurora sat in the chair with her back to the front door. "This place is cute. Are you Irish?"

"Oh, I have some Irish blood, along with German, Czech, and British."

"So you hate beer is what you're saying?" Aurora clutched the arms of the chair with slender fingers.

Stella laughed heartily. "Exactly." She settled into the chair, crossing her right leg over her left. "Tell me about your date problem."

"Wow. You're coming in hot." Aurora's confident grin was intriguing.

"Am I? I didn't mean to. I'm just puzzled, really, as to why a woman as beautiful as you are is having a hard time getting anyone to take you to a wedding."

"For one thing, my date wouldn't be just anyone. I have standards, but don't tell Becky. She thinks I'm considering an escort."

"Really? Any reason in particular you want her to believe this?"

"It's fun to tease her. She's a smidge uptight and highly opinionated." Aurora held her arms out wide.

"And this is the hill you've chosen to die on?" Stella asked, intrigued.

"Not necessarily, but I do think Becks is being a bit absurd. The wedding is months away. Plenty of time for me to hook a chick." Aurora cast an imaginary line to catch a fish.

Conor, in faded jeans and a Red Sox T-shirt, approached the table, tossed down two Guinness coasters, and then placed the beers on them. "I better not see you soaking up the head with a napkin." He waggled a finger at Aurora. "Two tourists from

Northern California did that last week, and I asked them to leave."

"They're probably used to wine," Stella said. "And don't worry about Aurora. I'll keep her in line."

Conor gave Aurora the once-over. "Not sure who'd come out on top of that." He retreated back behind the bar.

"Now I'm tempted to get out of line to see what methods you'd resort to for getting me to behave. Wrestle me to the ground?"

"You might enjoy that punishment too much."

"Depends on how you do it."

"I'll keep that in mind." Stella circled back to the conversation. "I'm still not understanding the dilemma. I bet girls are tossing themselves at you all the time."

"You don't expect me to confirm or deny that, do you?" Aurora tucked a lock of hair behind her ear.

"Not at all. It'd take the fun out of finding out on my own."

Aurora arched a playful brow. "Wouldn't want to do that." She raised her glass in the air. "I like Conor's style. It's crisp black and white. I hate when bartenders serve it before everything's had a chance to settle. Cheers."

"A true connoisseur, I see." Stella hoisted hers. "Cheers." After a lustful tug, Stella set the glass back down. "Tell me more about your perfect wedding date."

"Is there such a thing?"

"Not sure anyone is perfect, but you seem intent on finding a suitable candidate. I'm curious about the criteria." Stella steepled her fingers and rested her chin on the tips.

"Are you now?" Aurora crossed her legs, giving Stella a faint glimpse, *Basic Instinct* style. "Why?"

"I told you earlier. I'm a good problem solver."

"Ah, you're the type who likes to save damsels in distress." Aurora batted her long eyelashes.

"You seem very capable and in no need of saving."

"Yet, I don't have a date, and I've been informed it would be a wedding foul to go stag."

"I hate rules like that. If you don't want to bring a date, why do you have to?" After grabbing her glass, Stella relaxed into her chair, holding the beer in her right hand.

"The thought has crossed my mind. I hate being told I have to do something. It's the quickest way to piss me off."

Stella raised her glass again. "I'll drink to that. Not about pissing you off, but being strong enough to believe in yourself."

Aurora reciprocated.

"I don't know about your situation, but I've been living alone for a few years now and I'm the happiest I've ever been." Stella yanked a loose thread off her sleeve.

"Me too, although, I haven't been alone that long, but I aspire to be like you. We're not counting roommates, right?"

"No, roommates don't count. I don't understand society's need to force relationships on people. The last thing I want is a woman complicating my life."

Aurora's lips twisted up, and she flourished her beer before taking another sip. "I thought my gaydar pinged the first time we met."

"I have to admit mine didn't with you. Not on the first day."

"But you figured it out?"

Stella chewed on her bottom lip, not wanting to call out Aurora's flirting on the off-chance Stella had been misreading the woman the entire time. "I believe you dropped some clues. Like wanting a female date."

"I may have, accidentally of course." Aurora playacted innocence. "And I hear from many that I don't register on their gaydar. I'm too girly and garner the wrong type of attention."

"You mean only men check you out?"

"Correct."

"That's ridiculous. This is the twenty-first century. If you want to wear skirts and heels, go for it. It works for you, for sure." Stella's gaze traveled up from Aurora's feet, along her legs, continuing until landing on those lovely dark eyes.

Aurora held her pint glass with both hands right below her full lips, her elbows on each chair arm. "Is that right?" She took a sip. "I'm curious. I know you aren't in a relationship, but have you been *alone, alone* for the entirety of the last few years?"

"What do you mean?"

Aurora smiled seductively. "Really, Doctor, do I have to explain the birds and the bees to you?"

"Oh, that!"

Aurora prodded with an open palm. "I'm waiting."

"I never said I was against sex," Stella said, now convinced she hadn't misread any of Aurora's clues.

CHAPTER FOURTEEN

"THAT'S GOOD TO KNOW." AURORA RAPPED THE SIDE
of her head, indicating she was savoring that tasty morsel. "I've
always hated the saying *the birds and the bees.*"

"And yet, you used it," Stella teased.

"True." Aurora scrunched her brow. "Are women the birds
or the bees?"

"The birds since they lay eggs and bees pollinate flowers."

"God, what a simplistic view of something that's..." Aurora
shrugged, at a loss.

"That's what?" Stella pressed.

Aurora drank from her glass, buying some time. "We may
need another round for that conversation."

Stella rose. "The same?"

"Please, but it's my round." Aurora got to her feet, but
Stella didn't budge.

"We have a tab open, and I'm not sure I can trust you not to
pay for both rounds."

"Is this the way to start the evening? Accusations?"

"Can you behave?" Stella tossed back.

"About some things, yes."

"Does that include allowing me to buy the beers?"

"If you insist, but let me go to the bar. How else will you be able to check out my ass?" Aurora motioned for Stella to sit.

Stella still stood. "Sometimes I don't know what to say to you."

"I know. It's cute. Are you going to behave and let me order? Or are we ending instead of continuing what's shaping up to be a delightful evening?"

"That's blackmail." Stella's deep-blue eyes sparkled.

Aurora tsked. "Such an ugly word."

"The truth can be." Stella's smile could only be described as the type meant to get a woman to strip naked.

Aurora's insides went gooey with anticipation, but not wanting to get ahead of the situation, she said, "True. It doesn't always have to be, though. Have you made your decision? Another round, or do we shake hands and say good night?"

"Guinness."

"That was the answer I was hoping for." Aurora left before Stella could concoct a witty riposte.

At the bar, Aurora raised two fingers. After several moments, she asked, "Who's your team?"

"The Sox, of course." Conor glanced down at his shirt.

"I'm more of a Kilkenny fan," Aurora tossed out breezily.

Conor stopped pouring the first glass at the two-thirds mark and started on the second pint. "In that case, Limerick."

"You must be a happy man now that Limerick has ended their forty-five-year dry spell by winning the hurling final last August."

His expression brightened. "Are you from Ireland?"

"Feck no. You?"

"Both my parents were born there, but sadly, I was born in Boston." He hung his head in shame.

"I feel your pain. It's been a weird couple of years. I've considered jumping ship and asking my Irish relatives to let me move in. Although, I'm fond of having access to hot water twenty-four seven, so..." Aurora joggled her hands up and down, weighing both options.

"The immersions are something to get used to, for sure. Always takes me a few days when I'm visiting to remember I have to allow the water to heat up." He flashed a toothy grin. "I'll bring these out to you when they're ready."

"Not a minute before. And whatever you do, don't draw a shamrock on the froth. I can't respect any bartender who does that." Aurora pretended to wave a white flag, indicating she was only joking.

Conor grunted.

Rejoining Stella, Aurora said, "I'm having a hard time determining if he likes me or not." She retook her seat.

"Only an insane person wouldn't."

"I'm not sure about that. It seems I have an uncanny ability to attract the crazies."

Stella sized up Aurora. "I must be insane, then."

"Is that your way of telling me you find me attractive?"

"Do I actually need to verbalize it?" Stella raised one slender blonde eyebrow.

"Oh, no. What woman wants to hear that from anyone?"

Stella drummed her fingers on the arms of the chair. "I'm not sure if I'm coming or going with you."

"Does it have to be only one? I'm a big believer in two-way streets. Especially in certain areas in life."

Stella slanted her head, seeming to puzzle that one out, and Conor's appearance with fresh drinks gave the doctor more time to.

"Two special Irish milks." Conor winked at Aurora and departed.

"I don't think you have to worry. He only takes the piss out of people he likes," Stella said.

"Ah, you're showing your British roots with that phrase."

"I watched a lot of British crime drama over the summer." Stella raised her glass. "To the second round."

"That's good news." Aurora clinked Stella's glass.

"How so?"

"It would have been ominous if you said here's to the last round."

"You'd like another?"

"Maybe not tonight." Aurora was hoping for something else and soon.

"Another night?"

"My schedule did just free up." Aurora flicked a hand upward.

Stella's face tightened. "Did you like working at the school?"

"I see. We're going back to a safe topic." Aurora shifted in her seat, recrossing her legs.

Stella's eyes roved down Aurora's sculpted leg for the second time that night—according to Aurora's count.

"Humor an old lady," Stella said.

"I wouldn't call you old."

"You did earlier."

"Only in jest. You are nowhere near the old lady category."

"Older, then," Stella clarified.

"To answer your question, I enjoyed being on the medical campus. The office… it was an interesting experience. Most of the staff is a bit nutty. Harmless but difficult to control. It'd be easier to herd feral kittens."

"Why did you decide to take the temp job on the medical campus?"

"A couple of reasons, one being needing a paycheck. But, there's more. Back in my younger days, I wanted to be a nurse."

Aurora avoided Stella's gaze, speaking more to the beer in her hand.

"Not now?"

"I just don't think I'm cut out for it." Aurora shrugged, wishing she hadn't divulged that detail.

"Why not?"

Aurora looked up, her usual bravado gone. "It's hard to explain."

"I've been told I'm a good listener." Stella tugged on her right earlobe.

"I have no doubt, but it boils down to not thinking I'd make the grade."

Stella flinched as if Aurora had tossed ice-cold water in her face. "Are you kidding me? You're intelligent. Funny. Kind."

"Thanks, but you've only known me for a couple of months. I'm not that intelligent."

Stella set down her beer. "How did you get that thought in your head? About not making the cut for nursing?"

"A teacher made it crystal clear I wouldn't be nurse material."

Stella started to rebut this but resorted to taking a tug of beer. "Let me see if I can guess. It was a male teacher."

Aurora's brow furrowed. "How'd you know?"

"Because I've been told that by my fair share of men."

"You've been told you're an idiot?" Aurora shook her head. "No, I don't believe that."

"It's true, though. Many men find intelligent women intimidating. Add drop-dead gorgeous to that and..." Stella waved for Aurora to fill in the blank.

"Now I'm drop-dead gorgeous?" Aurora's voice purred, and she didn't hide the fact she looked Stella up and down. "You're not so bad yourself."

"We're talking about you. You are stunning, but don't try to steer me away from the actual topic. The nursing profession needs people like you. Have you considered medical school, instead?"

Aurora rolled her eyes. "Really, Doctor, things were going swimmingly for us. Now you're just blowing smoke up my ass."

"I'm not, though. You have everything it takes to be a great doctor."

"And you know this how?"

"Over the years, I've recruited and taught hundreds of doctors."

"Oh, that. That's…" Aurora didn't complete her thought.

"Aurora, don't let one asshole discourage you from chasing your dream. There are too many people in this world who love to crush hopes just because they can. If you want to be a nurse, go for it. If you want to be a doctor, fucking do it."

"I don't. Want to be a doctor, that is."

"Why not?"

"I like people. Not enough to be in a relationship, but ya know, I do want to help."

"I'm right there with you about no serious personal relationships, but I have to push back about your doctor theory. You don't think doctors help?" Stella's voice contained a hint of amusement.

"No, they do. But the way I see it, they're behind the scenes mostly. I want to be on the frontlines, doing all I can to help people through the scariest times in their lives."

Stella set her beer down on the table and leaned on her knees, clasping her hands. "Aurora, I'm pleading with you to please reconsider. Before that answer, I knew you'd make a great nurse because you have people skills. Now I know you might be one that changes the profession for the better." Aurora started to speak, but Stella silenced her with a raised palm. "If you're going to cut yourself down in any way, don't bother. I'm onto you."

"But you've only known me in the professional sphere. How can you say you really know me?"

"I'm good at reading people."

"Is that right?" The playfulness returned to Aurora's tone. "What am I thinking right now?"

"Dinner."

As if it had been waiting for its cue, Aurora's stomach rumbled.

Stella pointed to Aurora's stomach. "Take this as a sign."

"Of?"

"I'm always right."

Aurora's eyes darted upward. "It's well after seven. It doesn't take a rocket scientist to guess a person would be hungry at this time of night."

"Since you're insisting on paying for the second round, dinner is on me."

"Wait." Aurora closed one eye as if consulting a mental calculator. "How do you figure that?"

"Because I want to buy you dinner. That is if you'll join me."

"That depends." Aurora rested her chin on her palm.

"On?"

"Where you're taking me."

"I was considering one of my favorite places, but it's closer to where I live in Brighton."

"I'm in Allston on Commonwealth Avenue."

"Ah, just down the street from me. We can Uber to Ray's."

"Ray's pizza!" Aurora rubbed her hands together. "In my opinion, there's no other pizza place that's comparable."

"I agree. Is it a date?"

Aurora's stomach rumbled again, causing her cheeks to burn, much to her mortification. "I think that's a yes."

"We should get going before I have to administer life-saving measures. No beautiful woman will starve to death on my watch."

"Just the ugly ones?" Aurora asked.

"I try not to let anyone die, but only take a select few to pizza."

"Now I'm curious about my competition." Aurora rose to her feet.

"You don't have any."

CHAPTER FIFTEEN

THE PIZZERIA WASN'T FANCY, BUT STELLA HAD A feeling Aurora was much like Stella and preferred a more relaxed atmosphere with primo food. Besides, Aurora had been clear she wasn't looking for a relationship. This was the type of place no one in their right mind would go to on a first date if they wanted something serious down the road.

Their pepperoni pizza arrived at the table.

Aurora reached for the red pepper flakes. "Here's the true test. Any on your side?" She shook the round plastic container, causing the flakes to swirl.

"Love them. Do your best or worst."

"Is that a challenge? Finding the right flake to pizza ratio?"

"It is. Are you up for it?" Stella laced her fingers on the tabletop.

Aurora liberally covered the pie. Before setting them aside, she eyed the pizza with one eye closed and gave one last shake on her half.

Stella nodded, appraising the situation. "I couldn't have done it better."

Aurora did a half bow as much as she could considering she

was sitting. "I take great pride in my seasoning skills." She ripped off a slice, setting it on her white paper plate. "How long have you lived in Brighton?"

"A few years. How long have you been in Allston?" Stella chomped into a slice, silencing a moan. Ray's pizza was the best.

"Since college."

"That was last week, right?"

"Are you being ageist?" Aurora took a hearty bite, her eyes glazing over in satisfaction.

"Does that work in this case? It seems you would be the one more concerned about age."

"How do you figure that?" Aurora bit again into the pizza, closing her eyes as she chewed. After swallowing, she said, "This hits the spot."

Stella could watch Aurora eat pizza all night.

Aurora stared at Stella. "I'm still waiting."

Stella sighed and decided to get it out there before they went much further down whatever path they were on. "I'm forty-one."

"I'm twenty-nine."

"Twelve years." Stella let out a faint whistle.

"No wonder you're a doctor. You didn't even need your toes to calculate that one." Aurora waggled her brows.

"Oh, I did. You just didn't see me do it."

Aurora laughed. "Does it bother you? That I'm younger?"

"No. But, it's difficult for me not to wonder why you like hanging out with me."

"You're charming, funny, sweet, and you look smoking hot in your white coat." Aurora held four fingers in the air.

"I should have worn it home." Stella snapped her fingers in a *dang it* way.

"Seriously, Stella, I'm not bothered by your age. It's just a number."

"I've noticed the people who say that the most are younger than I am."

"Do you feel old?"

"No, I don't. Sometimes I'm shocked when I remember I'm in my forties. I thought I would feel forty when I woke up on my fortieth birthday, but I didn't and still don't. Actually, I feel like I did when I was in my twenties. Although, my left knee makes a hideous crunching sound when I descend stairs."

Concern etched in Aurora's brow. "Does it hurt?"

"Nah. It's just cringeworthy to hear."

"I think it bothers you that I'm younger, and you're trying to put it on me."

"Yes, a lot of forty-somethings hate it when someone in their twenties flirts with them. Absolute torture."

"Have I been flirting?" Aurora sipped her Coke through a straw.

Stella was pretty sure Aurora was pulling her chain, but there was some doubt. "Uh..."

Aurora's smile overtook her face. "You really can be adorable."

"In that sweet old lady way?"

"Oh my God, you're not old!"

The man behind the register looked up.

Aurora leaned over the table. "Let me be clear. I think you're fucking hot."

Stella held a pizza slice in the air, the tip falling downward. "I think you are."

"Great. Another thing we have in common. This could be fun." Aurora wiggled her butt on the bench.

"Does that mean we should have drinks and dinner again soon?"

"Are you wanting to end the evening already? It's starting to get very interesting."

Stella shook her head. "Not at all. And, my place is literally right around the corner."

* * *

STELLA SWEPT a loose strand of hair off Aurora's face. "You have amazing eyes."

Aurora's smile was delightfully shy.

Neither of them seemed willing to make the first move now that they were standing in the privacy of Stella's apartment.

Rain splattered the window, causing both of them to swivel their heads to the source. Unsure how to get the ball rolling now that Aurora stood in Stella's apartment, she turned to a tactic she hated when other people deployed it. "It's really coming down now."

"It is." Aurora seemed relieved by Stella's decision to latch on to the one thing any idiot could discuss during an awkward moment: the weather.

"Do you need a tea or hot chocolate to warm up?" Stella hitched a shoulder, realizing she was acting like a woman who'd never seduced someone, but truth be told, she was more than rusty.

"I never turn down hot chocolate." Aurora's confident tone didn't match the nerves practically swimming in her dark eyes.

"It will help us with..." Stella lost her train of thought when Aurora chewed on her bottom lip, the tip of her pink tongue briefly poking out. Could Aurora pick up on Stella's silent plea for help? Simply put, Stella wanted to feel Aurora's lips on hers. But how to get to that point? Go in for the kill? Play hard to get? Was there a middle ground?

Stella wheeled about toward the kitchen, a measly five steps away. "Hot chocolate. I'm supposed to make hot chocolate."

"Need help?"

Yes!

"I think I can handle it." *Nope, I can't.* Stella wanted to slam her head into the wall for turning down the offer.

"Do you have a robe or something I can borrow?"

Stella glanced over her shoulder to spy Aurora tugging her soaking-wet blouse away from her skin. "I should have offered to get you out of your clothes sooner."

"You're coming in hot again." Aurora's smile was emboldened.

"I didn't mean it that way."

A blush spread across Aurora's face. "Okay, then."

"No, I didn't mean it that way, either." Stella inhaled. "I'm sorry. I can't seem to say or do the right thing, and I'm messing everything up."

"No, you aren't. I find your bashfulness refreshing."

The urge to feel Aurora's lips on Stella's intensified, but she feared making a move on a woman more than ten years younger. Shouldn't Aurora be the one to show her intentions? More than she'd been doing all night? Or since they met, really?

Aurora moved closer to Stella.

Stella sneezed.

"Maybe we should both get out of our wet clothes," Aurora said, still inching closer to Stella.

Now that Aurora's intentions practically dripped from the intensity of her gaze, Stella faltered again. "Right. Bathrobes. We both need bathrobes." She stepped around Aurora and headed to her bedroom. When out of Aurora's sight, Stella muttered, "Real smooth, idiot." She found her bathrobe, but the sudden realization that she only had one entered her mind. Quickly, she shucked her pants and panties, pulled on blue scrub bottoms, and then dispensed with her top, replacing it with a T-shirt.

"I could only find one." Stella said upon her return, holding out the white terrycloth robe to Aurora.

"What? You don't want to share with me?"

"The robe?" Stella attempted to hand it off again. "Wait, you mean...? I'm not sure logistically how it would work for both of us to wear one robe."

"Might be fun to give it a try." Aurora took the garment.

"The bathroom is down the hall on your left."

"Be right back." Aurora amscrayed.

Stella filled the teakettle and flicked on the gas burner. She rummaged in the white cabinet for two Carnation hot chocolate packets she kept on hand for Mackenzie.

"Are you sure you don't want help?"

Stella jumped. "Jesus. You scared the crap out of me."

Aurora laughed. "I didn't mean to. Are you okay?"

"My heart rate is through the roof."

"Goodness. Hopefully, it's not a life-threatening situation. Maybe I should check it out." Aurora placed her hand over Stella's shirt, right above Stella's left breast. "It is going. Shall I kiss it better?"

"Depends on your goal."

"Meaning?" Aurora left her hand on Stella's chest.

"If you want to slow it down or not."

"What do you want?"

Stella's face moved closer to Aurora's as if by some magnetic pull.

Aurora's chest heaved with a deep breath.

Their lips met, but Stella pulled back as if compelled to do one final check to make sure she was reading Aurora's signs clearly.

Aurora grabbed Stella's face with both hands, smashing their mouths together with urgency. Stella didn't part her lips at first, but Aurora deepened the kiss, and Stella responded with an increased need. Her arms encircled Aurora, and they continued kissing.

The teakettle whistled, and without breaking their lip-lock, Stella turned the knob to the off position.

In between kisses, Aurora said, "I don't want hot chocolate anymore."

"Me neither."

Aurora's lips were much softer than Stella had anticipated. And Stella found it hot as hell that Aurora was taking control. In every facet of her life, everyone looked to Stella to act first. It was nice to have Aurora step in, making it clear by the way she kissed Stella there was more on the horizon, but there wasn't a rush. The kiss was quickly morphing into *the* kiss. The one against which to rank all others.

And that was before they kicked it into an even higher gear.

Aurora snapped her head back. "Here or the bedroom?" Her voice was thick with desire, and lust burned in her eyes.

Stella swallowed. It was as if she stood on the razor's edge, and the realization she was about to fall headfirst or backward paralyzed her. Which did she want? Sex with Aurora? Or to go back to no human touching?

"Stella, are you okay?" Aurora leaned down to peer into Stella's eyes.

Come on, Stella. Answer her.

"Hey, if you need to, we can slow this down. Go back to Plan A. Hot chocolate."

Stella turned her head and appraised the kettle. Her wanting hardened, and she responded with flipping her head back around and kissing Aurora hard. For what seemed like hours, they kissed. Finally, Stella said, "Bedroom." Stella led Aurora to the room, holding onto her hand.

Aurora pressed Stella against the bedroom wall. Their hands seeking the other's skin under their clothing. Stella fisted Aurora's silky hair, causing her to emit a soft moan.

Stella pulled away. "Should we slow it down? Savor..." Stella stopped herself from saying *the first time*, unsure if there would be another. Both had clearly stated neither wanted anything serious. She settled on, "It."

"I know. It's our first time and we should savor it, but I don't know if I can slow things down." Aurora's eyes shone with sexual longing.

"I don't know if I can put the brakes on, either." Stella placed a hand on Aurora's cheek. "Not with you looking at me like that."

Aurora leaned into her touch. "Like what?"

"Like you want to rip my clothes off and have your way with me."

"I do." Aurora didn't bother playing coy.

There was no going back now. Their bodies became intertwined once again. Kissing. Pawing. Groping.

Aurora jerked the collar of Stella's T-shirt to allow her tongue to trace along Stella's collarbone.

"Take me," Stella said.

A *fuck me* moan escaped from Aurora, and she ripped Stella's shirt off, casting it onto the floor. Stella yanked the tie of the robe, exposing Aurora's soft milky skin, perky breasts, and a tantalizing triangle. Stella's eyes roved over Aurora's offerings.

"I take it you like what you see."

"You're fucking gorgeous, Aurora."

"Is that your professional opinion, Doctor?" Aurora arched a teasing eyebrow.

"It is."

"You know, I've never actually played doctor with a real doctor. It's kinda hot." Aurora twirled the drawstrings of Stella's scrubs around her finger. "My turn." She yanked the strings, allowing the scrubs to plummet to the carpet, and Stella stepped out of them.

Kissing Stella, Aurora walked them backward, taking charge once again, and pushed Stella onto the navy, medium blue, and silver paisley comforter before climbing on top of her. Aurora's fingers tracked up and down Stella's side.

Aurora straddled Stella, putting Aurora's pert breasts on display. Stella massaged them, not quite believing she was actually doing this. Not after such a dry spell.

Aurora's eyes widened, and the hunger present darkened them to nearly black. She bit her lower lip again, and Stella adored this tick.

Aurora leaned down and licked the hollow of Stella's throat. Stella closed her eyes. Aurora licked and nipped her way to Stella's left breast. Aurora flicked the nipple, and it started to harden in her mouth. She applied pressure. Softly at first and then more.

"Oh," Stella moaned.

Aurora's mouth continued to torture the nipple in the most tantalizing manner.

It drove Stella mad with wanting, and her hips arched upward. Aurora rocked her hip into Stella. The two moving together, Stella clasping onto Aurora's back as if needing to pull the young woman as close as humanly possible. Enjoying the feel of Aurora's warm skin against her own.

Aurora peered into Stella's eyes, questioning, and Stella whispered, "Please."

Aurora's nod made it clear she knew exactly what Stella craved, and Aurora began her trek down, following a winding path that didn't seem to make sense, but that didn't matter. Stella's skin was aflame, while Aurora's mouth and tongue continued downward.

Farther and farther.

The eagerness spurred an overwhelming yearning Stella hadn't experienced in so long. If ever. Juices pooled between her legs.

"Jesus! I may burst." Stella shoved the back of her head deeper into the pillow.

"This wouldn't be a good time for me to stop, then?" Aurora teased and raked her teeth on Stella's pubic hairs, followed by Aurora running a hand up the inside of Stella's right leg.

"Uh, that would be so disappointing."

"And I'm not the type to leave a girl high and dry." Aurora looked down. "You aren't dry, though." She ran one finger along the slippery surface of Stella's outer lips. All the way up. Back down. Repeating the action until her finger was good and wet. Then she sucked her finger while maintaining eye contact with Stella.

Stella's chest heaved up, and her tongue licked her lips in anticipation.

"Did you want a taste?" Aurora dipped her finger in Stella's juices once again, and then placed it on Stella's mouth.

Stella couldn't take her eyes off Aurora, who slipped the finger into Stella's mouth. Leaving the finger there, Aurora's head dipped closer to Stella's pussy.

Stella sucked hard on Aurora's finger.

Aurora's tongue made contact with Stella's clit. Swiping it once, before exploring all of Stella's nether region. Stella reached back, holding onto the metal railing with one hand, the other fisted the sheets. She spread her legs further, granting Aurora full access.

Her tongue penetrated Stella. Hesitant at first, but quickly becoming more emboldened and plunging in deeper.

Stella groaned, "Oh, fuck."

Aurora's tongue moved back to Stella's bundle of nerves. Stella writhed, and Aurora slid a finger inside. The action set Stella's senses into the stratosphere, and again, she closed her eyes.

"Tell me what you like. Hard or soft?" Aurora asked.

Stella's eyes snapped open. "A bit harder."

Aurora replaced her tongue on Stella's clit and shoved another finger in. Deeper this time.

"Don't stop," Stella panted. "Whatever you do, don't stop."

Aurora circled the bud, all the while her fingers dove in and out, seeming to plunge deeper with each thrust.

"Oh my God." Stella squirmed, not wanting to buck around too much, but it was nearly impossible not to.

Aurora's tongue continued to circle, doing her best to stay in the right spot. She pulled away, "Do you want another finger?"

Stella nodded frantically.

"Okay. Tell me if it gets to be too much." Aurora inserted another finger, setting back to work with her tongue.

"You feel so good. So fucking good."

Aurora drove in deeper. Stella lurched up, which seemed to unnerve Aurora, and she removed her fingers and stopped lapping Stella's clit. "You okay?"

"Yes. You have no idea. Please, don't stop." Stella steered Aurora's mouth back into place. "And inside. Need you inside."

Aurora willingly complied, moaning as she reentered and going as far as she could.

It didn't take long for Stella to say, "I'm so…" Stella didn't have time to complete the sentence as the orgasm darted through her, pinging every nerve in her entire body.

Aurora plunged in one last time, curling her fingers upward, but her tongue didn't still, causing the orgasm to spill into another. Then another.

Stella's entire body shook.

And again.

After the fourth full body spasm, she fell back onto the comforter.

Aurora kept her fingers inside but rested her cheek on the inside of Stella's thigh.

"That was—"

"Yes?" Aurora prodded. She supported her head with a palm. The lower half of her face glistened.

"I've never…" Stella sucked in air.

"Never what? Surely you've had an orgasm."

"Yes. But not four in a row."

"Oh, that. Sorry, but not sorry. I didn't want to stop. You taste amazing."

"No apology necessary. It was fantastic." Stella's breathing was still ragged.

"Give me a minute, before…"

"Before what?" Aurora teased.

"You know what."

"Not sure I do. I'm the type that likes firsthand explanations."

"Is that right?" Stella rolled Aurora onto her back and straddled her, enjoying the feel of Aurora's bare stomach on her slick pussy. "I like a challenge."

"I fucking hope so, because I'm a challenge."

Stella gazed down, wondering if Aurora meant it was difficult to make her come or something else. Stella would find out soon enough. She leaned down and kissed Aurora, tasting her own juices. Stella worked her way to Aurora's ear and tugged her earlobe before dipping her tongue inside.

Aurora moaned.

"Step one to overcoming the challenge," Stella whispered.

"Cocky," Aurora teased. "I like it."

Stella captured Aurora's lips, deepening the kiss instantly.

"Now, time to find out what else you like. The ear is a definite yes. What about your nipple?" Stella took it into her mouth. So soft at first. She flicked it with her tongue and pressed her teeth gently into the nub. It roared to life in her mouth. "I'm counting this as a yes."

Aurora's moan added to the confirmation.

Stella sat up, straddling Aurora's midsection. "We've made

a mess of this comforter, and I think it's only going to get worse." Stella started to ride Aurora, who matched each thrust with her own. Her eyes admired Stella's breasts. "Are you a boob girl?" Stella teased.

"I'm enjoying the way they're moving right now."

Stella jiggled them a bit more, still riding Aurora.

Aurora attempted to fondle one, but Stella playfully slapped Aurora's hand away. "It's my turn to take charge."

"Just a feel, please," Aurora begged.

"This seems like something I can take advantage of." Stella leaned down and practically smothered Aurora's face with her tits. The pleasing sounds made it clear the action was much appreciated.

Stella kissed Aurora, sweetly at first, but it turned into an *I want to fuck you* kiss. Moving to Aurora's other nipple, Stella teased it until it hardened. One of her hands trailed down Aurora's stomach, enjoying the softness.

"Your turn. Fingers or no?" Stella asked.

"Yes."

Stella eased one in, amazed by how wet Aurora was before they really got going. Well, before Stella had a chance to properly reciprocate. Aurora got this turned on simply by fucking Stella. Amazing.

Stella's mouth continued working on the nipple, and her fingers explored Aurora's lips.

Aurora let out a gratified growling sound, urging Stella on.

Her tongue trekked down Aurora's stomach, pausing here and there for soft kisses or nips of the flesh. Stella could explore the alabaster skin for hours, never getting bored.

Arriving at Aurora's mound of hair, Stella deeply inhaled the musky scent.

Stella reinserted a finger, watching it slip in and out of Aurora. In a voice barely above a whisper, Stella said, "You feel amazing." She closed her eyes to focus solely on being inside.

The warmth. Aurora's muscles tightening around Stella's finger. She added another and dove in deeper.

Aurora elevated her buttocks off the covers.

"Another?" Stella asked.

"Yes."

Stella added a third. Aurora welcomed it by shuddering more. Stella couldn't rip her eyes away from Aurora's face, wanting to see the woman as she edged closer and closer to bliss.

Aurora thrashed more frantically, and Stella sensed she was edging even closer and thrust her fingers more. She took Aurora's bud into her mouth, the taste alluring and pungent. Stella knew she would crave this again and again. She shoved this troublesome thought out of her mind.

Aurora moaned louder and louder, propelling Stella to intensify her lapping of the clit and plunging in deeper, Aurora's intake of air greeting Stella's ears. Stella penetrated harder and harder. Aurora's breathing deepened, and she poured into Stella's mouth.

Aurora's body shook once, turning into trembling, and she reached for Stella's free hand. Their hands clasped, while Aurora bucked off the bed momentarily and then fell onto the bed, her back arching. Stella went in farther and pulled her fingers upward in hopes of triggering Aurora's G-spot. She was met with a groan and a full-body spasm.

"Hold your fingers right there," Aurora instructed.

Stella watched as Aurora came. Hard.

CHAPTER SIXTEEN

AURORA GROANED WHEN SHE OPENED HER EYES. NOT from the drinking the night before but from being unable to place where she was. She knew one thing for sure; she wasn't in her apartment.

"Good morning."

Aurora rolled over and stared into Stella's mesmerizing eyes peering down at her. "Hi. What time is it?"

"Early."

"Why are you awake?" Aurora propped up on her elbows.

"The curse of being a surgeon."

"Oh." Aurora sat up, yawning and rubbing her eyes. "I should leave so you can... do your thing."

"There's no rush. I'm not expected anywhere for another hour."

Then why is she up and showered? Was this the doctor's way of ushering Aurora out the door without the ugliness of coming out and saying it? "No, I need to go."

"I thought your schedule as of five o'clock last night was wide open." Stella spread out her arms.

"It is, which is why I have to go. Need to fill it with... something."

Stella clearly seemed befuddled by the answer but didn't press, moving out of the way for Aurora to clamber out of bed.

Aurora looked around for her clothing, not spying anything.

"I folded everything and put it on top of the dresser." Stella left the bedside and grabbed them. "Here." She seemed to hold onto the red satin bra for a second longer.

Aurora took it and mumbled a thanks on her way to the bathroom, where she hurriedly dressed. Why had she fallen asleep? It would have been so much better if she'd left after... everything.

Fully clothed, she found Stella in the kitchen, packing her work bag. She glanced up, looking uneasy or stressed. "Are you sure you wouldn't at least like a cup of coffee before you dash out? Or the hot chocolate I promised you last night?"

Aurora would kill for a cup of java to clear the cobwebs from her brain. "That's okay. I'll grab one on the way home. Last night was... lovely."

"Is this the part where you say you'll call me but then don't?" Stella's smile was wide.

Baffled as to how to take the statement coupled with the smile, Aurora blustered, "Uh..." Was that a hint that Stella was serious about the no relationship thing? If it was, it hit Aurora hard because she liked Stella and last night had been amazing, but she wasn't willing to stick her neck out only to have Stella chop it off. "You got it. I gotta dash. Bye."

Outside on Commonwealth Avenue, Aurora tried to shake off Stella's behavior. Was it a brushoff? Aurora mentally ticked off the evidence supporting her belief. One: Stella got out of bed and showered. Even the women Aurora had one-night stands with wanted more nookie in the morning before saying goodbye. If you were actually interested in the person, wouldn't that be a given? Two: She made it clear she had to head to work in an hour, but why was she shoving things into her bag like she was one second from dashing out the door? Three: the don't call line. That was just weird. On the flipside, Stella seemed sincere about making a cup of coffee or hot chocolate. She'd folded Aurora's clothes. Did that mean she was considerate, or she wanted Aurora to get dressed quicker?

Walking on Commonwealth Avenue, Aurora tried to gather her thoughts and perhaps scrape her pride off the sidewalk. Taking in her surroundings, she turned toward the direction of her apartment, which was only a mile down the road, but miraculously, they'd never bumped into each other. How had the two of them ended up working in the South End? It wasn't that far, but the subway didn't travel close to the medical school, which complicated the commute.

Her feet started to hurt, so she eased the heels off and proceeded to walk barefoot, the wet cement cold with each step. "So much for Stella taking care of my feet if I needed her to."

Outside of her apartment building, her phone rang. "Hello?"

"Is this Aurora?"

Who'd the person expect? "Yes."

"This is Alice Newman, the director of the AV and Scheduling department on the medical campus."

"Good morning." Why in the world was the director calling after Aurora no longer worked for the school? Interesting timing for their first contact.

"I know this will seem out of the blue, but would you like your job back? Permanently?"

"Excuse me?" Aurora stared at the T slowing on Commonwealth Avenue at the Allston stop, the brakes making a horrendous metal-on-metal sound. "I'm sorry," Aurora spoke loudly. "I don't think I heard you correctly."

"Would you like your job back?" Alice screamed.

"Uh…?"

"You'd make three dollars more an hour and have full benefits." The director continued to speak at an ear-piercing level even though the train had finally come to a complete stop.

"Wow. That would be great." Aurora's caffeine-starved brain tried to comprehend the situation. Did the previous scheduler not return?

"Can you start today?"

Aurora looked at her watch, but it wasn't there. Fuck, she'd left it at Stella's, and now the not-so-good doctor would think Aurora had resorted to one of the oldest plays in the book. "I can be there in an hour."

"Great. Come straight to my office in the B-building. 708. Not Scheduling. You got that?"

"Yes."

After ending the call, Aurora didn't mess around getting showered, dressed, and dashing out of her apartment in record speed. At the Hynes stop, she sprinted in heels to catch the number one bus, and Aurora arrived in the director's office with one minute to spare.

"Good morning. Alice Newman is expecting me," Aurora announced to the receptionist as Aurora tried to steady her heavy breathing.

"Name?" the woman, in her fifties with the typical New England middle-aged haircut that looked more like a well-worn brown football helmet, glared at Aurora.

"Aurora Shirley."

The woman lifted the phone and dialed. Into the receiver, she said, "There's an Aurora—yes, I'll show her in." As if it killed the woman to be nice, she plastered a fake smile that was clearly meant to say, *I don't like you, but…* "If you'll follow me."

The door was slightly ajar, and Aurora overheard, "I fucking know how serious it is. That office is a nightmare!"

The admin knocked on the door.

"Enter," Alice barked.

The receptionist motioned for Aurora to go ahead.

Taking a steadying breath and straightening her blouse, Aurora breezed in, hoping she looked confident, in control, but also obedient.

Alice was still on the phone. "She's here. I know. Yes, we all hope so." She replaced the phone on the base and rose. With a hand out, she said, "Ms. Shirley, it's a pleasure to meet you."

Aurora shook the woman's pudgy hand. At a loss for what to say, she opted for, "Good morning."

"It's morning, but I'm not sure how good it is. Please take a seat."

Aurora complied, crossing her legs at the ankles.

"Here's the lowdown. The Scheduling department has been... difficult for some time now, and it's been deemed that it's time for a fresh start. Shelly won't be back. Kip has been demoted from head tech to simply a tech. The regular scheduler is back, but she's wanting part-time hours. I've heard good things about you. Even Vera, Dean Andrews's assistant, has been singing your praises. But I need to know right here and now if you have the gumption to take the department by the horns and whip everyone into shape."

"The department?"

"Yes. The Scheduling branch. Hopefully, Bri will be in charge of the AV staff. I haven't had a chance to speak to her yet. I'm thinking she'll come in around two, meaning we'll have to hire a part-time tech for the evenings." Alice jotted something down on a notepad.

"As in be the one in charge of all the scheduling?" Aurora swallowed, speculating Alice was making battle plans on the fly.

"For the moment. Until we can flesh out the best course of action. It's no secret HR has been gunning for Scheduling and with good reason. Turnover has been atrocious, and that doesn't even take into account the chaos that occurs daily. Shelly didn't have the cajones"—Alice made a crude gesture —"to take the necessary action to get everyone to play nicely in the sandbox. I've been told you're smart. We need that. We also need someone who isn't afraid of a challenge, because it's going to be one. Kip isn't going to like the news about his demotion, but he's not your problem. You're only in charge of Kristin, whom you haven't met yet. Or have you?"

Aurora shook her head. How long had Alice known Kristin wanted part-time hours and that HR wanted Shelly out? And, had Shelly really only been making three dollars more an hour? Or was that what they offered Aurora since she was younger? A lot of this seemed fishy beyond belief. But it was also a permanent job offer with health insurance. Considering Aurora had woken up jobless, this was a surprising change. Although, what would Stella say? They'd gone to bed when both of them believed they weren't colleagues.

Alice regarded her. "I can tell from your cautious expression you're aware of the task at hand."

Aurora nodded, not wanting to risk saying something stupid like, "Is it wrong I slept with a doctor who also works for the school?"

"And to complicate matters, we need to start planning the White Coat ceremony ASAP. Have you heard of it?"

"Yes, of course."

"Great. I know you've just arrived and haven't had time to go to your office, but we're expected upstairs in five minutes for the first planning meeting. That okay?" It was asked in a way that implied it better be.

"Absolutely."

"I'll be in the front in a minute. I need to finish my conversation with HR and then call my office on the main campus."

Aurora imagined a few more f-bombs were in the making. She rose, nodded, and retreated to the waiting area that consisted of two institutional black chairs with hunter-green cushions that had faded from years of being in the direct sunlight. Taking a seat, she googled for articles about past White Coat ceremonies, but before the search page could populate, Alice was looking down at her.

"Ready?" the director barked.

Aurora got to her feet, the blister she'd earned last night making it clear she was in for a long day.

In the hallway, now that she wasn't rushing, Aurora noticed the difference in the surroundings. The floor was spotless. The conference rooms were professional looking with staff members groomed and dressed appropriately, even the ones in scrubs or white lab jackets.

"Just a heads-up, HR will be so far up your asshole you may as well get used to it now and ensure its spic 'n span." Alice's laughter was chilling.

Aurora clenched her entire body.

"Any hint of funny business will be catastrophic for all involved." Alice stopped outside a door. With her hand on the shiny silver knob, she said, "I hope you understand there won't be any second chances."

"I understand perfectly." Thank the fucking stars Aurora hadn't slipped about Stella.

"Good. Now, let's play nice with the important people." Alice rolled her eyes as if saying she'd rather deal with Aurora than what awaited her on the other side of the door.

They walked in, and Aurora's eyes landed on Stella's.

CHAPTER SEVENTEEN

"OH, HI," STELLA SAID. HER STOMACH SEEMED TO plummet to the first floor, and they were located on the seventh. "I wasn't expecting you." The last time she'd seen Aurora, the woman couldn't wait to get away. Stella thought she wouldn't bump into Aurora again, and it had been a bitter pill to swallow after the perfect night.

"We've had a last-minute change," Alice explained. "Aurora is stepping in for Shelly." Without another word, Alice took a seat at the end of the table.

On the far side of Alice sat the white-haired dean. To his right was Vera, an unfriendly looking woman in her fifties who gave the impression she knew how much power she held at the school—and that she didn't give a damn who she trampled for the greater good, whether it be for university affairs or her own gain.

Stella got to her feet. "Would either of you like a coffee?"

"Please. With four sugars." Alice answered, without sounding grateful.

Stella raised one eyebrow at Aurora, wondering how so much had changed since the previous evening.

"Yes, thank you." Aurora's tone was neutral.

"I'm curious. Is Aurora stepping in only for today? It's a bit unusual adding a newbie to the White Coat planning team." Vera's smile could intimidate the hell out of a murderer armed with a chainsaw.

"Shelly had a family emergency that's called her away. Rest assured Aurora is quite capable and if need be, she can handle the entire reservation."

Aurora's eyes flitted to Alice as if surprised by this. Or was there more going on?

Vera looked Aurora up and down, not showing whether she agreed or not. "I do hope the family emergency isn't too serious." Vera's tone implied she wasn't buying whatever Alice was trying to sell.

Knowing it was cowardly to duck out right then, but unable to watch the rest of this play out, whatever it was, Stella fled to fetch the coffees. The irony didn't escape her. Earlier, she'd offered to make Aurora a cup of coffee after a night of amazing sex, and now, here she was actually making Aurora coffee, and they were once again work colleagues. Was Stella being punished for something? Tested?

Stella returned with two cups, placing one in front of Alice. When she handed off Aurora's, she said, "I'm sorry, Ms....?"

"Shirley."

"I don't know how you take your coffee." Stella shrugged.

"Black is fine."

"Are you sure? I brought..." Stella fished out a handful of sugar packets and creamers from her lab coat pocket.

Aurora grabbed one of each. "Perfect. Thank you, Dr. Gilbert." She never looked Stella in the eye.

Stella navigated around the table, taking a seat directly across from Aurora and folding her hands in front of her. "What'd I miss?"

"We haven't started yet." Vera flipped open a manila folder.

"Here's a printout of the program and reservation from the last White Coat ceremony." She distributed the packets to everyone. "Last year went off without a hitch somehow." Her eyes seared into Alice's. "Will this year's event consist of the same AV staff?"

"That's to be determined. Kip will still—"

Dean Andrews huffed.

"Will not be involved," Alice corrected course.

Aurora reached into her bag, pulling out a folded-up paper that had printing on it, but Stella couldn't make out what it said. Aurora turned it to the blank side, and she jotted down *White Coat*, underlining it twice. The first bullet point, if Stella was reading it correctly, was: *AV staff?*

How in the hell did Aurora end up in this meeting of all meetings and seemingly in charge of Scheduling? They'd only been apart a couple of hours. This was like a bad dream. Wait. Was Stella dreaming? That seemed like the easiest answer even if highly improbable because she felt so very awake.

There was laughter in the room, and Stella realized she'd checked out for many minutes. One glance at Aurora's sheet, which was now chock-full with bullet points, confirmed Stella had missed a lot.

Stella tried to shake her funk and get involved, but her mind kept retreating to Aurora.

After an hour, Dean Andrews stood. "My apologies, but I have a meeting. Vera will stay to address the remaining issues."

No one said goodbye as the man goose-stepped out as if on a military parade ground.

The meeting dragged on for another forty-five minutes before Alice cleared her throat. "I think that's a good start."

Vera started to speak but seemed to think better of it. "When shall we get together again?"

"Same time next week?" Alice responded.

Vera consulted her phone. "Dean Andrews has a meeting."

"I don't," Alice countered.

"Fine." Vera seemed to log it into her schedule. "Next week, then." She turned to Stella. "Can you meet tomorrow at ten to go over our plan for wooing the woman I told you about?"

Stella felt heat rise up her neck. "Pardon?"

"Tracy Ang, who'll be the youngest med student. The Dean wants her to come here."

"Right! That woman. Yes, absolutely."

Alice got up to take her leave, Aurora following her lead.

"I'll walk you two out," Stella said.

In the hallway, Alice's shoulders relaxed some, which wasn't saying much. "Have you two met?"

Stella nodded. "Yes, Ms. Shirley helped me solve a problem. Two actually, for which I'm eternally grateful." Stella placed a hand over her chest.

"It was my pleasure." Aurora butchered the last word, but Alice didn't seem to pick up on it since she was reading her phone.

"I need to make a phone call. The joy of being me never stops. Aurora, I'll pop by the office before the end of the day to map out... things." Alice charged down the hallway, turning right and out of sight.

"And then there were two," Stella joked.

"Just so you know, I didn't intentionally leave my watch at your place." Aurora squirmed in her shoes.

"Okay." Stella hadn't noticed Aurora's watch, not that she stayed much longer after Aurora fled. "I'll look for it tonight."

"I didn't even realize until I was on the phone with Alice."

"About that. Care to fill me in about how you ended up in this meeting?" Stella crossed her arms.

"I'm just as shocked as you are."

Stella led them down the corridor, finding an empty supply room. "I was under the impression yesterday was your last day."

"It was. After I left... this morning, Alice called asking me back."

"In what capacity?"

"I think I'm in charge. Of Scheduling, that is, on a temporary basis until Alice can figure shit out, but I don't have much confidence that she will." Aurora flicked her hands up. "When I accepted, I had no idea I would be involved with the planning for the White Coat ceremony or that you would be either."

"Typical," Stella muttered.

"What does that mean?" Aurora bristled.

"I didn't mean it against you. It's par for the course for Alice, though. She's never taken the time to learn the importance of the scheduling branch of her department. Now, she's tossed you to the wolves to fail."

"What happened to you thinking I'm intelligent?" Aurora's shoulders squared.

"I do. That's not what I meant." Stella looked at her watch. "I'm sorry, but I have to run."

"Please, I don't want to keep you from whatever. All of you seem to think you're the most important people on the planet."

Stella sucked in a deep breath. "Can we talk tonight?"

"Do I have a choice?"

Stella took a step back. "Of course. I'd never force you to do anything you didn't want to do." Stella paused. "Aside from not expressing my thoughts well, have I done something else to upset you?"

CHAPTER EIGHTEEN

Yes, Aurora screamed in her head. "Nope. Just the stress of learning my new role, that's all." She couldn't help adding, "Ya know, being food for the wolves."

Stella's eyebrows knitted together. "Aurora, believe me when I say you're intelligent. That wasn't what I meant."

Aurora was annoyed, not just by the comment, but when Stella had inhaled deeply, her breasts moved in such a way, and Aurora was kicking herself for thinking of Stella naked. Having her flesh pressed against Aurora. No. Aurora was angry she wanted to see Stella naked again after the dig about her intelligence. Aurora steadied her voice to sound as flippant as possible. "Five-ish?"

"If I'm done for the day."

"Oooo-kay." Aurora flicked a hand in the air.

"I'll swing by your office to see if you can get together or not."

"No!" Aurora showed her palms. "I mean, call me if five will work, and I'll meet you outside. Please don't come by the office."

Stella gave her a puzzled look but didn't argue. "See you out front, then. Maybe."

Aurora made her way to the office. Upon entering, there was a scuffling sound. Aurora locked eyes on Kip, who was trying to put Isaac into a half-Nelson. "Knock it off."

"Who made you boss?" Kip pouted, his fat lower lip overtaking his top.

"Alice did." Aurora wasn't entirely clear that she had that much power, but knowing what she knew about Alice, no one would truly understand the perimeters of Aurora's duties. It seemed imperative to lay down the law right off the bat, or she truly would be fed to the wolves.

Kip blinked. "Wait, yesterday was your last day. I made cupcakes."

"As a temp. Today, I'm taking over for Shelly." Aurora set her bag down on Shelly's desk, which had already been cleared, including the computer.

A curly-haired woman with tortoiseshell glasses spun in her office chair, the one Aurora had occupied for the past two months. "I'm Kristin. Alice's admin called. Your laptop will be here within the hour."

"Thanks, Kristin. Nice to meet you. Are you glad to be back?"

"That remains to be seen." She laughed, her rosy cheeks turning redder.

"Wait. Is this for real? You're the boss now?" Kip planted his feet as if staking a claim.

"Of Scheduling. And this office. If you want to continue horsing around, you'll have to do that in the AV office down the hall." Aurora wanted to be clear she wasn't Kip's boss or keeper, and she wanted it known that all monkey business in Scheduling would be dealt with swiftly. None of the techs liked their office space since they were crammed into a former lab that had dusty machinery and a crumbling ceiling. "What happened at the last White Coat ceremony? What'd you do?" Aurora perched on the edge of her desk.

Isaac ran a hand over his head, taming the cowlick Kip's antics had rustled up. "Welcome back, Aurora. I was happy when I heard the news."

Kip turned on Isaac. "You knew Aurora was hired back?"

"Yeah. Didn't you read the email from Alice?" Isaac asked without a trace of accusation in his expression.

"No."

"You were cc'd on it." Isaac pulled up the email on his phone and stabbed his finger at Kip's address. "See, right here."

"It must have landed in my spam folder or something." Kip brushed it off with a dismissive wave of his hand.

Kip never read his emails. Aurora tucked this kernel away. "So, back to the White Coat ceremony. Did anything unusual happen?"

"Nope." Kip looked her right in the eye for a hot second before his gaze fell to his black and white Nikes.

"Don't you remember, Kip? You—"

"Nothing happened, Isaac," Kip snapped.

Isaac scratched his head. "But—"

"Nothing out of the ordinary happened, okay?" Kip's voice bordered on abusive.

"What time is Bri expected today?" Aurora asked, sensing she wouldn't get anywhere concerning the ceremony with Kip butting in. She'd have to ask Isaac in private, or perhaps Stella. Would it be weird to ask Stella?

"I don't know. She works the night shift, remember?" Kip ran a finger down the jobs board. "I'm needed in the auditorium."

After he left, Aurora checked the board and saw there wasn't a job. Not surprised, she added another mental note to track Kip's every move, including all his lies. Maybe she should start a spreadsheet to cover her ass. She believed it when Alice said HR would be up Aurora's ass. While she liked Kip, he was constantly screwing up on the job, and Aurora didn't want to get fucked by that. Should she try talking to him, or let Bri handle it?

"Dr. Howie called," Kristin said.

Aurora inwardly cringed. "And?"

"The boards in C432 are too white."

"They're whiteboards." Aurora wanted to call Stella to laugh over the situation, but...

Kristin nodded. "I tried explaining."

"Leave it with me. As soon as I get a computer, I'll find a room with not-so-whiteboards." Aurora didn't think that was possible, though.

"He doesn't like the color brown, either." Kristin added as if she'd had quite the conversation with Dr. Howie.

"I'm aware." Had Stella instructed Dr. Howie to call Scheduling directly? Or had he lost his patience when Stella was in the meeting earlier and the whiteboard situation had to be handled right then? "Do we have portable blackboards?"

Kristin nodded, but before she could say more, the phone rang, and Kristin answered in a professional tone. So far, Aurora deemed her as a keeper. Kip was going to be a challenge, given his mood swings. She was on the fence about Isaac since Kip seemed to pull his strings. Maybe without Kip's presence, Isaac would step up to the plate more.

"Is there an Aurora Shirley here?" asked a red-haired man.

"That's me."

"I'm here to hook up your laptop with all the bells and whistles."

"Great. Right here." Aurora gestured to her desk in the back of the room, which offered a semblance of privacy. "How long will this take?"

"Not long, but you don't need to be here."

"I didn't mean it that way. Would you like a cup of coffee?"

The IT man seemed surprised. "I like you already. Black, please."

* * *

A FEW MINUTES TO FIVE, Aurora was wiped, and she regretted agreeing to meet with Stella tonight. Truth be told, she wasn't eager to hear whatever Stella had to say. Sleeping with the doctor had been a huge mistake. Catastrophic. And she'd thought that before getting her job back. Stella's cold dismissal earlier made Aurora feel more like a call girl than... she didn't know what. Granted, Aurora had been telling Becky for some time that Aurora only wanted sex, but she hadn't counted on Stella. Was it possible Aurora had secretly hoped for more from the doctor? *This was the very reason you decided not to have relationships!* Feelings, wants, needs, and reality hardly ever meshed, only causing unnecessary complications.

But she'd promised, and if Stella called, Aurora wouldn't say no. She wouldn't want to hurt the doctor's feelings. Aurora wasn't the type to be vindictive. The only hope was for Stella to work late, which given the woman's profession, the odds were in Aurora's favor. The second hand went around one more time, raising Aurora's hopes. She started to pack it in for the day, logging off her laptop.

The phone rang, and since Kristin had left at three, Aurora didn't have a choice but to answer it.

"Scheduling."

"Do you still want to meet outside?"

No! "Yes, I can do that. I was just leaving, so if you can't tonight, I understand," Aurora rushed out.

"I'm heading out now."

"Okay. I'll be down in a moment. I just need to finish up here." Aurora looked around, crestfallen that the only tasks that needed doing were to switch off the lights and to close the door.

Stella was already outside and gave a friendly wave.

At least she was faking it well. "Hey."

"You look beat." Stella's face softened. "I hope your first day in charge wasn't that bad."

Aurora let out an exasperated sigh. "Kip."

"Ah. He's a smart guy, and one-on-one, he can focus. But he doesn't know when to stop when others are around."

"I'm getting that sense, yes. Anyway, what did you want to talk about?" Aurora shifted her feet, but it didn't help ease the pain from the blister that kept on growing.

"You okay?"

"My feet are killing me."

"I knew we shouldn't have walked last night. I won't make that mistake tonight."

"What do you mean?" Aurora switched her bag from her left to right shoulder in hopes of relieving the weight on her bad foot.

"I'm taking you to dinner," Stella announced as if that had already been agreed to.

"You took me to dinner last night, and look how that turned out."

"What do you mean?" The smile plummeted from Stella's face.

"You practically shoved me out of your apartment this morning."

"If I remember correctly, I offered to make you coffee."

"After you showered and made it clear you needed me to leave. Stat."

"I did no such thing." Stella seemed to mull over the morning's events. "Did I?"

"That's how I took it," Aurora admitted in all honesty.

"It wasn't what I meant. I was... I didn't really know the protocol, really."

"Protocol?" Aurora parroted.

"To the whole *sex with no complications* thing." Stella made a hand gesture implying she was in way over her head. It was cute, dammit.

"So much for that."

"What do you mean?"

"In case you've forgotten, we still work for the school. The *no complications* has snowballed into a smorgasbord of complications. Alice made it clear when she offered me the job: one wrong move and I'll be out on my ass. That's why I didn't want you popping by the office."

"It's not like we have the same cost center." Stella sighed. "But I see your point."

"Which is?"

"We need to have ground rules."

"For?" Aurora shifted her bag again.

"Us—I mean, for seeing each other casually outside of office hours. Last night was... fantastic, really. And I like spending time with you. I'm guessing Friday lunches won't be wise considering the turn of events. But they can't moderate our hours outside of work, can they?"

That sounded promising to Aurora. Had she misread this morning completely? "What kind of rules are you thinking of?"

"No trysts in the office for one," Stella said.

"Easily done on my part since I don't have an office. Not with walls around it, at least. Not even partitions."

"I do, but the walls are paper thin."

Aurora cocked her head. "And you know this how?"

"I can hear Dr. Miller—not having sex." Stella waved her arms as if on a runway telling a plane it was unsafe to land. "Talking on the phone."

"Oh."

"What do you say? Can I take you to dinner?" Stella gave Aurora the smile that turned her on, but a look of remorse overtook her face. "I'm really sorry about the miscommunication this morning. I feel terrible."

"No."

Stella's gaze dropped to the pavement. "I understand."

Aurora had to admit she was tickled to see how crestfallen Stella was about her assuming the word no meant Aurora had declined the offer. It wasn't what she'd meant at all, and she clarified, "Can I take you to dinner? It's my turn. We started tit for tat last night. I'd like to maintain that."

Stella's neck snapped up. "I'd like that."

"We should meet there, though. Probably best not to be seen leaving together."

"Yes, of course. I don't want to cause problems for you with Alice."

"It's mostly HR I'm worried about. Alice... I haven't figured her out yet. Any suggestions? For dinner? You know the area better. Allston seems to be on the other side of the world at the moment."

"Have you been to the Italian place two blocks over?" Stella pointed in the direction of Massachusetts Avenue.

"No, but give me the name and I'll find it." Aurora waved her phone, implying she'd use the GPS.

Stella supplied the name and walked off without saying another word.

Aurora took a seat on the bench, going over all the events in the past twenty-four hours. The prospect of seeing Stella again excited Aurora.

And terrified her.

CHAPTER NINETEEN

Two Sundays later, Stella didn't have Kenzie for the weekend. Still in bed, she contemplated going to the office to prep a lecture, but the thought of trekking to South Boston seemed daunting. Having Aurora over two nights in one week had been more than pleasant, but Stella was starting to show her forty-one years. Rest was probably needed, but every time she closed her eyes, memories of being with Aurora made it impossible to relax.

Instead, she put on running gear and headed to the Charles. Whenever she needed to clear her head, she pounded the pavement.

Never much of a music expert, she relied on playlists created by others on her streaming service. Today's list included one song after another about love. Falling in love. Falling out of love. Being destroyed by it. Or coming out stronger.

It was maddening.

What was the obsession with love?

And the dwelling that occurred when it ended?

People set themselves up when believing the myth of

happily ever after. It simply didn't exist. Those who claimed it did were deceiving themselves. The more Stella thought about it, the more she convinced herself the very idea of love was the greatest con thrust upon humanity.

After seven miles, Stella opted to make her way back home. She yanked out one earbud, slowing her pace to a walk for her cool down. It was only a hair past nine in the morning, but being Sunday, she didn't see too many others out and about. The water of the river drifted by, seeming peaceful, but Stella knew the current was stronger than it appeared.

A sculler flew by, totally in sync with his oars, arms, and legs. Hot on his heels was another. The same beautiful fluid movement.

That was something to believe in. The passion people possessed when wanting to become the best. Like the scullers. Or a basketball player. Judges. Doctors. Computer coders. Chasing perfection in one's hobby or occupation was something Stella could believe in. Support wholeheartedly, in fact. The tangible results: winning a race or championship, becoming a Supreme Court justice, saving a life in the operating room, or developing a program that revolutionized the world—those things mattered.

Love? She shook her head. How could it matter or even be measured in any fashion?

It wasn't like Stella kept track of how many people she'd helped. The ones that stood out the most were the ones she'd lost.

Returning from the Cambridge side of the river, Stella stopped on the Harvard Bridge, placing one foot on the bottom of the railing to stretch out her calf. Puffy clouds dotted the lapis blue horizon in the east. The water flowed beneath her. A lone goose bobbled on the surface, making it look effortless to float on the water. Two mallards were off to Stella's right. She wanted to peek under the surface. To see how the creatures paddled like hell to appear in control. The dichotomy was a thing of beauty. Something Stella strove for. Fight like hell without looking like doing so.

With a smile on her lips, she tapped her fingers to her forehead in a salute to the birds and continued the trek across the bridge. She crossed Storrow, turned onto Beacon Street, and then hung a right onto Commonwealth Avenue, heading back to Brighton. She still had a fair distance to go on foot, but she wasn't in a rush to get back to her apartment. The sunshine warmed her bare arms and legs. This was the best way to soak in vitamin D, and given the unpredictability of the weather, it was best to enjoy the sunshine whenever it struck. It could snow the rest of the year.

A handful of young people on a corner handed out leaflets to any who took pity on them and accepted the white sheets of paper. Stella tucked her head down, but at the last moment, when a piece was shoved into her line of sight, she looked up into Aurora's face.

"Oh, hey. I had no idea it was you doing this."

"Harassing you." Aurora didn't phrase it as a question, and her chuckle made it clear to Stella the young woman knew full well most didn't appreciate the group's tactics.

Stella scanned the slip of paper. "Organ donation awareness?"

"I know it's not April, which is the month dedicated to organ donation, but it matters to so many every day of the year."

Stella nodded. "It does." She swallowed. "May I ask why you're involved in the group?"

"It's a cause I can get wholeheartedly behind."

"Because?"

"Surely, you aren't against donations." Aurora's expression was misbelieving, but her upper body stiffened as if ready to do battle.

Stella's head whipped back. "Uh, no. I've performed countless kidney transplants. Some of my patients wouldn't be alive today without them."

"I didn't know that's what you did. I mean, I knew you were a doctor, but we never talked about your specialty."

"True." Stella laughed, "We've had more in-depth conversations concerning Dr. Howie and the White Coat ceremony."

"How come you didn't tell me?" Aurora asked.

"I don't know. This may sound weird, but to me, it's what I do. Sometimes, I get tired of people being somewhat in awe or whatever." Stella let out a rush of air. "That sounded pompous. I didn't mean it to."

"I am in awe, but not for the reason you think," Aurora confessed.

Stella cocked her head, peering into Aurora's bewitching dark eyes. "Care to elaborate?"

"Not here. I mean everyone here knows, but I don't want to spill my guts to you on the street. It's"—Aurora blew a strand of hair out of her eye—"I'm still processing some things."

Concerned, Stella said, "I'm all ears whenever you want to talk."

"What are you doing for lunch?" Aurora pounced.

"Talking to you." Stella glanced at her watch. "I can be ready around one. Will you be done here?"

"I was just about to head out. I only volunteered for the early shift because not many like to drag their asses out of bed on a Sunday. Ya know, they love to fight the good fight when it suits them." Aurora's smile contained shades of anger, or was it sadness? "I shouldn't say that. At least they show up. That's more than the majority of the world's population."

"How comfortable are your shoes?" Stella eyed the black leather shoes.

"Uh, they're fine." Aurora shook her head as if disoriented. "That was an abrupt transition."

"I didn't mean it to be. If you're leaving, I was wondering if you'd like to walk with me some, but I don't want you getting anymore blisters. We can chat. Stop for breakfast. I don't have any plans today, and I can't think of a better way to spend it than with you."

"Oh, wow. I wasn't expecting that. If I were in heels, we'd have to find transportation." Aurora motioned to her Sketchers. "And I took a precaution and have bandages on my heels since they're new shoes."

"If needed, I'm at your service." Stella did a slight curtsey.

"What do you charge? I mean, now that I know you're one of those fancy doctors. The ones people kowtow to in operating rooms." Aurora mimicked an *I'm not worthy bow* à la *Wayne's World.*

Stella laughed. "No one does that. Every member on my team is highly qualified, and it's a privilege to work with each one. But, to answer your question, my fee is just your company. Truth be told, I was on my way back to my apartment and I wasn't looking forward to being alone."

"That sounds kinda odd coming from you considering our conversations about not wanting to be in a relationship."

"Don't fear. I haven't gone back on that vow. That doesn't mean I want to be alone twenty-four seven. And, I find you fascinating." Stella raised the leaflet. "Even more so now."

"Because of this?" Aurora hoisted her remaining stack of papers.

"Not only that. Your passion. Dedication." Stella leaned closer to Aurora, "And you have the most amazing body."

"Ah, I think you let the true reason slip, my not so good doctor." Aurora fluttered her lashes.

"What happened to the bowing thing? It allowed me to peek down your T-shirt."

"Is that right?" Aurora playfully whacked Stella's arm. "You're going to have to earn another peek. Hold on a sec."

Aurora approached a frazzled woman, who clearly had only recently bounded out of bed. After they exchanged a few words, Aurora handed off the pamphlets with a quick goodbye hug before Aurora returned to Stella. "Ready?"

"Who's that?" Stella asked in a tone she hoped conveyed *I don't really give two shits but want to be polite.*

"Amy, one of the regulars." Aurora shrugged.

"Do you always hug your relief?"

"I'm a hugger. I'm guessing from your pinched face you aren't."

Stella shoved down the green-eyed monster since that probably wasn't allowed given their no-relationship status. "You could say that. I'd never survive living in Paris where it's customary to do the *kiss on the cheek* thing. I'd go mad."

"You don't mind when I kiss or touch you," Aurora whispered, bumping her shoulder against Stella's.

"Are you going to tell me soon or keep teasing me?"

"About?"

Stella hooked her thumb over her shoulder back in Amy's direction.

"Are you asking if I slept with Amy?"

"What? No. Even if you did, it's none of my business, if I'm understanding our arrangement correctly."

"Arrangement. Wow. You know how to make a girl feel special." Aurora's shoulders slumped, and she slowed her pace, or so Stella thought.

"I didn't mean it that way. I just don't know how to refer to... it."

"Does *it* need a label?"

"Guess not." Although it would help Stella if she did know. Given Aurora's pursed lips, it was time to change the subject. "I wasn't referring to Amy. I meant raising awareness for organ donation."

"Ah, that. It's been something I've supported for a handful of years now."

"What spurred it?"

"My dad. He has kidney disease." Aurora stopped at the corner, looking left then right. "I need coffee."

"Do you want to go to the café? Or we can catch a ride, and I can make you a Stella special."

"What's that, exactly?"

"Coffee with a smattering of grounds. Admittedly, I'm not the best when it comes to certain things." Stella shrugged it off.

"You can transplant a kidney, but you can't make a decent cup of joe?" There was amusement in Aurora's voice.

"That sums me up pretty well."

"I don't know about that, but I can manage making a cup of coffee sans the grounds, and I'd rather not talk with other people around."

"We don't have to talk—I didn't mean—I'm not trying to lure you back to my apartment for..." Stella didn't finish the statement, completely baffled why she always stuck her foot in it when around Aurora.

Aurora grinned but didn't speak. Instead, she got her phone out, tapping the screen. "Our ride will be here in one minute."

"I've never actually used Uber."

"You suggested it before, though."

"I read the news. The print version, of course, in an effort to stay hip without actually being hip, apparently."

"Ah, I've heard your generation likes to stay informed that way." A dark-gray Toyota Corolla pulled up. "Our chariot awaits, Princess." Aurora opened the door and waved Stella inside.

Sitting side by side in the back seat, neither woman spoke, the silence becoming deafening with each passing second. The driver, perhaps in sync with the mood that couldn't be labeled as tense or serene but somewhere in the middle, nudged up the stereo volume. It was a song Stella didn't know, but the lyrics made it clear the singer was nursing a broken heart.

After stopping at every possible red light and slamming on the breaks for a homeless man who'd wandered into the road, the car pulled up outside of Stella's apartment building.

"There's a sandwich shop around the corner that's decent. They serve breakfast on the weekends, and they deliver. Are you hungry?" Stella asked.

"Famished, actually."

"I have a menu upstairs, or we can stop in and get it to go."

Aurora shook her head. "Let's go upstairs."

Stella pulled her shirt from her stomach. "Probably best for me to hop in the shower."

"Is that your way of propositioning me to take a shower with you?"

Stella shook her head, laughing. "I know I've said this before, but I'm not sure if I'm coming or going with you."

"Again, why does it have to be an *either or* situation for you?"

"That's life, I guess. I didn't make the rules."

"You just abide by them?"

"Sometimes. Or I try to, but..." They crested the stairs, and Stella leaned over to retrieve a key from under her doormat.

"That surprises me."

Straightening, Stella asked, "What does?"

"The key under the mat. Seems too trusting for you."

"I don't like running with keys in my pocket. The rattling sound drives me bonkers."

Aurora tugged on the white cord threaded under Stella's shirt. "I thought that's what these were for." She clacked the earbuds against each other.

Stella slipped the key in the lock. "I'm anything but logical." Stella stopped herself from saying *around you*. "Let me get the menu. You can look it over while I hop in the shower."

"So you weren't propositioning me earlier?"

Unable to express her desire to listen to Aurora's story, Stella handed off the menu and took leave, not happy with the way she did so, but these types of situations always got the better of her.

The shower was quick, and when she slipped on a pair of jeans, her damp skin made the yanking up process a bit more laborious than usual. After putting on a long sleeve shirt, Stella twisted her damp hair into a knot on top of her head. Without wiping a spot on the fogged mirror to check her appearance, she made her way to the front room.

"Did you find something you want?" Stella asked.

Aurora consulted her watch, the one Stella had returned to her, and said, "I know it's kinda early for it, but I'm eyeing the Reuben with a side of onion rings."

"Excellent choice. The Reuben is my go-to with a side salad."

"A salad. Oh no! That doesn't go with a sandwich." Aurora made emphatic slicing motions with her hands in the air.

"It totally does," Stella said, knowing she sounded lame but couldn't conjure up a snappier comeback.

Aurora shook her head. "You have so much to learn from me. Soup and sandwich, yes. Sandwich and salad are a hard no. How do you not know this?"

"Can we agree to disagree?"

"I can agree that you're wrong. So very wrong."

"If that makes you feel better." Stella dialed the number and placed the order, requesting an extra side of onion rings.

"Are you caving on the salad already?"

"Nope. I happen to know the serving size is on the small side. Just covering my bases."

"Hope you don't mind, but I rummaged through your cabinets to brew some coffee. From my cursory look, I take it you don't cook much, unless it involves making a juice, given the looks of your Ninja and stash of bottles."

"Sadly, I never took to cooking. Even when I follow a recipe to the T, it doesn't turn out. I hate eating subpar food just to avoid having to toss the disaster. That seems wrong."

"I have a hard time believing you can't cook. I love to, but most of the time, I only make beans and rice. That might change now that I have a steady paycheck coming in, hopefully." Aurora handed Stella a coffee. "I wasn't sure how you took it."

"That doesn't seem fair. I know you prefer yours with one sugar and cream."

"Excellent memory. How do you like yours? I'll sear it into my memory bank." Aurora pressed her palm to her temple.

"Just milk."

"Easy enough."

"Where would you prefer we do this?" Stella waved, indicating either the table by the window or on the sofa.

"Remind me again what we're doing." Aurora's voice was meant to be provocative.

"Have you changed your mind about talking? No pressure from me, I promise. We can—what do you kids like to say? —*Netflix and chill.*"

Aurora laughed. "You do know the true meaning of that saying, don't you?"

"Watching a show or movie and relaxing."

"Not quite, Doctor. It means put a movie on and then have sex."

"During or after?"

"It can be either. Do you need to take notes for the next time you bring a younger woman to your home?" Aurora impersonated Stella frantically penning notes on a pad.

"I'm good. Usually, I don't invite people over."

"And yet, here I stand in your apartment." Aurora ran a hand up and down, emphasizing her presence.

"The first woman since my divorce."

"You're divorced?"

"Yep. A few years now." Flipping around, she said, "I opt for sitting on the sofa. Much kinder on these old bones."

"I'm cool with that."

"Is that code for anything?"

"What do you think it means?"

"With you, it can mean anything. It could be your way of asking for mushrooms with a side of ranch."

Aurora's jaw dropped. "You really aren't in touch with millennial lingo at all. It's kinda adorable." Aurora sat on the couch and patted the cushion next to her. "Before you ask for the hidden meaning, I only want you to sit next to me."

"With pleasure."

"Does that mean something else." Aurora waggled her brows.

Stella regarded Aurora. "I love looking into your eyes."

Aurora's gaze fell to her lap. "You probably say that to all the girls."

"Nope." Stella took a drink of her coffee. "Now your dad. Something's telling me there's more to the story, and if you want to talk, I'm all ears."

"How do you know? That there's more?"

"Earlier, I picked up on a sadness in your eyes. I've seen it many times before from family members."

Aurora nodded but took a moment, seeming to bolster her nerve. "He might need a kidney or... he may die. Surely, you know more about the disease than I do."

Stella took Aurora's hand in hers. "I know about the illness, yes, but I want to know how you're dealing with it."

"Why, though?" Aurora followed up with, "Our arrangement, as you like to call it, doesn't mean you have to care about what's going on in my private life."

"But I do, and I know how it can feel to be alone."

"It's hard to talk about, though. There's more to it. Something I recently found out about and…"

"I understand. I'm not saying you have to know how you feel about everything. Perhaps, though, talking about it will help you get to a certain point of understanding or accepting."

"The short version is my dad isn't my dad."

Stella blinked. "I don't want to put my foot in it, so can you tell me what that means?"

Aurora filled Stella in about her dad's kidney problem and learning that her parents had used a sperm donor. "The hardest part was learning I can't give him a kidney because I'm not a match."

Stella wrapped an arm around Aurora's shoulders. "That's a lot to take in."

"I'm sorry."

"No, I didn't mean it that way. I mean that's a lot for you to deal with. On top of that, you've been thrust into a new job supervising the Island of Misfit Toys."

"That's the least of it. At least the job gives me a sense of purpose. With the other stuff, I don't know what to do." Aurora fiddled with the hem of Stella's shirt.

"Do you love your dad?"

"Of course, I do."

"I know you're processing everything, and this may seem overly simplistic, but does the truth really change who he is in your life?" Stella said the words with compassion, sensing the issue truly troubled Aurora's heart and mind—even more than she was letting on.

"When you put it that way, the answer is simple, but there are other layers to it."

"Such as?"

"They lied to me. My entire life."

Stella nodded. "I can see that point."

"But?"

"But nothing. I imagine that knowledge cuts deeply."

Aurora clutched her chest. "It does."

"As the non-biological parent of a daughter, I can tell you, not contributing DNA doesn't lessen the love you feel."

Aurora stared at her, open-mouthed.

"You didn't know I had a child?"

Aurora shook her head.

"I assumed you'd guessed from the artwork on the fridge and the fact that I have a second bedroom, but didn't say anything because of... the arrangement."

"I'd assumed the paintings were from nieces or nephews or... I don't know. Kids of patients. None of my friends have kids, but they have family photos with younger relatives. It didn't dawn on me at all." Aurora raked a hand through her hair.

"Are you okay with me having a daughter?"

"W-what? Of course. I just wasn't expecting it."

"Look at me." Stella waited for Aurora to turn her head. "Are you okay with this?"

"It just took me by surprise. I'm processing. Do you see her much?"

"We have dinner every Tuesday night, and she stays with me every other weekend."

"That must be hard."

Stella's shrug implied not much could be done about it.

The doorbell rang.

Stella didn't move.

Aurora said, "I think lunch is here."

"I got it. Stay put." Stella went to the door, paid the man, and was back with Aurora as quickly as possible. "Shall I put them in the oven to keep them warm?"

"No, I'm an eater when upset. Just to clarify, I'm not upset about your news."

"I knew what you meant." Stella set the brown sack down

on the coffee table and went to the kitchen to get two plates. Sitting next to Aurora again, Stella said, "Whenever you need to talk or if you don't want to be alone, all you have to do is call me."

"You're a very strange fuck buddy." Aurora laughed, but the feeling didn't reach her eyes.

"I thought you said we didn't need a label."

"True." Aurora poured the onion rings onto her plate. "You know what would make me feel loads better?"

"What's that?" Stella asked, wanting to do anything to take the sadness from Aurora's eyes.

"If you'd eat one of my onion rings."

Taken aback, she blurted out, "Why?"

"Do I need a reason aside from wanting you to? I've seen you eat mac and cheese and pizza. You're not a total health food nut."

Stella eyed the fried and greasy pile. "It'd actually make you feel better?"

Aurora nodded.

"Okay. Here goes nothing."

CHAPTER TWENTY

"M OM?" A URORA SPOKE INTO HER PHONE AS SHE walked down the street on her way home from Stella's.

"Hi, darling. How are you?"

"Do you have plans tonight?" Aurora stood on the corner, waiting for the light to turn green.

"Do you want to come over? Your dad—"

"Can *you* meet me?" Aurora stressed *you*.

"Yes, sweetheart. Do you want to meet at your favorite place?"

"Do I have to bother ordering dinner, or can I dive in with—?"

"The fried ice cream. Meet you there in twenty."

Aurora squashed the thought she'd gain five pounds from today's gorging. First, onion rings. Now, fried ice cream. Briefly, she considered skipping every single meal tomorrow, but she knew that'd never happen.

Her mom, in a white tweed jacket, light blue dress shirt, and black jeans, waited out front of Mazatlán by the time Aurora arrived. "Come here." Her mom held her arms out for Aurora. "I've been worried about you."

"I'm okay."

"Don't lie to your mother."

Aurora melted into her mom's arms. "I needed this."

"Me too, sweetheart. There's nothing like a mother-daughter hug."

"What if I were a boy?"

"It'd be just as good."

"Do you wish I were a boy?"

Her mom shook her head. "Aurora you're my child, and I love you just the way you are. Nothing will ever change that. I've adored you since before you were born, and it's only increased from the moment the doctor placed you on my chest and I saw your precious face. Don't ever doubt that. Not for one second."

Aurora sniffled.

"You ready for dessert and some girl talk?"

Aurora was kinda talked out, but spending the afternoon with Stella had been nice in a bizarrely confusing way, which was why she'd called her mother right after leaving Stella's. Not only had Stella been kind listening to her, but the news of her having a daughter hadn't affected Aurora the way it should have. Initially, it had taken her by surprise. It did explain why a successful doctor was living in a two-bedroom apartment in Brighton. Child payments and everything else that went with divorce were costly. After it sunk in, though, the news wasn't so shocking, which was astounding. In the past, that had been a deal breaker. Kids added even more complications. Although, given their arrangement, as Stella was fond of saying, did it matter?

They were led to a quiet table in the back. The evening crowd hadn't arrived yet. Not surprising considering it was barely after four. Her family had always been early bird diners. Aurora ordered a fried ice cream, and her mom got the flan. Both opted for strawberry margaritas on the rocks.

When the drinks arrived, Aurora took a fortifying sip. "When did you realize you were falling in love with Daddy?"

Her mom set her glass down without taking a sip. "I wasn't expecting that question."

"Why not?"

"Oh, I don't know. You've heard the story. Dad and I were set up on a blind date by our best friends."

"And you two clicked right away. I know that part. But how'd you know he was the one, given how many fish there are in the sea?"

"I don't know if I can put it into words. I just knew." Her mom finally took a sip. "Have you met someone?"

Aurora stabbed her straw in and out of her drink. "No. Did you know before you married that he couldn't... you know?"

"No, we didn't know." Her mom placed her hand on Aurora's. "You have to understand. We always wanted you. When we realized your dad wasn't able, we did what we had to do so we could have you. It's the best decision we've ever made. You are the most amazing daughter."

Aurora pressed her fingertips to the sides of her head, holding it up. "I'm useless. He needs a kidney, and I can't give him one."

"You are not useless!"

"It's how I feel, though. And I'm angry."

"I know. I feel the same way, but my anger probably stems from a different source than yours."

"What are you angry about?"

"How unfair life can be. Your father has been the best husband and father he can be. He doesn't deserve this. Why do these things happen to good people?" Her mom's voice cracked.

The waiter set down their respective desserts while Aurora's mom fanned her eyes in an effort to control the damage to her mascara.

When alone, Aurora asked, "If you knew then that this would happen, would you still have married him?"

"Yes."

"No doubts at all?"

"None. You'll understand when you fall in love."

"I just don't see that happening for me." Aurora slumped in her seat.

Her mom stilled her spoon in midair. "Why would you say that?"

"Because I can't get the idea that I'm supposed to be alone out of my head." Aurora circled a finger next to her head. Was that still true? Or had Becky been right? Aurora filled her mind with stats from articles to believe the best course was staying single? No, it had to be true. Singlehood meant no compromise. Ever. Not to mention risking having her heart cracked into a million pieces.

"Why do you think that?"

"I'm stubborn. I don't want to answer to anyone. I like doing my own thing." Aurora thwacked her spoon against the fried coating of the ice cream, pleased with the cracking sound.

"You can't be yourself if you're in a relationship?"

Aurora jabbed her spoon in her mother's direction. "Exactly!"

"Your father hasn't placed any restrictions on me. He was the one who encouraged me to go back to school when you started kindergarten. He took care of all the school drop-offs. Cooked dinners." Her hand gesture implied *et cetera*.

"There aren't many like him, though." Aurora rested her chin on her palm, her upper body slumping.

"Are you sure about that?"

The image of Stella holding her after sex, the feeling that everything was perfect—she had to block that out of her head. It simply wasn't happening. Both had been clear about that right from the start. "I am."

Her mom shook her head. "For your sake, I hope you're wrong. My life would have been so lonely if I didn't have your father."

"But... he might leave." The thought of loving someone only to lose them to some illness, divorce, or a million other ways a person can be ripped out of her life... It was too much to think about.

"I'll always have our memories, though. A lifetime of them. With you and him." She squeezed Aurora's hand.

"I don't know if I can do it."

"Do what, sweetie?"

"Love someone the way you love Daddy. It's... I don't know. Confusing."

"Feelings are. And, of course, you can love someone with all your heart. You just need to find the right person and let it happen." Her mom's smile conveyed it was simple.

"The thought scares the bejeezus out of me," Aurora whispered in all honesty.

Her mom leaned over the table and whispered back, "It does to everyone."

"But—"

"Aurora. It can't be explained. You'll know it when it happens. Please don't fight it just because you're stubborn. Love isn't something you want to miss out on. Take my word for it."

CHAPTER TWENTY-ONE

In the dean's conference room, Stella had to force her eyes away from Aurora sitting right across from her.

But then Aurora started asking questions about past White Coat ceremonies, giving Stella an opportunity to look in the young woman's direction without raising any red flags. Or so she hoped.

"This is the first time the first-year students will recite the Hippocratic
oath. Is that correct?" Aurora lightly tapped her pen onto a notepad.

Dean Andrews nodded, but Vera answered, "Yes, it's a symbolic rite of passage that takes place in front of the students' families and friends. It's important that the event go off without a hitch—as much as possible. Again, I have to ask if Kip will be involved."

Alice leaned forward in her chair. "He'll only be involved behind the scenes. Covering AV for the graduate school's courses, not involved in the ceremony. Right, Aurora?"

Aurora nodded. "Correct. We're"—she motioned to Alice

and herself—"compiling a list of AV staff who will treat the ceremony with the respect it deserves."

"I saw Bri in the hallway yesterday afternoon. Is she back permanently? I always liked her." Dean Andrews glanced at his phone when the screen lit up. He put a finger in the air. "Hold on a sec." He typed a message or something and then waved for Alice to continue.

"She is. She's been made the head tech." Alice glanced at her phone.

"Any way we can limit Kip's ability to wreak too much damage and shuffle him to handle AV for the graduate school and Public Health? They'll scream, since they always do, but their classes don't involve that much recording and consist mostly of PowerPoint setup. Kip is smart, but he's his own worst enemy." Vera spoke directly to Alice, angering Stella.

"If that's what you want, we'll start it as soon as possible. Bri comes in at two and leaves at ten. We've hired a part-time tech to help with some of the night setups since she has more responsibility managing the team, but I'm sure we can find a solution and have Bri available for med classes." Alice turned to Aurora. "Can you look at the weekly schedules and arrange everything?"

"Absolutely." Aurora spoke confidently, but Stella detected an *oh shit* vibe.

Stella had to wonder about all the thoughts going through Aurora's mind. Vera had just thrown Kip under the bus and wanted Scheduling to make substantial changes to the department Vera had no say over. And Alice didn't fight back. Not that Stella disagreed with the request. But still. Scheduling was its own department.

Dean Andrews cleared his throat. "Vera and I are still setting up the speakers for the event. We hope to have a finalized list by the end of this month. That would be a good time to have our next meeting." Dean Andrews started to rise but seemed to second guess himself. "Oh, is there anything else we need to cover?"

Alice and Aurora shook their heads.

"Good. Until next time." He left the room.

Alice and Vera exchanged a few details about a different matter, and Stella blocked them out as she tried to make eye contact with Aurora, who had her head down, jotting notes on her legal pad.

A minute later, Aurora leaned over and whispered something to Alice before rising to her feet.

Alice nodded in her stern way with what seemed like a forced lack of emotion on her face.

Stella quickly said goodbye and dashed into the hallway to spy Aurora slipping into the bathroom. Stella hung back in the hallway, pretending to get caught up on email but mostly keeping a sharp eye on the door.

When Aurora exited, Stella said, "Hey, do you mind if I walk you back? I have some ideas about the ceremony."

"Do I need to take notes?" Aurora reached into her bag.

"That's not necessary. It's more big-picture stuff, not diving into the minutiae."

They rounded the corner into an empty hallway.

Aurora raised her brow at Stella to start.

"Okay, I don't really want to talk about the White Coat ceremony. I just wanted to make sure you were okay about the whole Kip situation."

"It took me by surprise, but it might be for the best. I'm not looking forward to the conversation with Kip, or Bri telling him and then him charging in, demanding if it's true or not. I'm pretty sure he'll think I have it out for him, when I actually like the guy. He doesn't seem to comprehend that his behavior has consequences. He's bright, and more than likely, he should be the one running the entire department. He's been here for donkey's years and knows things inside and out. I've heard he's applied for the position more than once, but Alice hasn't even given him a chance. Not even an interview."

"I think his problem is he's too bright for what he's doing, but he's too much of a kid to be taken seriously. From my experience, when I've encountered serious tech issues, he's the one that usually figures things out and gets it fixed."

They rounded another corner, leading to the bridge connecting to the medical school classrooms, the nice wood floors giving way to linoleum. The closer they got to Aurora's office, the worse the floor and walls became. The overhead lights drastically dimmed as if hiding the scuff marks on the walls and cracks and missing chunks of the floor.

Aurora seemed to be in tune with Stella's thoughts. "I feel like my office is in the ghetto."

In the stairwell, Stella scouted the area to confirm they were alone. "Has the planning of the White Coat spurred your desire to rethink nursing school?"

Aurora laughed. "I'm turning thirty this July. I think it's way too late to think about that."

Stella resisted the urge to run a finger down Aurora's cheek. "It's never too late to chase a dream."

"Come now. When you were my age, you were already a doctor."

"Not sure how that factors into your decision."

"It's sweet, really, and I do appreciate your encouragement, but I don't have what it takes. I'm simply not smart enough."

"I think you're wrong." Stella's phone beeped. After glancing at the text, she said, "I have to run, but this isn't the last time we'll talk about this. When will I see you again?"

"When do you want to?"

"All the time."

Aurora smiled. "That might be hard to arrange since we both have jobs. Are you free tonight?"

"Your place or mine?" Stella asked.

"I have a roommate, and if we want to continue flying under the radar, I don't recommend having many witnesses. Besides, I don't like being quiet." Aurora arched a seductive eyebrow.

"Mine it is, and I don't want to drop the nursing conversation."

"You are stubborn."

"So are you." Stella squeezed Aurora's hand. "Until tonight." Stella had to stop herself from kissing Aurora's cheek. She bounded down the stairs to the main floor, heading to the Cleaver Auditorium, where she'd been summoned by Dr. Greene.

When Stella arrived, she wasn't surprised to see Dr. Greene in a heated conversation with Kip. Should she call Aurora, or find out the issue first before adding more to Aurora's plate?

"I requested a recording!" Dr. Greene shook a finger at Kip. "Do you want me to show you the email?"

Kip took a step closer to Dr. Greene. "The reservation didn't include a recording. I'm only here to set up your PowerPoint. I have other jobs I need to do."

Stella didn't have a choice and rang Aurora's desk. "Did you schedule a recording for Dr. Greene?"

"What?"

"I'm in Cleaver with Kip and Dr. Greene. There seems to be some confusion over the reservation. Dr. Greene claims he requested a recording. Kip thinks it's a simple setup."

"Hold on." There was a rustling and clicks of a keyboard. "The reservation clearly states there's a recording with the Echo device reserved and a tech assigned." Hold on a second. "Oh, it was added late. It won't be on Kip's sheets, but he should have consulted the board first thing this morning to find out all the last-minute changes. I'll be right down."

Before Stella could say she'd handle it, Aurora had hung up.

Stella returned to the stage and found Dr. Greene and Kip standing within spitting distance, screaming at each other.

"I don't know how they do things in your department, but we don't have dictators in mine, and I don't take orders from you." Kip jabbed his thumb into his chest.

"Kip," Stella butted in. "Aurora is on her way down."

Kip's head whipped to her. "What does she have to do with this?"

"She's in charge of Scheduling—"

"No." He shook his head. "Once she enters the information in the computer, her job is done. This"—he waved to the podium and then the recording booth in the back of the auditorium—"is part of the tech world. Not Aurora's domain."

Not wanting to get into semantics, Stella once again tried to defuse the situation. "Kip, I think when you see the updated reservation, you may realize you overlooked—"

"Are you saying I'm unprofessional? Is that what you're saying?" Kip moved away from Dr. Greene to Stella.

"Kip!" Aurora called out as she stormed into the room. "Can I speak to you in the hallway?" she asked in a softer tone.

Kip looked to Stella and then Dr. Greene.

"Now, Kip. Please." Aurora's tone was authoritative.

With his chest puffed out, Kip marched from the room.

Before Aurora ducked out she said, "Isaac is on his way to the booth to set up the recording." She disappeared from the room.

Stella let out a breath and turned to placate her colleague.

"I never want to see that man again." Dr. Greene straitened his red and blue polka dot tie. "He's a madman! Calling me a dictator!"

Stella had to suppress a laugh, because Dr. Greene's splattering of white hairs on his head and thick black-framed glasses gave him a mad scientist look. "Aurora will take care of the situation. Is there anything else I can do to help you prepare for your lecture?"

"I forgot my printouts. Can you call my admin to bring them down?"

Stella was expected in the hospital, but she said, "Consider it done." Before he could bark another order, she stepped out of the room.

Aurora and Kip huddled at the end of the hallway. Aurora seemed to be holding her own, but oddly, she was miming driving a car, and Kip seemed to be soaking in whatever she was saying. Stella briefly met her eyes and waved. Turning around on her heel, she pulled out her phone to call her admin to phone Dr. Greene's admin as she hauled ass on her way back to the hospital, once again ruing taking on the course management role.

CHAPTER TWENTY-TWO

AFTER SHARING A PIZZA AT THE PLACE NEAR STELLA'S apartment, they walked side by side in a mostly comfortable silence. Or not. Aurora couldn't quite comprehend how she felt in the moment. If both of them were this comfortable not speaking, what did that mean about their arrangement? Was it turning into more? Because Aurora didn't feel this comfortable around many. If any.

"Is it weird I still feel like an awkward teen on a date, not knowing what to expect when we get to your place?" Aurora attempted to sound flippant, but there was more truth to her words than she cared to admit.

"Maybe it's because your teen years aren't that far back in the rearview mirror." Stella bumped her shoulder into Aurora's. "Kidding."

Aurora cranked her neck to look at Stella. "Are you, though? It's not the first time you've zeroed in on our age difference."

"I know. On paper there's a difference, but it doesn't feel that way when I'm with you."

"Let me guess. Because I act older than I am?"

"Yes." Stella didn't sound confident in her answer as if knowing it was the wrong one.

Aurora chuckled. "I've heard that all my life, when in reality, behind closed doors, I have nearly regularly scheduled freak-out sessions."

"All alone?"

"Sometimes. Becky has had a front-row seat for many."

"The roommate who's getting married?"

"Roommate and best friend since I can remember. Back to the matter at hand, though. What's going to happen when we get to your place?"

"What do you want to happen?" Stella's voice didn't give any indication about what she wanted.

"Ha! Way to put it all on me." Aurora laughed, trying not to sound bitter, but sometimes Stella's neutral tone was maddening.

"You did ask."

"I see. In your world, asking a question means you own everything about it. Okay, I'll put myself out there. I've been thinking about you naked a lot lately."

"Is there a *but*? It seems like there's a *but* coming." Stella's voice wasn't as strong by the second *but*.

"No *but* about wanting to be with you. I'm just wondering or worried rather about the long run. It goes back to my acting older than I am. It's hard for me to ignore what may be on the horizon. We've both stated we're not the relationship type—this is where the *but* comes in—but, I like you, Stella. I like you a lot."

"I like you. A lot."

"What are we doing then?" Aurora's voice teetered on the edge of happiness and concern.

"Can we just go day to day? Not define it right here and now. Not limit it either. See how everything plays out."

"O-okay." Aurora stuttered.

"Does your okay mean you're fine with the plan, or you wanted more from my answer?" Stella steered them around a tree root that had upended half of the sidewalk.

"Honestly, I think I need time to process your answer. I'm a thinker when it comes to these things."

"I'm learning that."

They reached the front of Stella's building, both of them standing on the sidewalk, staring at the door as if it contained all the answers neither of them could say.

"Do you still want to come in?" Stella asked.

Aurora gazed into Stella's sincere eyes. "Yes."

"We can take it one step at a time tonight, as well. First thing on my agenda is a shower. It's my thing. Showering at the end of a work day. It helps me transition from Dr. Gilbert to me."

"Rituals are important."

Stella motioned for Aurora to walk ahead of her.

Inside the apartment, Stella said, "Make yourself at home. I won't be long in the shower."

"How about I make us hot chocolate? It's getting chillier with each day it seems."

"Perfect." Stella kissed Aurora's cheek, but Aurora pulled Stella's mouth to her lips for a brief but deep kiss. "That's a nice change to my *home from work* routine."

Aurora laughed, swatting Stella's butt. "Go shower."

When alone in the kitchen, Aurora replayed Stella's comment about the kiss being a nice change to her routine. Did that mean Stella liked it enough for it to happen on a regular basis? Damn. How was this happening? Aurora wasn't supposed to have these thoughts. What happened to the woman who joked about protecting the rights of the singles? *That* Aurora wouldn't be wondering if Stella wanted a kiss every evening.

Hot chocolate. Focus on hot chocolate.

By the time Stella shimmied into the front room, towel drying her hair, Aurora held two steaming mugs of hot chocolate. "I couldn't find any marshmallows."

"What? You didn't ransack all the cupboards?" she asked in a sexy tone.

"I did. Do you have a secret hiding place I should know about?"

"*Should*, huh? I thought the purpose of a hidden stash was staying hidden."

"Oh no. The purpose is for me to find it."

"Good to know, but I'm pretty sure I'm out of marshmallows." Stella set the wet towel down on the kitchen counter.

"How does one live without them?" Aurora handed off one of the mugs.

"It's been touch and go for days now."

Aurora regarded Stella, a craving boiling inside. "I can only imagine."

"Are we still talking about marshmallows?" Stella returned Aurora's intense gaze.

"I have no idea."

Stella's shy smile was hot as fuck, and her freshly showered scent, lavender perhaps, was driving Aurora insane with desire.

Their lips met. All the tension in Aurora's body calmed. Or it was simply replaced with sexual needs.

Aurora set her mug next to the towel. "How do you do this?" She pressed her forehead to Stella's.

"Do what?" Stella also set down her drink.

"Make hot chocolate seem so unappealing. For the second time. I consider myself a connoisseur of sweet drinks."

"It's my superpower," Stella teased.

"What other powers do you have?"

"Like the secret stash, I can't tell ya. You have to find out on your own." Stella's eyes changed from teasing to wanting.

"I love a challenge."

Aurora tugged Stella's arms apart and lifted her T-shirt over her head. Aurora traced the outline of Stella's areola with a finger. "These have a power over me." Aurora continued tracing a circle around the nipple. "They're beautiful."

"You seem to have a power over them." Stella glanced down at her hardening nipple.

Stella shut her eyes, and Aurora thrust Stella against the pantry door.

"Oh," Stella moaned.

"You like?" Aurora didn't bother waiting for an answer, capturing Stella's lips. Her tongue forcefully pushed its way inside. It was more than clear to Aurora Stella indeed liked it, and her intensity begged for more.

Stella yanked away, panting. "While I'm liking the way this is starting, I have one request."

Aurora arched her eyebrows.

"You're dressed. That needs to be corrected. Now."

"Bossy," Aurora teased, but she started to remove her shirt.

Stella stopped her. "Allow me." A wicked smile appeared, and Stella slipped a hand under Aurora's shirt, cupping a breast before retracting the hand to fully expose Aurora. After getting the shirt off, Stella reached around Aurora to unclasp the bra.

Aurora's breath hitched, and Stella stared deeply into her eyes.

The bra fell to the ground, but neither woman wanted to break the gaze, speaking volumes without actually saying a word. Stella unzipped Aurora's skirt, letting it plummet.

Stella ran a finger over Aurora's lips. "So soft and inviting."

Aurora sucked the finger into her mouth.

Stella gulped in a breath, and she moaned. "Kiss me, please."

Again, they locked lips and deepened the kiss instantly. Without stopping, they clumsily stumbled into the bedroom, collapsing onto the bed in a tangle.

"Oomph." Aurora laughed, still bouncing a bit on the mattress.

"You okay?" Stella flicked hair out of her mouth.

"I thought doctors were supposed to heal people, not cause injury."

"I was never good with following certain rules."

"What other rules do you routinely break?"

Stella splayed her fingers as if she intended to count off more but said, "Another thing you need to find out on your own."

"With pleasure!" Aurora attacked Stella's mouth again, unable to get enough of the way Stella tasted.

Stella pinned Aurora's arms down with one hand above them. Stella's free hand walked all the way down Aurora's right side, the soft touches bringing forth a tingling sensation, making Aurora moan in yearning. Stella dispatched Aurora's panties, Aurora helping by lifting upward.

"Please, Stella. Make love to me."

A faint smile appeared on Stella's lips, the shimmer in her eyes indication of her desire to do exactly that. Her fingers separated Aurora's pussy lips, not going inside but teasing. Aurora pressed her hips upward in an attempt to get Stella to move past the foreplay and inside. God, Aurora wanted to give herself to Stella and allow her total control.

"Something tells me you want...?" Stella's finger rested right outside Aurora's entrance.

Aurora's hips gyrated again as if she couldn't stop herself from pleading for release.

Stella entered, and Aurora claimed Stella's mouth with her tongue. While Stella eased in and out below, Aurora kissed Stella hungrily, needing closeness in every possible way.

Aurora ground into Stella. "Your scrubs are getting soaked."

"Can you blame me? You're smoking hot." Stella slowly pumped her fingers. Her sapphire eyes aflame. "You're so fucking wet." She drove in deep and stayed. "I love this feeling. Being inside you."

Aurora cupped the back of Stella's head. "Me too."

Stella made to move lower.

"No. I want you up here with me."

"Are you sure?"

"I want to look at you." Aurora snaked a hand down, landing on her clit.

Stella sucked in a breath. "What are you doing?"

"I know kidneys are your specialty, but I'm pretty sure you're familiar with female anatomy and what works. Do you want me to stop?"

Stella shook her head.

Aurora continued to stimulate herself. "Kiss me."

Stella did, and her fingers went deeper inside Aurora. As they kissed, Aurora increased her efforts below, matched by Stella sliding in and out.

Within moments, Aurora was on the brink. "Look at me, Stella."

Stella looked at Aurora with such passion Aurora was determined not to close her eyes. She didn't want to break the connection growing between the two.

The orgasm steamrolled Aurora, and she could no longer keep her eyes open. Stella, still thrusting below, kissed each of Aurora's eyelids, as if saying it was okay. She understood how much the experience meant for the both of them.

Stella lay on top of Aurora, both women breathing heavily. "I'm not squashing you, am I?" Stella asked.

"No. I like you on top."

"I hope so, because I like being here."

"Don't get too comfortable."

"Why's that?"

"I need a taste." Aurora rolled Stella onto her back, making quick work with Stella's scrubs.

"Young people are always in such a rush."

Aurora eyed the glisten on Stella's lips. "It's not just the young who seem to be in a rush." Aurora's mouth inched closer.

Stella moaned when Aurora entered her with her tongue, lapping at Stella's warmth and wetness.

Stella held the back of Aurora's head. "I don't know how you do this, but no one has made me feel this wonderful."

Aurora reached for Stella's hand, lacing their fingers, as Aurora moved to Stella's clit, circling it. Stella poured into Aurora's mouth. Aurora guided two fingers into Stella and pumped in and out. Her hips moved in sync.

It wouldn't take long now.

Aurora wanted Stella to come. The sounds coming from her signaled it wouldn't be long. Stella's body writhed, and Aurora's mouth and fingers didn't stop until Stella finished the second time.

CHAPTER TWENTY-THREE

STELLA PULLED AURORA UP INTO HER ARMS, NEEDING Aurora close as if to reassure herself Aurora was real. That *this* was real. The experience and feelings.

"Wow!" Aurora said, her breathing steadying.

"Yes, wow," Stella held Aurora tightly. "You're amazing."

"You're not so bad yourself." Aurora sat up. "I need water."

"Coming up." Stella didn't bother getting dressed and padded to the kitchen.

She opened the fridge, reaching for a bottle. Twisting the cap released a hissing sound, and there was some spray of cold water, which felt good after sex. She pulled two Harpoon pint glasses from the cabinet, filled them, and returned to the bedroom.

Aurora fluffed a pillow and sat up in bed.

"Now there's a sight to return to." Stella handed Aurora a glass.

"Thanks." Aurora took a swig. "Seltzer?"

"Yes." It hit Stella that she should have asked what Aurora wanted. "I hope black cherry is okay."

"It's my fave. What brand?"

"Polar."

"Also my fave. It's weird, really."

"How so?" Stella skirted the edge of the bed.

"It's not the first similarity."

"Polar Seltzer is a New England thing." Stella shrugged.

"I know, but still. There are times I feel this connection with you. As if I've known you longer than the few months."

Stella crawled back into bed, pulling the covers over them. "I know what you mean."

"What's your favorite type of food?" Aurora quizzed, closing one eye and inspecting Stella.

"Mexican."

"Me too!" Aurora settled into Stella's arms. "Even the medical connection. I know I'm only part of the support staff, but it's cool to be part of the process of making doctors."

"Everyone on campus plays a role, but since you brought it up, can we circle back to the nursing school topic?"

Aurora groaned, going limp on the bed.

"Don't be that way. I have contacts who know the ins and outs of the various nursing programs in Boston. I can have them talk to you. Help you with your application. Many of them have summer, fall, and spring start dates. And you can go full- or part-time."

Aurora buried her head into the crook of Stella's neck. "I just don't think I have it in me. I'm too old to go back to school. Classes. Homework. All of that sounds exhausting."

"Maybe. Maybe not. You won't know until you try, and I'll help you study."

"Oh, really? During sexy time?"

"If that's the best way for you to remember things." Stella walked her fingers down Aurora's stomach and farther south. "Your thigh bone is connected to your hip bone." Stella laughed. "Or we could just study. It might do me some good to refresh my memory about some things."

"That's a scary thought considering you cut people up."

Stella refused to take the bait and gripped Aurora's hip. "Please, just think about it. You're young, but take it from an old fogey like me. Time has a way of flying by."

Aurora propped her head up, staring into Stella's eyes. "Is there something you wished you'd pursued but haven't?"

"I don't know if I have anything career-related, but I wish I trained myself to read more. Not medical journals. I get my fill of those. But I can't remember the last novel I read unless for the quasi book club with my daughter. We're working on the Harry Potter series, but I think it would be good for me to read more books. Or just have more down time."

"What kind of books do you like?"

Stella scratched her chin. "Oh gosh, I don't even remember. I used to love Sue Grafton's alphabet series."

"It's a shame she won't finish it."

"What do you mean?" Stella's face crumbled into confusion.

"She died before she got to Z. Her family says for them, the alphabet will always end with the letter Y."

"Aw, that's sweet but terribly sad."

Aurora's eyes darkened. "Maybe you should start them over again at the letter A."

"I'll make you a deal. You talk to one of my friends about nursing school, and I'll buy the first one in the series."

"You're blackmailing me." Aurora groaned playfully.

"In a way. Are you complaining?"

Aurora took a deep breath. "You're impossible."

"It's one of my traits. Depends on the person whether or not they take to it."

"I'll consider it." Aurora yawned.

"Did I wear you out?"

"Kinda, but I'm not ready to sleep. Do you know what series I loved reading when I was a kid?"

Stella shook her head with a curious smile.

"*Anne of Green Gables.*"

"Never read it."

"Have you seen any of the shows?" Aurora asked, bewilderment in her expression.

Another shake of the head.

Aurora laughed. "There goes one of my theories about our connection."

"What do you mean?"

"In the series, Anne Shirley married Gilbert Blythe."

Stella started to speak, but then she puzzled it out. "Our last names."

"Yes. It's silly, really, that I even thought it."

Stella rolled on top of Aurora, a knee separating Aurora's legs. "Not silly. It's cute." Stella rubbed her hip into Aurora's wetness.

"Whatcha doing?" Aurora teased.

"I can't get my fill of you."

* * *

TWO FRIDAYS LATER, Stella popped into the bathroom at work after her 8:00 a.m. lecture.

"Oh, hey. This is a pleasant surprise."

Aurora slowly turned around from the sink, her eyes red and puffy.

"What's wrong?" Stella moved closer.

"I just got off the phone with Becky. She accused me of purposefully trying to sabotage her wedding."

"That seems harsh. I know planning a wedding is stressful, but that doesn't give her the right to say that to you." Stella ran a finger down one of the tear tracks on Aurora's cheek. "Is it the date thing?"

Aurora nodded. "I don't know why she's so intent on me finding a date right now. The wedding is months away, and I don't want to bring just anyone. She's my best friend. This is the most important day in her life, and..."

"And what?"

Aurora wadded up a tissue and dabbed under her eye. "The one person I want to bring can't go with me."

Stella's jaw stiffened. "I see."

"It sucks." Aurora attended to her other eye.

"Who is this person?"

Aurora pulled the tissue from her face. "You don't know?"

Stella shook her head, crossing her arms.

"You. I want to bring you."

A wave of relief whooshed through Stella. "Why can't you bring me?"

"Because we aren't dating. Not officially."

"What do you call what we're doing?"

"I know we agreed to see where things go, but according to our employers, we don't know each other outside of work."

Stella uncrossed her arms. "True. But what's the likelihood anyone from work would even know if I was your date to Becky's wedding? It's not like we live in a small town."

"I don't know. I don't think anyone from the school is invited. Becky's an accountant, and Nathan is getting a PhD in some geeky field. Economics, maybe."

"You see, and even if we do bump into someone we know, we can say you're pathetic and couldn't find a date so I agreed to help out."

Aurora snorted. "Thanks for that."

"I'm teasing of course. You're such an amazing person. Anyone would kill to be your date."

"What about you?"

"I thought I said I would go."

"No. Would you kill someone?" Aurora's eyes shone with humor.

"Uh, I'm a doctor, and I'm bound by the whole *do no harm*

thing." Stella shrugged there was nothing she could do to change that.

Aurora laughed. "Is that the only reason you haven't killed someone?"

"I'm sure there are more reasons, but I'm kinda distracted right now and can't think of any."

"What's distracting you?" Aurora's eyes shone in the way that spoke directly to Stella.

"You. Remembering you in my bed the other night."

"You're such a sweet talker and in the ladies' restroom of all places."

Stella's eyes panned the area. "No one is in here."

Aurora shoved Stella's shoulder. "No way. I'm not having sex in a bathroom."

"I wasn't talking about sex. But what about a kiss? These"—Stella pointed to her lips—"miss yours."

"Is that right?" Aurora inched closer to Stella.

"It's hard to survive each hour without getting a taste of you."

"Well, Doc, I'm not sure if this is the smart thing to do. I mean, we're at work, and I distinctly remember one of the ground rules was no nookie at work."

"True, but aren't rules made to be broken? I told you I like to break the ones that need breaking, and this, right now, qualifies."

Aurora rolled her eyes. "There's another issue, though." She pressed a finger against Stella's lips.

"What's that?"

"The longer I make you wait, the better the release."

Stella sucked Aurora's finger into her mouth.

Aurora yanked it out. "You aren't playing fair."

"I'm playing to win."

"What's the prize?"

You.

Stella hefted a shoulder. "I guess we have to wait to find out. Only fair considering you're making me wait"—she placed her mouth next to Aurora's ear—"for the release."

Aurora pulled away. "Nicely played. I do love the way your brain works."

"It's working hard right now." Stella tapped her temple.

"Doing what?"

"Remembering the sounds you make when I'm making love to you."

"Again, this doesn't seem like appropriate work conversation."

"It's hard not to think of that when you look hot as hell in your skirt and heels."

"I have to admit"—Aurora ran a finger up and down in the air—"the white coat and scrubs are a turn-on."

"Got a thing for doctors?"

"Just one in particular. I'll introduce you to her someday."

"You're killing me, Aurora."

"I can see it in your eyes, Stella."

"It's not just evident in my eyes." Stella glanced down at her nether regions.

"I can only imagine." Aurora took a step closer to the door. "I have to get back to the office for a meeting with Kip. We finally worked out the schedules, with temps for the evening shifts until Bri hires someone, and today's the day he finds out about his new work load, as in not covering medical classes anymore."

"Oh, good luck. Do you want to get together later to let me know how it went?"

"Sure. Where should we meet."

"Care for a Reuben?"

"Your place? Is that what you're saying?"

"If I remember correctly, we're not supposed to be seen in public. Aside from Becky's wedding."

Aurora stepped closer and whispered in Stella's ear, "I'm starting to see the reason why you set these ground rules."

After the door closed behind her, Stella entered a stall to do some damage control. Her panties were practically soaked all the way through. "Oh, Aurora, the things I want to do to your body."

Someone came into the restroom, but unfortunately from the squeak of the person's sneakers, it wasn't Aurora rethinking the nookie rule.

CHAPTER TWENTY-FOUR

BECKY SAT AT THEIR USUAL TABLE. "YOU'RE ACTUALLY on time. Color me shocked as hell?"

Aurora took her seat. "Shut your pie hole. I'm hardly ever late."

"Your manners still suck." Becky ran one finger over the other, imitating a teacher scolding a child on the playground. "Where have you been spending your nights? For weeks now, you disappear a handful of nights each week."

"Wouldn't you like to know?" When the waiter stopped at their table, Aurora said, "My usual, please, Andy."

"You got it. Becky?" The slightly pudgy twenty-something blushed a bit, confirming Aurora's suspicion he had a crush on Becky.

Becky ordered her usual. Andy stared for one second too long before bolting.

Becky folded up a corner of her cocktail napkin. "So, are you going to spill or not?"

"About?" Aurora attempted to play coy.

"Where you've been spending your nights."

"I don't kiss and tell."

"Yes, you do. With me at least."

"I do not! Besides, you're practically married. Your sex life is on the endangered list, and I wouldn't want to make you jealous." Aurora crossed her arms, enjoying teasing Becky, but there was another reason she didn't want to confess about Stella.

"Thanks for that."

"According to articles I've read—"

"Stop right there!" Becky made an X in the air, her way of saying *go no further*. "I haven't even been on my honeymoon yet. I don't need these thoughts... I'm already not getting much since we live in different states."

"Get all sexed up while on your honeymoon, because after that—" Aurora made a throat slashing gesture, unable to stop herself from needling her opinionated friend. It had always been their thing. Teasing the other mercilessly.

"Speaking of my wedding, how's the date hunt?"

"Wouldn't you like to know?" Aurora rested her elbows on the table, propping up her chin.

"Yes. I would. I'm hoping your smug look means you've found a date."

"It's possible I have narrowed down my options. So many fish in the Boston pond."

"Is it the person or one of the persons you've been spending the night with?"

"Not going to tell you anything." Aurora acted out zipping her lips shut.

"Please tell me you aren't still considering an escort."

"What if I am?"

"How much is she costing you?" Becky's eyes glimmered with opinions. All negative and judge-y.

"Not a cent if I play my cards right."

"You found yourself a free escort?" Becky looked dubious at best.

"I did."

"Oh God. What's she like? Will she make the cut?"

"What cut?" Aurora stiffened in her seat.

"This is my wedding, Aurora." Becky pressed her hands on the tabletop. "No street whores. Think Julia Roberts from *Pretty Woman*."

Aurora bonked her forehead. "Why didn't you tell me sooner? All these nights, sampling different ones to see whom I like best."

Becky waggled a finger. "Stop fucking with me. Who are you bringing?"

"I think you'll be pleased."

Becky waved for more.

"Would a doctor suffice?"

Becky's eyes widened. "Really?"

"Yes."

"You have a date with a doctor?" Becky leaned over the table.

"Not sure I'd call it a date, since we're only colleagues, but a doctor offered to save me after she found me in the restroom crying."

"Why were you crying?" Becky had the decency to seem concerned.

"Oh, I don't know. Maybe because you had just called me the worst maid of honor in history." Aurora delivered the line with more oomph.

"I didn't say that!"

Aurora shot back, "You did. I'm quoting your exact words."

Becky slouched in her seat. "I'm sorry. The stress—"

Aurora squeezed Becky's hand. "It's okay. I get it. I do. You have a lot going on, and since Nate's away, all of it is falling on your shoulders. This is a good reason for me not to get married. I'd be three times as bad. You're nice to begin with, and look what it's turning you into."

"Stop. You love to pretend to be a badass, but you, Aurora, are one of the sweetest people I know."

Aurora shook her head. "I am not. Don't ever say that again."

"Aurora Shirley, you are the sweetest best friend anyone could have."

"You're dead to me."

The statement seemed to have zero impact on Becky, probably because it wasn't the first time she'd heard it. "What's the doctor's name?"

Aurora pressed her lips together.

"I'll buy you dessert if you spill."

Aurora recrossed her arms, but her resolve was flagging. Damn Becky for knowing her sweet tooth.

"I'll buy you two desserts, won't yell at you for leaving dishes in the sink, *and* I'll do your laundry for a week."

"Cheater!" Aurora glared at her best friend. "Stella."

"Dr. Stella?"

"That's her first name. I'm not giving you her last. You're unbalanced enough these days to call her up and instruct her what to wear to your wedding."

Becky rebuffed that idea with a flick of the wrist. "Do you have a crush on this doctor?"

"Most assuredly I do not. I've told you. I'm not a relationships kind of girl," Aurora mumbled more to her lap.

"Really? Is that why your face lit up when you mentioned her name?"

"Nice try. I know for a fact it didn't." *Did it?*

"It most definitely did." Becky sipped her drink. "Wait, is that where you've been spending your nights? With Dr. Stella Whatever?"

Aurora motioned for Becky to keep her voice down.

Becky hunkered down in her seat and whispered, "What?"

"Nothing. I just don't want you spreading false rumors about a work colleague. That's all."

"Oh, so does the mysterious lady or ladies of the night know you have a date with a hot doctor your crushing on?"

"How do you know Stella's hot?" Aurora wished she didn't let this nugget out.

"Have you looked in the mirror lately? You're easily the most beautiful dyke in Boston."

"That's not true!"

"It is. Okay, this person who's monopolizing your time, does she make you happy?"

"I like having sex with her, if that's what you're asking." Aurora couldn't quite figure out why she wasn't telling Becky the truth, but something was holding her back. Perhaps it was not truly understanding what she had with Stella. They'd started as fuck buddies, but were they still? Did fuck buddies ever morph into... more?

"Then why can't she come with you to the wedding? Why the need for the doctor?"

"Because you don't invite someone you're only fucking to your best friend's wedding." Was Becky really believing sex girl and Stella were two separate people? Or was she giving Aurora enough rope to hang herself? It was hard to read Becks sometimes.

Becky eyed her but didn't press. "Are you really happy with this arrangement with sex girl?"

"You forget, my dear Becks, I'm not like you. All I need from someone is sex. Not a ring on my finger or anything." Aurora flagged down Andy for a dessert menu.

"But does it make you happy?"

"Out of the world sex does have incredible mental health benefits. I feel clearheaded and energized." Aurora held her palms upward, her thumbs and forefingers forming a circle in a meditative pose, and hummed, "Ommmm."

"So, the only reason you're with sex girl is for your mental health?"

"Absolutely." Aurora forced herself to stare into Becky's questioning eyes.

"Uh-huh. If you want to believe that, go ahead, but I know the real reason."

"Sure, you do. I need to use the ladies' room. Can you order dessert? Remember, you promised two. Choose the ones that sound best."

"Coward!"

Aurora sought refuge in the bathroom before she accidentally spilled the beans about Stella. That she was falling for Stella. No! Aurora stared at her reflection in the mirror. No. She shouldn't tell anyone. That made it real, and it couldn't be real. Or could it?

CHAPTER TWENTY-FIVE

STELLA STRIPPED OFF HER WORK CLOTHES AND GOT under the streaming hot shower water. She had less than fifteen minutes before Aurora was due to arrive for a quiet night in.

Meaning Stella only had time for a quick rinse and hopefully wouldn't get her hair wet. Or not too wet.

It'd taken her forever to settle on an outfit, wanting to appear casual but not sloppy. Her typical scrub pants and white T-shirt she lounged in after work were out, but most of her jeans had seen better days. And trousers seemed an odd choice for a night in. Finally, she found a pair of jeans that clung to the right spots and looked like they'd been purchased in this century. No wonder her ex always wanted to get Stella to the outlet malls, but Stella could never seem to find the time. Her fashion sense was severely impaired, and now she didn't know who to call to help *zazz* up her selection, as the kids say these days. Perhaps her sister Rosie, but her sister was older, and Aurora—wait, did Stella want to dress younger because she was with someone younger? If that were the case, she should enlist

Charlie, her niece, to help. But she was away at school and not due to return until winter break.

There was a knock on the door, and Stella took one last look in the mirror before starting the night.

"Hey there." Aurora breezed past, planting a kiss on Stella's cheek. "It's fucking cold out." Aurora shimmied about, warding off the chill. "Wow, it looks nice in here. Did you clean, or do you have a service?"

"A little of both."

"Impressive." Aurora inhaled deeply. "What's that smell?"

"That depends. Is it good or bad?"

"Delicious. Are you cooking dinner?" Aurora took another deep breath.

"I thought I'd give it a go. You know what they say; it's never too late to try something new."

"Who says that?" Aurora grinned.

"I do."

"Is this another one of your attempts to convince me to apply to nursing school?"

Stella clamped her hands over her mouth and shook her head.

"Does that mean no nursing talk or no talk of any type?" Aurora ran a finger down Stella's front.

Stella stared at Aurora's finger resting on the waist of her jeans. "I'm totally down with not talking."

"I bet you are. Oh, here." Aurora handed Stella the bottle of red she'd been holding onto.

"Thanks." Stella set it on the kitchen counter. "Let me help you take off your coat."

"I could get used to this."

"What? Manners?"

"Yes. It's weird." Aurora chuckled softly.

"You young people today, always in a rush."

"Yes, we're the downfall of society, until you have an internet question or need help with a PDF."

"True. Does this mean I can have your number on speed dial for all my daunting computer tasks?" Stella joked.

"Don't you already?"

"News flash, I'm not that old. I do know my way around a computer."

"Is that right? We may have to test that skill."

Stella opened the oven to check the status of her chicken parmesan, one of the three meals she could muster when pressed.

Aurora eased onto one of the barstools at the small kitchen island. "Do you need help with anything?"

"Can you open the wine?" Stella handed over the bottle Aurora had brought along with an opener.

"Need someone with steadier hands?" Aurora opened the corkscrew.

"Yes. It's a well-known fact surgeons have shaky hands."

"Your malpractice insurance must be through the roof."

"Absolutely." Stella pulled out a spring salad mix from the crisper and balsamic vinaigrette dressing from the door of the fridge.

"Of course, you're including a salad. I'm onto your veggie agenda." Aurora shook the wine opener at Stella.

"Have to do my part. It's part of my Hippocratic Oath."

"Thou shall force green stuff on your date?" Aurora asked in what Stella assumed was a Greek philosopher voice.

"Yes. It's why all the chicks dig doctors."

"I always wondered about that." Aurora placed a finger in the dimple of her chin.

"Don't spread the word, though. I don't have a lot of free time, and I'd much rather spend these hours with you."

Aurora leaned on the countertop, her cleavage becoming more prominent. "Is that right? I'm starting to wonder if your whole *I only want a casual relationship* shtick was a ruse right from the start."

"That entirely depends on one thing." Stella reached for a glass of wine and took a sip.

"What's that?"

"If it works."

Aurora's eyes gave Stella the once-over, and then they panned the room. "Let's see. Candles are lit. Your meal smells yummy. You look absolutely scrumptious in your jeans and tight shirt. There's wine—"

Stella tipped her glass in Aurora's direction. "Which you brought."

"Yes. I didn't think the sandwich place would have booze. Little did I know I was in for a treat tonight."

"There's even cheesecake for dessert, which"—Stella stabbed the air with a palm—"full disclosure, I didn't make. I picked it up from a place near the hospital. They make the best cheesecake in the entire New England area."

"Which place?"

"Tony's."

"You've got to be kidding."

"What?"

"That's my favorite place for cheesecake."

Stella licked a finger and made a mark in the air. "Another tick in the similarity column."

"It's getting uncanny."

"In a good or bad way?" Stella mentally crossed her fingers.

"Depends." Aurora's smile was alluring.

"Guess it's my turn to ask why."

"Not sure I'm ready to answer the question yet."

"Take all the time you need." Stella flipped around in hopes of seeming like the answer didn't disappoint. "You ready for salad?"

Aurora hopped off the stool. "I'm always ready for you."

"You have such a way with words."

"Because I'm so subtle?"

"I think we may have different definitions for that."

"I may prefer mine right now, and I've been wanting to do this since I stepped into your apartment." Aurora pulled Stella up against her and kissed Stella softly on the lips at first before kicking it up to the next level, leaving Stella breathless when they broke apart. "That's out of my system."

"Permanently?"

"Uh, no. But it'll sustain me through dinner."

"Good to hear, because..." Stella couldn't fill in the blank.

"Because...?"

"I've found a reason to cook again." Stella had to suppress a groan. Could she sound more idiotic if she tried?

Aurora, though, melted against Stella. "When I met you, I had no idea you could get tied into knots like this. It's kinda adorable. If dinner didn't smell so good, I'd take you to bed right now."

"The oven can keep it warm, you know."

"True. But good things happen to those who wait." Aurora planted a kiss on Stella's cheek and then took a seat at the table.

"I'm counting on it."

Aurora placed her napkin in her lap. After Stella set the salads down, she took a seat. Aurora asked, "Am I right in assuming you don't cook often for your daughter?"

"Not as much as I would like. Kenzie seems to prefer pizza on Friday nights and restaurants on Saturday. For a kid, she has a refined palette. Since the divorce, I do everything I can to make her happy." Stella forked in a bite and crunched down on a crouton.

Aurora swallowed a sip of wine. "Do you wish you saw her more?"

"Yes, but we don't want to disrupt her schedule too much, although now that my ex is dating, that might change."

"Oh, I didn't know she was dating. How's that for you?"

"Fine."

"I see."

Stella placed her fork next to her salad plate. "Is that a good *I see* or a bad one?"

"It's not bad, really. I'm just surprised this didn't come up sooner."

Stella rested on her forearms. "It wasn't like I was hiding it. We started with some ground rules."

"Ah, yes. The no nookie in the office."

"And the no relationship part. Mentioning child custody and an ex-wife dating to just a... bed mate—"

Aurora laughed. "That's the most polite way I've ever heard of referring to a fuck buddy."

"Do you still think of me as only that?" Stella wanted to retract the words as soon as they flew out of her mouth.

"No. I won't lie." Aurora leaned over the table. "I love the bed mating part." She jacked up one eyebrow. "But I like spending time with you. Not just the sex."

"Me too."

"So, do we need to have a deeper conversation about... things?" Aurora's face showed slight discomfort.

"At some point, yes," Stella dodged.

"Is that your way of saying you aren't ready for that conversation?"

"We can talk about it now, if you'd like." Stella braced for whatever Aurora had to say.

"Way to put it on me!"

Surprised, Stella smiled. "I didn't mean to. It's just... this is all new to me. Dating again. I seem to be out of my element. I didn't even know the meaning of Netflix and chill."

"Don't put more on me because of some generational

notion you have in your head. This is new to me as well. Dating a woman with a kid. I haven't even told anyone about us. I wasn't sure if we've reached that stage yet. The whole meeting friends and family."

"I haven't either. I think part of my reasoning is I've been enjoying our time together. Is that selfish of me?"

"I feel the same. The holidays are rapidly approaching, and the days will zoom by. It's nice to have these quiet nights before…" Aurora's wave implied *and all that jazz.* "It almost seems a shame to spoil what we have right now."

Stella reached for Aurora's hand on the table. "Let's take it one day at a time and enjoy us in our own way."

CHAPTER TWENTY-SIX

AURORA ROLLED OVER IN BED TO STARE INTO Stella's sleeping face. God, she was beautiful all the time, but there was something special about seeing her face when asleep. More relaxed. Natural. No racing thoughts going on behind those beguiling eyes because Aurora was one hundred percent certain Stella's mind never settled during her awake hours.

They'd been seeing each other for months now, and it was hard to remember a time when Aurora ever felt this comfortable with anyone. Everything in her life seemed better. The sky was bluer. Bird chirps were sweeter. The scent of spring flowers wafting through the open window were more fragrant.

Aurora ran a finger down Stella's cheek, causing the woman to stir but not wake. Aurora continued the trek over Stella's chin, down her neck, between her breasts, finally resting her palm on Stella's belly.

"Hey." Stella's voice was groggy.

"Hey back. How'd you sleep?"

"Like the dead."

"True, I don't think you moved once. At one point, I was

tempted to place a mirror under your nose." Aurora tweaked Stella's nose.

Stella smiled, stretching her arms over head. "Usually, I toss and turn."

Aurora climbed on top of Stella. "Is that right? Maybe I should put you to bed every night. I'm pretty sure a doctor should get rest before wielding a scalpel."

"So, it'd be more of a public service?" Stella cupped her hands behind her head.

"Yes. I'm that kind of person. Always thinking of others." Aurora licked Stella's nipple.

"It's one of my favorite things about you. The thinking of"—Stella let out a moan when Aurora sucked the nipple into her mouth—"others," she breathed out.

Kissing her way to the other nipple, but before giving it attention, Aurora asked, "What are your plans for today?"

"Uh, haven't put any thought into it. You?"

"Taking you on a date."

Stella raked her hand through Aurora's hair. "Is that right? Does this date involve leaving the apartment?"

"Sadly, it does."

Stella feigned being put out. "That's pretty much the saddest thing I've heard all day, considering." She glanced down at her erect nipple.

"It's pretty much the only thing you've heard all day, but I have good news."

"I'm all ears."

"We don't have to leave right away, and I haven't made any plans for the morning, so if you play your cards right, I'll make leaving the house totally worth your while." Aurora ground a hip into Stella.

"Which card do I have to play?"

"Shut up and kiss me."

Stella, perhaps taking Aurora's *play your cards right* tip, didn't hold back and pressed her lips against Aurora's with passionate wanting.

"That's a perk of sleeping with a doctor. You wake raring to go." With the tip of her nose, Aurora traced Stella's right areola.

"Usually, I'm jumping out of bed for an emergency or something. This"—her breath hitched when Aurora bit down on the nipple—"is a much better way to wake."

"There's one problem, though." Stella rolled Aurora onto her back and nuzzled her neck and hair. "I'm used to being in control." She inhaled deeply. "You smell so good. Natural." Stella nipped Aurora's earlobe and licked the outer edges of the ear.

Aurora moaned. "Keep doing that, and you can always be in charge."

Stella's tongue worked its way down. Along the side of her neck. Paying attention to the collarbone. Landing on Aurora's nipple, which was standing up at attention.

After giving the left breast attention, Stella moved to the right breast but clasped the left nipple between a thumb and forefinger.

"Harder," Aurora begged.

Stella did with both nipples.

It set Aurora on fire.

* * *

STELLA, still with Aurora's right nipple in her mouth, looked up and seemed to acknowledge Aurora's pleading look. A ray of sunlight danced in Aurora's eyes. "Wait," Stella said around biting Aurora's nipple. "It'll be worth it."

"I don't know if I can. I need you. Now."

Stella's mouth stayed put, but her hand skated down, past Aurora's slight mound of hair, and then worked its way back up. Aurora attempted to direct the hand back to where she wanted it.

Stella laughed. "Do I need to tie your hands?"

"Wouldn't that be against your oath or something?"

"I'd have to check. I don't remember sex being part of it. Are you going to behave?" Secretly, Stella hoped Aurora wouldn't.

"Why should I? You aren't." Aurora playfully stuck out her tongue.

"That settles it." Stella twisted away. "Remember you asked for it."

"Please don't stop," Aurora begged.

"I don't plan on it, but you aren't listening to me." Stella levered up, rooted around in her dresser, and returned with three scarves. She proceeded to tie one of Aurora's wrists to the wrought iron bedpost. Then the other. She tugged on each, checking her work. "No cheating. I take being in charge seriously," Stella said in what she hoped was a commanding tone. This was new territory for her.

"I'll do my best, but I do love having my hands on you."

"Not counting that out later." Stella straddled Aurora's waist, holding onto a scarf with fringe. Stella moved it lightly over Aurora's skin, sketching arbitrary letters all over Aurora's body, but a thought struck her. "Can you guess the letter?"

Aurora's face pinched with concentration. "I... no, T."

Stella nodded. "And this?"

"E."

"This one will be a bit harder, so really focus."

Aurora closed her eyes. "O... no, Q."

"Nicely done."

Aurora guessed the remaining letters: U, I, E, R, and O.

"Are you tracing random letters or spelling something?" Aurora asked.

"Oh, just random letters," Stella fibbed as she continued

tickling Aurora's skin. How could Stella confess she'd spelled *Te quiero*, which meant I love you in Spanish? It was the cowardly way of saying the words without the risk of not hearing them back.

Aurora writhed on the bed. "Doctor, you're killing me."

"Not a bad way to go if you ask me." Stella ran the scarf over Aurora's pussy. "From the evidence forming on the sheet, I think you're loving this."

Aurora eyed Stella's naked body, her gaze landing between Stella's legs. "I can say the same about you."

Stella positioned her pussy over Aurora's and started to rock back and forth.

"Oh God!" Aurora tried to free herself, perhaps in need of touching Stella.

"Do you need a safe word?" Stella asked, stilling.

A squirt gushed out of Aurora. "No. Whatever you do, don't stop."

"Just in case, say *Green Gables*."

Aurora smiled. "Got it."

Stella flipped around, now facing Aurora's feet, but still straddling Aurora's body. Bending all the way over, Stella nipped Aurora's inner thigh and continued downward, assuring each toe received attention.

AURORA ADMIRED Stella's creamy and firm white ass on prominent display, ruing that she was unable to touch it. Would it be terrible to utter *Green Gables* solely to get her hands on Stella's scrumptious buttocks? God, there wasn't a part of Stella's body that Aurora didn't cherish. Even the back of the woman's knees were sexy as hell. How was that possible? The desire to touch Stella increased dramatically.

Maybe Stella sensed Aurora's need, because Stella's ass

inched closer and closer. Stella's fingers explored Aurora's slick lips. Slowly, Stella separated them.

Aurora sucked in a breath.

"I love that sound," Stella said.

"You have a way of making me do it."

Stella's finger started to ease inside.

Aurora inhaled deeply again.

Stella glanced over her shoulder. "I hope you never tire of me."

There was vulnerability in Stella's stare. "Not sure that's possible. Quite the opposite. I need you." Aurora motioned with a finger for Stella to scoot her ass closer.

Stella flourished an eyebrow, seeming to contemplate the request.

"Really?" Aurora blurted. "You don't want... it? Me?"

"Oh, I do, but the longing in your eye... It's sexy."

Aurora gazed deeply into Stella's eyes, detecting more than sexual need.

Stella held her gaze for a moment before moving right where Aurora wanted, gently easing down onto Aurora's eager mouth. Aurora's tongue tasted Stella's wetness, realizing how much Stella had savored torturing Aurora. How had neither of them climaxed yet?

And, did this act require a deeper level of trust? Was Aurora overthinking sixty-nining? Probably.

Stella's attention to Aurora's clit knocked Aurora out of her head and into the moment. Her tongue plunged inside. Stella moaned and reciprocated by burying her face into Aurora.

Both women lapped at the other's clit. Stella had the slight advantage by being able to insert a finger inside Aurora. Not that Aurora minded.

Both of their bodies trembled, yet neither stopped. Aurora's legs started to quiver. Stella groaned into Aurora's pussy, not stilling her tongue. Taking Aurora's clit into her mouth, Stella pushed her fingers in hard and deep.

Aurora intensified her circling of Stella's clit, in hopes they'd climax together. Aurora was so fucking close, and holding it off took effort, especially with Stella plunging in and out.

Right when Aurora thought it was a lost cause, a gush escaped from Stella and her legs spasmed.

Aurora's orgasm took siege, just as Stella seemed to start coming.

Neither stopped until both were fully satiated.

"Fuck," Aurora whispered.

Stella fell on top of Aurora, her body jerking from an aftershock.

"Morning sex rocks," Aurora said.

Stella swiped a tongue over Aurora's clit. "You aren't done, are you?"

"I'm in your hands, Doctor. Or tongue."

Stella chuckled but got to work.

AURORA SLIPPED on her jeans from the previous day after taking a shower with Stella. "Do you have a T-shirt I can borrow?"

Stella waved to her closet. "Take whatever you want."

Aurora moved some items around on the hangers. "Let's see. White shirt. Another. And another. Oh, look, a light gray one. You know you don't actually have any colored shirts?"

"White's a color. So is gray."

"Okay. You don't have any shirts that have eye-popping color. Not even navy. Why no navy?" Aurora looked over her shoulder.

Stella shrugged. "I don't like to think much, so I usually wear the same thing."

"Ah, like Mark Zuckerberg." Aurora turned back to the shirts.

"Probably for a different reason."

"You aren't destroying human civilization with your work." Aurora eyeballed the choices again.

"Exactly. I like to save lives, and it's possible I don't have much of a fashion sense," Stella muttered the last part.

"Want to know a secret?" Aurora gave Stella her attention.

"Always."

"It's something I find absolutely adorable about you."

"Is that right?"

"It's not the only thing."

"What else do you find adorable?"

"Only one secret at a time." Aurora flipped around and selected the gray shirt since Stella had on a white one. "We can't be twins quite yet. Way too lezzy for me."

Stella sat on the edge of the bed. "Will you at least tell me what the plan is?"

Aurora shook her head, enjoying the easiness between them. "Nope. But we need to head out."

"It's something we can't be late for?" Stella fished.

"You can, but I don't like to. Chop-chop!" Aurora clapped her hands.

Outside Stella's apartment, she asked, "T or walking?"

"T and one's coming." Aurora took Stella's hand, and they ran to the tracks in the middle of Commonwealth to catch the train heading to Hynes Convention center.

A group of guys in their twenties in Red Sox T-shirts and hats cut them off at the door.

After forcing their way onto the train, Stella muttered, "I hate game days and dealing with packed trains."

Aurora stopped in her path. "Is that the only reason you hate game days?"

"Is there another reason to hate them? Usually, though, I don't mind on the weekends. It's on a work night, when I have to squeeze onto the T with a bunch of fans after being on my feet all day, that it bothers me. That is if I can squeeze on. Sometimes, I have to watch two or three go by before there's room. I run home a lot more during baseball season." Stella guided them to the back of the train, where there was some room next to the steps.

"Have you been to a game?" Aurora's heart practically beat in her throat.

Stella seemed to mull this over. "I'm sure I have. When I was a kid."

"This should be interesting," Aurora said into her shoulder.

"What?"

"Oh, nothing."

"Do you feel okay? You've gone a tad pale. You didn't over exert yourself this morning, did you?" Stella placed the back of her hand on Aurora's forehead.

Aurora smiled. "Don't worry. You didn't break me." She placed a hand on Stella's shoulder. "But if you don't like my plans, please just tell me when we get there, and we'll do something else."

"I can't imagine me hating anything we do together." Stella widened her stance as the train came to a jerky stop.

"We'll see." Aurora rocked onto her heels, holding onto the bar, her gaze sweeping all the fans on the train.

They arrived at Hynes. "This is us," Aurora said.

Stella didn't budge, seeming not to hear over all the commotion of the majority of the people leaving the train.

Aurora tugged on Stella's shirt. "Hurry."

"Oh, sorry. Are we getting off here?"

Aurora gave her a wicked smile. "Depends on your definition."

Stella laughed.

Once outside of the station, Aurora guided Stella left on Massachusetts Avenue, and then they waited at the corner to cross, to continue their way onto Boylston Street. "Any chance I can tempt you into buying a shirt today? A red, blue, or green one?"

"Are you particularly fond of those colors?" There was a playfulness in Stella's tone.

"I may have a reason for those colors today." Had Stella really not guessed their destination?

"While I'm intrigued, I'm not sure I want to ruin my streak of wearing a white shirt every day for the past ten years."

"Has it only been that long? Maybe there's hope for you yet."

"Come on, wiseass. Are you going to tell me what we're doing?"

"You haven't guessed?" Aurora waved for Stella to take in the scene as they hooked a right onto Ipswich.

"I'm praying were not going to church." Stella's eyes were on St. Clement.

Aurora chuckled. "Nope."

"I haven't been in this direction in ages. I'm totally at a loss."

"Hopefully, you'll figure it out soon. We're only a few minutes away now."

"Why do you sound scared?" Stella squeezed Aurora's hand briefly.

Aurora moved them to the side of the sidewalk. "When I made plans for today, I didn't know you hated the Red Sox."

"I don't hate them. Why do you think that?"

"You said you hated game days."

"I hate when the train is crowded. I grew up in Boston.

There's no way I could survive four decades without being a loyal member of the Sox Nation."

"But you don't remember going to Fenway. How is that possible?" Aurora tossed a hand in the air. "That nullifies your claim to being part of Sox Nation."

"I'm more of an armchair fan."

"Hypothetically, if I surprised you with tickets to Fenway, would you be happy? Or grin and bear it?"

"Wait." Stella yanked on Aurora's arm. "Are we going to Fenway?"

Aurora gawked at Stella. "Yes, Doctor."

"I feel rather foolish not putting the clues together sooner." Stella laughed at herself.

"Why else would we be turning onto Lansdowne Street on a game day?" Aurora gestured to the craziness around them. Hot dog and sausage vendors. Tourist and locals rushing to the gate. The World Series Champions banners overhead.

"I thought you were taking the longest and busiest route possible to one of my favorite restaurants." Stella wore a sheepish smile.

"Which place?"

"Joey's Dogs."

"You love Joey's?" Aurora squealed. "We should have dinner there. I love the buffalo—"

"Dog. That's my go-to."

"Curly or regular fries?" Aurora slanted her head.

"Curly. Do they even have regular?"

"It's like I'm dating myself, but no, that sounds terrible." Aurora waved away the thought.

"Come on. We have a game to see. Who are they playing?"

"Tampa Bay."

A woman bumped into Aurora. "Sorry. Oh hey, Aurora. I haven't seen you in forever."

"Annie." Aurora tossed her arms around the brunette's neck. "It's so good to see you. Are you here with Ray?"

"Yep. Speaking of, I need to track him down." Annie stood on tippy toes to scan the crowd. "Call me. We should have drinks soon." Annie made a *call me* motion with her hand and then disappeared into the crowd.

"Oh, sorry. I didn't introduce you," Aurora said to Stella.

"No worries. How do you know Annie?"

"We went to school together. She's even more of a rabid fan than I am. I don't think she's missed a home game since she was in diapers."

"You love having people in your circle with connections."

Aurora cocked her head. "What do you mean?"

"Annie. That's pretty close to Anne of Green Gables."

"I guess so, but her full name is Annabelle." Aurora didn't like the look in Stella's eye and couldn't figure out how or why she'd even made the connection.

"Oh." Stella looked away. "Do you come to games much?"

"Yep. I inherited my grandfather's season tickets."

"Is this a typical Saturday for you then, during the season? How is it baseball season already. Seems like the calendar year just ticked over and *wham!*" Stella's easygoing smile was back in place.

"I know. And to answer your question, this is a typical Saturday when the Sox are at home." Aurora pulled out her phone and clicked on the ticket app. "I was going an evening or two a week, but now that I'm working longer hours, I'm not sure how often I'll make it this season."

"That's a lot of baseball." Stella didn't seem excited about the prospect.

"Depends on the season." Aurora guided them to their gate. "If you're a good girl this afternoon, I'll reward you later."

"I thought you liked it when I wasn't good," Stella said with a straight face.

"Empty your pockets," Aurora instructed.

"Was that an attempt at being naughty?" Stella seemed befuddled by the thought.

Aurora laughed. "No, but if you want to avoid getting frisked by a stranger, I don't recommend setting off the metal detector." Aurora gently shoved Stella toward the screeners.

"I don't really like being touched," Stella commented.

"That's not what I've experienced."

Stella grinned. "I meant by people I don't know."

After they cleared security, Aurora placed her phone in the scanner, moving it around to find the right angle. The green light gave them the all clear.

"You survived the first test," Aurora said.

"You did all the work."

"I meant you avoided being frisked." Aurora waggled her brows and whispered in Stella's ear, "I wouldn't mind searching your body, though."

"The police officers over there might object if we got naked."

Aurora eyed the three male cops. "They might not."

Stella scoffed. "Way too many people for my liking. I much prefer having you all to myself."

"Sounds promising."

"I like to keep my promises." Stella glanced around. "May I buy you a beer, my dear?"

Aurora's heart lurched. "Yes. You absolutely may."

Stella leaned in to give Aurora a kiss, but Aurora ducked away. "Stella! What if someone from work sees us?"

"I'm really not sure I care, but I don't want to get you in trouble at work." Stella leaned in. "You were the one talking about getting me naked not so long ago."

Stella's phone beeped.

"Oh, that's a Fenway foul." Aurora jabbed an elbow into Stella's side.

Stella smiled, but it fell from her face after glancing at the screen.

"Everything okay?"

"No. Kenzie fell off her bike, and Kim's taking her to the ER."

"We should go."

Stella didn't budge. "It's okay. I don't want you to miss the game, but I need to go."

"Are you sure you don't want me to go with you? How serious is it?"

"I don't know everything, but Kim thinks Kenz broke her wrist." Stella brushed her lips to Aurora's right cheek. "I'll be fine. Besides, I'll need updates about the game. Please, stay and enjoy it."

"Okay. Will you keep me updated about Kenzie?"

"Of course. I'm really sorry." Stella quickly kissed Aurora's cheek again before disappearing into the crowd.

Aurora stood next to one of the beer lines, losing the will to sit through a game by herself. But would it be better to go home alone? Aurora got into the line, thinking it best to make the most of the day, although the thought of Stella rushing away—no, that wasn't it. It was Stella not wanting Aurora to go with her. That rankled.

By the seventh inning, Stella had texted a photo of a cast, which Aurora assumed was on Kenzie. Aurora texted back she hoped Kenzie wasn't in too much pain and that the Sox were up by three.

The only reply Aurora got was: *Go Sox.*

CHAPTER TWENTY-SEVEN

"WHO KNOWS YOU BEST?" STELLA ROLLED ONTO HER side on the mattress and laid her arm over Aurora's stomach.

"Becky." Aurora ran a finger up and down Stella's arm.

"The one who's getting married?" Stella had to admit she was curious about Aurora's relationship with her roommate and why Aurora never invited Stella over. Was the reason solely to keep their relationship under the radar, or was there something Aurora wasn't telling Stella?

"Yes. We've known each other since we were kids. She was one of the few people who stood by me when I came out in high school. That was... let me remember, 2005 or 2006 maybe, and you'd think it would have been easier considering it was this century, but so many, even today, don't realize how stressful it is. And not all of my friends were accepting, which is kinda shocking considering I grew up in Boston. The city is known for being a liberal bastion, but that doesn't mean every Masshole is. Just the other day, I had an Uber driver, a female, who's a rabid Republican. She spent the entire time bashing the Green New Deal and socialism."

"Did you tell her you're gay?"

"I opted to keep that to myself. She scared me a little. A petite blonde with so much anger she can't keep it bottled up. You'd think she'd be more concerned about getting a decent tip and rating than ranting about her beliefs. Totally unprofessional."

"The true believers of any ideology usually can't hold it in. How'd your parents react to the news? About you being gay, that is?"

"Oh, they were supportive right out of the gate, but it was a change for everyone. It was Becky, though, who was my rock. She stood by me through thick and thin." Aurora laughed. "Her love didn't even waver when she learned I had a minor crush on her."

Stella untangled herself from Aurora to reach for a glass of water on the nightstand. "Oh, really? Is she gay or bi? I'd just assumed she's marrying a man, but now I'm realizing I never actually asked."

"She is. I think I've mentioned his name, Nathan."

"In today's world, a person can go by any name, and it's difficult to guess gender." Stella thought of Kim's new girl, Rooney, which was gender neutral.

"True, but Nate is a man."

"Is she bi, though?" Stella swallowed more water.

"No. I don't think so. There was a brief time when Becky considered the possibility. In high school, guys weren't falling over themselves to ask her out. She's uber smart and an odd mix of being opinionated but also the no-nonsense type when it comes to certain things. Becks can be somewhat intimidating to most men, and women, I think. Her confidence and intolerance for any BS can be off-putting. Not to mention, she's way better at math than most on the planet. I keep telling her to open her own accounting firm, which I think she's contemplating after she settles down with Nate."

"Did she consider you?" Stella steadied her breathing. Or

tried to. Why was this getting to Stella? Better yet, did Stella have any right to question this considering her relationship with Aurora hadn't been firmly established?

"We kissed when we were juniors. It just kinda happened. She stayed the night, and we were in my bed, talking. There was this moment between us. It's hard to explain, and it makes me laugh now." Aurora's laughter was lighthearted.

"You kissed Becky?" Stella's voice was on the edge of screeching level.

"Yep." Aurora didn't seem to pick up on Stella's reaction and pressed on, "It was a total disaster, and we both knew within a hot second it'd been a mistake."

Was that true, though? "How?"

"It was like kissing my sister. Once we both realized the other felt the same way, we got out of bed and gargled with Listerine, laughing."

Stella glugged the water, trying to keep the words forming in her mind from burbling out of her. It all sounded innocent. *Don't overreact, Stella.*

Aurora sat up. "Can I have some? I'm parched."

"Sure." Stella handed her the glass, still reeling in her thoughts. "How did you get over the crush?"

Aurora gulped the water. "It wasn't that hard after the disastrous kiss. I'm not even certain it was a legit crush now that I think about it. I was really shy and, to be frank, horny. She was the only girl I felt comfortable around. I think it was more about proximity, not true feelings." Aurora fanned her face with a hand. "Saying that out loud to you proves to me how silly it was to begin with. Oh, to be young again—no thanks. I'm amazed the majority of us survive adolescence. What a confusing time." Aurora laughed again. "I'm sure most of us are scarred by those years."

Stella offered a noncommittal shrug, her mind continuing to

torment her, racing about the kiss and whether or not Aurora was downplaying the significance.

Aurora plowed on. "Besides, don't most have a crush on a friend at some point in their life?"

Stella stared directly into Aurora's eyes, becoming more certain Aurora wasn't being completely honest. "I never did."

"What about your ex-wife? Were you two friends before you dated?"

"No."

"How'd you meet?" Aurora seemed genuinely interested.

Was that weird?

Stella answered, "Accidentally. I was leaving a coffee shop and ran smack dab into Kim, spilling a coffee all over her silk blouse. I offered to have it dry cleaned and insisted she give me her phone number so I could follow up."

"Did she take you up on the dry cleaning?"

"No. But she later confessed she thought I was adorably awkward and she felt sorry for me, so she gave me her number. When I called, we ended up talking for three hours."

"That's sweet."

"You are such a strange woman. I don't know many who would like to hear the woman she just had sex with talk about how she met an ex."

"I'm assuming since you two divorced you don't want to get back together. Or is there something you want to tell me?" Aurora narrowed her eyes, but the stern look gave way to a smile.

Stella shook her head. "Uh, no. No confession needed. What about you? Are you absolutely certain you still don't harbor feelings for Becky?"

"One hundred and ten percent positive!" Aurora squirmed. "I'd rather chop off a finger than consider anything with her."

Somewhat mollified, Stella reached for Aurora's hand.

"Please, don't ever say such a thing. I for one am quite fond of your fingers."

"Is that right, Dr. Gilbert?"

Stella nibbled on Aurora's index finger before sucking it into her mouth. "Very much so."

Aurora moaned.

Stella grinned, but it receded. "Besides Becky, who else has broken your heart?"

Aurora shook her head. "Becks never broke my heart."

Yeah, right. "Okay. Has anyone?"

"Of course." Aurora rolled onto her back. "Oh, gosh. That didn't happen until college. I was madly in love with my girl-friend. We were together every day for months. We became that annoying couple that completed each other's sentences. I swear, if I had a thought, she knew it." Aurora's expression turned dark. "Then one day, she just... disappeared." Aurora blew a breath onto her fingertips, slowly pulling them away to hammer home the woman floated off like a ghost.

"No word from her at all?"

"Nope. I bumped into her a few years later, and she practically ran away from me."

"You never found out what caused her to cut off contact or...?" Stella shrugged, at a loss for why anyone would do that to a person, most importantly to Aurora. Or had Aurora's relationship with Becky scared the woman off?

Aurora shook her head. "I knew she wasn't out, and her family was the super strict catholic type. According to her Facebook page, she's married to a man and has four kids."

"Wow." Stella hadn't expected that. "That must have hurt."

"It did. I'm not sure if it would have been better if she actually broke up with me instead of just running away. I'd like to think I'd understand her plight. She was close to her family, and she worried a lot about what they'd think of her if they knew about us. But she didn't give me a chance to be there for her or at least try to understand. Although it's hard to say for sure if I'd be okay with just being friends. Maybe it worked out for the best. For me at least. I have no idea what it's like for her being married and having kids." Aurora flicked a hand in a hopeless gesture. "I hope she's happy, but I know she'd claimed to many on several occasions she had zero attraction to men and even less desire to have children. Of course, at the time, she was still so young. From the photos, it seems like she loves being a mom. Do you think that's enough for someone? To be happy in one part of their life but not all?"

"It's hard to know. How many of us are entirely happy in life?" Stella's thoughts drifted back to Becky, but something else niggled at her mind. "How'd you meet your girlfriend in college?"

"We were the lezzie stereotype, and were roommates our freshman year."

"I'm seeing a theme with you and love," Stella said in what she hoped was a playful tone.

"What's that?"

"You fall for friends."

"Not all the time. Besides, I told you, I didn't fall for Becky. It was a confusing time. That's all."

"So there's no deep feelings at all? Or do you think that's the reason why you didn't want to find a date for Becky's wedding?"

Aurora burst into laughter. "Wow! That's a crazy thought. Really, Stella, it's a good thing you became a surgeon."

"Why's that?"

"Psychobabble doesn't seem to come naturally to you." Aurora wrapped her arm around Stella's bare stomach. "If you haven't noticed, right here and right now, I'm insanely happy."

This snapped Stella out of her funk. "What's the reason for this bliss?"

"Not what. Who."

"Who's the reason?"

"Need an ego boost?" Aurora took Stella's hand and kissed her fingertips.

"I hate making assumptions. It's the scientist aspect of me. Liking hard facts."

"Uh-huh. Keep telling yourself that after dishing about your wedding date theory."

"I was only teasing. Are you going to answer me?"

"Do I have to use words? Or can I act out my answer?"

"Like charades?"

Aurora captured Stella's lips, deepening the kiss. "Does that help you understand?"

"I might need another clue to fully understand."

Aurora laughed. "You're terrible. I love it."

"When you say terrible, do you mean in a good way?" Stella, now on top, pinned Aurora's arms above her head.

"Good Lord. How much ego boosting do you need tonight?" Aurora wiggled her arms free of Stella's grasp and held her.

Stella kissed the hollow of Aurora's throat. "I'm okay with physical answers if you're too shy to name and shame."

"There's no shame involved. Sex with you is…" Aurora acted out mind-blowing.

"Good to know. I'm kinda partial to it these days."

"You weren't before?" Aurora arched one eyebrow.

"Interesting question."

"And the answer would be…?" Aurora waved for Stella to fill in the blank.

"It seems to be getting better lately."

"Because…?"

Stella laughed. "You are incorrigible."

"How so?" Aurora asked innocently, batting her long lashes in that way of hers, letting Stella know Aurora was aware she was being shameless.

"Because you're fishing for compliments."

"Name one woman who doesn't like compliments."

"I don't."

"Really?" Aurora burst into laughter. "You've been working hard for some the past few minutes."

"Have not. Just wanted a clear and concise answer."

"Is that right?"

Stella stared wide-eyed.

"If you say so, but this seems like it could be fun. I'll sneak in a compliment at some point and see how you react."

"Now I'm not going to believe any of them out of fear."

"I'm terrible that way. Absolutely terrible."

"Yet, for some unexplainable reason, I like being with you."

Aurora's head tilted back, and she laughed. "Wow! You really know how to make a girl feel special."

CHAPTER TWENTY-EIGHT

"IT'S YOUR TURN IN THE HOT SEAT. WHAT WOMAN has broken your heart?" Aurora sat crossed-legged on the bed.

"N-no one, really," Stella stammered.

"You've never had your heart broken?" Aurora asked, not believing the answer but unsure how far to push Stella, who seemed uncomfortable with the question.

"I was always busy with everything and didn't have a lot of time to date."

"But you got married," Aurora stated without trying to insinuate she didn't truly believe Stella. Or if it were true, why had Stella married in the first place?

Stella nodded. "True."

"I'm guessing it wasn't an arranged marriage." Aurora ventured further down the path, trying to get to the truth without ruffling feathers.

Stella shook her head, seeming slightly amused but looking as if she was fighting a smile.

Aurora would be lying if she claimed she wasn't overly curious about Stella's marriage, including the reason or reasons for the dissolution. It was as if for months both of them had avoided this conversation. Aurora hadn't been able to pinpoint why Stella never brought it up, and her reluctance to do so made Aurora gun-shy aside from nibbling around the edges. But this seemed like a golden opportunity to press. "And you divorced."

"Also true." Stella settled on her back, closing her eyes.

"That didn't hurt you at all? Not even a tiny bit?" Aurora held out her thumb and forefinger, despite Stella not looking at her.

Stella sighed and reopened her eyes. "Divorce isn't fun. Not by a long shot."

"Yeah, but I'm not sure I'm buying she didn't break your heart."

"What do you know about it? Have you ever been married?" Stella snapped.

Aurora motioned for Stella to bring it down a level or twenty. "Easy. I wasn't trying to upset you. I promise."

"I'm sorry. Like I said, divorce isn't pleasant, and it brings up bad memories. Lawyers get involved. There's a lot of paperwork. Wrangling of finances. For the most part, we were able to skip a lot of the painful aspects for Mackenzie's sake."

"Sometimes I forget you have a daughter."

Stella seemed puzzled. "Why?"

"A couple of reasons. One: I've never met her. Two: you never mention her unless you absolutely have to. Like when she broke her arm and you had to leave our date at Fenway."

"I just mentioned her, though."

"I know, but it's like you don't want me to know about her or something." That was starting to get to Aurora. How could they be more than whatever they were if Stella didn't let her in?

"Really, Aurora, it's not like I've hidden Kenzie from you. All the photos with me and Mackenzie, here and in my office, not to mention her bedroom. The paintings on the fridge. Toys." Stella's open palm in the air suggested *et cetera*.

"But why haven't I met her?"

"It's hard to know when it's best to do that. We started out as fuck buddies. You don't introduce a fuck buddy to your daughter." Stella shrugged.

Aurora stared openmouthed.

"That was too harsh, wasn't it?"

"Uh, yeah. Besides, I was under the impression that we've morphed into more than fuck buddies. We've had a few conversations about it." Aurora willed her tears away.

"I know. It's just... hard to know what's right when it comes to Kenzie and you." Stella's voice was more vulnerable than normal.

This softened Aurora some. "I understand, I think."

"I'm not trying to hurt you or anything. I'm not explaining this right." Stella sighed. "It's hard for me to get a read sometimes on what you want. And I don't want to..."

"What?" Aurora reached for Stella's hand, threading their fingers, sensing a longed-for crack in Stella's protective shield.

"I don't want to get hurt." Stella's eyes fell to their conjoined hands.

"I thought you were the type that didn't get hurt when relationships ended."

Stella looked into Aurora's eyes. "It's possible that would change if you left."

"Really?"

"Yes."

Aurora leaned in for a kiss. "I don't plan on hurting you."

"What about your aversion to relationships?"

"I'm realizing it was my fear of not finding... you."

"Is that right?" Stella beamed.

"I wasn't the only one who said they didn't want a relationship. Has your opinion of them changed?"

"You can't tell?"

"Call me silly, but I'd like to hear it loud and clear." Aurora cupped a hand behind her ear.

"I already told you."

"You told me you want us to be in a relationship?"

"I told you how I felt."

"Uh, I'm sure I would have realized that." Aurora searched her memory bank but came up empty.

"You may not have noticed."

Aurora cocked her head. "Care to explain how I wouldn't notice?"

"The scarf."

"What scarf?" Aurora narrowed her eyes, not following Stella in the slightest.

"When I spelled out letters on your skin. They weren't random letters."

"Oh, that day. But, I don't remember them. What were the letters? Better yet, what did they spell?"

"Te quiero."

"Sounds Spanish."

"It is." Stella's face was blank.

"What does it mean?"

"Look it up."

"Oh my God!" Aurora shook her hands in the air. "Why can't you just tell me?"

"And ruin the fun?"

Aurora reached for her phone on the nightstand, but Stella stopped her.

"Look it up later."

"Why?" Aurora couldn't understand delaying finding out.

"I'm shy."

Aurora groaned. "You aren't playing fair."

"I'm aware."

"It almost makes me want to torture you."

Stella gripped Aurora's ass cheeks. "Torture, huh? As a doctor, I'm not sure I can condone certain types."

Aurora squeezed Stella's nipple between her fingers. "Is this out of bounds?"

Stella dug her head into her pillow, her eyes closed. "So far you're staying in bounds."

Aurora applied more pressure.

"Still okay."

Aurora released her fingers.

Stella's eyes popped open. "Hey. No fair!"

"No one said torture was enjoyable."

"I thought the torture involved the squeezing of the nipple."

"Nope. It was the stopping." Aurora looked at the alarm clock on Stella's bedside. "I have to get home for dinner with Becky."

"You're getting out of my bed to have dinner with another woman?"

"I am."

"I'm not sure I'm liking this turn of events. Are you sure you don't still have a crush on her?"

"I'm sticking with my answer of one hundred and ten percent. I'd invite you, but we'll be discussing wedding crappola, and it'll just bore you."

"I don't mind."

"You want to come?" Aurora climbed out of bed. "Uh, really?"

"I don't have to if you want to be alone with Becky."

"It's not that I want to be alone with her. It's just... Becky isn't the type who appreciates a change in plans."

Stella sat up in bed. "Are you sure she doesn't still have a crush on you?"

"Yes, considering she never did." Aurora looked around. "Any idea where I tossed my bra?" She scanned the possibilities. Not on the carpet. Or the chair. The stool was free of any type of clothing.

"We started in the bathroom. Remember? We had to shower after our run."

Aurora snapped her fingers. "Yes. It's starting to come back to me."

"Are you sure you're the younger one?"

"Not my fault this hot cougar fucked my brains out and I can't remember shit."

"I'm a cougar now?"

"Pretty sure you meet the criteria. Or do you prefer MILF?"

"You didn't just say that!" Stella's nose crinkled.

"Try being in my shoes." Aurora cringed, mostly for effect.

"You aren't wearing any."

"Nothing gets past you."

"Not true. I never guessed you had feelings for the bride-to-be."

"I don't!" Aurora tossed her hands heavenward.

"But I can't join you tonight."

Aurora rolled her eyes in an exaggerated way. "Seriously. This is how you want to end an enjoyable Saturday? Fighting about absolutely nothing?"

"I didn't want it to end yet," Stella pouted.

"It doesn't have to, you know. I'm only committed to dinner. And Becks is trying to lose weight for the big day. No dessert."

This piqued Stella's interest if the rise of her eyebrow was any indication.

"Dinner and then...?"

"Dessert here. What do you have on offer?"

"You want to see a dessert tray to determine if it's worth the trip?" Stella bit down on her lower lip.

"Now there's an idea. No wonder you're the one with the medical degree."

"Please. You're heads above me. If only you'd give yourself a chance."

Aurora placed a finger on Stella's lips. "No nursing school talk. Not right now. I'm trying to sear this image into my mind so I can survive dinner with the bridezilla." Aurora took a step back to look Stella's naked body up and down.

"Still not sure why you're leaving my bed to be with the bridezilla."

"I'm deranged like that."

"Now you tell me. Shall I come with you and hide in the shadows in case you need protection?"

Aurora laughed. "She's not that bad, and maybe it's time you two do meet. I'll arrange something with her if you're ready for that."

"I think I am."

Aurora leaned over and kissed Stella. "See you soon."

CHAPTER TWENTY-NINE

STELLA SAT AT HER DESK, HOLDING HER FOREHEAD IN her hands. If she had to deal with one more work issue, she'd scream.

The desk line rang.

Without opening her eyes, she fumbled for the receiver and brought it to her ear. She said, "Dr. Gilbert," in a brusque voice.

"Do you have a minute?" It was Aurora.

Stella's bad mood dissipated like a fog giving way to sunshine. "I always do for you."

"Aw. I needed to hear that. Can we meet after work at the Irish pub? I want a pint or five."

"As a doctor, I don't recommend five."

"It's either I drink myself into a coma, or I may start committing murder." Aurora let out an exasperated sigh.

"Let me take a wild stab in the dark. Kip?"

"And Isaac."

Stella groaned. "Are you wrapping up for the day?"

"I have a meeting with Alice in a few, but it'll be short considering they always are. Then I can head out. I can meet you there a little after five-thirty. That is if you can escape work that early."

"I can. In fact, I may scram now while I have the chance to vamoose without being seen. Maybe I'll tie some hospital sheets together and shimmy out the window."

"You having a bad day as well?" Aurora's voice showed concern.

"It's been one thing after another. I never knew becoming the point person for the school and hospital involved so much hand-holding. I mean, I work with doctors. Fucking stupid and petty doctors. And don't get me started on the students."

"I work with nerdy AV techs who think they're the only ones who know LCD stands for liquid crystal display. I gotta jump, sweetheart. See you soon at our place."

Stella replaced the phone, a smile forming. Aurora had called her *sweetheart* and said *our place*. Both had nice rings.

Her phone rang again. Briefly, she considered not looking at the caller ID but caved, only to wish she hadn't when she saw Kim's number.

"Hello."

"Stell?"

"Yes. Everything okay? Is it Mackenzie? She's not having issues with her wrist, is she?" Stella gripped the phone tightly.

"Everything's fine. Kenz doesn't like the cast, but there's nothing to worry about. I was wondering if we could get together one night next week for dinner," Kim said.

Stella opened up her planner. Try as she might, she could never trust her Outlook calendar. She was the type who had to see the entire week's schedule on paper. "Does a particular night work better for you?"

"Thursday. The Italian place we like."

Stella clicked her pen. "What time?"

"Eight-ish."

Stella marked it down. "Care to tell me what this is about?"

"I'd rather tell you in person."

Stella didn't like her tone. It wasn't sharp or commanding. Much meeker. So unlike Kim. "Are you okay, hun?"

"Yeah, I'm fine. You haven't called me *hun* in I don't know how long."

"I guess that's part of divorce."

"I guess you're right. I hope you have a nice weekend, and I'll see you on Thursday."

Stella hung up again, sighing. Then her self-preservation kicked in, and she packed up, taking the back stairs to avoid another pitfall that would derail her escape.

Outside, the sun hung low in the west, the air warm and smelling of hyacinths. Stella inhaled deeply. Spring had always been her favorite season. The promise of a fresh start.

Then she sneezed.

It also promised headaches and runny eyes, but her allergies were a small sacrifice after enduring the cold and bleak winter months in Massachusetts.

She purposely chose one of the side streets through the south end that wasn't near her home. Or rather the home where her ex lived. Not that she was avoiding her daughter, but the phone call with her ex had her on edge. Or was it her protectiveness roaring back to life? Either way, it wasn't what she wanted to focus on at the moment.

Aurora had called because she'd had a bad day, and Stella wanted to be there for her. That meant shoving thoughts of Kim out of her mind.

As soon as Stella arrived at the pub and was in the process of ordering a pint, Aurora texted she was on her way.

"Make that two, Conor." Stella held up two fingers.

"Jay-sus, Stella. I didn't peg you as the type, but you do look like you've been through the wringer this week."

Stella loved Conor's thick Boston Irish brogue, especially his pronunciation of *Jesus*.

"I'm living the dream. Living the dream."

"Makes me glad I'm a simple man." Conor grunted.

Stella laughed. "Says the man with three ex-wives."

"And about to get married to the fourth."

Stella's jaw hit the floor. "When did this happen?"

"Just last weekend." He leaned on the bar, making his hairy arms more pronounced. "Get this. She asked me." He removed a toothpick from his mouth and pointed it at Stella.

"Wow! How very progressive of you." Stella grinned.

"I'm trying to get with the times. She's a sweetheart, in a bossy way, and I never have a moment's peace." His eyes darted upward.

Stella laughed. "You're a sucker for those types."

"How about you? Do you ever plan on settling down again?"

Stella sucked in a breath, not because the idea scared her, but she didn't want to put the cart before the horse. She and Aurora were getting along well and growing closer, but did that mean they'd become so much more and even cohabitate? She didn't want to dissect that with Conor and said, "I'm about as settled as I plan to be. Kenzie keeps me grounded, and I have work."

"What about the new girl?"

"Aurora?" *Was it obvious to Conor that Stella was gaga for the girl?*

"Yeah. I like her. She's the type that keeps a person on their toes. Everyone needs a woman like that."

"She does do that, but it's way too early to think anything else other than meeting for beers and... st-stuff." Stella stumbled over the last word.

He rubbed the ginger scruff on his chin. "Is that what you fancy doctors call it? Stuff?"

The door opened, letting a sliver of sunlight into the darkened pub.

Conor straightened and jerked his head to the door.

Stella turned and smiled at Aurora's profile.

Conor greeted Aurora and then said, "Take a seat. I'll get these beers out to you soon."

"Thanks." Stella went to Aurora and gave her a hug. "That bad?"

Aurora shook, as if warding off the bad juju from the day. "It's looking better. When I have a beer in hand, everything will be right with the world." She pressed her palms together as if meditating like a Buddhist monk. Laughing, she said, "Shall we claim our usual table?"

Stella had to control a grin from overtaking her entire face. "Sounds good. I can't wait to hear about your day."

Aurora sat heavily in the chair, the leather creaking. "It wasn't like anything monumental happened. Kip, though—he has a way of wearing me down. Like a waterdrop tunneling a path through a rock surface over a millennium. Every day in the office seems to drag on and on." Aurora's body went limp in the chair.

"What'd he do today?"

"He started making bets with Isaac about absolutely everything. It started off innocently, and since they were entertaining themselves, I didn't intercede right away. What did I care if they were placing bets about how many minutes would pass before the next phone call? How many professors would come to the office? Vendors? Students having issues with study rooms? Those I could handle, and no money was actually being exchanged. Then before I could process how they even reached this point, Kip got it into his head that his farts were more flammable than Isaac's. He yanked out a lighter and started to get on the floor." Aurora leaned forward. "I swear, Stella, not once did I ever imagine I'd scream at one of my coworkers, *You will not light your fart on fire in the office!*"

"Did you actually scream that?"

Aurora nodded. "When he wants to be, he can be a total fucking nightmare. How is it certain men never grow up?" She smothered her face with a palm.

Conor arrived with their beers.

"Thanks," Stella and Aurora said in unison to Conor's retreating back.

Aurora raised her glass. "Cheers."

"Cheers, my dear." Stella sipped the drink. "You have some foam on your lip." She brushed her own mouth to demonstrate where.

Aurora patted it with a cocktail napkin. "Tell me about your day."

Stella's mind flashed to her ex, but she shoved that issue to the side. "Just the usual. Dr. Howie isn't happy with..." Stella looked at the low-hanging ceiling. "I can't even remember what the issue was now. Something inconsequential but he loves to get his boxers in a twist."

"I'm betting he wears briefs." Aurora's face lit up. "Maybe that's why he's always uptight."

"That's an interesting theory. Shall we place a bet?" Stella rubbed her thumb over her fingertips, indicating she was about to win easy money.

Aurora laughed. "I'm trying to picture you finding out the answer. Drop something and ask him to pick it up?"

"Can't. His lab coat shield's us from that. Mine does as well."

"A true shame because you have the cutest ass."

"Do I?" Stella looked over her shoulder, trying to assess it herself, but it was too hard considering she was sitting.

"You do. Have I not told you that before?"

Stella pretended to run through a mental file of compliments. "I don't seem to remember that one."

"Says the woman who said she didn't like compliments."

Aurora took another sip, the stress seeming to wash away. "I love Friday nights."

Stella relaxed into her seat, stretching out her legs. "They are nice. And, I didn't bring any work home with me this weekend."

"That's a change."

"It is. I'm blaming you." Stella flourished her beer at Aurora.

"I'll happily take the blame for you being kind to yourself."

Stella eyed Aurora, trying to determine if this was the time to bring up the thorny issue. "Maybe your day is another sign that you should pursue nursing. You clearly love the medical school environment. Why else would you put up with Kip's antics? You're capable. Dedicated. Intelligent."

Aurora mimed *yeah, yeah.* "So you keep saying, and I put up with Kip because I like to eat. Before I got the temp job, all I could afford was rice and beans. With Becky moving out soon, I may be back to that."

Stella opted not to focus on the Becky comment, since any mention of the woman's name got under her skin, even if she knew that shouldn't be the case. They were having a pleasant evening. Besides, Aurora wasn't Kim. Was she? "I'm serious, Aurora. I'm not saying being a nurse would be less stressful, but it does help when you're doing something you love."

Aurora held the pint glass pressed against her right cheek. "How would I manage? I'd have less free time, even if I went part-time at work and school. As it is, I barely spend time with Becky, my parents..." Her voice trailed off as her gaze drifted away.

"I understand." Stella would appreciate Aurora not spending any time with Becky. "I went through it with medical school. But don't focus on that part. Remember. She's getting married"—Stella couldn't bring herself to say her name—"and the first year of marriage is the hardest. Everyone thinks it's the honeymoon stage, but it's not. It's the year two adults have to adjust to living with each other, knowing they're legally bound to wake together every single day. It's a lot of pressure."

"Are you saying Becky won't have much time for me, so I should find a way to fill my hours? I can think of something else I'd rather do than study." Aurora trailed a finger down her neck, stopping at her cleavage.

"Oh, you'll need that to relieve the stress, and I happen to know a doctor who will personally advise you about how to manage your stress levels." Stella leaned forward in her chair and took Aurora's hand. "All teasing aside, you'll have the best tutor on the planet."

"You have a high opinion of yourself today, Miss I Hate Compliments." Aurora squeezed Stella's hand as if saying she was only teasing.

"I hate to see you wasting your potential managing Kip."

Aurora tossed up one hand, letting out a whoosh of air. "I'm not his manager, thank God. Although, Bri doesn't seem to know what to do with him either. I have to wonder if Kip was the sole reason she temporarily jumped ship to the main campus."

Stella smiled. "God you're beautiful."

"When I'm bitching?"

"All the time." A quiver went through Stella. "All the fucking time."

"Drink up. I'm finding a reserve of energy, and I don't want to waste it."

Stella didn't waste time finishing her beer. "Can you make it to my place, or shall we get a hotel room?"

"I'll try to hold on, but can we Uber? Not sure I can behave on the subway."

"I wouldn't dream of asking you to."

CHAPTER THIRTY

A BIRD'S CHIRP AND THE SCENT OF FRESHLY BREWED coffee woke Aurora. Opening her eyes, she smiled at Stella sitting on the edge of the bed with a cup.

"Morning, sunshine." Stella's endearing smile made it worthwhile for Aurora to push away her tiredness.

Aurora rubbed her eyes and then propped herself up with a pillow. "You know, when you get up early and make coffee, which is sweet, really, there is a downside to it."

"What's that?"

"It denies me the chance of having my way with you first thing." Aurora held the cup with both hands, the caffeine fumes invigorating her.

"It's the surgeon in me, but I don't see why we still can't be frisky."

Aurora sipped her drink. "And let this go to waste? I need a jolt in the morning, or I'm completely useless."

Stella ran her hand up Aurora's smooth leg, landing on her hip. "I know. Why do you think I make you a cup first thing? Some of us are morning people. You aren't one of those people."

"I know. I fucking hate mornings." Aurora grinned over her mug.

"For a hater, you seem rather perky."

"It's hard to be grumpy with you around. Maybe you were the answer all along to my difficulties with mornings." Aurora took another drink. "Do you know the second-best part of mornings with you?"

Stella arched an eyebrow.

"Shower time with you."

"I already showered."

"You can never be too clean."

Stella laughed. "You love getting your way."

"I do. And, are you really complaining right now? Me. You. Hot water. Do I actually have to point this out?" Aurora took another drink.

Stella tapped a nail against her front teeth. "Why did I shower earlier?"

"I have no fucking clue. It's not the first time I've stayed the night. We spend every other weekend together. I've been trying to give you a break since you're older, but you really do need to get with the program."

Stella slanted her head, squinting one eye. "How many weekends has it been?"

"Who knows? Usually two a month, and it's been what… six months? Once it gets above three, I can't keep track." Aurora pitched her right shoulder, carefully so as not to spill any precious coffee.

"Yeah, right." Stella shook her head. "Do you want another cup before the shower? Or something to eat? I don't want you passing out on my watch."

"Would you give me mouth to mouth?"

"I'm legally bound to," Stella said with mock seriousness.

"Is that the only reason?"

"In that situation, yes. Although, if you revive quickly, I may include some tongue action."

Aurora tossed her head back, laughing. "Do you teach your students how to be naughty?"

"Kissing is naughty?" Stella feigned confusion.

"I happen to know all the things you like doing with your tongue."

"You didn't answer my question. Coffee, muffin, or sex?"

"Yes."

Stella licked her lips. "In any particular order?"

"Use your best judgment, Doctor."

Stella rose from the bed and put out her hand. "Shower."

"A very wise choice."

CHAPTER THIRTY-ONE

THE SHOWER, WHILE SPOTLESS, WASN'T THE LARGEST Aurora had been in. While Stella hadn't mentioned it, Aurora suspected Stella, not for the first time, was on the hook for child support and possibly alimony. It was something they should talk about at some point, considering they seemed to be progressing way beyond fuck buddies, but Aurora sensed Stella's resistance to talking about things like that.

Stella tested the water by placing her hand under the stream. "I think it's ready."

"Why are you still dressed?" Aurora tugged on the waist of Stella's scrubs. "I'm not getting in until you do."

"Blackmail so early in the day."

"Call it whatever you want." Aurora didn't care about hiding her ulterior motive, just as long as she got her way with Stella.

Stella rolled her eyes. "I was planning on getting in. I wasn't sure if you wanted some time alone first."

"Nope. Strip."

Stella did.

They stepped under the hot water, and Aurora started to

fully wake. She was the type who had to shower before starting her day. She reached for the shampoo.

"Here, let me." Stella pumped the shampoo twice and started to lather Aurora's hair.

Aurora tilted her head back, shutting her eyes. "That feels good."

Stella massaged Aurora's scalp, and each rake of Stella's nails banished the darkness from Aurora's mind. How much of Stella's paycheck went toward her daughter and ex? Okay, maybe the darkness wasn't receding entirely.

Stella guided Aurora under the water to rinse the shampoo, leaving Aurora under the therapeutic water while Stella prepped a healthy amount of conditioner. Again, Stella massaged the hair product onto Aurora.

"Can you do this every morning?" Aurora practically purred like a kitten getting a belly rub. "This is the only way to start a new day."

Stella grinned. "I'll have to check my schedule." She squirted lavender shower gel onto a round mesh sponge. Starting with Aurora's backside, Stella attended to every square inch of skin. "Flip around for the front."

"You don't have to ask twice."

"I was counting on that." Stella delicately sponged Aurora's front, spending more time attending to the breasts. When Stella hunched down, Aurora's breath hitched. Stella swiped one leg then the other. "Now for the most important part." Stella glided her tongue along Aurora's lips, stilling briefly on her clit.

Aurora, in the corner of the shower tub, braced herself with an outstretched arm. She lifted one leg onto the lip of the tub, the water cascading over Stella's body, plastering her blonde locks to the side of her face. She glanced up, grinning, yanking wet strands of hair out of her mouth.

"Don't drown," Aurora said.

Stella snaked upward and ringed an arm around Aurora for a kiss. The type that promised so much in the not-so-distant future. Not just in the moment. But... Aurora really needed to find the guts to open up the discussion of where Stella thought their relationship was going.

Stella moved Aurora up against the wall, a hip pressing into Aurora's hot zone, effectively shutting down that thought for the moment.

"I love the way you look at me," Aurora said.

"How's that?"

"Like I'm the only person who matters."

"That's very true right now."

Stella's hand searched down below, seeking entrance.

Aurora clamped down on Stella's bottom lip when Stella inserted two fingers with force.

They continued kissing passionately, while Stella pumped her fingers in and out. Seconds ticked by. Then minutes. Stella broke free, and Aurora pressed the back of her head against the cold, wet tile.

Stella gazed into Aurora's face with a look that was hard to describe. Determined? Loving? A mixture of both? Stella made her way down, nipping at one erect nipple but not staying long.

Stella was fingering Aurora with much more urgency, so when Stella's tongue flicked Aurora's sex, she let out a moan. All the hairs on Aurora's body stood at attention. She pinched one of her nipples between a thumb and forefinger. Her other hand cupped the back of Stella's head, as a way of diverting the stream of water.

"Oh my God!" Aurora exclaimed.

Stella kicked her lapping into a higher gear.

"Oh, Stella. Don't stop!" Aurora fisted Stella's wet hair. "Oh, God, don't stop." A prickling of light behind her eyelids indicated Aurora was close. So fucking close.

Stella drove her fingers in deep and arched them upward, ushering forth an earth-shattering tremor.

"Jesus!" Aurora's arms reached out for the walls as her legs trembled.

A second wave rumbled through Aurora, and Stella rose to support Aurora, peppering her face with sweet kisses.

After, Stella said, "I can't get enough of you."

Aurora sighed contentedly. "Same here."

Stella continued to support Aurora's body with an arm.

"Seriously, why don't we do this every morning?"

"I'm not sure we'd ever leave the apartment if we did. Not to mention, it might be awkward the days Kenzie is here."

"Right. I forgot that part. I can't be here when she is." Aurora's insides went cold.

Stella cupped Aurora's face. "That's not—I'm sorry. I never meant to make you feel that way. I guess I never stopped to think fully how the Kenzie factor impacted you. Especially in the beginning since we spent more time doing the naked tango."

Aurora tried to smile, but every time Kenzie's name came up in conversation, it was hard to overcome the doubt that crept into her mind. Granted they'd started out as a no-relationship couple if there was such a thing. But that was over with, so why didn't Stella consider introducing Kenzie to Aurora? Wouldn't that be something someone would do if they were serious about the other?

Stella gazed deeply into Aurora's eyes. "What's going on in there?"

Aurora didn't have the necessary energy to broach the subject. Or so she convinced herself. "You just fucked my brains out in a hot shower. Do you really think any thoughts are going through my head? Although, if you offered me breakfast in bed, I wouldn't say no."

"Are you going back to bed? We need to work on your stamina."

"I plan on having more coffee and a muffin. Then I want to eat your pussy."

Stella turned off the water. "One coffee and muffin coming right up."

"That anxious for more?"

"Hey, I had a dry spell for quite some time before you, and now that you've reignited my sex drive, I can never say no."

"To me? Or to sex?" Aurora closed one eye, not sure what to expect.

"To you. Sex is just the cherry on top."

Aurora wanted to believe Stella, but there was the Mackenzie issue.

Not meeting Stella's daughter seemed like a big fucking deal that kept getting bigger. Was she making too much about it? Because when Stella gazed into her eyes, Aurora felt the intensity of the stare. And the feelings swirling inside. God, Stella was a dream come true. How could Aurora trust Stella, though? Especially since they danced around the big conversations, of which Aurora knew she was partly at fault. Hearing anything other than *I love you and want to be with you no matter the obstacles* was simply too much to risk.

Stella toweled off and eased on a robe. "Are you okay?"

"Yep," Aurora said, wishing it were true.

CHAPTER THIRTY-TWO

STELLA ARRIVED A FEW MINUTES EARLY AT THE Mexican restaurant and claimed their usual table. She cracked open *A is for Alibi*.

"Sorry, but you have to leave. This is where I meet my sister once a month. We have a standing reservation for this table."

Stella glanced up from the paperback to scowl at her sister. "Very funny."

"Holy cow! What have you done with my sister?" Rosie set her purse down on the table. "There's no way my blood sister would be early and reading a novel to pass the time. She's the type to always read emails or medical journals."

"Are you implying I'm a clone?" Stella asked, amused and slightly pleased with shocking Rosie some.

"It's the only explanation." Rosie flashed a *duh* look.

"Maybe I'm turning over a new leaf."

"Which leaf is that? More importantly, where can I find it? Because I have some ideas of things we can both change."

Stella didn't like the sound of that. Even incremental changes were scary. "What's with you tonight?"

"Oh, I thought we were trying on new personalities this

evening." Rosie pretended to play the drums, ending with imaginary cymbals.

"Are you on something?" Stella leaned over the table for a clear look into Rosie's eyes. "Legitimately?"

"I wish. Can you prescribe me something that'll get me high?"

Stella shushed her sister. "Stop that!"

Rosie snapped her fingers for the waiter, placing her usual order. After, she turned to her sister. "Are you going to tell me what's going on?"

"Clearly, I'm having dinner with an insane woman." Stella gestured to Rosie, implying that was the only evidence needed for such a statement.

"You've been doing that for years. Are you just noticing?"

"I am. I give you credit for hiding it well. I'm more familiar with kidneys, but I have to wonder if menopause causes women of your age to lose their minds."

Rosie waggled a finger in Stella's face. "You take that back. I am not menopausal. Nor am I close to that... stage."

"I hate to break it to you, but you are close and getting closer every day."

"Maybe this is why you're alone. Not many like fun haters who spread terrible rumors." Rosie snorted. "I'm so not menopausal."

"Are you showing signs? Is that why you're a bit more defensive than usual?"

Rosie shoved up her shirt sleeve, causing her gold bangles to rattle.

"Hot flash?" Stella joked.

Rosie groaned. "All right. Spill why you're feisty and in a good mood. For you, this counts as a good mood. It's almost like you've been getting laid or something."

Stella squirmed under Rosie's inspection.

Her sister's expression went from merriment to realization.

"Oh my! That's it, isn't it? You have been getting laid." Rosie did a little jig in her seat and then tapped her fingertips together. "Give me the deets."

"The deets?"

"Yep. Don't skimp, either. I love George, but the excitement of a new relationship—it's hard to harness it after waking in the same bed for years and hearing him fart first thing every morning."

Stella glared at Rosie. "I'm not going to share a thing with you to help you with whatever illusionary dream you're chasing. Every morning?" Stella pinched her face.

"I don't want to talk about George."

"You're the one who brought him into the conversation."

"Will you just share for once? Act like a normal sister? Or I'll start to shout at the top of my lungs that you're peddling illegal prescriptions."

Stella waved for her to stop teasing. "You'd never do that to me."

"I'll give you to the count of five before I start screaming. One. Two. Three. Four." Rosie formed a bullhorn around her mouth.

"Fine. What do you want to know? I would like it noted that I never ask you for details. Not the private ones."

Rosie frowned. "But those are the details every normal person wants to hear about."

"I'm not telling my sister about my sex life. Period." Stella punctuated her resolve with a brisk head nod.

"Who else can you tell, though? It's not like you have girl-friends, and by that, I mean friends who happen to be female, not ones you're boinking."

"I don't need to tell anyone. I'm perfectly happy not sharing anything about it."

"*It?* That's an interesting way to describe someone." Rosie didn't bother hiding condemnation in her expression.

"I'm not going to fall for that."

"Fine!" Rosie sipped her drink. "At least tell me her name. It is a woman, right? You haven't changed completely?" She pointed to Stella's book as if that were damning evidence.

Stella shook her head. "Yes, it's a she. Aurora."

"Aurora. I'm not sure I've ever met an Aurora. Kinda youngish sounding."

Stella shifted in her seat, keeping her eyes cast downward.

"She is. Oh wow! My uptight baby sister has game. Consider my mind…" Rosie finished the thought with her fingers simulating an explosion. "I can't believe you're sleeping with someone younger and I'm not."

"You're married!"

"I know. For the second time and I'm wondering why I bothered."

That nabbed Stella's attention. "Everything okay? Besides the farting issue?"

"Yeah, yeah. It's just one of those weeks when his very presence drives me crazy. Do you know how loudly he swallows his coffee?" Rosie demonstrated by gulping her drink. Then she cringed. "If I have to hear that one more time, I may go postal."

"Because you're perfect?"

"I am without a doubt. How can you even question that?" Rosie narrowed her eyes in an accusatory fashion.

Stella tsked. "You, dear sister, make me glad I'm not married anymore. Speaking of, Kim called to meet me for dinner. Then she cancelled but said we should get together soon."

Rosie traced the lip of her glass. "That's out of the blue, isn't it?"

Stella nodded.

"Do you know why?"

"Nope. She just said she had something she wanted to tell me."

"Does she know about Aurora?"

"I don't see how."

"Kenzie hasn't met her, then." Rosie gave Stella a knowing look.

"No. We haven't reached that stage, and I don't know if we will." Stella wasn't able to pinpoint why she was resistant to introducing Kenzie to Aurora. Becky was an issue, but was she the only one that caused Stella to hit the breaks when it came to moving forward in the relationship?

"Are you sure? I haven't seen you this relaxed in I don't know how long, but your eyes are darker now. What's up?"

"Nothing."

Rosie splayed her fingers on the table and ducked her head to peer into Stella's eyes. "There's something there. Don't make me threaten you again."

"It's just—have you ever had a crush on your best friend?"

"Okay. I wasn't expecting that question. What's the source? I know Aurora's not one of your former BFFs considering she's younger. How much younger by the way? Like a tadpole when you were in medical school?"

"You're demented, you know that?"

Rosie cupped her ear. "I didn't hear a number."

"Twenty-nine."

Rosie whistled. "Still in her twenties. Score!" She raised her hand for a high five.

Stella ignored it. "Well, not for much longer. Her birthday is in July. So, have you ever had a crush on your best friend?"

Rosie, seeming to not want to waste the energy, beckoned their waiter to order chips and guacamole. After, she answered, "Nothing's coming to mind. Are you afraid Aurora has a crush on hers?"

"She did. Back in high school."

"In high school? Why does that matter now?"

"She's the maid of honor for said best friend."

"Exactly. The crush was over a decade ago. Wait. Are you

saying you think Aurora's actually in love with this other woman?"

"No, of course not." *Was she?* "It's just weird, isn't it? They did kiss, though."

"In high school?"

Stella nodded.

"Please don't go all Stella-like. Kissing one's best friend in high school really doesn't warrant much attention. Everything about adolescence is weird. It's a total mind fuck. Besides, I seem to remember a certain young woman who developed a crush on her best friend."

"I did not!" Damn. Why had Stella overreacted to that?

"If you say so, but I remember you pining over Kate your junior year."

"If it makes you feel better to believe that, go ahead." Stella stared at the cover of her novel, trying to recall the right word for the particular shade of green.

"It's amazing how much you don't know about yourself." Rosie seemed to take a cleansing breath. "How did you even find out about Aurora's crush?"

"She admitted it."

"Because?" Rosie quirked one eyebrow.

"She was sharing her coming out process and how Becky stood by her side even when Becky found out Aurora had a crush on her."

"And the kiss?"

"Apparently, they shared a moment during a sleepover."

"Just a measly kiss?"

"I think so. At least, that's what she said." How could it be, though, during that time of Aurora's coming out process?

"Sounds pretty innocent." Rosie rubbed her chin. "What's getting your panties in a bunch? Did she admit she still has feelings for her friend? Did she say being part of the wedding would be difficult?"

"No. She hasn't said any of that."

"Talk to me. What's bugging you?" Rosie pantomimed having to shake it out of Stella.

"I'm just having a hard time knowing she had a crush on Becky and now I'm going as Aurora's date to the wedding."

"She's taking you to her best friend's wedding, and you're worried she's in love with Becky? Oh, Stella. You're worse off than I thought." Rosie pressed her fingertips into her forehead as if having to hold it in place.

"What does that mean?"

"You have serious trust issues. I mean, have you considered therapy? Because from what you've told me, there's nothing to stress about. I think this has a lot more to do with Kim than Aurora, and that's just not fair to Aurora. She can't be held accountable for another person's mistakes."

"This has nothing to do with Kim," Stella protested.

"Can you look me in the eye and say that you don't think all women cheat after Kim broke your heart?" Rosie motioned for Stella to meet her gaze. "I'm waiting."

"I'm not being irrational. Just cautious. Aurora wants to meet Kenzie, and I don't want to take that step until I know for certain."

"Know what?"

"That... we'll work."

"Oh, Stella. There's no guarantee that any couple will last until the end of time, but that doesn't mean you have to live like a nun for the rest of your life."

"I'm not. Don't you remember wanting the details?"

"I'm more concerned about your jealous streak at the moment. The lengths it'll go to sabotage any chance at happiness."

"What jealous streak?" Stella scooted back in her seat.

"Please, don't give into it. Not all women will cheat. I know what Kim did hurt like hell. Especially considering who she slept with. But you have to trust again. Do you care about Aurora?"

"It's not as simple as that?"

"It is, and it isn't. That's love."

"I'll get to judge for myself if Aurora still has a thing for Becky."

"You aren't going to do something stupid, are you? Like hire a PI?"

Stella shook her head. "Not at all. We're going to dinner with Becky next week."

Rosie seemed overly relieved, but her eyes clouded over once again. "Just don't go with guns blazing like some macho male that turns off women."

CHAPTER THIRTY-THREE

AURORA GOT OFF THE C LINE TRAIN TWO STOPS FROM the end of the line at Cleveland Circle and hung a left onto the side street where her parents lived in a spacious two-bedroom apartment. They'd moved there a few years back, wanting to downsize but still needing to be close to the city. Her parents had never been the traditional suburb types, and Brookline was about as rural as they'd go.

Her mom was outside with Ralph, their rescue dog that seemed to be a smashup of every tiny dog breed. Her mom waved and smiled broadly. "I'd thought we'd take Ralphie for a walk at the reservoir."

"Which one?"

"Chestnut is bigger."

"Dad isn't coming?" Aurora peered around, which was pointless since her father hadn't been the type to join these walks even when he was healthy.

Her mom shook her head, but her expression showed nothing but happiness. "He's resting right now."

Aurora sensed her mom was being brave so as not to worry Aurora. She'd play along for her mom's sake. But needing a second, Aurora leaned down and let the dog kiss her face, allowing her to swipe away a tear. Ralph let out an excited yip. "Lead the way, Ralphie."

Her mom smiled.

"It must be so nice to be a dog." Aurora straightened, back in control of her emotions. "At least a pampered one like Ralph."

"I'm hoping to come back as a spoiled pet in my next life. And I plan on getting fat and sassy."

"You're already sassy," Aurora joked.

They made their way to the reservoir along Beacon Street, which was still relatively quiet for a late sunny weekend morning in May. Stella was with Kenzie, meaning Aurora hadn't seen her since passing in the hallway at work on Friday afternoon. Ralph happily sniffed the sidewalk, stopping occasionally to leave a trace.

"How is Dad really doing?" Aurora asked.

"Let's hold off on that until we get to our bench."

Aurora didn't like the sound of that.

"It's not bad news. I promise." Her mom avoided Aurora's eye.

"Okay." Hearing it wasn't bad news hadn't alleviated Aurora's fear one bit.

They walked by the pizza place she and Stella had been to a few times, and the workers must have been prepping for the day because the smell of baking crust wafted in the air.

"Shall we pick up a pie for lunch on the way back?" Her mom asked.

"Sounds great. Want me to pop in and place the order so it's ready when we swing back by?"

"Good thinking! No wonder the school hired you full-time. The usual please." Her mom stood off to the side of the entrance with Ralphie sniffing the ground.

Aurora walked through the glass door. She didn't recognize

the man dressed in a white short sleeve shirt and black trousers, but she hardly ever came here on the weekend. "Can I place an order to be picked up in an hour or so?"

"Of course. What can I get you?"

"A large super veggie, extra mushrooms if possible." Her father loved them. "And garlic bread with cheese and jalapeño poppers."

He wrote the order on his pad and then punched it into an old-fashioned register that belonged in a museum, not a thriving pizza place. "Do you want to pay now or when you pick up?"

"Now, please." Aurora handed over her debit card.

He tucked a pencil behind his ear. "Okay. Everything will be ready by noon."

Aurora met her mom and an extremely wiggly Ralphie on the sidewalk. "All set for noon. Now, let's get this beast some exercise." Aurora took the retractable leash from her mom.

They crossed at the corner and climbed the stairs leading to the trail around the water. Two female runners, happily chatting, zoomed by on the dirt path.

"Are you going to tell me the news soon?" Aurora asked.

Her mom smiled. "You've never been patient."

"Considering everything running through my brain, I think I am being extremely patient."

"I'm sorry, sweetheart. I'm not trying to be cruel."

Aurora shortened Ralph's leash as they circumnavigated around a gaggle of geese, who flapped their wings, some of them spitting. Ralph, who Aurora suspected was terrified of the birds, pretended not to see them and kept his nose to the ground on the far side of the dirt path, away from the feathered bullies.

Her mom waved to the first bench on this side of the water. It wasn't their usual, but Aurora wasn't going to complain. Ralph knew the drill when Aurora hooked his leash to one of the bench legs, and he happily rolled around on the brown grass.

"You're kinda scaring me," Aurora confessed.

"I'm not trying to. Your uncle is a match."

"That's great news, isn't it? In case Dad needs a kidney."

"Yes." Her mom squeezed Aurora's thigh. "You know me. I always worry about everything. It comes with being a mom and wife."

Aurora held her mom's hand. "It has to be so very hard for you. Watching Dad go through this."

Her mom pressed her lips together.

"It's okay to talk about it. You can tell me anything. I'm old enough now."

"Almost thirty. How do I have a daughter who's almost thirty?"

"You don't look it. I hope I'm still in such great shape when I'm your age."

"Flattery will get you everywhere." Her mom laughed. "I'm fine, I promise. I'll be greatly relieved when it's over."

"Over?" Aurora reached for her mom's hand. "Then it's a go? He needs a kidney?"

Her mom nodded.

"Has the date been set?"

"That's being worked out, although, it looks like we won't make Becky's wedding after all."

"I'm sure she'll understand. You two have always been like parents to her. Sometimes, I thought you liked her better."

Her mom chuckled. "Only because we were never actually in charge of her, and she's not as stubborn as you are. Stubborn daughters can be difficult."

"Says the woman I inherited it from."

"Oh, I'm aware. Your father reminds me every day I'm set in my ways."

Aurora's eyes skimmed the water's surface. "I wish I could

be the donor. It would be so much easier. Uncle John isn't exactly a spring chicken."

"I know you do, but that's life. We can't always have what we want. Let's just be glad it's working out." Ralph jumped into her mom's lap and licked her face. "He always seems to know when I need love."

Aurora motioned for the dog to get onto her lap. "I need some love, Ralphie."

He happily obliged.

"What's going on with you these days?" her mom asked.

"Just life."

Her mom bumped Aurora's shoulder. "I'm not buying that. Are you still upset about the news concerning the sperm donor?"

"I still don't get it. Why did you lie to me?" Aurora looked her mom in the eyes.

"I never saw it that way because it wasn't a big deal to us. Your father was so excited about you before I even conceived. He has always wanted to be a father, and he's so proud of you, Aurora. So very proud."

"Have you always wanted to be a mother?" Aurora knew the answer, but she needed confirmation.

"Yes."

"But why the secrecy? You literally almost had thirty years to tell me, and you only did when it became absolutely necessary."

"It just never came up." She looked into Aurora's eyes. "You were always his daughter. Blood relation or not. Neither of us ever saw it any other way."

Aurora broke off eye contact, focusing her attention on Ralphie. "That seems to be the theme in my life. Not telling or sharing everything."

"You know, the opening up thing is a two-way street. Tell me what's troubling you."

"It's about a woman."

"Tell me the parts I don't know." Her mom chuckled quietly.

Aurora's eyes darted to the puffy white clouds overhead. "You think you're so smart."

Her mom gave Aurora the *confess all* stare, so Aurora did. After, her mom's eyes skimmed the horizon across the water. "Are you ready to have a child in your life?"

"Yeah, I am. I know I haven't met Kenzie, but if she's anything like Stella, how could I not love her?"

"Is Stella the birth mom?"

"No, but it's no secret I've learned some traits from Dad, and well…"

"True. He doesn't like to finish difficult sentences either."

Aurora laughed. "In a way, it's been good for you and Dad that I met Stella when I did."

"Why's that?"

"How do I explain this without it coming out wrong? It's been eye-opening to know how much Stella loves her daughter, who biologically isn't hers. All the sacrifices she makes and how hard she works."

"Kids have that effect. They're hard not to love."

"It's difficult to explain or to understand entirely, but Kenzie already holds a spot in my heart. Do you think I'd be good with a kid?"

Her mom squeezed Aurora's thigh. "No doubt about that. I know you don't like pressing buttons in case they set people off, but I think you need to have a *come to Jesus* talk with Stella soon. It'll only fester, and you tend to wait until it's too late."

"I think I got that from my parents."

Her mom turned to face Aurora completely. "I deserved that, but don't discount what I'm saying. If you love this woman, talk to her. No good will come from avoiding the conversation."

CHAPTER THIRTY-FOUR

"WOW! YOU LOOK AMAZING." STELLA'S EYES TOOK IN the tropical floral print dress, with the hemline several inches higher up Aurora's thigh than Stella would prefer and a halter top neckline that appeared to plunge all the way to her navel. The flesh colored strappy high-heeled sandals highlighted the curves of Aurora's calves. If there was a definition for a *fuck me* outfit, this was it.

"What? This old thing." Aurora wore a *cat ate the canary* grin.

"I know I asked to meet Becky, but can we cancel? Because..." Stella hooked a thumb over her shoulder to the bedroom.

Aurora laughed. "That wouldn't be the best way to impress Becky."

"I'm not trying to impress her. Are *you*?"

Aurora wore a confused expression. "Uh, no. Are you ready?"

Stella glanced down at the white palazzo pants and striped navy and white boatneck shirt Aurora had helped pick out. "Do I look presentable?"

Aurora took a step back, appraising Stella. "Just barely."

"Geez. Way to make me feel even more intimidated."

"Why are you intimidated?"

"I'm meeting your best friend, and you look like you're taking a spin on a runway. Not to mention, I'm out over my ski tips, being the oldie in the group."

Aurora hooked her arm through Stella's. "You need to stop thinking that way. You are not old. Do you mind if we get a car? These shoes are killer."

"Do you need to change?" Stella secretly hoped Aurora would.

"Is that your way of saying you lied earlier and you don't like my outfit?"

"Are you kidding me? Although, it may be hard for me to keep my hands off you." To prove this, Stella ran a hand down Aurora's front.

"Let's get going. The sooner we get dinner over with, the sooner we can come home and you can have your way with me." Aurora let out a sexy growl.

"You said a car, right?" Stella whipped out her phone and requested one on the newly uploaded app.

"You're terrible." Aurora nibbled on Stella's ear. "I absolutely love it."

"Oh, if you only knew all the dirty thoughts running through my mind right now. The car will be out front in two minutes. We better get going."

In the backseat, Stella said, "Do you know I meet my sister once a month at Mazatlán?"

Aurora faced her. "What's your favorite dessert there?"

"I don't get it often but the fried ice cream."

Aurora grinned. "The streak continues."

They rode in silence, Stella stealing looks at Aurora's smooth legs, wishing they were wrapped around her.

The driver pulled up at the curb. After getting out, Stella

helped Aurora out of the car, standing close. "You even smell tasty."

"I'm getting the impression I need to dress like this more often. Apparently, I've been denying you."

"I'm trying not to hold it against you that you pulled this out for our night with Becky instead of a date with me."

"Oh, please. It's not like I haven't worn anything sexy before."

"True, but this may have set a really high bar." Stella held her hand in the air slightly above her head.

Aurora placed a finger on Stella's chin. "Lucky for you, I like a challenge. And clothes. A win-win for me."

"And me." Stella leaned close to Aurora's ear. "I want you. Can you rethink the no sex in a bathroom rule?"

"Oh my God, you look fucking gorgeous."

Stella turned to the mousy-brown haired woman that was much taller than she was expecting.

Aurora tossed her arms around who Stella guessed was Becky. "Thanks, doll."

Doll?

Aurora continued, "You look adorbs. What's your shirt say?" Aurora yanked Becky's casual black blazer to reveal the goods. "Another Star Wars quote. You're such a nerd. Don't ever change." Aurora put an arm around Becky's neck. "This is Stella."

Stella held out a hand, which was received meekly. Surprising since Becky was a shoo-in for a rugby player. "It's a pleasure to finally meet you."

"I didn't think you actually existed."

"Yet, here I stand." Stella winced, recalling her sister's advice not to go macho-jerk on Becky.

Becky turned to Aurora. "I'm famished."

"You're always famished."

"It's the stress. Why did I say yes to Nathan? It's ruining my life." Becky didn't seem hard-pressed.

"Oh, stop. You're gaga over the guy," Aurora said. Becky motioned to her shirt and jeans. "Do I seem like the type of girl who goes gaga over a guy?"

She had a point, which rankled Stella further.

Aurora rolled her eyes. "Let's get a margarita in her before she really starts to spill the beans." Aurora put an arm out for Stella and then one for Becky. "It's so great to have both of my girls finally meet."

Stella swallowed a reply and walked inside, blind with the green-eyed monster.

CHAPTER THIRTY-FIVE

AURORA SIPPED HER STRAWBERRY MARGARITA, laughing at Becky's joke. Out of the corner of her eye, she spied Stella fidgeting. Aurora placed her hand on Stella's thigh. Stella stiffened at first but relaxed after a second.

"I'll be right back." Becky rose and headed for the bathroom.

Aurora took the chance to ask, "Are you okay? You've been pretty quiet."

"I'm fine."

Aurora regarded Stella. "Usually when someone says they're fine in that tone, it means they're lying. What's wrong?"

Stella's expression eased somewhat. "Nothing. I might be a little nervous; that's all. Out of practice."

"What do you mean?" Aurora's brow furrowed.

"Outside of work, I'm only around you, my sister, and my daughter. I think I need to brush up on my social skills." Stella seemed to go out of her way to seem as lighthearted as possible, resulting with Aurora becoming more concerned.

"Are you sure that's it? You seem tense in a pissed off way."

"I'm not. I promise."

"Okay." Aurora wasn't buying it, but she didn't want to start an argument with Becky due to return any moment.

Becky reappeared. "So, I hear you're a surgeon. What's it like slicing someone open?"

"Becks!" Aurora laughed, releasing some of her tension. "Can we not talk about that right before I eat enchiladas."

Becky pinched her face. "For someone who wants to be a nurse, you're kinda squeamish-y."

"Pretty sure that's not a word. And, to correct the record, I wanted to be a nurse." Aurora picked up her knife and jabbed the tip onto the tabletop. "That dream is dead."

Becky looked to Stella. "She's never dramatic."

Stella actually laughed.

"Can you talk some sense into her? I can't seem to get through to her." Becky tapped her own noggin. "Hard as a rock, she is."

"Channeling Yoda?" Aurora asked.

Becky flipped Aurora the bird, then turned back to Stella. "Can you?"

"About nursing school or just in general?" Stella joked.

Becky's eyes widened. "Oooh, I like this one."

"Gosh, Becks, you make it sound like I've introduced you to a ton of women."

"Not lately, no." Becky leaned back for the waiter to set down her tamale platter. "There was a string of them in college, though."

Aurora kicked Becky under the table.

"Ouch! Was that a secret?" Becky leaned over the table, presumably rubbing her shin. "What are you wearing? Spikes?"

"I wish. If you haven't noticed, I really like Stella. So, no more talk about other girls. Capisce?" Aurora did her best mafioso impression.

Becky studied Aurora and then Stella, before taking a sip of her drink.

Aurora squeezed Stella's arm, before tucking into her enchiladas. "Oh, wow. These are fab. You have to try a bite." Aurora loaded up her fork and handed it to Becky.

Becky gave Aurora her fork with a bite of tamale. Aurora proceeded to load up what was Becky's fork and prompted Stella to eat off it. Stella hesitated. "Trust me. It's delish," Aurora prodded.

"She's not lying. Not about that." Becky laughed, all the while moving in her seat. "Ha! I knew you'd try to kick. Hope you broke a toe."

"No breaking toes." Stella turned to Aurora. "No broken bones. Not tonight."

"But I sleep with a doctor. Are you saying you won't put me back together?"

"I would, but I prefer not to."

Aurora whispered in Stella's ear. "I have much better plans for later."

Stella blushed.

Becky grinned.

Aurora eyed Stella's plate, placing a hand between Stella's legs. "Can I try your carnitas?"

Stella swallowed. "Help yourself."

Aurora did, leaving her hand and enjoying the warmth of Stella's pussy. "Spicy," she teased.

Stella smiled and then guzzled ice water.

"Aside from ruing your decision to get married, how's life, Becky?" Aurora asked, not wanting to ignore her best friend.

"Not bad. Nate's flying home in a few days."

"I should hope so. The wedding is two weeks away."

"Eleven days and seven hours, but who's counting."

"The accountant," Aurora quipped.

"You think you're so funny. How's your speech coming along?"

Aurora snapped her fingers. "Oh, I keep forgetting that part."

"Nice try. Do you want me to write it for you?"

"Will you?" Aurora sounded hopeful.

Becky groaned. "Because I don't have enough on my plate."

Aurora looked at Stella. "She acts like I'm at fault for everything." She turned to Becky. "You're the one who decided on having a wedding when I told you not to."

"What do you mean?" Stella asked.

"I thought it would be so romantic if they ran off into the sunset together, eloped and not trouble the innocents."

"Innocents!" Becky scoffed.

Aurora gave her a glare that made Becky wilt some in her seat.

"Be careful of this one, Stella. She's been known to eat her mates after... mating." Becky hiccupped.

"I think you've had enough to drink." Aurora gave Becky her water, which was full.

"Please. I'm going to be married soon, which means I have one foot in the grave. I plan to live it up while I can." Becky snapped her fingers as if expecting the waiter to pop up from the floor. When no one appeared, she took Aurora's drink. "Thanks, doll."

Aurora rolled her eyes. "You'd think a giant of a woman could hold her liquor."

"I haven't eaten in days. I can't seem to drop the last few pounds that I banked on losing when I did a juice cleanse."

"Please. You're beautiful the way you are. Don't you dare starve yourself!" Aurora pointed her fork at Becky, which Becky took and plunged into her tamale. "Something's telling me we'll be escorting Becky home tonight."

Stella nodded, not looking all that thrilled about the prospect.

Becky seemed to be in her own world.

"Although, we haven't had a chance to... in my bed." Aurora tried to impart what she wanted with a meaningful glare.

"Fuck. That's the word you're looking for." Becky reached over for a bite of Aurora's meal. "Man, these are good. So good."

Aurora caught their waiter's eye and made the *check please* motion.

CHAPTER THIRTY-SIX

STELLA STOOD UNDER THE DEEP BLUE SKY, STARING across the vibrant green grass at Aurora in a lilac bridesmaid dress. Aurora looked absolutely stunning with her hair in a messy updo. She was in mid-conversation with an older woman with gray hair, and by the looks of it, they were quite close. The woman placed her hand on Aurora's arm, whispering something in Aurora's ear. Aurora tossed her head back, laughing.

God, she was sexy.

"Hello," a woman in her sixties addressed Stella. "Are you a friend of the bride or groom?"

"Actually, I'm here with Aurora, the maid of honor."

"Oh, everyone here knows Aurora. You must be Stella. She asked me earlier today to keep an eye on you. To make sure you don't slip away." The woman laughed. "Okay, she didn't really say that, but Aurora has a hard time keeping a hold of a woman."

"Is that right?" Stella asked. "I'm sorry. You're at an advantage since you know who I am, but I don't know your name."

"Celia. Mother of the bride."

"Lovely to meet you. You must be so proud of... your daughter."

The woman supplied her daughter's name, perhaps thinking Stella had forgotten it. "I'm amazed this day finally arrived. I know it's the trend. Getting married later in life, but Becky dragged her feet. Nathan wanted to get married almost right after their first date, five years ago, but Becky took a lot of persuading."

"Is that right?" Stella's hackles started to rise. "What was her reason for resisting?" Or who?

"Oh, you know. Fearful about settling down. Becky never played the field much, and I think part of her thinks she cheated herself by not exploring."

With men or women? Stella's eyes sought Aurora, but she had moved away from the woman she'd been speaking to, and now Aurora was nowhere in sight. "That's a frank assessment."

"Becky hates my candor. But, when you get to be our age, why not? Am I right?"

Stella dipped her head, not liking being compared to Celia, who was at least fifteen years older and had a daughter getting married. Kenzie wasn't even a teenager yet.

"Oh, one of the caterers is trying to get my attention. Would you excuse me?" Celia squeezed Stella's shoulder. "Don't run off. Aurora would never forgive me."

Stella reached for another glass of white wine from one of the waiters. After a sip, her eyes roved over the venue in search of the MIA Aurora, finally landing on her standing next to the bride. Both were laughing, but then the mood changed, and from afar, it appeared there were tears. Aurora wrapped her arms around Becky's neck, and the two embraced. Like they fit completely together.

Stella glanced around to see if anyone else had noticed this interaction, but everyone seemed to be blind to the connection between the so-called best friends and roommates.

Nathan, much to Stella's relief, approached, and Becky leaned against him, resting her head on his shoulder.

Aurora moved on to another woman to chat. Jealousy perhaps or keeping other things incognito?

Stella made her move and approached. "There you are." She kissed Aurora's cheek, not caring they were out in public. Stella hadn't recognized any of the guests. Besides, both of them tacitly gave up on the ruse that they weren't dating. They stayed professional at work, but outside of it, they started to be more affectionate.

"Is this the doctor lady?" the portly woman, who had to be nearly ninety years old, asked.

Aurora laughed. "Trudy, I'd like you to meet Stella."

Stella shook Trudy's pudgy hand.

"Are you really a doctor?" Trudy looked her up and down.

"Guilty."

"Do you deliver babies?"

"Not since my residency."

Aurora whispered in Stella's ear she'd be right back.

"My father had a lady doctor in his office. They were OBGYNs. It caused quite a stir when my father hired her, but he was a feminist. Even more so than my mother or I, really."

Stella, not wanting to get embroiled into a conversation about feminism, attempted to steer the conversation to safer waters. "Are you with the bride or groom?"

"I'm Becky's grandmother."

"I don't believe it. You seem too young to be a grandmother."

Trudy gave Stella a dismissive wave. "Trust me, honey. I'm older than God. At least, I feel that way with the way my bones creak. Just getting out of bed is risking my life. Be a dear. Track me down a scotch on the rocks." Trudy shooed Stella to get on the task sooner rather than later.

"Of course."

Aurora met Stella at the bar. "I saw Trudy bossing you around."

"After telling me she's older than God and risks her life every day simply getting out of bed."

"She's been saying that since I was yea high." Aurora held her hand waist height. "Take my advice. Drop off the drink and say you have an emergency. Don't engage in idle chitchat. Unless you want to bang your head against a wall. Because no matter how much you'll want to, it's never appropriate to punch out an opinionated old lady. Especially not at a wedding with so many witnesses."

Stella gave the scotch order to the bartender and then turned her attention to Aurora. "Is that why you bailed?"

"Yep, sorry. I know it's terrible. I totally left you on your own, but it was for the best. No way do I want to ruin Becky's special day, and I haven't quite mastered ignoring Trudy. She knows exactly how to get under my skin in under five seconds flat. I'm still traumatized by some of our conversations about girls who like girls. That's how she puts it." Aurora mimed strangling Trudy. "If I don't see you in five minutes, I'll send Celia to save you." Aurora kissed Stella's cheek. "Good luck."

Stella clutched the tumbler, wondering if she could have one of the waiters drop it off, but the two who zoomed by didn't make eye contact. Had they been warned?

"Here you go, Trudy." Stella handed off the tumbler. "If you'll excuse me—"

"Did Aurora tell you to drop and dash?" Trudy barked.

"What? No."

"Then you won't mind keeping an old lady company." Trudy leaned on her cane with one hand.

Stella smiled to the best of her ability. "Absolutely."

"You are brave. Everyone else has come up with an excuse. My favorite was my own daughter telling me she had to clean the toilets. In her dress and heels."

"At least she came up with an excuse. I couldn't think of one."

Trudy cackled. "So you *were* warned!"

"I was."

"Aurora?" Trudy arched a penciled-in eyebrow.

Stella placed a hand over her heart. "I'll never tell."

"You don't have to, dear. She's terrified of me. Too bad she doesn't know how much I like her."

Stella motioned for Trudy to take a seat on a white metal bench. "Why's that?"

"She's the only friend of Becky's with pluck. Becky is sweet, caring, and loyal. She needs someone like Aurora by her side to protect her."

"What about Nathan?"

"He's a lot like Becky. Not the protective type. I know this isn't politically correct, but he's the bookish type. Becky needs a bulldog." Trudy growled like a dog.

Bulldog? Did she mean bull dyke? No way would anyone refer to the extremely fem Aurora as one. Stella couldn't stop herself from asking, "Are you saying you wished Becky married Aurora?"

Trudy's steely-eyed gaze never left Stella's. "And here I thought I was talking to the bright one in the group. They'd never work out together. But, after a woman is married, she loses a part of the bond with her best friend. There's no way around it. And, when the child comes—"

"Is Becky pregnant?"

Trudy hefted one shoulder. "All I'm saying is the dress was let out days ago. Considering she's been exercising and trying to lose weight—"

"Are you poisoning Stella's mind?" Aurora placed a hand on Stella's shoulder.

"Moi?" Trudy laughed. "She's the dangerous one."

"Yeah, yeah. You're always innocent even when plotting against your own granddaughter." Aurora shook a finger. "I heard the pregnancy comment. How dare you? Becky isn't pregnant, and the dress wasn't let out. What a terrible thing to say."

"Figures. I doubt Nathan can seal the deal."

Aurora shook her head. "Why do you hate him? He's a good man."

"Good, yes. The best, no."

Aurora groaned. "In your opinion, no one is the best. What do you expect Beck's to do? Never marry."

"I've been happy since my husband dropped dead thirty years ago. God, why didn't the man have the decency to die earlier?"

Aurora let out an exasperated sigh, but she ended up grinning. "You're an evil woman."

Trudy placed one hand over the other in her lap. "You know better than most, Miss Aurora."

Guests started to find their way to their assigned seating.

"Chow time." Trudy motioned for Aurora and Stella to help her to her feet. "Remember what I said," Trudy told Stella before tottering off to the main table.

"What'd she tell you?" Aurora asked when the coast was clear.

"I have no idea," Stella replied.

"Is it weird that I admire the nasty woman? I'm terrified of her and limit my interactions, but I have to respect how she's survived all these years all alone. And for better or worse, she speaks her mind." Aurora clung to Stella's arm.

"She has a certain amount of charm in the *never turn your back on her way.*"

"Exactly. Fierce! We're over here." Aurora led them to the table closest to Becky's. After taking her seat, Aurora whispered, "I'm so not looking forward to my speech."

Stella reached for Aurora's knee under the table. "You'll do great. Just be you because you are amazing."

"Oh, that was sweet." Aurora waved a hand in front of her face. "I'm so emotional today. I don't want to wreck my makeup."

Stella offered a tight-lipped smile.

The waitstaff started serving up the meals.

Aurora leaned over. "I requested the chicken for both of us. I hope that's okay. The salmon option seemed iffy."

"Excellent choice. I'm not in the mood for food poisoning."

"Are you ever?" Aurora asked with a smirk.

"When you put it that way, no."

"You okay? You seem a bit off today."

"Me? I'm fine. Just out of my element here. I'm used to being the one in control."

"Poor you, having to take a back seat for once." Aurora kissed Stella's cheek.

"Never a problem when it comes to you." Stella wished the words were true. No, they were. She just didn't want to take a back seat to Becky.

The hubbub under the tent increased tenfold as the guests tucked into their meals and the staff plied everyone with wine.

When there was a chance, Aurora introduced Stella to their dining companions.

"Aurora, when can we expect you to get married?" A woman in her forties asked.

"Joan! You are such a pot-stirrer. We're here to celebrate Becky's happy day, not plot against me."

"Plot!" Joan laughed. "Good to know your view of marriage hasn't changed."

"If memory serves me correctly, you and I have never discussed the topic. This is why"—Aurora pointed her knife blade at Joan—"Becky stuck you at my table. For me to keep an eye on you."

Mitchell, her husband, laughed. "If you can keep her under control, I'd be eternally grateful." He made a praying motion with his hands, his eyes turning heavenward.

"I don't know what you two are talking about. I'm a perfect angel. Have been since I popped into this world."

"And by that you mean kicking and screaming every moment since that terrible day in human history." Aurora sipped her wine.

Mitchell burst into laughter. "She's got you pegged."

"Sure, she thinks that now. Which is right where I want her. Unsuspecting to my true nature." Joan cackled.

Stella watched this exchange, wondering if everyone at this event was an unlit fuse ready to activate, but Stella couldn't guess what would happen if they did.

"Of that I have no doubt. It's why I love you. Nice people are so fucking boring." Aurora sliced a bite of chicken.

Joan raised her wineglass. "I'll toast to that!"

Mitchell and Aurora joined in, with Stella one beat behind.

Joan turned to Stella. "What about you? Are you opposed to the institution of marriage?"

Stella raked a hand through her hair, not pleased to be put on the spot. "I'm pleading the fifth."

Mitchell nudged Stella's side with an elbow. "That's a good plan with these two around. Stick with me, and we may survive the day by the skin of our teeth."

"Cowards," Aurora and Joan said.

Someone clinked a knife against a glass. Stella lifted her gaze to the father of the bride. The speeches were starting. Stella stole a glance at Aurora to see her pallor seep a shade whiter. Stella gave Aurora's thigh a squeeze. Joan gave Aurora a thumbs-up when Aurora rose to her feet.

"I have to admit, when Becky asked me to be her maid of honor, I blocked out this portion of my responsibility. Getting up in front of all of you to tell you how wonderful the bride is and how lucky I've been to be her best friend since we were mere babes—you see, I'm not used to lying. At least not in front of such a large crowd."

There was laughter in the room.

Aurora smiled, her eyes tearing up. "I kid only because while I'm absolutely thrilled Becky has married her knight in shining armor, I feel somewhat cheated. I'm not the type who likes to share. And now it's legal. I have to share Becks with…" Her voice choked up. "With an amazing man, so there's some consolation to that. But, I should warn you, Nathan, if you think I'll sit idly by when you upset my best friend, you have another thing coming. I've got my eye on you." Aurora pointed to her eyes and then at Nathan's. "One wrong move and I'll let you have it, because no one will ever get away with upsetting my Becky."

"Geez, Aurora, when did you join the mafia?" a man two tables over taunted.

"Join? I run it," Aurora quipped. "All kidding aside, please join me in raising a glass to Becky and Nathan. May you two always be happy now that you've made the jump into holy matrimony." Aurora raised her glass, but again she made the *I've got my eye on you* gesture to Nathan, much to the guests' delight.

Becky mouthed, "I'll always love you."

Aurora sat heavily in her seat, her tough veneer melting like an ice cream on a hot summer day.

Stella blocked out the remaining speeches, unable to get one phrase out of her mind: *my Becky.*

The speeches done, the music started up for the dancing portion of the night. Mitchell set his napkin to the side and rose. "Aurora, will you do me the honor of dancing with me? This one is a hater." He jerked his head to his wife.

"Only because I value my toes. Best of luck to you, Aurora dear." Joan shook her fingertips in a good luck wave.

Stella slightly fumed but forced a smile when the two made their way to the dance floor.

"Mitch has always thought of Aurora as a daughter," Joan said.

Stella wondered if Joan had picked up on her jealous vibe.

"Aurora tells me you're a doctor and a professor. That's impressive but fitting for Aurora."

"Why's that?" Stella asked.

"She's special and deserves to be treated right."

Stella watched Aurora giggle when Mitch trampled on her foot. He blushed but shrugged it off.

"If you don't want to have to amputate one of her feet by the night's end, I recommend rescuing her now. I'll be your wingman and take the hit for the team." Joan stood.

Stella tapped Mitchell's shoulder. "May I?"

He bowed and teamed up with his wife, who pulled him into a slow dance as the music switched gears.

Aurora wrapped her arms around Stella's neck. "How are you surviving?"

"Barely. You didn't warn me I'd be swimming among sharks."

"There are quite a few characters on the guest list. It was one of the reasons Becky and Nathan considered eloping." Aurora played with a strand of Stella's hair on the back of her neck.

"Have you recovered from giving your speech?"

"I honestly don't have a clue what I said. I didn't prepare a word ahead of time. When the best man pulled out a paper to read from, I thought to myself, *Oh, fuck. I'm going to look like a jackass.* Did I?" Aurora stopped swaying to the music.

"Not at all. The depth of your feelings for Becky came through loud and clear."

"I hope so. I adore her." Aurora restarted the dance.

"Are you really that upset she's married now and off the market?"

"Off the market? Why would that affect me?"

"Oh, you know. That whole missed chance to fulfill your high school crush."

Aurora's feet stilled. "What are you saying, Stella?"

Stella whisked Aurora off the dance floor.

Aurora glared at Stella, crossing her arms and tapping a foot. "I'm waiting."

"I think a part of you is still in love with her."

CHAPTER THIRTY-SEVEN

AURORA REMAINED SPEECHLESS FOR SEVERAL LONG seconds. Shaking her head as if trying to dislodge water from her ears, she said, "Did I just hear that right? You're telling me at Becky's wedding that you think I'm in love with her?"

"It's obvious you're upset about the marriage. Hence why you dragged your feet in finding a date. And now I'm wondering why you didn't craft your speech but waited to the very last second to think of something, only to not-so-discretely declare your longing."

Aurora's eyebrows darted upward to her hair. "My longing? And here I thought my speech was about how special Becky is. You know, making it about the bride on her special day."

"Oh, it was exactly that. How special she is and how Nathan isn't good enough for her. Trudy thinks like you do, by the way." Stella put up a hand. "Wait. Didn't you say you couldn't remember what you said?"

Aurora closed her eyes and groaned. "You're right, Stella. All of this has been one elaborate con. Months and months of scheming so I could fulfill my dream of being the world's worst maid of honor by declaring my love for the bride in my speech after she's married. It was the perfect plan until you called me out." Aurora's chest heaved up and down. "And to know I have Trudy's blessing just makes it even better. Jesus! You've just met Trudy. But you believe her more than me. You should know the woman always has ulterior motives. Apparently like me if you're in the right."

"What ulterior motives?"

"She had a terrible marriage and thinks any woman who gets married to a man is tossing her freedom away because that's how it was when she was younger."

"I'm sure that's part of it, but—"

"Please don't tell me what you think, considering you've only had a five-minute conversation with the woman I've known all my life." Aurora flicked a tear away, trying to regain her composure as two women entered the bathroom.

"You see. You're crying because—"

"Because I'm fucking pissed at you." Aurora dabbed another tear. "There are such things as angry tears, and just so we're clear, I'm mad as hell. This has been such a nice day, and you had to go out of your way to sabotage it. Was it because you weren't the center of attention? The successful doctor playing second fiddle to me, the lowly support staff? You acted weird when we had dinner with Becky, and this. I don't even know how to explain what you're doing now." Aurora placed a hand on her chest.

"You think it's because I'm used to being the center of attention?"

"I think it's part of it. Because if I give too much credence to your insane theory—"

"That you're in love with Becky."

"In love with...?" Aurora shook her hands in the air. "I can't believe we're having this conversation. Especially at her fucking wedding." Aurora took a fortifying breath. "Ya know, it's funny. You don't seem to trust me, and I sure in fuck can't trust you."

"You can't trust me? Are you serious?" Stella shook her head, not seeming to believe a word. "I'm the most honest person I know."

"You must be the only person you know because that's the only way you can classify yourself as the most honest."

"That doesn't make any sense!" Stella wiped her brow. "What evidence do you have that I'm not honest?"

"You've been lying to me for weeks. No, not weeks, but months!"

"About what?" Stella asked in exasperation.

"Caring about me."

"How do you figure that?"

"Why else won't you introduce me to your daughter?" Aurora had finally said it at the worst possible time, but it was out there.

"From what I read, it's not wise to make introductions until six months." Stella stood her ground.

"We've been together for longer than that."

"We started as fuck buddies. I don't even know when we turned into whatever we are." Stella huffed.

"How romantic of you." Aurora shifted the weight on her feet, her left heel feeling like it was being clawed by the back of the shoe.

Neither spoke.

The music switched to a more upbeat song, not that they were near the dance floor.

"You know, it might be best for you to leave," Aurora said.

"Wait. What?"

"I can't deal with you right now. I should be socializing with the guests, having fun after all the planning, and need I remind you this is my best friend's wedding day? Even if you believed what you say you believe, you honestly…" Aurora tried to steady her voice. "Couldn't you have waited until we left the venue? How did you think this would go? You'd yell at me and then we'd go back and dance? Have some cake and then go home for makeup sex?" Aurora glared at Stella. "Leave. Now."

A flicker of panic shot through Stella's eyes. "Can we talk later?"

"What's the point? You clearly don't trust me."

"You don't seem to trust me either."

Aurora nodded. "We've made a huge mistake thinking we could be more than colleagues with benefits. That's the problem when emotions become factors."

"What emotions?"

"Okay, then. Good to know I'm the only one who fell in love. That makes this whole scene even better." Aurora made a tick in the air. "You don't feel anything for me, and I'm a fucking idiot for thinking you did."

"I never said that," Stella's gaze dropped to the ground.

"You never said you didn't."

"Aurora, please. We need to talk about this." Stella reached for Aurora's hand but was rebuffed.

Taking a step back, Aurora stated, "I don't see the point. It's becoming clear you aren't the type to trust. Ever. It's not in your DNA. The doctor who lives an orderly life. A kid every other weekend, plus Tuesday night dinners. No one can easily slot into the time and role you give them, all the while living up to your standards, which means not having a past at all, no matter how innocent. A high school crush. You're seriously throwing all of this away because I admitted I had a crush over ten years ago. Unbelievable!"

"My standards? Like what? Don't cheat?"

Aurora staggered on her feet, her vision swirling. "So now I've cheated on you. Oh, wow! This just keeps getting better and better. I didn't. I cried at my best friend's wedding because it's the end of our childhood friendship. Things between Becky and me will never be the same. That doesn't mean I'm in love with her. It just means I'm a fucking sentimental fool. Why can't you get that into your head?" Aurora bonked her own head.

"Because cheating is what people do," Stella stated it as if it were the gospel truth.

"I don't. Never have. Never will. Even when we classified the relationship as fuck buddies, I wasn't fucking anyone else because that would have been wrong in my book."

"I wasn't either."

"Because you don't let people in!"

"I did with you!" Stella's lips curled.

"Apparently, ever since I told you about the crush, you've been harboring this thought that I'm a cheater. Why didn't you tell me sooner and not today of all days?" Aurora pressed her palms together. "Listen. I want to get back to the wedding after I gather myself in the bathroom. When I come out that door"— Aurora pointed to the restroom—"I don't want to see you. When I'm socializing and pretending that I didn't just break up with you, I don't want to see you. Are you understanding what I'm saying?"

"You're breaking up with me?" Stella sounded floored.

"You've accused me of being in love with Becky and cheating on you. Why would you even want to be with me?"

"Because I like you."

"Like me. You can't even say the word, can you? You can only spell it in Spanish and in a way to make it nearly impossible for me to know." Aurora paused to gather the strength to say, "Please, Stella. If you like me, do as I ask and leave."

"Can we talk later?" Stella repeated the request with nervousness in her tone.

"Fine!" Aurora ground her teeth. "I'll call you when I get home, and we can continue whatever the fuck this is." She stormed into the bathroom and slammed one of the stall doors closed, collapsing against the metal door, willing herself not to cry.

The main door opened, and Aurora swore under her breath. If that was Stella, she may kill the woman.

"Aurora?" It was Becky's mom. "You in here?"

"Yes," Aurora said in a singsong voice, dabbing her eyes with cheap toilet paper.

"Everything okay?"

"Absolutely." Aurora wiped under both eyes and emerged from the stall. "Hasn't this been a wonderful day?"

Becky's mom grinned. "It has, but I can't believe my baby is leaving."

Aurora purposefully didn't bring up that Becky had been living away from home since she was eighteen, eleven years ago. That wasn't the point. Becky's mom may be the only one else at the wedding who understood the sadness Aurora felt. The two embraced.

When they pulled apart, Becky's mom said, "Oh, I was supposed to track you down because they're getting ready to cut the cake."

"Right. We don't want to miss that."

They hugged again briefly and then went out to participate.

Back among the guests, Aurora's eyes sought out Stella, but she didn't see the doctor. Great. Now the woman listened to Aurora. Never mind. It was for the best.

Becky sidled up to Aurora. "Can you believe I'm married?" she squealed, bobbing up and down.

Aurora didn't respond but hugged her best friend, clutching tighter than normal.

"You okay?" Becky whispered into her ear.

"I'm just so happy for you," Aurora tried to fight off the tears but failed.

"Where's Stella?"

"Oh… there was an emergency at the hospital. You know. Doctors." Aurora made a la-di-da motion with her hand.

Becky pulled away and studied Aurora's expression. "It's

weird, isn't it? We won't be roommates anymore. I can't believe when I get back from my honeymoon, I'll have to box up everything in the apartment and leave. Leave my Aurora Borealis."

"I know. But Nathan might find it weird if his wife didn't sleep next to him, and no way am I letting a stinky boy into my personal space," Aurora joked. "You know you're excited to move into your new place. The first will be here soon, and you won't have to deal with my dirty dishes in the sink ever again."

"I'm going to miss yelling at you."

"You're good at it. Maybe I can come over occasionally and just leave my dishes at your place."

"That would be wonderful." Becky clapped her hands together. "I have to go now and cut the cake."

"Do me a favor. Smear it all over his face. For me."

"You got it. Thank you for everything you've done. Every girl should have a best friend like you."

CHAPTER THIRTY-EIGHT

STELLA RETURNED TO HER APARTMENT AROUND seven on Wednesday night after what could only be categorized as a complete and total flop of a day. Her morning lecture had been lackluster, with three students actually falling asleep. She knew her students were burning the candle at both ends, but no one had ever fallen asleep before. Never.

She'd sat in on several meetings, only to be rewarded with an ass chewing by Dean Andrews. Dr. Howie was causing problems about yet another room assignment, meaning she had to email Aurora to plead for help. While Aurora's response had been professional, quick, and effective, the coldness of the transaction left Stella feeling a hole in her life. Aurora's text the night of the wedding had been much colder and succinct: *I don't see the point in talking about us, so I'm not going to call.*

Stella bobbed her head while standing in her kitchen, deciding what to eat for dinner. Order in or heat up a frozen meal? It was relatively early in the evening, but if she opted for plan B, she could be in bed by nine and put this day behind her.

In the grand scheme of things, it was only one day. Everyone had bad days. It wasn't a reflection of the Aurora situation. Stella's happiness wasn't dependent on another human being. It was down to Stella to boost her spirits. She didn't need another human to fill a hole in her life. That kind of talk was only found in romance novels. It simply didn't exist. Stella, and Stella alone, was in charge of making her life be what she wanted it to be. She absolutely did not need Aurora. Or any woman for that matter.

So what should the first step be?

Order a nice meal. Something healthy. Japanese. That sounded wonderful.

After placing an order, she tidied up the apartment. How had it become such a pigsty in three days? Her outfit from the wedding was still on the barstool, where she'd stripped down as soon as she walked through the door Saturday night. It needed to be sent to the cleaners, and the rest of her laundry needed to be gathered and placed in the basket. She'd start a load as soon as she got home tomorrow, not able to muster the will to do it right now.

Yes. Cleaning and making plans were already helping her mood. Action. Stella was a woman of action.

She glanced at her watch. The food should be there in mere minutes. What could she do to make it special? Candles. She should light some candles. Why only have them when dining with Aurora or anyone else? Was there a law that a single person shouldn't pamper herself? Absolutely not. In fact, if more did, there would be a lot less angst in life. She should write a manual for how to live a happy, successful, and fulfilling life alone. There had to be a market for that. She could interview others, like Trudy, but how would she get her number without Aurora's help? Never mind. That wasn't necessary. The point being singlehood wasn't a curse but a blessing. Something to embrace.

Step one for a satisfying meal alone: set table, light candles, play relaxing music. Stella selected Mozart.

Step two: a healthy meal.

Eating a tub of ice cream was the worst possible thing to do. It'd only make her feel worse. *Whatever you do, Stella, don't go to the freezer.*

The doorbell buzzed.

Stella did a fist bump. She was fucking rocking this single life. A complete and total success. She hadn't felt this good in weeks. Smiling, she gave the delivery guy a ten-dollar tip, much to his surprise.

Step three: spread the good cheer by doing a good deed, like making someone else smile.

She'd only set out on this new life in the past hour, and so far, Stella was smashing it out of the fucking ballpark. Her thoughts flitted to their aborted date at Fenway, which Stella had always meant to correct. But Stella stamped it out of her mind as if squashing an ant invading a picnic spread. The chance to get that right was now dead.

Stella took a seat at the table with the meal, the steam rising from the succulent beef, making her mouth water. Using chopsticks, she ate slowly, enjoying each bite to the fullest.

Step four: don't rush dinner. Her days were packed with work, meetings, never-ending questions from faculty, students, staff, and patients. Take the one meal at the end of the day and savor every single blissful second. She closed her eyes, letting the music infiltrate her mind and soul.

Step five: do a quick rundown of all the positives in her life. Mackenzie. She had a daughter she adored and treasured. Rosie. While her sister could be a smart-ass and loved to give her shit, no matter what happened, Rosie would be there for her. Two people Stella would lay her life down for. How many had that? Why did she need more? Not with her career. She simply didn't have time for a girlfriend. Correction. She didn't want to make time for one because one wasn't needed to complete her. *Complete her!* What a fucking crock of shit peddled by shysters who didn't understand the single lifestyle.

After finishing her meal and cleaning up the kitchen, Stella sat on the couch, the music still going, with a glass of wine. This was the life. So quiet. Peaceful. It was as if she were floating over her own body, seeing the healing powers of a healthy mindset and routine. She vowed to do this every single night. Take care of herself. Be happy. Because it really was a mindset. No one else could make her happy. Only Stella. And her daughter and sister. Life complete. Stella made a huge check mark in the air with her index finger.

In fact, she should give Rosie a call. Just to say hello. Let her sister know how much Stella cherished their bond. Family. That was what mattered. Stella had always been a family woman. That was why it'd torn her apart when her ex had wrecked everything. Now, Stella only saw her daughter every Tuesday and every other weekend.

That would not happen again. Never. No woman was going to wreck Stella's life.

Aurora was only an illusion. Causing Stella's mind to feel like the missing piece had finally been snapped into place, completing the picture-perfect life. But Aurora couldn't be that piece. The only people Stella needed were herself, her daughter, and her sister. The simplicity of a happy life was a beautiful thing, but having more than that complicated the shit out of it. And for what? To chase an illusion? Like a delusional person wandering in the desert chasing after mirages? Love was for weak-minded people who weren't happy because they simply didn't appreciate themselves.

That was the key.

Loving thyself.

Stella asked Alexa to play music, not specifying a genre or playlist. The first was a sad song about a relationship ending. The next a hateful one about another relationship crashing and burning. By the time she'd heard seven out of ten songs about the pangs of heartbreak, Stella reached for her phone to call Rosie.

"Well hello, baby sis. To what do I owe the pleasure?" Rosie's voice was pleasing, all the while dripping with sarcasm. Just the way Stella expected her to be. Perfect!

"Hey."

"Hey. That's all you got? Are you getting a cold? Your voice sounds funny."

Stella drank some water. "I'm fine. I swallowed wrong earlier, and my voice is still shaky." This was a lie and a useful lesson. Before calling Rosie, Stella should loosen up her vocal cords to sound perkier. Not like she hadn't talked to a soul for the past few hours, which she hadn't. Well, she had mumbled *thanks* to the delivery guy.

"Are you sure? I'm picking up on a different vibe. What happened? Last time we had dinner, you were on cloud nine. *In love with Aurora.*" Rosie sang the last line.

"I was never in love with Aurora. I see that now."

"That doesn't sound good."

It didn't feel all that great either. *No, don't go down that path.*

"Care to fill me in, Stell?" Rosie said.

"Aurora and I have decided to part ways." Stella picked a hair off the back of the sofa cushion. It was a long black strand. She had to force herself to drop it onto the floor and tear her gaze away from where it landed.

"What in the fuck happened?" Rosie barked.

"What needed to," Stella said in a cool, calm, and collected voice.

"I'm going to need more."

"It's simple really. I called her out about still being in love with Becky—"

"The woman who's getting married?"

"The one who got married on Saturday."

"Tell me again why you think Aurora is in love with her bestie, who is now officially married to someone else."

Stella provided the highlights of the wedding, the speech, and the confrontation.

Rosie groaned, and Stella could picture her massaging her brow in the way Rosie did when she thought Stella was being a grade-A heartless asshole.

Stella pushed on. "I feel great, though. Back to myself."

"And when you say that, do you mean back to being alone, bitter, and miserable?"

"No. Well, yes to alone, but that's my natural state. I function better this way. I'm happier this way. I think many people need to learn to be with themselves. That's the key to happiness. Love isn't. Unless it's loving yourself." Stella nodded emphatically.

"What fucking bullshit have you been reading? The guidebook of how to become an unhinged sociopath?"

"Seriously." Stella sat up on the sofa. "Listen to me. I've figured out the key."

"To the looney bin?"

"Why do I share these things with you?" Stella crashed back against the couch.

"Because you know I'll give it to you straight. You fucked up. Big time. Not only did you accuse Aurora of being in love with Becky, which doesn't make any sense because your only evidence is a confession about a crush back when she was a kid and being Becky's maid of honor—"

"She cried at the wedding!"

"So did others I'm willing to bet. That's what happens at weddings. Jesus, I went to a wedding last month, and I'd never met the bride or groom, but I still cried. They're emotional for normal people. Which you clearly aren't. Because only a fucking stubborn idiot would pull what you pulled at the wedding! Have you tried to figure out what else could be the cause of those tears?"

"Like what?"

"You mentioned they've been roommates, and I'm assuming Becky pays half the rent. Maybe Aurora is freaking out about money. Or, perhaps she's sad about losing a roommate and best friend. Both in all likelihood, along with so many other things. She must have felt like someone tossed so many thoughts and feelings into her head and then hit puree."

"You weren't there. You don't know."

"Willing to bet I have a much better clue than you, dear sister. Jealousy warps even the most sensible minds. I warned you about this."

CHAPTER THIRTY-NINE

AURORA'S WORK LINE RANG THE MOMENT SHE walked in to start the day, and something told her she wasn't going to like the news.

"Scheduling. Aurora speaking." She forced herself to sound confident and in control in an attempt to mitigate the situation.

"We have a problem," Alice said.

Aurora clicked her pen, ready to jot down notes. Stay calm. Aurora was the problem solver. All she needed to do was stay fucking calm. "Hit me with it."

"All the Dean's booze is gone."

She clicked her pen several times. "Can you repeat that?"

Alice let out an exasperated breath. "The Dean is hosting an event tonight, and all the alcohol was delivered to the cold room last night. The door was supposed to be locked, but when facilities went to the room this morning to retrieve it, all of it was gone."

Aurora pulled up the reservation in the system. "Yes, the directions are clear. The alcohol was scheduled to be delivered yesterday at four. And the door was locked by Bri." Aurora spun in her chair to retrieve the job sheets from the plastic tray.

Rifling through them, she said, "Hold on. Okay, yes, Bri initialed the job as complete."

"If she locked the door, then how did the alcohol disappear?"

Aurora flipped the pages to the night shift. "Oh, shit."

"What?" Alice snapped.

"There was a blood lab last night."

"How does that factor in?"

"Kip had to unlock the cold room for the lab tech to get the bags of blood." The first time Aurora found out they stored blood and alcohol in the same cold storage room, her stomach had flipped a gazillion times. Now, it didn't even phase her. Although, losing the Dean's booze was doing a number on her central nervous system. "Let me call Kip and check with him."

"I have to go to the main campus. Can you handle this?"

Aurora didn't believe Alice had to dash to the other campus along the Charles River, and even if she did, the situation seemed to warrant more urgency. Still, she said, "Leave it with me."

Aurora set the phone down, the cold panic turning into a tsunami. She'd never been involved in firing someone in her life, but she feared that was about to change.

Kip could be an unmitigated disaster, but Aurora didn't want to give up on the man. He was brilliant in his Kip fashion. Annoying, yes. Combative, yes. But the man had more tech knowledge crammed into his brain than all the other techs put together. Aurora worried he wasn't being challenged enough to reach his full potential. Assigning him to unlock a room for someone to collect lab supplies was downright insulting.

There had to be a way to channel his positive traits as a win.

Didn't there?

Aurora called the security office, relieved when Frank answered. Recently, he'd helped her figure out which student had been breaking into a classroom that was off-limits in the evening. It was one of five classrooms that couldn't be used as a study space, and clearly, someone found this offensive or whatever. Medical students could be unbelievable, thinking no rules applied to them.

"Frank!" Aurora squealed in delight. "Man, I'm glad you're working today. I need your help. Last night, someone got into our cold room. Can you check the footage and see who?"

"In the C building?"

"Yes." Aurora consulted the job sheets again. "Start checking the video after six at night. That was the last time someone on my staff was there. Better yet, start at four. That's when it was delivered."

"I'll get right on that, but what was delivered? What am I looking for? And please don't say bags of blood."

"No. No vampires are involved. Hopefully, at least. I don't need more fodder for my nightmares. It's a shitload of booze for an event for the dean tonight, so this is an emergency."

Frank laughed. "Okay. I'll be in touch."

Aurora's next step was to text Isaac and Bri to get to the office ASAP. Since the most recent schedule changes per Alice, although Aurora suspected the order came from Vera, both started their day at eight.

Kip wasn't expected for another two hours, but she didn't want to wait a minute longer so she dialed his phone, wondering if he'd pick up before his shift started.

"Kip here." He sounded friendly.

"Good morning, Kip."

"Hey, Aurora."

"Hey back at you."

"You're acting weird. Why are you acting weird?"

"Oh, I'm just checking up on something for Alice. Last night, when you unlocked the cold room for the lab tech, did you lock the door before you left?"

"Yep. I distinctly remember doing that."

"You are one hundred percent certain?" Aurora pressed.

"Absolutely. I saw all the booze. No way would I leave it unlocked." She could picture him bobbing his head the way he did when sure beyond a doubt about something.

"The alcohol was still there when you locked the door." Aurora jotted that down on her notepad. "Okay. I'll have security focus on the footage after that time, so hopefully we'll get to the bottom of it sooner rather than later."

"Bottom of what?"

"All the liquor is gone."

"Gone, gone?" His voice was barely above a whisper.

"Yes. I'm calling a staff meeting. Any chance you're near the campus?"

"Close enough. I'll head there now."

They disconnected, and Aurora had to wonder why the Kip she'd just spoken with wasn't the same Kip when he was physically present.

Alice rushed in, her white blouse and scarf looking as if she'd pulled them out of the hamper. Hopefully, they didn't smell like it. Not that Aurora planned to get close enough to check. Besides, what adult didn't do the sniff test on clothing to see if they could get another wear out of it?

"On my way out, I thought of something, and it seemed faster to come here than phone. We should call security," Alice said as she sat heavily in the empty desk chair behind Aurora.

"Already done. Frank is looking at the footage."

"Good. Frank is the only one there with half a brain."

Aurora was willing to bet Frank had a lot more ambition than the woman breathing heavily in wrinkled clothes, who clearly wasn't in a rush to get to the main campus, solidifying Aurora's suspicion that Alice hated conflict. Had the woman debated about whether or not she should get more involved? Given herself a stern lecture in front of the mirror to buck up the nerve to act like a boss?

Isaac and Bri entered the office, both with confused expressions, which morphed into fearful when they spied the angry looking Alice. Their boss had two expressions: uninterested or pissed. Aurora had to wonder how she had moved up in the department because both attributes weren't what Aurora associated with effective leaders.

"Would you like a cup of coffee? Do you have time?" Aurora asked Alice.

Alice glanced at her phone, for the time presumably, or maybe it was just a habit she developed to look more important than she was, and nodded. "Four sugars, please."

So much for Alice having to haul ass to the main campus on the other side of town. "You got it. Isaac? Bri?"

"I'll go with you." Isaac strode to the breakroom, with Bri hot on his heels.

Aurora inserted a Keurig cup for Alice and hit start.

Isaac whispered, "What's this about?"

"Kip and booze."

"Kip doesn't drink," Isaac said.

Aurora didn't know that, but did it really matter? "Kip was the last to enter the cold room, and this morning all the Dean's liquor is gone."

"All of it?" Bri's eyes grew three sizes. "There was a lot. Why didn't you tell me earlier?"

"I just found out." Aurora reached for the sugar packets. "Bri, what time did you leave last night?"

"A little after five-thirty. I stayed late since the schedule was packed."

Kip was still the last one on the clock after the blood lab. Aurora didn't like the way things looked for him. But he sounded so confident on the phone. She didn't know what or whom to believe.

She wished she could talk to Stella and ask advice about how to handle Alice. Or just for a hug. This day was snowballing into a shitstorm, and it wasn't even eight-thirty.

Aurora made herself a black tea. "You two going to make something?"

They nodded.

Aurora briefly contemplated staying in the breakroom until their drinks were good to go but knew that was the cowardly way. "See you out there, then."

She handed Alice her coffee when Kip rushed in.

"Kip. Just the man I wanted to speak to." The left side of Alice's lip snarled like a wild animal.

"Aurora told me on the phone about the cold room situation." Kip stood confidently, but Aurora sensed he was putting up a brave front.

"That's an interesting way to phrase your fuckup." Alice set her coffee down as if needing both of her hands free.

"I locked the door. I've never left the door unlocked. Never."

"There's a first time for everything, and you picked the worst possible time to screw up." Alice drummed her fingers on the desktop.

Isaac and Bri returned, their heads cast down.

"I demand to check the security footage." Kip stood with his arms crossed.

"If I were in your shoes, I wouldn't make any demands. I have half a mind to fire you right here and now."

"On what grounds?" Kip demanded.

"For not doing your job!" Alice's face became cherry-red.

"You have no proof."

"We're checking the tapes, Kip. I'm dead certain we'll find you're in the wrong. You're always in the wrong. If you weren't Dani's nephew, I would have fired you long ago."

Who was Dani?

"Please. You're the one who should be fired. No one here

likes you!" Kip stood on his toes, perhaps in an effort to seem giant size.

Isaac and Bri looked as if they were praying the floor would open up and swallow them whole.

"That's it! You're on leave until we get to the bottom of this fiasco. And if I find you didn't lock the door, you'll be let go immediately. If I were you, I'd dust off my résumé and start looking for a new job. I don't give a fuck who your aunt is." Alice grabbed her coffee and stormed out.

Aurora wished Alice had stuck to the original plan and never come to the office, because this didn't help solve the problem. It only exacerbated an already terrible situation.

Kip turned to Aurora, his eyes imploring her to intercede. "I locked the door. I know I did."

"We'll find out soon," Aurora said.

"But you believe me, right?"

She wanted to. She really did. "Of course, Kip."

He wasn't done and turned to Isaac and Bri, who cowered in the back corner. "And you two? Do you believe me?"

They nodded, although Bri's nod didn't elicit much confidence.

Kip's shoulders sagged. "Now what?"

"Go home. I'll call you as soon as I can with whatever I find out."

"This isn't fair. I should be able to view the footage. Alice has had it out for me since day one, and I don't trust her."

You haven't helped yourself either. "Leave it with me, Kip. I'll get to the bottom of everything. You can trust me." Aurora believed he had the right to stay and watch the footage, but she didn't think the battle with Alice would help the situation. "Please, Kip. I'll give it to you straight as soon as I know everything."

He stared at Aurora, tears in his eyes. "This isn't right. I know I locked the door."

"Frank will get to the bottom of it."

Everyone left the office.

Once again, Aurora had the urge to call Stella. She needed a shoulder to cry on, but Stella wasn't an option from here on out. Aurora's mom had too much on her plate with her dad recovering from surgery. And Becky was on her honeymoon.

Aurora had to survive this all alone.

CHAPTER FORTY

AROUND THREE IN THE AFTERNOON, STELLA STEPPED out of the office for some fresh air. It was her new thing. Taking small breaks when she could to be kind to herself. Wasn't that the new trend? Being kind to oneself? What was it called? Self-care? And since she wasn't teaching any summer classes, Stella had more time on her hands. Although, all the admin stuff she'd been pushing to the side now had to be tackled. Not to mention being a doctor at the hospital.

She found a bench under an oak tree that provided some protection from the sweltering late-June sun. Unfortunately, there was no escaping the humidity. And the dog days of summer hadn't even arrived.

Stella closed her eyes, trying to clear her mind from anything and everything. She sucked in a lungful of air and slowly released. Repeating the process while attempting to keep her mind from wandering. But each time she chased one thought away, another flittered into her brain. It seemed a useless task. How did people meditate for any length of time? She'd been trying for—Stella consulted her watch—three minutes, and she hadn't been able to clear her mind at all.

The one thought she wanted to permanently banish from her mind was the most powerful: What was Aurora doing right now?

Stella was willing to bet Aurora hadn't given her a second thought since the wedding. Becky. Aurora wanted Becky. Stella had been a fool to believe otherwise.

She opened her eyes, and Aurora stood thirty feet away from her, talking with someone from security. From the looks of the conversation, Aurora was animated and stressed. Stella wondered if she should go to Aurora. Find out what was wrong.

Even upset, Aurora looked stunning in her sleeveless blouse, skirt, and heels.

A stab of doubt skewered Stella right in the gut. Was Rosie right? A lot of people cry at weddings and Aurora was only doing what anyone in her shoes would have done?

Aurora bid the security guy farewell and made her way across Whitaker Green, her brow furrowed and her arms wrapped around her chest as if in physical pain.

Stella wanted to rush to her. Talk to her. Ease whatever emotions she was feeling. Hold her tight and kiss her. God, she missed Aurora more than she thought possible.

Whoa!

Where did that come from?

What happened to being better off alone?

But it was hard to deny Stella wanted to be close to Aurora. To talk to her. Have romantic dinners. To go for long walks, hand in hand, chatting about everything and nothing. To wake up with Aurora in the morning. Every damn morning.

Stella had been such an ass. She didn't want self-care. Or alone time. She wanted the woman inching closer and closer, yet seeming so far away.

Oh God! If this was really how she felt, what she'd done was even worse. Because Stella had wrecked Becky's wedding day for Aurora. And for what? Had it simply been to reinforce her belief, which was based on what? One bad relationship. Which hadn't always been bad. Kim and Stella had been happy for many years—until Stella had become too involved with work and forgot about what was important in her life.

It didn't excuse Kim's actions, but Stella couldn't place all the blame solely on her ex's shoulders. Why was Stella figuring this out now? Too late, of course, because that was Stella's luck. Oh, why didn't she have this epiphany weeks ago, which would have saved her from destroying something beautiful with Aurora? Stella had loved Kim, but her connection with Aurora was different. Stronger. Had Aurora been the one?

Aurora had confessed her love for Stella, and what had Stella done in return? She accused Aurora of harboring feelings for Becky. All because of a silly crush and one measly kiss.

Sitting on the bench, staring at Aurora from this distance, one simple fact infiltrated every fiber of Stella's being. Stella was madly in love with Aurora. It was suddenly clear to Stella. Oh, the irony. She palm-slapped her forehead.

Before Aurora reentered the building, she turned around. Stella hoped Aurora would see her and... what? Rush to Stella? Wave? Smile? None of that happened, and Stella wasn't even sure Aurora had seen her, although she'd have to be blind not to, unless the glare from the sun was the reason. Stella clung to this hope because if Aurora had seen her, not reacting was proof positive Stella had fucked up beyond reproach.

CHAPTER FORTY-ONE

AURORA SHIELDED HER EYES FROM THE SUN, thinking she saw Stella sitting on a bench. But the uber-busy doctor wasn't the type to take a break in the afternoon to sit outside. Aurora had recommended it once, but Stella laughed, saying the only breaks she got was to dash to the bathroom. If she was lucky.

Besides, the profile of the woman on the bench didn't have Stella's self-assuredness. No way would Stella slouch, propping up her chin in such a lazy way. That didn't fit the cocksure doctor. Not one iota.

Aurora walked through the glass doors and nearly slammed into Alice.

"We need to talk," Alice said. "In private. Not in the office."

"Okay. I think the classroom at the end of the hall is free."

Alice glanced to the right and then left as if making sure she wasn't being spied on. Aurora wondered if Alice was on medication but hadn't been taking her pills and needed some type of intervention.

In the classroom, Aurora waved for Alice to take a seat, but the woman chose to pace back and forth in front of the whiteboard.

"Kip," Alice started. "We need to fire him."

Aurora perched on the desk, holding onto the edges with her hands. "Actually, I don't think that's necessary. I talked to Frank. Kip locked the door, and all the bottles have been accounted for. The head of facilities sent a team to get them early this morning, and they're now where they should be. It was a misunderstanding and a wild goose chase."

"That's all well and good, but that doesn't address the bigger issue."

"Which is?"

"Kip's insubordination."

Why did Alice insist on pulling Aurora into the Kip problem? Bri was his manager, but for some reason, Alice latched onto Aurora. "Granted, he can be frustrating, but—"

"He makes me look like a fucking moron. Repeatedly. And I'm positive he's doing it on purpose. I won't let him make me look like an ass one more time. This alcohol thing was a disaster. The dean doesn't think I know what's going on in my own department."

You don't.

"I'll call Vera and explain what happened. It actually didn't have anything to do with us. This one is on facilities for not letting us know they accessed one of our rooms without permission. And without letting their entire department know they took care of it much earlier than planned."

"How'd they get in?"

"Uh..." *Could Alice be this clueless?* "They have keys to all the rooms in the building."

"They shouldn't. We should have to let them into our rooms."

"We'd have to have someone follow each facilities member all day and night since they set up all the rooms, not to mention clean them, and the offices." Aurora didn't want to point out the obvious but decided maybe she should. "We only have three full-time techs. And depending on the night, one to two temps. It's simply not possible."

"They should call every time they enter a room."

"They'd be calling every minute of the day. I don't have someone in the office who can solely field these types of calls. Kristin only works part-time." Aurora wasn't sure if Alice noticed Kristin wasn't even in the office today. Bri was covering the phones while Aurora was running around trying to solve the problem.

"Hire someone!"

Aurora ignored the spittle that flew out of Alice's mouth. "Tell you what. I'll meet with Tom, head of facilities, and we'll craft an action plan for these types of scenarios to avoid confusion. I agree when it comes to something important like this, we need to know when they're going into one of our spaces and taking items we're storing."

"Okay, that sounds good. But Kip—"

"I'll talk to him. Let him know he needs to clean up his act or else."

"Really lay into him!" Alice shook a finger in Aurora's face, much to her annoyance. Alice had no issue telling Aurora what to do but couldn't confront Kip on her own.

"Got it. Anything else?"

"No. I need to go. I have a dentist appointment." Alice didn't make eye contact with Aurora.

Liar, liar, pants on fire. "Oh. Good luck."

"I won't be back in the office after it. I need a break. This ordeal has been so upsetting." Alice placed the back of her hand on her forehead, like a woman about to faint. "I'm glad I got this sorted."

Aurora stopped her eyes from rolling. She'd been dealing with it, and from her viewpoint, it turned out to be much ado about nothing. If Alice had thought to call facilities before sounding the alarm, all of this could have been avoided. It wasn't Kip making Alice look incompetent. It was Alice never bothering to learn the protocols of scheduling or anything to do with her departments. How could she manage anything without knowing what she was managing?

After speaking with Vera in the Dean's office, Aurora tracked down Kip for a heart-to-heart, letting him know he wasn't on leave, making the executive decision to do so, simply to save Alice from looking even more like an ass if Kip filed a complaint with HR.

In the breakroom, Kip took a seat on the opposite side of the round table, his arms crossed, but it appeared he was hugging himself more than being combative. "I locked the door."

"You did," Aurora confirmed.

He perked up. "So I'm not fired?"

"Nope."

"Then why are we talking?" He slanted his head and studied Aurora, looking like a confused puppy.

"I want to know what's going on with you."

"What do you mean?"

"Do you like your job?"

He shrugged. "Yeah."

"I know you like to joke around, but there's a time and place to do that."

He stared at the tabletop, not speaking.

"You're the best tech we have on staff. You're also the most difficult to work with. One minute you're clowning around; the next you're berating people for your mistakes. It's unacceptable. I know you're a good man. You baked me cupcakes for my last day. But, Kip—"

"Did you trick me, earlier? Are you firing me?" His expression darkened.

"Is that what you want?"

He shook his head.

"What do you want?" She placed her palms on the table.

"To be back in the recording studio."

"Why were you taken off the rotation?"

"Alice hates me."

"Why do you think that?"

"She had a relationship with my aunt. When they separated, Alice took it out on me."

This was an interesting morsel Aurora knew nothing about, but it did explain why Alice confided in Aurora if Alice suspected Aurora was gay. A lesbian bond.

"And how did you react to that?"

Kip inhaled deeply.

"I'm waiting."

"I may have dedicated a song at last year's after-party for the White Coat ceremony that made it clear I was on my aunt's side."

Aurora closed her eyes, imagining all the songs it could have been, hoping it wasn't the first that popped into her mind. "Dare I ask?"

"An Alanis Morrisette song." His shoulders drooped.

"You Oughta Know" seemed to be the ultimate breakup song with explicit lyrics, and Aurora had the dubious honor of having this song dedicated to her in a bar once.

"Oh, Kip."

He slouched even more in his seat. "My aunt explained to me that I shouldn't have done it."

No shit, Sherlock. It was a miracle Kip hadn't been fired, and his aunt must have played a huge role in saving his job. "I understand it's tough seeing a family member go through something painful, but did you ever consider taking the high road? Not humiliate her in front of the dean at last year's White Coat after-party?"

"But my aunt means the world to me. And Alice treats me like I'm fucking clueless when she doesn't even know the difference between VGA, DVI, and HDMI cables. How is she in charge of the AV department if she doesn't even know the basics?" His shoulders stiffened with defiance.

Aurora understood his frustration. "But embarrassing her in front of others doesn't help your cause, Kip. And it puts me in a really awkward situation. Can you try to ignore when she steps in it and come to me to vent instead?"

"It's hard to stop myself. I'm not an idiot, and I don't appreciate being treated like one," he pouted.

"No, you aren't. I'll never treat you that way."

"I know. You're actually nice. How'd you end up in the loser department? You should be one of the doctors or something. You're smart."

"So are you. And just so you know, I don't see anyone on this staff as a loser. I won't tolerate you thinking that about anyone here."

"I don't. It's how *they* treat us." He leaned over as if about to spit on the floor but seemed to stop himself.

"I know some do, but not all. Tell you what. Let me take a look at the schedule to see if I can get some recording shifts for you."

"You'd do that?" His face lit up.

"I'm not promising anything, but I'll do what I can. If it doesn't work for the summer classes, there's always fall. If I give you a chance, I expect you to be professional at all times. No more of your pranks. Stop yelling at people, especially professors. If you find yourself in a situation where you need to scream, call me." Aurora lowered her head to make eye contact. "Am I making myself clear?"

"Why can't you be the big boss? Everyone likes you."

Aurora smiled. "Thanks. I appreciate that."

Kip glanced at the clock. "I have a setup in ten minutes. That is if I'm really still on the job."

"Of course. Thanks for the talk."

He smiled. "Do you know what HDMI stands for?"

"High-definition multimedia interface."

"Or?" he pressed, smiling.

"High-density multichip interconnect."

"You really should be running things."

"Why not you?"

The grin on his face made Aurora's heart soar, but it fell quickly. "I wouldn't want to take your place or Bri's. I like both of you."

"That's the only thing stopping you?"

"And Alice."

"We need to come up with a plan. Now scoot, or you'll be late."

"Scooting." He did a two-finger salute.

Taking a moment to check her phone for an update on the Sox score from the game that had been rained out the night before, Aurora glanced at a nursing school ad that popped up. "What's stopping you?" Aurora asked herself.

CHAPTER FORTY-TWO

THE FIRST THURSDAY IN JULY, KIM HAD CALLED Stella early in the day to rearrange the dinner Kim had cancelled. They planned to meet up at one of their old favorites in the South End. An Italian restaurant that boasted the best food with zero fanfare, which turned out to include not many other patrons when Stella waltzed in at seven.

Kim already sat at their usual table.

Stella took a seat.

"I wonder if the chef even bothered coming in tonight," Kim joked.

"I hope so. I'm not in the mood for ravioli out of a can."

Kim laughed. "Have you been cooking more?"

Stella swatted away the memory of cooking for Aurora. "Not really."

"Kenzie does love your Friday night pizza and movie tradition. She's forcing us to adopt it on the Fridays she's home."

Stella picked up on the use of *us*, which meant that Rooney was becoming part of Kim's new family. Surprisingly, the thought didn't stir Stella's jealousy. Instead, it saddened her. Not because she missed Kim, but Aurora.

Damnit. Once again, she was realizing how much of a fool she'd been.

"You okay?" Kim's expression showed sincere concern.

"Not really. But you didn't call me to chat about what's wrong with my life."

A waiter approached to take their drink order. Kim ordered a bottle of Malbec, Stella's favorite.

While the waiter fetched the bottle, Kim asked, "Are you sure you don't want to talk?"

Stella nodded.

After the wine had been poured, Kim said, "I have some news."

"Good or bad?"

"Good, I think."

Curious, Stella motioned for Kim to get it out.

"Rooney asked me to marry her."

"Oh," Stella said, setting her glass back on the table. "And...?"

"I said yes."

"Wow. That's weird... I mean, it's great for you but weird to hear."

Kim smothered Stella's hand with her own. "I know. I've been trying to figure out a way to tell you. It's why I cancelled the other dinner. I'm not sure how I would react if I heard the news from you. I don't want to hurt you, Stell. Not more than I already have."

Stella simply nodded, letting the news slowly sink in as she tried to figure out how she truly felt.

"Talk to me. How are you handling this?" Kim shook Stella's hand.

"I'm okay." Stella squeezed Kim's hand. "Really. It's just a lot to take in."

"I imagine. Rooney's great with Kenzie. I want you to know that."

"I know you wouldn't be with anyone who wasn't. Are you happy?" Stella asked with sincerity.

"I am."

"I'm glad."

Kim examined Stella's face. "Something's bothering you. You looked troubled even before I dropped this news on you."

Stella stared into Kim's light green eyes. "I messed up big time."

"Do you want to talk about her?"

"How do you know it involves a woman?"

"The sadness tinged with confusion in your eyes. There's only one source for that kind of pain."

Stella sucked in a deep breath. "I don't know. Do you really want to hear about my female troubles?"

"I'm always here for you. I always will be. I also know talking has never been your greatest strength. Especially when feelings get involved." Kim delivered the statements without any judgment.

Still, Stella snorted, knowing Kim had been on the front lines for years dealing with Stella's reticence.

"It used to drive me crazy. I'd want to have a heart-to-heart, but you'd shut down. Or accuse me of the absolute worst."

"I'm sorry. I've been doing a lot of soul-searching, and I'm realizing how difficult I was in our marriage. And still am, apparently. Not with you, but with..."

Kim's expression softened. "You have some very admirable qualities, too. You just need to learn to be yourself and to trust the woman in your life."

Stella massaged her eyes. "You're a little too late."

"Tell me what happened."

"I'm not sure I can. It's just too painful to admit. Besides, you'll only say I told you so."

"I promise I won't." Kim flashed scout's honor with her

hand. "But I know you best, or I used to know you best. It might do you some good to talk to me."

Stella let it all out while they ate spaghetti and the most amazing meatballs. By the time Stella couldn't fit in one more bite, Kim stared down at her plate.

"I'm not surprised," Kim said.

"Isn't that the same as saying I told you so?"

"No, it's not. For some reason, even though you're a fucking brilliant doctor and absolutely stunning, you've never been able to feel worthy of others. Do you know how many times you accused me of cheating?"

Stella looked away.

"The next part of what I want to say may sting some, so brace yourself." Kim paused. "Are you ready?"

"As I'll ever be."

"I don't know how to say it, now…"

"I think I need to hear it. Please." Stella acted out ripping off a Band Aid.

"Not that this excuses what I did, but I believe one of the reasons I cheated was because part of me thought I might as well since you always thought I was."

Stella remained rigid in her chair.

"Like I said, that in no way excuses my behavior."

"Does Rooney know about it?"

"Yes. I told her early on."

"And she's okay with…?" Stella was at a loss of how to put it.

"Being with a cheater? Is that what you were going for?" Kim's face was neutral.

"I didn't mean it that way. Or at least, I couldn't think of a nicer way to phrase it. Really, it's not my business anymore."

"I know you didn't mean to be hurtful. It's just a difficult topic for both of us. I wasn't trying to attack you or be defensive. After you left, I started therapy to work out why. I can't take back the pain I caused you. I wish I could. I really do. I'll always love you. I'll always cherish all the good times. And no matter what, you'll always be in my life. We have the most amazing daughter, and she deserves two parents who are kind and loving to each other. I hope you can confront your demons because I have no doubt once you do, you'll be the most amazing partner for someone. Believe in yourself so you can learn to trust others."

"But I don't know why I do the things I do."

"Are you sure?" Kim stared at Stella. "I think deep down, you do. Most of us know what lies beneath. It's being able to face it—that's the difficult part."

* * *

STELLA CRUISED by the staff's announcement board, barely giving it a glance, but one of the loopy-handwritten notices in purple caught her attention. A room for rent. The phone number was Aurora's. Had Rosie been right? Aurora was freaking out at the wedding not only because Aurora was losing her best friend, but also a roommate who was paying half the rent? It wasn't a lost chance at love causing Aurora to act weird but financial worries?

Did that mean Aurora was only eating rice and beans?

Stella bonked her forehead with the side of her fist, which only made her head hurt and didn't solve the problem: winning Aurora back.

Or at least getting Aurora to give Stella the time of day. They'd had a White Coat meeting earlier in the week, and Aurora basically ran out of the room minutes before it was over under the guise of having a scheduling emergency. Stella hadn't bought it. Even if it had been true, Aurora's emails had been so overly professional to the point of indifference. To Stella's mind. She was well aware if she showed them to anyone on her staff, they wouldn't pick up on it, but they lacked Aurora's playfulness.

Given this evidence, how could Stella get Aurora alone?

Stella emailed her sister with *SOS* in the subject line and nothing in the body of the text.

Rosie rang her immediately. "What's wrong?"

"You were right."

"You sent an SOS to tell me I was right?"

"Yes."

Rosie muttered something under her breath. "Are you aware of the definition of an emergency? I'm always right, so that's not exactly earth-shattering news. Fuck, Stella, I thought you were in the hospital."

"I am. It's where I work."

"I meant as a patient!" Rosie responded.

"I'm not that lucky. That would be a good ploy, I think. Maybe that's what I should do."

Rosie made a beeping sound. "Back it up. What plan are you concocting about ending up in the hospital? That sounds like a terrible idea, and I'm pretty sure when you tell me the whole thing, it will only make it worse."

"What if Aurora thought I was dying and rushed to see me? Then I could apologize."

"You want the woman you love to think you're dying so you can apologize? This seems like a good plan to you?" Rosie's voice lacked her usual sarcasm and instead conveyed that she thought Stella was acting like an idiot.

"It's all I got. How do you suggest I get her to talk to me?"

"Oh, I don't know. Have you tried calling her?"

"Her work line, yes. And, I've emailed."

"Email. Wow. You really are the romantic." Some humor was returning to Rosie's voice, which only irked Stella more.

Stella groaned. "Why'd I think you could help?"

"You're calling for my help?"

"That's what the SOS meant."

"Come over to my place tonight. We'll devise a plan. Until then, do not fake a near-death experience to impress her or something. That is not a good idea. Are you listening? Do not do that! Didn't you tell me her dad has kidney disease?"

"Yes, why?"

"That makes your idea a hundred times worse. She has enough death worries at the moment. Why are doctors so fucking self-involved?"

"I'm trying not to be. That's why I called you!"

"Bring wine tonight. I can't think and deal with your idiocy without wine."

Stella started to argue, but Rosie had hung up.

Fitting. Stella's track record with the female species hadn't been stellar lately. Would Kenzie have a solution? Did Stella want her daughter to know her mom was an idiot?

At eight, Stella knocked on Rosie's door. Her phone buzzed with the message: *Door is unlocked, Einstein.*

Stella ground her teeth and opened the door.

"Hope you brought the vino!" Rosie shouted. "If not, go back out, find some, and then come back."

Stella found her sister in the family room, sitting on the couch with her legs underneath her. Stella set the bottle on the coffee table. "I guess I'll get the glasses."

"Thanks. I have no desire to get up until bedtime." Rosie stretched her arms overhead and yawned.

Stella returned with two glasses and a corkscrew. "Long day?"

"Nope. Just being lazy and taking advantage of your plight like any older sister would."

Stella uncorked the wine. "At least you're honest."

"First lesson about women: none of them is completely honest. Really, didn't you have to study psychology or whatever before they allowed you to take a scalpel to a patient?"

"It's considered a soft subject by hardcore medical types," Stella lectured.

"I'm assuming you're in the category. Okay. Tell me about Aurora. How you met."

"At the school. I told you that."

Rosie sipped her wine and then raised the glass to inspect the red liquid. "Ah, you do like her. This is decent." She took another drink. "I need to know details. Women love details. If you want to woo her back, you're going to have to prove you know and care about her. So, tell me everything. Don't leave anything out. Even how many times she shits in a day."

"How would I know that?" Stella asked, aghast.

"Stop stalling. Lay it out for me."

After Stella talked for well over an hour, Rosie started to pepper her with some questions, making Stella go back to a certain point, but then Rosie wouldn't say why she'd asked for clarification, frustrating Stella, who didn't like to be left in the dark, and she was feeling even more lost the more she talked about Aurora.

Finally, Rosie asked, "Is there a conference room, preferably the nicest with a view that's easily accessible to you?"

"There's one on the sixteenth floor. It's the Dean's space for when he needs to impress a financial donor or doctor he wants to recruit to the school."

"And the view?"

"You can see all of Boston, especially at night."

"Does Aurora schedule this space?" Rosie tapped her manicured nails onto the wineglass.

"No. As I said, it's the Dean's space."

"Good. Reserve it for tomorrow night."

"Why?"

"I'm getting to that. Do you have pen and paper? I'm going to tell you exactly what to do." Rosie waved for Stella not to dillydally. "Hup, hup! Times a ticking on this operation."

* * *

THE FOLLOWING MORNING, Stella called Vera. "Good morning. I hope you had a delightful night."

"What do you want?"

"A favor. I want to reserve the dean's conference room for tonight. I need to impress Tracy and, more so, her parents. They're wavering about letting her start med school so young." Stella didn't feel great about this lie, but she wasn't sure she could say, "Here's the deal. I fell in love and messed up, and this is part of my grand gesture to win said girl back. What do you say?"

"But she's accepted!" Vera snapped.

"I know, but they're getting cold feet. The fall semester starts in weeks. I need to reassure them that I'll look out for their daughter."

"Should the Dean be there?" Vera sounded a bit shaken.

"I don't think so. I think this needs a woman's touch." Stella hoped Vera didn't offer her services.

"That makes sense. Will seven work?" Vera sounded slightly more confident.

"Yes, thank you. This is the only night she and her parents can make it while they're in town."

"I won't be here if you need me."

Perfect!

"Trust me. I won't need you."

Vera sighed, as if second-guessing the scenario. "This is highly unusual. Are you sure you're up to the task?"

"You charged me with recruiting Tracy. Let me get us over the finish line."

"Okay, whatever. There's not much I can do, anyway. Come by to grab the key. Do you need AV for a presentation?"

Stella had to stifle a laugh. What did Vera envision?

Graphics of Stella holding Tracy's hand her entire time at school?

Vera continued, "You'll have to arrange that with Aurora. I have too much on my plate today."

"Don't worry. She's my next phone call. Thanks, Vera. I owe you big time." Stella gave herself a high five.

Counting to ten, she dialed Aurora's work line.

"Scheduling."

"Aurora?" Stella asked in spite of recognizing Aurora's voice.

"Yes," Aurora said in a neutral tone.

"This is Stella Gilbert."

"Dr. Gilbert, how can I help you?"

Stella opted not to call Aurora out on being so formal. "I have an unusual request I'm hoping you can help me with."

"Ooo-kay."

"I need to impress someone tonight and have reserved the dean's conference room on sixteen."

"Do you need AV?"

"Nope. I need you to unlock the door. Vera can't stay, but she said your office has a key."

"Sure. I can schedule a tech to open the door—"

"Actually, I need you to do it."

"I won't be here."

"But I haven't given you a time yet."

"I'm leaving at five on the dot."

Stella squeezed her right forearm with her left hand. "I'm sorry to ask you to stay until seven, but this is important. It'd put my mind at ease if I knew you were the one in charge."

There was a sharp intake of breath. "Our techs are perfectly capable—"

"Usually, I wouldn't even request this, but it's that important to me. It has to be you." Stella waited, but there was dead air. "I'll forever be in your debt."

"Fine. Seven o'clock tonight?"

"Yes. I'm sorry for the last-minute request."

Stella thought she heard Aurora mumble something about doctors, but Aurora said, "It's part of my job."

There was a click.

Stella dialed Rosie's number. "She bought it!"

"That's great news, Stell. Don't fuck this up. I don't think I can come up with another idea to bail you out. Not so soon, anyway."

Stella laughed. "Yes, you can. You eat this shit up, but I'm hoping I don't have to prove that."

"It's true. I do love romance. Shall I start thinking of how you're going to ask her to marry you?"

"Whoa! You have a lot of faith in your plan."

"I have a lot of faith in you, little sis. Knock her dead. Wait, no. Don't do that. I'm learning I have to be very clear with you."

"Thanks..." Stella settled on, "for everything."

"Is that your way of saying you love me?"

"Yes."

"I recommend saying those words to Aurora. The actual words. Not some Stella code. Don't hold back."

CHAPTER FORTY-THREE

AURORA GLANCED AT THE CLOCK ON HER COMPUTER and then the one on the wall. It was a quarter to seven. Her stomach growled. There was an apple in the fridge in the breakroom, but it wasn't hers and she didn't want to be that coworker. The type to help themselves to someone else's stash when desperate. She'd only brought enough beans and rice for her lunch, which she'd eaten hours before. To kill time, she'd gone for a walk, but that had only made her hungrier.

She growled, cursing Stella's name. Stella used to joke that Aurora needed meals on a regular basis. Why had the doctor insisted Aurora stay late? There was absolutely no reason why a tech or even someone from facilities couldn't unlock the conference room door.

Aurora could be home, eating rice and beans for the seventh straight day. But no. Stella was full of herself, insisting the head of Scheduling cater to her. Just because Aurora's department was a service one, not one that brought money in for the university. Aurora was getting used to the doctors treating Scheduling as serfs, but she'd never expected this behavior from Stella. Who in the hell did Stella think she was to demand Aurora stay until seven just to unlock a door? She was tempted to send a tech. If there was a problem, she'd still be here, but Aurora feared she'd lose her cool when she saw Stella. Because right now, Aurora wanted to throttle the pompous doctor.

Aurora's phone alarm went off, letting her know it was time to head upstairs. Standing, she shoved one arm and then the other through her blazer.

When she pressed the elevator button, she swore when too many seconds whooshed by without one of the three doors opening. Would Stella berate Aurora if she was one second late? The old Stella—never. The new? Who knew?

Finally, the doors on the left slid open, and Aurora jammed her finger on the sixteenth-floor button and then the one to close the doors, not wanting to waste another second. Fortunately, it didn't stop along the way. When the doors opened again, Aurora straightened her blazer and blouse.

Outside the conference room door, she noticed a flickering light inside. "What the?" Aurora slid the key into the door and turned the handle.

Stella was already in the room.

"What are you doing in here?" Aurora rattled the key. "I thought you didn't have access."

"I may have fibbed slightly." Stella showed her palms.

Aurora tossed up her hands. "Unbelievable! I have a million other ways to spend a Friday evening. I can't believe you right now. Do you even have an appointment?" Aurora glanced about, not seeing anyone.

"Yes."

"With who? The president? Of the country? Because right now, I don't see any other reason for this charade."

Stella shuffled on her feet.

"Well? Who exactly is this big shot you want to impress?"

Stella pointed at Aurora.

Aurora scouted over her shoulder and then looked back at Stella, even more confused.

"You," Stella said.

"Me what?"

"My appointment is with you."

Aurora placed a hand on her chest. "You scheduled the dean's conference room to have a meeting with me on a Friday night?"

"To have dinner." Stella moved to the side to showcase the spread on the table. "I ordered your favorite things from the Italian place near here. Butternut squash ravioli to start. Chicken piccata for the main course and then mint chocolate chip cannolis and tiramisu to finish."

Aurora blinked.

"Please, Aurora. Will you at least sit and hear me out?"

Aurora eyed the food, and the delicious smells made her stomach grumble. "I don't understand."

"I know. I want to explain." Stella pulled out a chair for Aurora.

Aurora remained standing.

Stella placed a hand on her chest. "Just... please."

Aurora took a seat.

Stella poured a glass of wine and placed it in front of Aurora. "Are you hungry?"

"For an explanation."

Stella sat. "I wanted to apologize for acting like an idiot at the wedding. There was absolutely no excuse for my behavior. None."

"I agree."

Stella folded her hands on the table. "This is difficult to say." She moved her hands to her head, pressing her index fingers to the sides of her forehead. "My ex... she had an affair with one of the doctors at the hospital." Stella shifted. "Actually, there's more to it. Kim had an affair with one of the doctors I was insanely jealous of because she was the doctor everyone looked up to." Stella raked a hand through her hair. "When I found out about the affair, I don't know what hurt the most: my wife cheating on me or the fact that the other woman was the one I hated." She sucked in a deep breath.

"Is your ex still with this doctor?"

Stella shook her head. "As soon as I found out, Jess jumped ship and moved to Chicago to avoid a scandal."

"Wow," Aurora said, not sure what else to say.

"When you told me you had a crush on Becky—"

"That was years ago, Stell. I was just a kid." Aurora had to quell the anger in her tone.

"I know, I know. But when I started working with Jess, I was already married to my ex. At a staff party, Jess got drunk and confessed she had a crush on Kim and was insanely jealous of me. In full honesty, I'd always accused Kim of cheating, even when she hadn't. I don't know how it takes control over me, but it does." Stella wrung her hands.

"The jealousy?"

"Yes. As you can probably imagine, Kim didn't really appreciate that." Stella raked a hand through her hair. "I'm sorry. It's hard for me to talk about this stuff."

"Define *stuff*," Aurora said in what she hoped was a tone that didn't sound accusatory.

"Baring my soul."

"I've noticed that, yes."

Stella smiled, but it dissipated. "I think the reason I didn't introduce Kenzie was I wanted to make sure... I didn't want to introduce someone to her unless I knew the woman would stay. The past few years have been difficult for her, and she's been worried about me."

"Why?"

"Because I've been alone for years. Kim is getting married, and Kenzie's worried about what will happen to me."

"That's a lot for a daughter to take on," Aurora said.

"That's what I think, but she takes after her mom, wanting to take care of everyone."

"She got it from both sides, then."

Stella started to speak but then nodded. "I'm really sorry about... everything. I've started seeing a therapist. Getting it under control is a huge priority for me."

"I wish you told me all of this sooner. It would have helped me understand certain things. I couldn't figure out why you acted so weird when we went to dinner with Becky. I thought you simply hated her, perhaps because Becky got drunk so easily, but didn't want to tell me that."

"I did hate her but for the wrong reason." Stella's eyes dropped to her refolded hands on the table's surface. "I understand if explaining everything doesn't smooth things over, but at least enjoy dinner. I'm afraid you're living on rice and beans now that Becky's out of the apartment."

"You remembered that detail." Somehow, this cheered up Aurora.

"I may not be good at talking, but I do listen."

Aurora's stomach rumbled again.

"Have one last dinner with me."

"Seems like the least I can do." Aurora picked up a fork and popped one of the raviolis into her mouth.

"Are you sure? We can go someplace else if this isn't to your liking." Stella waved to the offerings. "Whatever you want."

"No, this is perfect. Besides, we won't have a private view like this anywhere else." Aurora pointed to the Boston skyline. "There's just something about this city."

With her eyes on Aurora, Stella said, "There is. Thank you for sharing it with me."

"Too bad we can't make it a Friday night tradition."

"Why can't we?"

"Don't you think the dean would catch on if you keep

asking for the conference room? How in the world did you convince Vera to hand over the key?"

"I lied. If anyone asks, I'm wining and dining a very special prospective student."

Aurora laughed, covering her mouth to avoid spraying bits of food all over the table. "No one is going to ask me anything. I'm from the department everyone pretends doesn't exist until the shit hits the fan."

"That's not true. Ever since you took over, Scheduling has vastly improved. Even Kip has been different."

"I think the problem is Alice."

Stella nodded.

"How do I take her out?" Aurora regretted bringing that up.

Stella laughed. "Let me noodle it."

Aurora jabbed her fork at the lit candles. "You are aware of all the rules your breaking? Just the candles alone are a big no-no."

"Are you going to bust me?"

"Depends."

"On?"

"Can I get back to you on that?"

"That sounds promising."

"Does it?" Aurora sipped her wine.

"I'm hoping this isn't really our last meal together."

"It's a lot yummier than rice and beans." Aurora wanted Stella to dangle a bit longer.

"Have you really been eating them?"

Aurora nodded.

"No bites on the ad you placed in the staff lounge?"

Aurora shook her head.

"Do you have a plan B?"

"My parents."

"How's your dad doing?"

"He's going stir crazy. It's been weeks, and Mom still won't let him out of her sight."

"Here's to hoping you don't have to move back in with your parents." Stella raised her wineglass.

Aurora clinked hers to it. "Praying for a miracle."

They locked eyes. The flickering light danced in Stella's gaze. "I missed you," Aurora confessed.

"I've been so lost these past few weeks."

"If you don't kiss me soon..." Aurora didn't complete the thought.

Stella leaned over the table with Aurora meeting her half-way. Their lips pressed against each other, both seeming shy to make the next move. Finally, Aurora deepened the kiss, Stella greeting Aurora's tongue with her own. They both rose from their seats, only briefly breaking their lip-lock.

Aurora fisted the hair on the back of Stella's head, needing to pull Stella further into her orbit. Stella seemed to understand Aurora's desire and walked Aurora backward, until she was pressed against the floor to ceiling glass wall. Stella inserted her knee between Aurora's legs, all the while Stella's hand slipped under Aurora's shirt, kneading the flesh.

Aurora moaned into Stella's mouth.

Stella cupped Aurora's breast, running a thumb over the silk, causing the nipple to harden.

"Stella," Aurora moaned. "We shouldn't... not here."

"No one is around, and the blinds on the door are closed."

"But..."

Stella kissed Aurora again, muting all protests. Not that Aurora truly had one. Stella unbuttoned Aurora's blouse and reached around to unclasp the bra, sucking Aurora's nipple into her mouth. Aurora pressed her head against the window, her hands clutching the side of Stella's head. Stella's hand tried to slide into her pants, but the belt blocked her. Not deterred, Stella dispatched the belt and undid the button and zipper.

"Some might think you're a surgeon or something."

Stella smiled, staring into Aurora's eyes. "Something." Stella eased her fingers under Aurora's panties. "I've missed how wet you get."

"I've missed you getting me wet."

Stella entered Aurora with two fingers, causing Aurora's eyes to snap shut and her body to tense. Stella moved them in and out, while the pad of her thumb circled Aurora's clit.

"I need you," Aurora said.

Stella captured her mouth, kissing Aurora hard as if that was the only way to prove how much she loved Aurora. Because right then, right there, Aurora didn't doubt for one second Stella Gilbert's love.

One of Aurora's hands held Stella's face to hers, while Aurora's other hand slipped under Stella's shirt and dug into her back. "Oh, don't stop."

Stella went in deep, curling her fingers upward, causing Aurora's knees to go weak. Stella supported Aurora, not stopping. Even with the air conditioning blasting in the building, Aurora's entire body was aflame.

And she was close. So fucking close. Aurora buried her face into the crook of Stella's neck, holding onto her. "I love you," Aurora said into her ear.

"I love you so much, Aurora."

Aurora held on tighter.

Stella plunged in deep, sending Aurora over the edge.

CHAPTER FORTY-FOUR

STELLA, GROGGY FROM SLEEP, SENSED SHE WASN'T alone in bed. Could it be? She rolled over, bumping her elbow into Aurora's head.

"That's an interesting way to wake someone." Aurora lowered Stella's hand off her head to her chest.

Stella cupped Aurora's breast. "My aim isn't perfect until at least one cup of coffee."

Aurora laughed. "I'm surprised you're still in bed. Usually, you're up and showered before I open my eyes."

"I forced myself to stay put," Stella joked.

Aurora's eyes tapered. "You had to force yourself to stay put while we're both naked in bed? You really know how to make a girl feel special."

Stella squeezed Aurora's nipple. "Does this help?"

"Some but I'm still puzzled by your statement."

"Truth be told, I only woke seconds before rolling over. Most mornings, I'm not good at downtime."

"Sleeping is downtime?"

"Sleeping in falls into that category."

Aurora turned her head and squinted at the clock on her nightstand. "It's two minutes after seven."

"I know. It takes you forever to wake, forcing me to resort to desperate measures." Stella squeezed Aurora's nipple even more.

"Hitting me in the head."

Stella made a *whoopsie* face.

"You're seriously warped, you know that? It's Saturday morning."

"And we're burning daylight." Stella waggled her brows.

"I'm so sorry to torture you this way. How will you survive?" Aurora crooked a finger, indicating she wanted a good morning kiss.

"A demanding torturer." Stella rolled on top of Aurora, planting her lips softly onto Aurora's. After the sweet kiss, Stella swiped hair off Aurora's face. "You're so beautiful."

Aurora smiled. "Do you remember the first time we woke up together? I thought your *early bird catches the worm* routine was your way of kicking me out without having to say *get out of here*." She laughed.

"I wondered why you rushed out. You didn't even let me ply you with coffee."

"Can you blame me? When you wake up in a woman's bed for the first time and she's nowhere in sight, it's not comforting."

"No wonder all the others never called."

"Yeah, you've dated so much. If I remember correctly, I'm the first since you split with your wife."

"Ah, since you brought up that subject, I have a question for you?"

Aurora arched her brows. "Not sure if I should be scared."

"Don't be scared. Ever. I think it's time you met Kenzie."

Aurora didn't react right away.

"Is it too soon since getting back together?" Stella tried to disguise the disappointment in her voice but failed.

"Not at all. I'm just in shock. Everything seems to be happening so fast."

Stella stared at Aurora with a questioning expression. "We've been dating since the beginning of the school year."

"True, but only seriously—"

"I was always serious."

Aurora smiled. "I know that now, even though you kept saying it wasn't. You really know how to give a girl mixed signals."

"Says the pro at that." Stella lightly pressed a finger onto Aurora's nose.

"I know. You intimidated the shit out of me. And, I had my own issues to overcome in order to open up completely with you."

Stella's expression softened. "How are things with your parents?"

"Good. Really good. Dad's recovering from the surgery. I know it's not a cure to his disease, but it's keeping him here longer. I don't want to spend the time we have left upset. I don't understand everything—not completely, but I know both my parents love me. Not a lot of children can say that."

"That's all that matters. I want the same for my daughter. Kim and I have always tried to shield Kenzie from the ugliness of divorce, but she's a smart cookie. She reminds me so much of Kim it scares me."

"Are you saying she got her brains from Kim?"

"She is the birth mom."

"Yes, but she's also your daughter. There's a lot to be said about the whole nature versus nurture argument. All of it matters. I know this as a fact since I seem to take after my dad more than my mom. I'm sure Kenzie sees how hard you work and admires you for it."

"I hope she doesn't resent me later. I want to do better. With you. With Kenzie. I don't want to wake up twenty years from now and realize I blew it."

"Good to know you don't put too much pressure on yourself and all before your first cup of coffee."

"You joke, but I'm serious."

Aurora cupped Stella's face with both hands. "I tease because that's what I do to lighten the mood. I think it's great to have goals, but you also need to know it's a process. You can't wake up on a Saturday morning and expect your entire life to change simply because you're willing it to. Baby steps. Like staying in bed a little longer with your smoking hot girlfriend."

"You are."

"Show me."

"Is that a direct order?"

"If you need it to be, yes. Fuck me. In a good way. Don't waltz out of here and never come back."

Stella gazed intently into Aurora's eyes. "I don't think I could even if I wanted to. I feel like a whole new person. No. That's not exactly right. I feel whole. For the first time."

"I love you, Stella Gilbert."

"I adore you, Aurora Shirley."

"Shirley and Gilbert—we should have known right from the start we were meant to be together." Aurora's eyes misted.

"Yet, we complicated the heck out of it." Stella shrugged.

"Just like the characters in the book."

"Not exactly. I don't think they started as fuck buddies."

"I wonder how it would have changed their story if they had."

"Shall I start writing our story and see the parallels?" Stella joked.

"Yes, because you have so much free time. Why not add fan fiction to your résumé?"

"I'd rather add tutor to my duties. Have you given nursing school any thought?"

The sexiest smile spread across Aurora's face. "That's right. You don't know. I've applied and been accepted. I'm starting this fall. I haven't told Alice yet that I either need to cut down on my hours or quit to find a part-time job. My parents are going to help me out financially. Another reason I'm considering moving back home. I'll need to cut all extra expenses, but I think it'll be worth it in the long run."

"I happen to know someone who'll be willing to order meals for you. And maybe I'll start cooking on a regular basis. Kenzie's been wanting to take cooking lessons. Do you think it's too late for this old dog to learn a new trick?" Stella was usually bashful.

"You're far from old. And I think it's a great idea for you and Kenzie to spend more time together. All children need their mothers."

"She's going to have even more moms now that Kim is marrying the paleontologist."

"Are you okay with that?"

Stella nodded. "I am. It's time."

"For Kim to marry?"

"For me to forgive and move on."

"Look at you. Growing up right before my eyes."

"Such a wiseass." Stella kissed Aurora's forehead. "A cute one."

Aurora responded with a kiss, which switched from sweet to *I need you right now*. She rolled Stella onto her back.

CHAPTER FORTY-FIVE

THEY STOOD OUTSIDE OF FANEUIL HALL, WATCHING A group of dancers entertain the summer crowd. Everyone clapped their hands or cheered on one of the dancers as he backed up, ran, and then completed a backflip over a volunteer. The crowd cheered even louder.

Aurora reached for Stella's hand, threading their fingers.

"Nervous?" Stella asked with a knowing look.

"A bit."

"Don't be. She'll love you." Stella squeezed Aurora's fingers.

"I hope so. Is she as intimidating as her mother?"

"Which one?" Stella arched a brow.

"Oh, God. I'm screwed." Aurora's voice showed her nerves.

Stella chuckled. "No, you aren't. Kenzie will adore you like I do. How could she not?" She boosted Aurora's hand to kiss it.

Aurora nodded but didn't feel all that buoyed by Stella's words. She'd never been with a woman who had a child. Not that she hated kids, but what did she know about them, really? Why hadn't Aurora considered this before now?

They weren't there to watch the dancers. This was today's meeting spot for the kid drop-off. Kim and her fiancée were meeting Kim's parents for lunch nearby, and Kenzie, according to Stella, loved all the food stalls inside the marketplace.

"Mom!"

Both Stella and Aurora turned around, and Aurora spied an adorable eleven-year old girl with glasses slam into Stella's open arms.

"Hey, kiddo." Stella held her daughter close briefly. "Let me get a load of the new specks."

Kenzie turned her head to give Stella the profile shot.

"Looking good!" Stella pulled Kenzie back into an embrace.

The two women who approached looked to each other with curious expressions after taking in Aurora's presence.

Stella straightened. "Kenz, I'd like you to meet Aurora."

Kenzie tilted her head up, her button nose crinkled. "Nice to meet you."

Aurora smiled. "It's a pleasure."

"I'm Kim," said a woman who looked so much like Kenzie it took Aurora by surprise. No wonder Aurora had originally assumed the photos in Stella's place were of a niece.

Aurora shook her hand.

"And this is Rooney." Kim motioned to the nerdy woman to her side.

Aurora shook Rooney's hand.

Stella and Rooney nodded at each other, friendly-like but clearly not entirely comfortable around each other.

"She's a dinosaur expert," Kenzie squealed. "Go ahead. Ask her a question."

Aurora laughed. "What's your favorite dinosaur, Kenzie?"

"All of them!"

"She's an equal opportunity kind of kid," Stella joked and spoke to Kim, "What time should we meet up?"

"Does four-ish work?"

Stella nodded. "Enjoy your lunch. Say hi to your parents for me."

"Will do, and thanks for pitching in today." Kim addressed her daughter, "Behave for your mom."

Kenzie waved *yeah-yeah.* "I know the drill. No kicking, screaming, or crying, or I won't get ice cream later."

"Who said we're getting ice cream?" Stella asked in a mock-serious tone.

"I'm a child of divorced lesbian parents. It's the least you can do." She crossed her arms and closed one eye.

Stella rolled her eyes, and Kim laughed.

Kim and Rooney departed, walking hand in hand.

"Are you ready for lunch?" Stella asked Kenzie.

"I hope you two can keep up. I'm a growing kid and have a monstrous appetite." Kenzie rubbed her belly.

Aurora eyed Stella to see how she received this, but Stella answered, "You talk a big game, Little Mac. Let's see if you can live up to it."

"Rookie mistake. Challenging me." Kenzie plowed inside the market, threading her way through the crowd, intent on the Indian place.

Aurora quirked a brow at Stella.

"She has a sophisticated palate for someone her age. Another reason why I'd like to get us into cooking classes together." Stella sidestepped a woman doing her best to keep her two-year-old from tottering into oncoming legs.

"I'm holding you to that," Kenzie called over her shoulder. When she got to the front of the line, she said, "Mango lassi, please."

Stella started to hand Kenzie a five, but Kenzie pulled out a wallet from her purse. "I got this one."

"I see someone has been doing her chores."

"That's me. The chore machine." Kenzie paid the man.

"Do you want one?" Stella asked Aurora.

"I'm holding out for dessert."

"This is kinda like a dessert." Kenzie sucked the yogurt

drink through a straw, heading further into the melee of tourists and locals.

"She's kinda intimidating, in a cute way. Much like someone else I know," Aurora whispered into Stella's ear.

"I'll take that as a compliment." Stella reached for Aurora's hand.

Kenzie glanced over her shoulder and spied them holding hands. She seemed to nod in approval.

After she finished her drink, Kenzie rubbed her palms together and announced, "I'm ready for Greek, now."

"Indian to Greek. A bold move, Kenz." Stella stood on tippy toe to look around. "On your left, just up ahead."

Kenzie ordered an appetizer sampler that included hummus and tzatziki with pita and stuffed grape leaves. She looked to Aurora with widened eyes, "You getting something this time?"

"How could I turn down Greek food? My grandmother came from there." Aurora ordered a gyro.

Stella got a Greek salad wrap.

Food in hand, Stella led them to the staircase leading to a sitting area on the second floor, an elaborate dome overhead. Old business signboards hung on the brick wall. Stella steered them to an empty table to the side that had a view of the first floor.

Kenzie dipped a small chunk of pita into the hummus, kicking her feet as if sitting down was a challenge.

Aurora slid Stella a look, implying *I see she has your energy levels.*

Stella shrugged one shoulder, taking a bite of her wrap.

"Kenzie, what grade are you in?"

"Sixth." She nibbled on a stuffed grape leaf and then dabbed her mouth with a paper napkin. "Are you two dating?"

Aurora looked to Stella for guidance. Stella gave Aurora a go-ahead nod.

"Yes, we are."

"Good. It's about time Mom dates."

Aurora stifled a laugh. "You think so?"

"I do. I've been worried about her."

"Hey there. It's not your job to worry about me. It's my job to worry about you." Stella placed her hand on Kenzie's head.

"Worry is a two-way street, Mom."

"She's got you there," Aurora said.

"This is going to be an interesting afternoon." Stella's grin made it clear she meant no harm.

"Mom's getting married," Kenzie continued. "You need to catch up."

"Love isn't a race," Stella countered. "Are you okay with your mom getting married?"

"Yeah. They really like each other. And Mom is much easier going about dessert at night." Kenzie quirked her head. "Do you two love each other?"

"I walked right into that one, didn't I?" Stella asked Aurora.

"You did."

Kenzie cupped her ear. "I'm still waiting."

"Would you be okay with that?" Stella seemed unsure how to answer.

"Yep. You deserve love."

Stella gaped at her daughter. "For someone so young, you're very wise."

"I'm not that young. I'm in the double digits."

"You are?" Stella teased and proceeded to count on her fingers.

"Mom!" Kenzie shook her head, laughing.

"Hold on, I'm only on six. I'm getting there."

Kenzie looked to Aurora. "Good luck with this one."

CHAPTER FORTY-SIX

THE SECOND THURSDAY OF AUGUST, STELLA STOOD to the side of Whitaker Green, as first year students, friends, and family took photos. Most days of the year, the lawn was a place for students and staff to eat their lunch on warm days. Today, the space had a massive white tent and hundreds of metal folding chairs.

"Great job, Stella." Dean Andrews shook Stella's hand. "This has been one of the best White Coat ceremonies I've been part of. Will I see you at the wrap up party tonight?"

"Yes, sir."

Vera beckoned Dean Andrews, and Stella thought the man groaned before heading for his bossy admin.

Aurora sidled up to Stella. "I don't envy him."

"The woman runs his life like a general in the marines."

"If you become dean, will you inherit Vera?"

"Please. Don't ever speak those words, or I may never sleep again." Stella rubbed her forehead.

Vera waved Alice over, and Aurora's boss looked as if she'd prefer eating twelve bad oysters than do Vera's bidding. But Alice obeyed.

Stella laughed. "Kip did a fantastic job today. How'd you keep him in line?"

"I believed in him."

"What a novel idea? You mean that's a better way than Alice's berating the poor man?"

"Shocking news, I know. People want to feel appreciated."

"The department is going to miss you."

Aurora's eyes swept the green as her team started to break down the AV equipment. "Who knows? Maybe we'll join forces again. You know, when I take over the entire university."

Stella let out a bark of laughter. "I think you'd make a good match for Vera."

Dr. Howie waved at Stella.

"If you'll excuse me. Time to mingle and see how much money I can wrangle from jubilant families and friends." Stella squeezed Aurora's shoulder. "See you at the party."

"I'm thinking of skipping."

Stella stopped in her tracks. "Hard no. If I have to go, I need you by my side."

Aurora grinned. "You say the sweetest things these days."

"I have my new roommate to thank for that. And now that we're out as a couple at work, you can't ditch me." Aurora had moved into Stella's apartment the weekend before.

Aurora goggled. "Roommate! I take back my sweetest things comment."

"I thought you might." Stella stepped closer and whispered, "Is it wrong I get turned on when you feign being mad at me?"

"Why do you think I do it? Now go. Earn your paycheck. One of us has to."

Stella was greeted by a first-year student and her parents. "You must be so proud of Tracy. We're thrilled she chose our school."

Tracy's mom beamed. "She's had her heart on being a doctor since she was five years old."

"You knew way before I did," Stella confessed. "My daughter has her heart set on being the first doctor in space."

Tracy laughed. "I need to meet her. Sounds like we would get along."

Stella panned the area in search of Kim and Kenzie. Spying them to the right, she said, "If you're serious, I can introduce you to her now. Kenzie insisted on coming this year, although she was heartbroken to learn she wouldn't be getting her own white coat." Kim had volunteered to tag along since she knew both Stella and Aurora would be busy ensuring the ceremony went off without a hitch.

Along the way, Tracy's mom looped her arm through Stella's. "We appreciate you looking after our baby. She's so young, and we worry about her."

"Thank you for trusting us. I wish I was so put together when I was only sixteen."

"I don't know where she got it from. Between you and me, I was a nightmare at her age, and it scares me to think I became a mom when I was only two years older than Tracy."

"You've done a fantastic job raising her."

"Thank you."

They reached Kenzie and Kim. Stella waved to Tracy. "Kenzie, I'd like you to meet the youngest student ever to start her medical career here. Tracy, this is my daughter."

Tracy shook Kenzie's hand. "Very nice to meet you. Now give me the lowdown. What's your mom like? Really?"

"Oh, you've come to the right place." Kenzie motioned for Tracy to step aside from the group so they could talk in private.

"I may be in for it," Stella joked.

Kim smiled. "You must be so proud of Tracy."

Tracy's father grunted. "And terrified."

"Don't be. Stella is many things. Protective most of all." Kim's tone implied she meant every word.

Another family approached Stella, and Kim gave her *don't*

worry, I got this smile. Stella greeted the Matthews family and congratulated Mike on starting his career in medicine.

By the time the after-party started for the staff members who had worked their tails off for the ceremony, Stella was half dead on her feet. She asked Aurora, "Do I look as tired as I feel?"

"Nope. Quite the opposite."

"Good. Because I have to go up there"—she pointed to the podium—"and give some final remarks. Wish me luck."

"You don't need it. You're a natural."

"No pressure then." Stella made her way to the front of the lounge and tapped the microphone, getting everyone's attention. She started off saying, "I would like to thank everyone, from the professors, guest speakers, AV staff, admins, caterers, and security for coming together and pulling off a fantastic event that kicked off their students' careers in medicine. A day they'll remember for the rest of their lives."

She rattled off more particulars and shout-outs. And then she came to the heart of her remarks. For her at least. "Please give Aurora a big round of applause." The crowd readily complied, many hooting and whistling. "Some of you may have heard that we're losing her next week. You know, before I say more, Aurora can you come up here?"

Aurora gave Stella the hairy eyeball, which Stella promptly ignored and continued waving Aurora up on the stage. The crowd cheered, and Aurora walked slowly to the stage.

When Aurora stood beside her, Stella continued, "I'd like to be the first to wish Aurora the best of luck in nursing school. We may be losing a valuable member of our team, but the field of medicine is gaining from our loss. Please join me in raising a glass to Aurora."

EPILOGUE

FIVE YEARS LATER

Aurora took a step on the ladder.

"What are you doing?" Stella rushed up behind her. "Get down right now."

"I'm hanging up the sign for Kenzie's party."

"I can do it. Please, step down."

Aurora sighed but complied. "I'm perfectly capable of hanging a sweet sixteen banner."

Stella placed her hands on Aurora's expanding belly. "You are, but this little one is my biggest worry."

"So, what? I'm just the incubator for your second child?" Aurora crossed her arms over her chest.

Stella's eyes skimmed over Aurora's cleavage. "It's just not fair I can't play with or touch them."

"Sorry, sweetheart. They're too sensitive. Off-limits."

"Hello!" Aurora's mom shouted.

"In the living room," Aurora shouted back.

Her dad and mom, with a wrapped gift, entered.

"Look at this!" Her mom's eyes panned all the decorations

in the room. "It looks like you're having royalty over. So much purple!"

"It's her favorite color," Aurora said. She kissed her mom's cheek and then her dad's.

"How are you feeling? Do you need anything?" Her dad eyed Aurora's protruding belly.

"Can you make the heat go away? Considering we planned this baby, I'm shocked by how I didn't factor in how hot and humid it could be in September. It's like my calves have swallowed my ankles, and my entire body has tripled in size. I swear the humidity and my water retention are competing with each other." Aurora laughed, but everyone else expressed concern.

Her mom patted Aurora's back.

Kim and Rooney entered the room, pulling the attention from Aurora, who was tired of everyone fretting over her. Aurora was only pregnant, something women had done since the beginning of time. Her dad had survived a kidney transplant.

Kim said, "Oh, wow. Aurora you shouldn't have done this. Not in your condition."

"Am I invisible?" Stella asked.

"It's no secret your idea of decorating is one wrinkled bow," Kim countered.

Aurora nodded. "True, but she's been sweet as pie and hasn't let me do much except boss her around."

Stella spun around. "Yet, you still climbed onto the ladder when I left the room for one minute!"

"Oh, geez. Are you two fighting on my birthday? I think that's a parenting foul." Kenzie, no longer a child, but not quite an adult, stood in the room.

"No fighting. I promise." Stella hugged her daughter. "You weren't supposed to be home yet."

"It's not a surprise party, Mom. I've invited all my friends."

"I know, but..." Stella wrapped one arm around her daughter as a way of completing the thought.

Kenzie pressed her hands together. "How can I help?"

"News flash, Kenz, this is your party." Stella placed her hand on Kenzie's forehead. "Are you feeling alright? Usually, I can't get you to clean your room."

"I'm not going to let Aurora do everything."

Aurora smiled. "You really are the best."

"Am I really that bad?" Stella asked. "No one thinks I help out around here."

"Oh, you do. You're the best when it comes to taking care of the yard. Shoveling. You make the best chicken parmesan." Aurora tapped her chin. "Did I cover everything?"

"So funny."

"The backyard still needs setting up if any of you are game."

Everyone left, but Aurora and Stella remained behind.

Aurora kissed Stella's cheek and whispered in her ear, "You're very good at bedroom things."

Stella whispered back, "We need this one to pop out so we can get back to that."

Aurora cradled her baby bump. "And I miss seeing my feet. Oh, and wearing heels."

Stella laughed. "That ranks up there with the other. Good to know."

"When I wear them, it usually leads to one of my favorite pastimes, searching out all your hidden freckles like the one right below—" Aurora placed a finger underneath Stella's right nipple.

"Excellent point. Do you still have that outfit you wore when I met Becky for the first time?"

"What'd I wear?" Aurora tried to recall.

"It was a floral thing that barely covered all your assets."

"Oh, that. I may. I have no idea if I'll ever fit into it again, though." Aurora took in her belly.

"Doesn't matter. You're absolutely beautiful. And if I haven't told you this lately, I adore you, Mrs. Gilbert."

"Right back at you, Dean Gilbert. Shall we join the rest of the fam and get ready for the party?"

"I can't believe Kenzie's sixteen. When did that happen?" Stella released a shallow sigh.

"Time can be cruel. The way it flies by."

"We need to try to slow it down so we can enjoy this." Stella kissed Aurora on the lips.

"Why are you torturing the pregnant lady?"

Stella wheeled about, shaking a fist at Rosie. "It's nearly impossible to have alone time in my own house."

Rosie rolled her eyes. "Where's Kenzie? I've got her BMW parked outside."

"W-what?" Stella sputtered.

"She's such easy pickings." Rosie laughed.

"Everyone's outside. Enjoy the time now before all of the teenagers descend." Aurora looped her arm through Rosie's. "What was Stella like when she was sixteen?"

Aurora and her sister-in-law made their way to the backyard, Stella a step behind them.

"Oh, much like she is today. Although, she has wrinkles now."

Aurora looked over her shoulder and said, "Don't listen to her. You're still hot as hell."

Stella formed a heart with her fingers and mouthed, "I love you."

Aurora couldn't hear the word enough from the woman she'd fallen for, and Stella told her every single day since they'd gotten back together. Cradling her baby bump, Aurora couldn't help but feel she was the luckiest woman in Boston, if not the world.

AUTHOR'S NOTE

Thank you for reading *Reservations of the Heart*. If you enjoyed the novel, please consider leaving a review on Goodreads or Amazon. No matter how long or short, I would very much appreciate your feedback. You can follow me, T. B. Markinson, on Twitter at @IHeartLesfic or email me at tbm@tbmarkinson.com. I would love to know your thoughts.

ABOUT THE AUTHOR

TB Markinson is an American who's recently returned to the US after a seven-year stint in the UK and Ireland. When she isn't writing, she's traveling the world, watching sports on the telly, visiting pubs in New England, or reading. Not necessarily in that order.

Her novels have hit Amazon bestseller lists for lesbian fiction and lesbian romance.

Feel free to visit TB's website (lesbianromancesbytbm.com) to say hello. On the *Lesbians Who Write* weekly podcast, she and Clare Lydon dish about the good, the bad, and the ugly of writing. TB also runs I Heart Lesfic, a place for authors and fans of lesfic to come together to celebrate and chat about lesbian fiction.

Want to learn more about TB. Hop over to her *About* page on her website for the juicy bits. Okay, it won't be all that titillating, but you'll find out more.